SINS
OF THE
BEES

ANNIE LAMPMAN

PEGASUS CRIME

NEW YORK LONDON

Sins of the Bees

Pegasus Crime is an imprint of
Pegasus Books, Ltd.
148 W 37th Street, 13th Floor
New York, NY 10018

First Pegasus Books hardcover edition September 2020

"Ode to the Beekeeper" from *Bringing the Shovel Down* by Ross Gay, © 2011.
Reprinted by permission of the University of Pittsburgh Press.

Interior design by Sabrina Plomitallo-González, Pegasus Books

ISBN: 978-1-64313-533-5

10 9 8 7 6 5 4 3 2 1

Printed in the United States of America
Distributed by Simon & Schuster

For my family of men—my tribe, my genus, my species:
Stephen, Phinehas, Benjamin, Isaiah

—◦—

Apis mellifera: *The common honeybee. Order: Hymenoptera (Hymen is the Greek god of marriage, hence the union of front and hind wings); Suborder: Apocrita (ants, bees, and wasps); Superfamily: Apoidea; Family: Apidae (bees); Tribe: Apini; Genus: Apis; Species:* mellifera *(honey-bearing)*

—The Beekeeper's Handbook

Ode to the Beekeeper

who has taken off her veil
and gloves and whispers to the bees
in their own language, inspecting the comb-thick
frames, blowing just so when one or the other alights
on her, if she doesn't study it first—the veins
feeding the wings, the deep ochre
shimmy, the singing—just like in the dreams
that brought her here in the first place: dream
of the queen, dream of the brood chamber,
dream of the desiccated world and sifting
with her hands the ash and her hands
ashen when she awoke, dream of honey
in her child's wound, dream of bees
hived in the heart and each wet chamber
gone gold. Which is why, first,
she put on the veil. And which is why,
too, she took it off.

                                        —Ross Gay

PART ONE

....

*Here, then, as everywhere else in the world, one part of
the circle is wrapped in darkness; here, as everywhere,
it is from without, from an unknown power, that the
supreme order issues; and the bees, like ourselves, obey the
nameless lord of the wheel that incessantly turns on itself,
and crushes the wills that have set it in motion.*

–THE LIFE OF THE BEE

PROLOGUE

AUGUST 2001

The show was finally over, white linen-draped tables lined with smudged champagne glasses and crumpled cloth napkins, the crumbs of catered cake. Isabelle wandered the vaulted room, haunted with the reverberating disruption of the *Maidens*—all her watercolor girls framed on soft gray walls, girls too young for their rounded stomachs and long-suffering pain, girls whose eyes still cried out to her in entreaty.

Like O'Keeffe, Isabelle had returned to the Santa Fe desert looking to find healing in its austerity, to escape what she hadn't ever been able to leave behind. But it was always there in her work, as inescapable as her memories. Study after study of the same subject. What she'd run from, what she'd always been running from—fifteen and alone with the wreckage of herself, her own stomach swollen with unwanted life. All the girls, holding themselves so still for her, their faces shuttered in retreat, their bodies burgeoning.

After she'd fled the compound, fled Len Dietz and all he was working to enact—his promised land, his army of god, his holy family—she'd kept painting them, these girls, from memory, her mind delivering flashing snapshots just when she thought she'd finally forgotten their sorrow, their doomed fate.

She'd thought then, as she often had over the past twenty years, of running back to Eamon, back to the island after all this time gone—decades now—but instead, as soon as she'd escaped Almost Paradise, she'd painted Eamon's honeysuckle bonsai from memory in one fevered, post-Y2K, post-*Wedding of the Maidens* session. She'd named the honeysuckle painting *In Eden*, and when it had gone out in a small traveling art tour, on an impulse she hadn't been able to halt, she'd sent Eamon a copy of the show's magazine along with a packet of the painted girls, but she'd never heard anything back. She couldn't blame him—not after her sudden abandonment so long ago—but she had despaired following each empty-mailbox day.

In Eden was the only subject-matter departure of the show. Derek had hung it by itself in the back alcove, said people would buy the others, all the girls, just because of it, and he'd been right, the honeysuckle calling its children home, seedpod babies cradled tight in its roots.

The show had been the success Derek had predicted from the start. He'd toasted Isabelle before he'd left, leaned close, said, "I told you so," his face brushing her hair, his lips grazing her cheek. A man young enough to be her child, smitten with a sorrow that didn't belong to him.

Isabelle went back to the alcove and sat on the bench herself, studying the lovers' bodies in the honeysuckle's trunk, each one mirroring the other.

"To you, Eamon," she said finally, lifting her glass.

Derek had tried to put the honeysuckle painting up for sale, too, said it would bring top dollar, but Isabelle told him it wasn't hers to sell. That she needed to take it to its rightful owner.

She stood and gently lifted it off the wall. "It's time to go home," she said.

———

She gave her apartment one last check—a cleaned-out fridge, emptied cupboards, a tidily made bed, and bare wood floors. An old lady's spartan domicile.

She didn't know when she'd be back, or if she would ever be. She was tired of trying to pacify people who would never understand. People from a world where you could live happily ever after. A world where a mother didn't give up her firstborn daughter, her only child. A world where virgin child brides weren't given over to a fifty-some-year-old man to impregnate for his end-of-the-world new millennium and told that it was god's will. A world where you didn't bury pregnant girls or their stillborn babies under a cult's palaver tree, declaring it divinity, heaven just another form of the girls' hell.

She grabbed an age-softened flannel shirt and flattened it against the bed, smoothing the creases before folding it for packing. A thing kept for so long. When she'd been going through the apartment before the show, she'd found it in the far reaches of the back cupboard, and when she'd pulled it out, there it was, still caught in the shirt's folds after all these years—the island's damp musk and cedar, a hint of salt air. She buried her nose in the shirt and inhaled. Even in summer, the island's fog had chilled her. *Trawler Island*. So long ago. She thought of the young woman she'd been then and wanted to go back, tell her to stay.

———◦•◦———

Her suitcase packed, everything ready, Isabelle went to the bathroom and pinned her hair back, looking at herself in the mirror—the network of spider lines around her eyes, the softness along her once-distinct jawline, her hair turned from bright auburn to streaks of silver and gold.

She opened the box on the counter and folded back the tissue inside. She'd kept Eamon's marriage present all this time—honeysuckle bonsai earrings. His beautiful tree cut out in profile on wooden circles, its sweeping canopy painted green, the lovers still visible in its trunk. She fit the earrings carefully in her ears and studied their dangling grace against her long neck. She would take what came. That was the deal she'd made with herself. There would be no running this time. No more questing, searching. No more questioning. Only acceptance of whatever outcome there would be.

———◦•◦———

After the cab dropped Isabelle at the bustling airport and she got through the rushing push and stress of security, she made her way through the throngs of people to the boarding gate waiting area and sat in a corner with her suitcase and the honeysuckle painting parked in front of her. The TVs suspended around her played out a familiar scene of summer wildfire—billowing smoke and dramatic shots of flames licking up into the sky from the tops of towering pines perched high along an austere canyon rim. It looked like the apocalypse the Lenites had prepared for with Y2K, the new millennium, the end of the world—which, of course, had never come.

But then the camera panned out to a full canyon view and Isabelle had a quick shock of recognition. She knew that place. She had *lived* in that place.

Breathlessly she scanned the ticker-tape headlines running along the bottom of the muted screen: "*Four hospitalized after an Idaho Fish and Game helicopter was shot down . . . Hells Canyon Visitor Center Occupation over . . . Fourteen suspects in custody on multiple charges, including arson . . . Wildfire still raging out of control in steep canyonland . . . Len Dietz, founder of Almost Paradise and occupation organizer, arrested . . .*"

Her body washed cold and her scalp prickled with goose bumps as the TVs flashed from one scene to the next—the compound filmed from above, swarming with SWAT and ATF, the air filled with black smoke. She watched without breathing as they showed scenes from the occupation, replaying wobbly insider home videos of Len pacing and preaching, his long hair glistening like a pelt on his back, his silver seeing-eye pendant swinging on his chest over his crisp white shirt, laundered and pressed by his child wives, who faithfully bore the fruit of his loins, propagating his holy army in preparation for the end times of the new millennium, everything ramping up to humanity's sure and swift destruction, the four horsemen of the apocalypse well on their way, Len Dietz and his followers ready to join their rushing charge.

Then the footage switched, showing Len handcuffed and booked, glowering at the camera with his piercing blue eyes, charged with enough crimes to hold him, but not enough to call those back from the graves they'd been sent to. Never enough to make up for all the pain and destruction he'd enacted upon one after the other of his followers who believed he was someone who could save them from themselves, save them from the end.

All the girls who'd had no choice: Rebecca, Leah, Naomi, Ruth, Rachel, Miriam, Hannah, Eve, Abigail, Jerusha, Johanna, Esther. Girls baptized in the waters of the Snake River winding deep in Hells Canyon under the sheer peaks of the Seven Devils Mountains. Girls who never stood a chance against a force so large, so overpowering.

Everything felt tipped sideways, Isabelle's emotions reeling out—what she'd tried so hard to contain, to work through, to express in painting after painting. That pain. The wounds she would always carry, for failing them, failing herself. What she'd gone to the compound trying to achieve, paying witness, purposely connecting herself to something she'd been running from since she was a girl herself, trapped in her stepfather's gaze, her body bearing the fruit of his dark touch.

"*The flames of hell unleashed*," one of the flashing TV headlines read, the drama of the reportage building. Fire, the one thing that had been able to do what nothing else had. The one thing that had been too big, too powerful, for even Len to direct, the force of his will burned away by the very thing he'd sought to unleash.

But all the footage showed only the men—Len's soldiers. Isabelle imagined Faith huddled like a protective mother around all the maidens and their surviving babies. Where was she now? Where would she go, now that the compound was swarming with the authorities? Where would all the girls go—those lucky enough to have been spared—their lives driven by the unrelenting wind and flames that had once been Len Dietz himself?

When she had finally escaped to Santa Fe and changed her last name, making sure there was no record of her anywhere, that she hadn't been followed, Isabelle had risked sending Faith one last painting—a thank-you for what help Faith had offered her in the end, secreting her out of the compound in the middle of the night, keeping her true purpose and feelings

hidden from the rest of them. The painting was a farmers market scene from
that first time they'd met, Faith dressed in her homemade dress and apron, a
scarf tying back her long blond hair as she stood at her booth full of garden
produce and fresh-baked pies, looking as if she'd just stepped off a nine-
teenth-century Scandinavian farm, carrying all the world's burdens on her
shoulders. Something nobody could ever take from her, those burdens. Baby
after baby, girl after girl, woman after woman. Faith as midwife, witness to
every dark thing Almost Paradise had tried to keep hidden.

Two years ago, when Isabelle had been with Eli and selling her paintings
at the Two Rivers farmers market every week, Faith had come up to her
booth and told her that Almost Paradise was looking for an artist to do a
series of commissioned paintings, and that they'd all agreed Isabelle was
the one they wanted for the job. Isabelle had heard all the rumors, good and
bad, about the cult—you couldn't help it if you lived in town, even though
most of the residents supported them—but she'd immediately seen Faith's
offer as a sign. A way to finally take back the past. A way to finally make
some kind of difference in the future.

When Isabelle had agreed to take the job, she'd thought she knew what
she was getting into, that her work would serve as the only strength she
needed. That perhaps she could make recompense at last, shed light on Len
Dietz's dark secrets, opening them up for the world to see, and therefore
stop. But she'd come to realize that each painting she did was like dropping
a pebble into a lake, the power of Len's darkness swallowing everything
in its wake. She'd been nothing more than another of the cult's targeted
women, just like all the others.

Almost Paradise had been a well-formed entity by the time she'd
come onto the scene—a local establishment: thousands of acres on the
rim of a plateau overlooking the Snake River, along with the compound that Len had branded his "covenant community." He'd been
preaching his particular brand of doomsday, antigovernment religion
in the area for decades with some success, but after President Clinton's

election, he'd started accumulating followers and converts—the end, he said, all but sure with the changing political tides, Armageddon written on the wall.

With his Vietnam War background and local roots, people listened when Len told them the government was after them, that the New World Order was coming for them all. People who wanted to become Almost Paradise residents just had to agree to a community covenant, which required that they be god-fearing Christians who would stand and fight with one another should any resident's rights be threatened. But those "rights" ended up having more to do with Len's desires than anything else. He had built his own order—one that conscripted all of Almost Paradise's unmarried girls and women to him. The virgins were his official wives, the nonvirgins his wife-concubines, and all of them were meant to bear his children, build his holy family. The men and teen boys became his soldiers, and the other married women the compound's servants. Len was their leader, their ruler, and they were all to obey. By the time Isabelle had gone to the compound, a few dozen families lived there or in the surrounding area, and the town of Two Rivers was their support system, protecting the Lenites as part of their own. Anyone who didn't comply was marked an enemy, an outsider, and retaliation—through threats or actual violence— was expected.

Watching the footage on the airport TVs—all the bearded, camouflaged Lenite soldiers shackled—Isabelle wondered if any of them had understood what was coming. All this fire and loss. The end of everything they had been working so hard to create. "God's Family" gone.

When the flight attendant called for boarding over the speakers, it was all Isabelle could do to stand, to walk onto the plane and stow her carry-on with the honeysuckle painting above her, to sit at her window seat. The runway lights rushed underneath them as they took off, the dark outside growing larger and larger until it seemed it would swallow them whole. All that injury. All that sorrow. Gaping like an open wound.

She had worked hard to keep the outside world at bay for the past year after she'd come back into society, but it had found its way to her anyway, pressing in, overtaking her.

She leaned back, closed her eyes, tried to push away the flashing images of the girls' faces, but the plane bucked in the air, everything rattling and shaking as if coming apart, and perhaps it was. Perhaps this was meant to be her end, too—all her documentation gone, all the girls left nameless and forgotten, their faces adorning strangers' walls, forever muted.

• • • • •

Later, as they landed, Isabelle gripped her seat, the plane shuttling in hard and rough, a headlong rush, early-morning light breaking a bright horizon line. She felt drunk and swirling. She could barely find her way out of the airport to a taxi, everything strange and disconnected feeling, as if she'd been transported from the flames into this cool world, thick fog obscuring the buildings in gray.

When she got to the terminal, the ferry was just coming in, blowing its foghorn in short blasts, mist swirling from the water, the light soft. Air that made her feel as if she were breathing water—the smell of salt and seaweed, wet wood. This place. She'd forgotten its quiet magic.

She remembered the way she'd sucked in her breath the first time she'd seen Eamon's honeysuckle, the way it seemed to breathe, to pulse as if it were alive, the lovers' bodies shaped inside it. Eamon's trees had moved her like no art ever had, her paintings only a shadow representation of what he'd been able to bring out in trunk and branch, in whorl and knot.

She'd thought about calling or writing ahead, had thought about finally giving Eamon all the letters she'd written to him from her bunker room in the compound, but in the end, she hadn't. She couldn't see how a series of despairing love letters from inside a self-imposed cult internment or an out-of-the-blue phone call after two decades gone would be any better than just showing up, even if there was a chance Eamon wouldn't be on Trawler anymore, although Isabelle couldn't imagine him anywhere else. It seemed he'd always been a part of the island.

Over the years, she'd tried not to imagine the life they might have had. The family they might have made together. But it had been her choice, trying to find her way on her own, make it through all her own hauntings.

She walked to the ferry's front deck and stood watching the gulls sail around, the jellyfish float translucent in the water. Below her, the ferry attendants waved on the first row of vehicles. The drivers nudged into their front-row spots and parked. The farthest vehicle was a jalopy of a truck—a patchwork of turquoise and rust, several boxes strapped in the back. One was a bee box, Isabelle realized with surprise. It had been a long time since she'd seen one—in Two Rivers before Almost Paradise, when she'd been so briefly with sweet Eli and his bees and chickens, the lilac in his front yard that she had pruned, trying to form the honeysuckle bonsai from memory, trying to soothe her soul.

A tall, lean man got out of the jalopy truck and patted his leg. A dog jumped out behind him—a husky mix that looked like a wolf, a dark stripe down its nose and a mask over the top of its eyes, its ears tattered, its white tail wagging like a peace flag.

The man walked with the dog to the front deck, the Salish Sea stretched out beyond them. They stood still, looking out as if it were their first time seeing so much water. She could remember that feeling—how awed she'd been by the sea, the island.

The ferry's engines kicked in, surging them forward and out, the wind picking up, blowing in her face as they gained momentum, leaving a trail of white frothing water behind. She looked down again, watching the man climb into the back of his truck and check the bee box, securing its ties. Then he opened one of the cardboard boxes next to it and carefully lifted out a small potted tree. Isabelle's heart stopped. It was a bonsai, although not much of one—two bare trunks wired together, a sweep of twiggy branches. A bonsai in training. She'd seen Eamon form the same thing.

The man lowered his head, and it looked for all the world as if he were in supplication—praying to the tree, praying to the bees. When he jumped out of the truck, he brushed off his hands on his jeans, then closed the dog in the truck cab, windows left down. She could barely hear him say, "Stay," over the engine noise, the dog watching with concentrated concern as he left.

She wondered what his story was—a man and his dog and honeybees. A man with a bonsai tree heading for the islands. She imagined him going to make a new start just as she and Eamon had. Find all the things you didn't know were missing.

She shook her head at herself—she was getting musing in her age.

The wind blowing cold and wet, she went back into the cabin, walking past the vending machines and bathrooms, making her way to the other end so she might look at the map hung under Plexiglas on the far wall. She knew the way, had studied the ferry's route before coming, but now that she was here, she wanted to look again, see the green blots of islands on blue water, the mainland receding into memory. Over twenty years, gone in a breath. As if it were her first time going to Trawler all over again. She and Eamon starting their life together. Nothing else in the way. Both of them optimistic, sure that the life rolling out ahead of them was all that they wanted, all that they had planned. A family coming. A beautiful life in the making.

She could feel the thrum of the ferry's engines vibrating through her legs as she traced the dashed line that marked their path then—the same path she was on now. She stopped on the smallest island, her finger pinning it. *Trawler*, it read in bold cursive, cartoonish drawings of the old hotel, the beach and dock, a few gulls and cormorants perched on pilings.

"That's where you're going as well?" a voice asked from behind her.

She turned. Of course it would be the young man with the honeybees and bonsai. Of course he would be going to Trawler. Hadn't she known it as soon as he'd gotten out of his truck?

"Have you been before?" he asked. There was a sorrow in his eyes she recognized. A life lived through tragedy.

"Decades ago. Too long to really claim any kind of kinship," she said. "Your first time?"

Glancing at the map, he nodded. "I just wish I'd been able to come sooner," he said, his voice layered with deep sadness, regret. Something she knew only too well.

"Don't we all," she said. She held out her hand. "Isabelle Fullbrook."

He shook with a firm grip even though she could see his thoughts were held elsewhere, as captured as she had been, coming here the first time.

"Nick Larkins," he said. "Nice to meet you."

CHAPTER ONE

MARCH 2001

Silva drove east, away from the coast, away from Trawler. This time, she wouldn't stop until it was over—whatever that meant. Even if it meant things were exactly what she thought they were: irrevocably stripped away, severed, uprooted.

She urged the Dodge into high speed, double-clutching the way her grandfather Eamon had taught her—that long throw, the smooth coolness of the oak knob under her hand, rounded and gleaming with varnish. Reassuring. The road atlas fluttered on the seat beside her, threatening to take wing out the open window, the route to her grandmother's lover highlighted in yellow. *Two Rivers, Idaho.*

Once as a child digging through Eamon's old boxes, Silva had found a photo of Isabelle. An older version of herself, except, like Modigliani's women, Isabelle's gaze had held something tragic, a fated sorrow. Silva had studied herself in the mirror for days afterward, angling her face until everything was the same except their age and the depth of their mourning.

She knew now that it had only been a matter of time.

On the freeway, cars streamed past her, parting around Eamon's 1970 Dodge Power Wagon like water around a rock. When a convertible cut in too close, Silva hit the brakes and flung her arm out as if the five bonsai packed on the pickup's bench seat beside her were loose children she had to protect from being tossed. She remembered Eamon doing the same for her at five years old, the Dodge snarled in traffic during a trip into the city. She'd frowned at all the vehicles and asked Eamon why everyone didn't just go home.

The place she'd just willingly left behind.

She rested her hand on her stomach, absorbing her own body heat. A tender bit of growth rising out of the ashes. Her, the fetus inside her, and now perhaps Isabelle, too. A fractured family of castoffs formed out of the severed pieces that made up the sum of their existence.

Before Eamon, before Silva's mother's accident, home had been a commune with a giant garden lined with bowers of vining hops clustered with papery flowers and plate-size leaves that cast a patchwork of shade. The "New Community," they called themselves, the women working the garden together, weeding, planting, tending with a kind of maternal tenderness Silva missed more than ever—a deep inner ache that matched the biology of change happening within her, cells dividing, copying a new iteration of her, of those who'd come before her. She could remember what it felt like to be part of a family, one unit functioning together, joined by purpose and belief, there to help one another—even if now it seemed naive to believe in such things.

She'd lost her mother the day after the summer solstice party, a pig roasting in a pit, men stocking sauna wood and setting up teepees, and women weaving the children hops and field-daisy wreaths. Silva, five years old at the time, had run and played late into the night with her friends, crowned in their wreaths. They'd eaten shreds of roast pig rolled up in lettuce leaves and snuck sips of home brew. She could still remember the sharp bitterness, the cold wash of fizz. They'd watched steaming people stumble out of the sauna, women's breasts and men's penises loose with heat, and fallen asleep by the bonfire, blankets thrown around them like petals.

The next morning, Silva's mother had driven into town for more supplies and never come back. Fire pits drifting with ash, people coming and going. Silva had waited hours, days, feeling as if she were the one drowning, the air a wave that sucked her under and kept her. The same way she felt now.

She climbed Snoqualmie Pass, sharp-toothed mountains cloaked in trees and snow, fog hanging, Vs of Canada geese pushing northward, leaving the security of their southern warmth behind, pulled forward by a season of breeding and rearing.

When Silva had taken a job on the mainland a few months before, Eamon hadn't wanted her to leave, wanted her to stay on the island and take over the arborist business he and Isabelle had made, stay near him. Silva had told him that she couldn't stay forever, that she needed to find her own way. The work he'd taught her had become second nature by then—trimming, transplanting, aerating, grafting. She didn't have to think, just had to follow her hands. She'd made forays into the suburbs of Seattle before—Woodinville, Mukilteo, Gig Harbor—but had mostly stayed close to home, close to Eamon. The way it'd been since he'd first picked her up and brought her to Trawler.

Over the years, Eamon had told Silva the story many times—how after Isabelle had left him, he'd gone back to the same places on the island over and over again, hoping to find her standing at her easel with her watercolors, returned to him. Said it'd always been her pattern, leaving everything behind scattered in her wake. Pieces torn asunder and flung about, left to the mercy of the wind. A kind of survival that felt more like death than living. But then the phone call had changed everything: the authorities reporting Isabelle's twenty-two-year-old daughter dead in a car accident, run into the river, hair suspended around her, tires balanced on some underwater boulders as if she'd settled there by volition, as if she were enjoying the view. Her five-year-old child left behind. Isabelle's granddaughter. Silva. A child neither of them had known existed.

Eamon hadn't known much about Isabelle's early life—pregnant at fifteen from an abusive stepfather; the baby, Silva's mother, given up—but in the end, none of it had mattered. The trail of crumbs had led to him—nobody else but the broken foster-care system available to take in Silva. Even though Silva wasn't his blood, Eamon was the one to be her guardian. A five-year-old with no family left but him and a runaway grandmother who didn't know she'd fostered a family line that was still going—if only barely.

Silvania August Moonbeam Merigal. A small, quiet girl with an outsize name. Eamon later told Silva that when he'd picked her up, he hadn't expected the uncanny resemblance—her pale skin, fern-green eyes, and copper hair making her an exact replica of Isabelle. Along with the sorrow she carried. He said that first day on the island, when Silva had refused to come inside—standing lithe and pale well into the evening's gloaming, legs as long and thin as a heron's, perched waiting on the shore like a shorebird herself—that she'd reminded him so much of Isabelle it'd taken his breath away.

When Eamon had first come for Silva, he'd presented her with a juniper bonsai in a moss-covered tray. He'd had her repeat its style until she could pronounce it correctly: *Sokan*—twin-trunk. The smaller tree emerging from the larger, forever protected. The juniper's pungent smell forever a part of that passage, the ferry, bells clanging, engines surging, the smell and stretch of salt water, the green mass of trees rising out of the Straight that Eamon had pointed to and called home.

Silva had been awed by Eamon's bonsai. They had formed the habit of his days and so formed the habit of hers. Every morning he'd scrutinized them, eyes owl-like under his magnifying glasses, Silva beside him. He'd told her he could read a tree's future, could divine the way it would become something other than itself, the way it would anchor and transform. Like his muse—the hundred-year-old honeysuckle bonsai he'd inherited at sixteen from his mentor, who'd collected it in the wilds of Japan. Eamon had carved its shape into marriage earrings for Isabelle, and he had later modeled it as his business logo.

The honeysuckle's trunk was fissured into two shapes—a woman's body wrapping into a man's, her long legs tapering off into a heap of moss, her breast a small knot in the upper trunk, the lovers leaning over the edge of the pot, the woman bent into the man, their branches sweeping out behind him, as if blown for years, they had succumbed to the way of the wind.

Eamon had been that wind. Each day he'd examined the tree, magnifying glasses on the end of his nose, trying to see the future of each nodule and root. He'd articulated the lean of the trunk by forcing the roots to grow away from the lee side, letting lead branches grow until they achieved the sweep he saw in his mind. But the lovers had been there from the beginning, their outlines alive in the trunk, the branches, alive as flesh to him, breathing and pulsing with existence. They had always been at the start of everything. Or at the end of everything—although he hadn't known that yet.

The honeysuckle had been the focus of Eamon and Isabelle's final battle— Eamon silently tending the bonsai with fixed attention as Isabelle yelled and cried and stormed out of his life for good, accusing him of only caring about his "fucking trees," even though all he'd ever really cared about was her. After she'd left, Eamon had driven, looking for Isabelle all over the island, his arms tensed on the steering wheel, his tools shifting and bouncing as the truck's back end skittered and bucked over the potted blacktop. He'd finally stopped at the farthest point along the island's wildest stretch—Isabelle's favorite hidden spot—bramble overrunning the gravel on the shoulder and rooting into cracked pavement, subsuming the road. Made his way down the wet dirt trail to the long crescent lighthouse beach, seagulls bobbing on the water, and stood staring out. He'd thought he would find Isabelle standing at her easel as always, a paintbrush full of watery pigment in her hand, her body a collage of paint smears, oblivious to everything but the scene directly in front of her, trying to re-create the world as she saw it: fragments made into something newly whole, pieces of herself joined back together. Speaking riddles about purpose and clarity, forgiveness and recompense, relentless in her effort to define some undefinable thing, to make sense of what could never make sense. All that carried pain, all that heartbreak.

After painting, she had always come home and thrown her still-damp canvases into the fire one by one until they burned to ash, no matter how much Eamon had begged her not to, no matter how much he'd begged her to let him keep them instead. There wasn't even one remaining after she left. All those haunting self-portraits she'd created over and over again. Eamon had tried to secret one away once, a small landscape portrait titled

Burial—a red-haired woman standing waist-deep in the Sound, her arms raised over her head, the tide swelling around her pregnant stomach, lapping at her breasts—but Isabelle had found it and burned it, too. In the end, the honeysuckle bonsai was the only thing Eamon had that still connected him to Isabelle—her body wrapped into his within the tree's trunk, the two of them forever together.

Over Snoqualmie Pass, past the last line of trees and dropping into the eastern Washington lowlands, Silva rolled down her window, let in the dry air—the smell of land so parched that to look at it was like experiencing thirst for the first time. All the coastal trees and moisture replaced by a vast expanse of rolling desert, open road miraging into lakes of sagebrush, squat herds of tumbleweeds waiting to take flight. A land as foreign as moonscape. Places she'd never wanted to be, places she couldn't think of living—no water, no sea, no gulls, no trees.

Two months ago, when the mainland job hadn't turned out to be what she wanted after all—swarms of people everywhere, everyone invested in the chaotic, cutthroat business of making maximum money in minimum time—she had decided to go back to the island, tell Eamon she'd finally made up her mind: she would settle there, on Trawler, keep the family business going. It was her only home and future, the only one that made any kind of sense.

She'd gone back to the island happy, anticipating Eamon's joy when she surprised him with the news he'd always wanted, but instead she'd found him lying on his bed, color drained from his skin, the honeysuckle uprooted next to him, its branches stripped, it trunk laid bare, as if in direct consequence of her abandonment, no one there to help him, no one there to help her.

She'd dragged him out to the Dodge and driven too fast, bracing his keeling body as she skidded through the corners. At the docks they Life

Flighted him out, the blink of the helicopter's lights in the sky, the dock swaying under the lap of the tide, clunking gently against its moorings.

By the time she'd caught the ferry and arrived at the mainland hospital, Eamon had been entombed in tubes, his skin putty-gray. Nurses brushed past, adjusting IVs, checking monitors, before the doctor came in and told Silva that Eamon's heart was failing, that it looked as though it had been in trouble for some time. Even though it wasn't what the doctor meant, Silva knew that both of their hearts had been compromised long ago.

She'd sat next to Eamon all night, smoothing his blankets, watching the movement of his breath, begging him to stay, stroking his knobbed and crooked knuckles, as hard as tree knots, as though he were turning into a tree himself, but he lay silent and died in the dark of early morning, his last breath like the rustling of leaves.

The nurses had come in officious and busy, handling Silva as if she were a task to be checked off, having her sign the cremation orders that forever consigned her to a family of ashes.

On Trawler, people had left casseroles and condolence cards as Silva slept in Eamon's bed—a dead dreamlessness that did nothing but make her more exhausted. She would wake and stare at the ceiling's water stains, which bled out like amoebas on the white tiles, feeling as though she were the one bleeding out, her mourning a numbness creeping up each limb. Everyone gone to the water now. The beach shore below the cabin where Eamon's ashes drifted, the white grit of them shifting beneath the water like a shadow presence left behind.

Finally, Silva had forced herself up, took the ferry to a seedy place on the mainland where the men eyed her as if they knew her, knew all she might be willing to take, all she might be willing to give to escape her sorrow. And she accepted everything they offered, drinking and inhaling until her limbs loosened in the thick air, until the music undulated into waves of pixilated light, until in the night's dark haze, someone took her to a mattress in a back room, the air saturated with the sickly ripeness of bare flesh, heads nimbused above her, her body suppurated beneath the metallic slap of strangers' skin. She had pawed the air like a drowning swimmer fighting for the surface until she'd finally lifted, suspended above herself on dark currents that cast her loose and drifting, severed from the weight of earth's gravity.

In the dusk of early morning, someone had finally taken her back to the ferry, and she'd stumbled home to the cabin along dense, overgrown trails, branches whipping her face and tearing at her legs, spider webs clinging tenuous and sticky to her face, everything transmuted, as if she'd come to in another land, as though she'd been gone forever, a lifetime spent and over.

Aloneness had enveloped her in an aura she could not evade, an emptiness that swallowed her whole. The bonsai dripped puddles into pocks of dark earth, and she had wanted to lie down, let the rain beat against her and never get up. Become one with the soil.

Buried in the fog of her mourning, it had taken her a long time to understand the scope of her damage—that night an irrevocable growth swelling inside her like a tumor. She pictured the embryo inside her growing monstrous— different pieces of the men that night forming its legs, its arms, its head, until it overgrew her body and she burst open like a flower blooming red.

She had rowed Eamon's boat out until the island was a shadow in the dark, then shipped the oars and drifted, contemplating the water's black depths. When she leaned over and saw the strange white halo of her own face reflected back to her, she stopped.

Instead she'd started running—ran with a kind of anguish nothing could assuage. She ran the woods along the shore, paths she followed by the indentations of smell and sound, her feet beating a constant rhythm past the cedars, past the ferry, past the docks, the island traced into the pounding rhythm of her legs. At the docks, she dumped crabs from fishermen's buckets and threw them back to the sea, watching them shimmy their way back into deeper waters.

The evening she'd finally decided to take herself to the water, let it claim her and the embryo growing inside her, she'd been going through Eamon's boxes looking for the picture of Isabelle, wanting to compare herself to it again, both of them the same age, equal in their sorrow now. Instead, she found a packet with a short note addressed to Eamon in a woman's scrawling cursive, written on stationery embossed with *McGregor's Honey Fresh Hives*—a honey business with an address from Two Rivers, Idaho. The packet's postmark from not even a year earlier.

Holding the packet in her hands, she'd had a feeling of suspense, of something profound waiting, something full of a deep meaning she couldn't name. Sitting under Eamon's worktable's yellowed lamplight, she'd pulled out a flat, tissue-paper-wrapped packet addressed to Eamon *"for safekeeping."* She stared at the faded, ink-bled letters, mistrusting her eyes, everything suddenly too dark to see, to understand what anything meant.

The tissue paper had torn easily—too flimsy to hide anything, meant for gift-giving: colorful, cheerful. And then into Silva's lap tumbled all the girls. Paintings of twelve girls with swollen abdomens and barely budded breasts, girls too young to be rendered so, their bodies in finely detailed exposure as they stared out into the unknown, their gazes a marker of their tortured fate, all of them with the same braided coronet and the same somber gaze, dressed in the same high-necked, old-fashioned wedding dress, as though they were playing dress-up for a staged antique-photo session, their rounded stomachs protruding in various degrees, each of their faces reflecting a kind of impending, sepulchral doom. A painted biography of the kind of loss and searching Silva already knew in her own cells. What it felt like to have everything of yourself stripped away until you were forced to leave your own body in surrender, cells dividing inside you until they replicated the reality of your own capture.

Before they'd fallen in her lap, the paintings had been tucked in a dog-eared magazine featuring a traveling art exhibit that had reached its halfway point in Moscow, Idaho—a small college town that proclaimed itself "The Heart of the Arts." And it hadn't taken Silva long to find it, a photograph of a small watercolor titled *In Eden*. The details of the painting were distant and blurred, but Silva had recognized the subject matter with an immediacy that stuttered her heart.

The tree was loosely stroked, softer in watercolor than it was in Eamon's journal sketches, but it was the honeysuckle bonsai, there was no doubt about it—the same curves of fleshly bodies, the same flowing wildness, the trunk-twisted lovers perfectly captured, leaning both into and away from each other, intrinsically intertwined, as clear and evident as if they were standing in front of Silva naked and in the flesh. Except, in this version, the honeysuckle's roots were laid out bare, and cradled in each root's branching reach was the bud of a newly formed infant—twelve of them like unfurled seedpods waiting for the sun's reach. Eamon's honeysuckle, uprooted as it had been beside Eamon as he lay dying—the tree so much a part of him, there was no way for one to live without the other.

As a child, Silva had always imagined Isabelle living nomadic and loose blown, existing somewhere lush and tropical and far enough away that nobody would ever find her, living a life without consequences. The same life Silva wanted to live. Instead, she'd been so close it made Silva's head spin. Sending Eamon her tortured paintings for "safekeeping."

Silva had always wondered what it would take to harden your heart enough to purposely abandon someone, to hurt them so deliberately. She realized now that Isabelle had never quit loving Eamon. She had just forever doomed him to a broken heart.

Eamon had told Silva that at first, after Isabelle had left, he'd planned on tracking her down, bringing her back home, but he hadn't been able to bear the thought of finding her in the arms of another lover, looking back at him from a distance he couldn't span. He'd convinced himself that it was too late to change anything. But over the years, he said he couldn't help wondering if all Isabelle had needed was for him to search her out, show her proof of how much he cared. That perhaps that's what she'd been looking for all along. Letting her go might have been the biggest failure of all; he'd just been too dilatory and heartbroken to see it. He said he would never make the same mistake again.

Silva had clutched the envelope in her hands. *I found you*, she wanted to yell, imagining Isabelle stopping, paintbrush in hand, listening to her voice echoing across the distance. She wasn't an imagined part of Silva's own existence—she had an address, a town, a lover, a date and time of being. Less than a year and a state away.

That night Silva had dreamed of a trio of females twirling on a cliff top in dappled light, their hands brushing the seeded tops of grasses above the sea's surface far below. But when they turned and faced her, the shock had woken her up cold. Three versions of herself staring back at her: her child self, her current self, and her older self. *Sankan*—triple trunk. Isabelle, Silva, and the baby.

Rain drenching the world gray, fog drifting like shadows, Silva had gotten up and packed her things, loaded the five bonsai, locked the cabin, peeled the ragged honeysuckle stickers off the Dodge's rusty doors, and driven to the early ferry with desperate finality. A journey into the wilderness, tracking the flight path of a grandmother she'd never met. A woman who had made a practice of leaving behind anything that mattered. A woman who didn't even know she existed. A woman who had become her only remaining family link, whether she wanted it or not.

———

Silva rested her hand on the outside of the Dodge's door, its red oxidized paint chalking her palm and fingertips. Together, she and Eamon had planned on repainting it again, repairing the rust. A '70 4x4 half-ton short-bed Power Wagon, the pickup in a previous life had been beaten into the ground by overzealous wildland-fire crews who didn't care that Kelly humps were meant to keep vehicles off old logging roads, who didn't care that skid roads were meant for skidders. Over the last few decades the truck had grown rusty on the edges, saggy in the middle, and weak in the U-joints— not unlike Eamon himself, who had begun to seem not exactly slow, but mellow. Content to spend long hours studying the ways his bonsai had matured into grace.

Silva had helped Eamon overhaul the pickup when she was fourteen, wire brushing, block sanding, taping, and masking. They'd painted it fire-engine red, the interior glass black, Eamon remounting the silver-scripted *Dodge* insignia on each fender, replanking the flatbed with smooth-sanded boards, and punctiliously trimming everything in the tight-grained oak he'd hoarded for years—oak the emblem of strength and survival. Of longevity and stubborn endurance. Oak trim on the dash; an oak cover over the radio and temperature controls; an oak knob for the gearshift; and oak for the glove-box door, its honeyed interior stamped with both their initials and the date of completion. Long enough ago that the rust had come back.

The Dodge smelled like home—sawdust, tree fungus, and loam, the five antediluvian bonsai bearing silent witness like a host of wizened judges ready to hand down sentence, each one a direct coniferous communication to Eamon. Each ancient style a language he'd taught her to speak: *sokan*—the twin-trunk juniper, a parent and child growing from the same roots; *ishizuki*—the rock-grown Sitka spruce, a sparse and stately oceanic sentinel; *moyogi*—the curved-trunk western red cedar, a primeval wizard with a long, shaggy beard; *shakan*—the slanting deadwood larch, a fiercely wild and mysterious shapeshifter; and *fukinagashi*—the windswept bristlecone pine, a silver-trunked mystic. Five primordial shamans seemingly more dead than alive but with enough strength to outlast every catastrophic event that had come their way.

She could still see Eamon at his bonsai table, clairvoyant with his otherworldly gaze. He had always known what she hadn't. It was a thing's roots that determined the shape of its life.

Eamon had taken Silva everywhere with him—every job, every outing. Rowing the Sound, walking the forest, he would point out well-formed saxifrages and madrones, explaining the ways of growth, and even as a five-year-old, Silva had been able to tell with a quick glance if a leaf-edge was dentate, crenate, or serrate. Whether a bonsai was cascade (*kengai*) or semi-cascade (*han-kengai*).

As a child, she had peered past her bedroom door, watching at night as Eamon watered and misted one bonsai after another, the damp earthy smell of wetted soil permeating the air. She would slip back to bed and dream of dirt and leaves, of branches twining around her in an embrace until she, too, was transformed.

My little dryad, Eamon had always called her, delighting in this, their shared kinship—trees a language she'd always been able to understand. As Silva had grown, all they'd had to do was gesture, tilt a shoulder, flip a hand, and the other understood. She had spent her first years in Trawler walking the beaches, sorting pea-size pebbles and tide-tumbled rocks, as Eamon explained the leavings of gut piles and empty claws. He'd taught her everything he knew, and she'd soaked it up like island moss, following heron tracks and exploring the foraging of crabs, gathering leaves and driftwood and the dry husks of beetles. They'd explored the woods around the island that held the unspeakable stuff of divinity: white clusters of wood nymph blooms, nests of junco and wren, the bone-sharp castings of owls. They'd rowed around the island, digging plants, collecting shells, scouting for whale spouts and the smooth slip of seals. The sound of the water, the oars creaking and dipping. Those had been her favorite moments—everything family life should be.

In Eamon's absence, Silva had taken over—misting, trimming, caressing, nurturing each ancient bonsai with the same care he had used. She thought perhaps that's all she wanted to do now—nurture. Having someone, some-thing, completely dependent on her was very different than always being the dependent one, the one left behind. There was the possibility of something else—something so new that even considering it felt dangerous.

———

Outside, the land transformed again, the highway paralleling rolling hills sprouted with spring crops—wheat, barley, canola, lentils, chickpeas. A feast in the making. Silva's appetite was something new and unexpected. A body forming the shape of new life.

She had been afraid to leave anything behind. Along with the five bonsai, she'd packed the seed collection her mother had helped her start when she was young, Eamon's antique bonsai tools, the packet of Isabelle's girl paintings and the art magazine she'd sent Eamon, and Eamon's mildewed bonsai journals, full of fifty years of notes and sketches.

Each bonsai journal showed a stage of who Eamon had been and who he'd become. Silva had named his earliest work "The Isabelle Influence"—sensuous, full-bodied trees curved into soft draping arrangements, trees that blossomed and berried: jasmine, gardenia, bougainvillea, honeysuckle. Afterward, Eamon's bonsai had become more and more austere and spare—conifers gnarled into their most essential form.

Silva wanted to study the journals until she found the answers she was sure were hidden there—how to regrow all that had been torn loose and uprooted, how to repair heartrot and root rot, how to splice in severed growth, graft in new DNA—although she was afraid there was no real coming back from a lifetime of suffering that kind of damage.

Finally, eight hours into the drive, Silva reached Moscow, where Isabelle's *In Eden* had hung. Below a backdrop of towering grain silos, tweedy, wool-coated professors and hipster students strolled the sidewalks, intent on their scholarly lives. Silva wanted to stop and ask if they'd seen it, if they'd felt what she had: a sense of almost electrical recognition and connection, the heartbreaking beauty of each branch and leaf and blossom, the striking reality of the lovers' bodies sculpted into its trunk. An intimacy that had left her stunned, as though she'd stumbled upon a painting of her own naked body, as vibrant and exposed as light, illuminated for the whole world to see. The honeysuckle, Eamon, Isabelle, and Silva reflected back to one another.

She'd planned to stop at the gallery just to be in the same space the painting had been in, but instead she drove through town without stopping. Even though she was chasing a lead that was over a year old, even though she'd hardly eaten, had hardly even stopped for bathroom breaks despite her bladder's new insistence, she felt as though if she stopped, she would lose Isabelle forever, each minute weighted with the permanency of development: *lungs, fingers, toes. A beating heart.*

She dropped down into the paper-mill-stink of a river valley town, then climbed back up to high prairie, stilt-legged barns and houses perched on the edge of land too dry to support more than brush and bony-hipped steers. At the driveway of one weather-beaten farmhouse, a woman drove a tractor to a field, the two cow dogs trotting alongside its tall tires giving Silva hard stares over their shoulders. Dust devils and chaff traveled along the ditches, drafts of air dipping and rising with the unexpected coolness of a creek inlet and the recent hatching of insects.

She held on to the drift and swerve of the Dodge, dropping elevation again, passing a historic Native American battleground—the Battle of White Bird Canyon, fought June 17, 1877, between the Nez Perce Indians and the United States government. People who fought to stay together in a place that had always been theirs, the Salmon River carving its path through their canyonland home. *The River of No Return.*

Eighteen-wheelers blew by, sucking the Dodge into their wake, leaving Silva white-knuckled, holding onto the loose steering wheel as if she were steering an errant boat through the rising chop and curl of the Straights on a storm-threatening day, the water calling for her to join it.

The island's every feature was imprinted into her being. The madrones and Sitkas lining the shore above the beach like denizens of another place and time. Black-capped chickadees calling their own name, Swainson's thrushes trilling watery. It was early March—time to cut back dead wood, prune rose cane and privet, the spring wind bringing with it an invisible signal of growth, everything burgeoning under its touch, buds bursting open and suckers surging upward, growing straight and unseemly from the branches of lilac, forsythia, willow, and flowering plum. Eamon's bonsai, too, had spurted into new growth, and she'd been busy pinching eruptions of green from branches long trained to be bare.

Leaving the island had been a tearing away, a stripping down. Like this steep-walled rough canyon with its spines and striations—its fragility disguised by severity. Its exposure like pain, raw and unencumbered.

Finally, she passed a sign announcing *Two Rivers—Population 422* and found herself driving through a corridor of sharp-peaked houses sheathed in mismatched siding and corrugated tin, their porches hung with "Don't Tread on Me" flags, junked cars and walleyed horses mired in mud yards behind sagging barbwire fences. She wondered if Isabelle had been counted, too, along with the beekeeper she'd lived with. McGregor of the healthy hives. Eamon's replacement.

As a child, Silva had loved nothing more than being on the water with Eamon, imagining herself, like Isabelle, on tropical shores, each wilder and more exotic than the last. Like Isabelle's namesake island: Isabela of the Galápagos, birthplace to primordial beings. But Isabelle had come to this land, the antithesis of tropical. Although nobody could argue its wildness. A rough sprawl of empty spaces meant to drive you away rather than pull you in. A confluence of wild waters near the place Isabelle had called home, at least for a while.

A group of older ladies planting petunias and marigolds in half barrels on the street corner just past a weedy, overgrown baseball diamond watched as she parked next to Build It Best, the only place in town with a room available. A hardware store whose front windows displayed a grizzly reared in attack, yellowed teeth and claws prominent.

When Silva had called ahead to make a reservation, the town's only motel was booked full of government tenants. The receptionist hadn't seemed too happy about it, calling them "idiot feds" before catching herself. She'd given Silva the hardware store's number, and Silva had just been happy to find a place to stay, though now she questioned her decision.

She stayed in the Dodge for a moment, taking stock of her surroundings. Down the street, a few people chatted outside a drugstore, and on the corner the women were back to planting petunias. Otherwise the town was quiet, studded with billboards advertising wild-game processing and huckleberry desserts. She tried to imagine Isabelle on the sidewalk on a late-spring afternoon, chatting with townspeople, but Silva's childhood imaginings hadn't ever consigned Isabelle to such a place—a place with a kind of roughness that brooked no frivolity, although like most of the town's businesses, Build It Best was squared off in a western facade with an upside-down horseshoe nailed over the doors. A few stores had hitching posts installed outside for added western flair. Even the movie rental place across the street had a western facade, advertisement posters of explosions and scantily clad women framed in rough-sawn lumber and a life-size John Wayne cardboard cutout, six-shooter drawn, in the front window.

Making sure their delicate branches weren't smashed, Silva repositioned the bonsai, the bristlecone pine alone older than this place, at least in terms of colonial history. *Pinus longaeva*, the oldest non-clonal living organism on earth. Methuselah, a wild bristlecone and one of the oldest trees known, sported over five thousand growth rings, germinating somewhere around 3050 BCE in the wilds of the US, even before the Egyptians built their pyramids. A gnarled but diminutive tree that had outlasted everything else, including the American westward "progress" that had helped populate Two Rivers—something, like her driving need to find her long-lost runaway artist grandmother, Silva doubted the townspeople would appreciate.

CHAPTER TWO

Date: September 1, 1999
Title: Baptism of the Virgins
Subject: The Twelve Maidens of Almost Paradise & Len Dietz
Setting: Larkins Beach, Snake River, Hells Canyon
Medium: Watercolor and graphite on cold-press
Size: 12×12

Dearest Eamon,

It is September first. Our anniversary. Remember that dark drive, our headlights on water, the sound of Canadian geese flying over? Twenty years ago. A time like coming home.

The grasses here are blond and brittle already, dry husks rustling with the canyon wind, the sky bleached pale, the sun's power leaching color from everything it has touched as the season hardens, the nights grown cold, the air alive with the movements of birds flocking for fall. The river makes me think of you, this water winding its way past me. But everything makes me think of you: the water, the shoreline, the deep currents. And the trees, of course, though none are like yours. Is it ever possible to go back? To make something wrong right again?

Let me try to explain: I have come here to pay witness. To record and capture for the rest of the world just what the depth of this female subjugation looks like. Desperation, despair, desolation, disempowerment. Patriarchal abuse. Though perhaps I have also come here to make sense of my past, to understand myself, to make amends for the wreckage of my own life. But this place is a poison spread. It is the hardest thing I've ever done. And you know just what kind of "hard" that means, for me, even though it's been decades since I left, since we last saw each other, since everything changed. But some things never do change, no matter that everything else around them does. You always knew everything I ever knew about anything.

Today, the first of my commissioned Almost Paradise paintings is done, leading up to the grand finale: the Wedding of the Maidens, which will be held on the coming millennial, January 1, 2000—Y2K, The End of Everything, the Apocalypse, the beginning of Len Dietz's reign, of his Holy Family of God, of his marriage to the Twelve Maidens. These child brides, these girls conscripted to his insanity.

The painting of them is a pink light-wash that belies the torn heart pulsing in its center. Something you would still recognize, I think— all that beating pain, all those ragged edges peeled back, revealing that unfathomably dark and bleeding middle.

I set up on the beach, as I have so many times before. I arranged each brush, each tube of color. I angled the easel. I settled my feet wide in the sand—a power stance. Ready, I thought. But there was no preparing for it. When I opened my eyes, when I looked up and breathed out, there was nothing but them—these girls, each one like a newly captured and injured self. When he lowered them, one by one, into the water, I couldn't breathe, my heart like a broken bird beating against the bones of my chest. I thought I would faint, thought I would fall, too, just as they had, but instead I let my hands go free, and I painted face after face under those lace veils, under that silvered water, drowning themselves in their own mistaken faith. But what choice have they been given? What choice might they otherwise make? He is their lord and savior. He is their ruler and king. He is their master and their keeper. He is their father and their lover. He is their abuser, who dictates everything that will ever be done to them, for them, and against them.

And I do nothing but paint.

I never told you what I needed to, what I should have said right at the beginning: that what that man—my "father"—did to me would never be undone, no matter how long it has been, no matter how far I have run from him, from myself, from everything that has come. Where are the words for such things? How do you speak such things into the daylight, or even into night?

I have never been able to face it except through my paints. And now, maybe, these letters, even though I will never send them. How could I do that to you? All these years gone, and only now can I speak it, laying down each word like a brick mortared into a wall we could never break through. Your trees, my paintings—our language of grief and longing, and love, too. Everything we wished we could be and say and do for each other, but didn't. . . . I didn't. You did. Every day. Do you know what that meant to me then? What it means to me now? There are some things that defy words, that defy images—your actions like the air I breathed, the water I drank, the food I ate. Except in the end, not one of them could sustain me. Nothing could. Not with the black hole inside of me forever sucking in all the light, voracious and insatiable.

Now the darkness is on the outside, the small light of my soul like a candle held against the black expanse of this compound's sky. I wish I could burn it all down. I wish I could grab the girls by their hands and pull them all to safety. I wish I could shelter them with you on the island, just as I found shelter there. But this storm is not yours to break. This storm belongs to the broken.

And so I will carve their names into paper, I will sing my heart to yours, I will blot color until it bleeds truth. I will call their names out in my sleep until I can again find myself. Please keep them safe for me.

> My love to you always,
> Isabelle

CHAPTER THREE

MARCH 2001

Silva brushed herself into a semblance of tidiness—her clothes limp and wrinkled, her hair a wind-blown mess—before pushing through Build It Best's glass doors, wincing as a raucous cowbell attached to the inside handle announced her entry. Confronted by dozens of head mounts on every wall, she stopped. Black glass eyes gazed back at her with reproach: elk, mountain sheep, deer, moose, caribou, mountain goats. A dusty wolf and tattered mountain lion crouched, snarling. It looked like a horror movie set waiting for the unwitting protagonist to wander in.

Nobody there, she went to the front counter, which was arranged with fishing tackle and ceramic Idaho potato penny banks next to bumper stickers that read *Welcome to Idaho, Now Go Home.* Liquor bottles stood stacked high on shelves behind the counter, a bright yellow sign declaring: *We know who you are, so don't even try!* The newest warted-gourd postage stamps were lined up next to the cash register under the display-case glass, and various items of "moose-bead" jewelry were draped over blue velvet on the shelf below: shellacked moose pellets strung onto necklaces and bracelets. Objects that seemed purposefully adventitious in a place hostile to outsiders.

Finally, a heavyset bottle-blonde with a nametag that read *Becky* with a smiley face came bustling from the back of the store, looking Silva over from head to toe in a sweep that landed on Silva's hair and stayed there, wavering, as though she were taking in a strange beast.

"Can I help you?" Becky asked uncertainly, as if worried Silva might demand more than she could provide.

"I have a reservation?" Silva tried not to show her discomfort, being in this town, searching for a ghost.

"Ah, Sylvia from Trawler Island?" Becky asked, her brows arched quizzically under curls that adhered to her forehead, her smell a mix of baby power and candy. "We don't get many visitors. Not from a place like that. Sounds exotic." Her tone hinted at accusation.

"It's no place special," Silva said quickly, though it wasn't true. The cabin, the water and salt air, the smell of kelp and damp sand. Already it seemed a place she'd left a long time ago—something that had happened anciently, alone again, fighting for herself. She felt as out of place as Eamon's bonsai on the Dodge's front seat. As out of place as Isabelle's painting of the honeysuckle. None of them with any kind of belonging in a place like this.

"Come to see all the action?" Becky asked, some kind of deeper inquiry behind her forced small-town friendliness. She rubbed a small, newly inked tattoo on the top of her wrist—three small parallel lines inside a circle that she touched as carefully as a scabbed-over wound.

"Just passing through."

Silva wondered if Becky had known Isabelle. A year wasn't a long time, and Two Rivers was the kind of place where everybody knew everyone else—even those who were just passing through. The kind of place where a woman like Isabelle would have stood out, caused a stir.

"Well, we'll get you taken care of right away," Becky said, bustling into action. "Town's full up. You're lucky to have a spot." She glanced at Silva again in unspoken assessment as she pulled out a pad covered with names and dates. "Just sign here and we'll get things in order."

As Silva signed the paper, Becky pawed under the counter for a key on a green plastic fob then picked up the phone intercom, her voice echoing hollowly throughout the store. "Rick, come to the front desk, Rick." She shook her head at Silva. "He's probably jawing with Delbert. I swear that man could talk the hind legs off a mule. We'll get you all settled in just a minute, honey." She uncapped a tube of ChapStick and applied a thick layer, the smell of chemical-cherry making Silva's stomach lurch. "You be sure to let us know if there's anything you need. We aim to please around here, no matter what they're saying about us in the news. . . ."

"I'll get my things together," Silva said before Becky could tell her why this tiny, dried-up town or its people would be in the news. Before Silva could question her own motives again.

She knew what it was like to live in a place where everyone wanted to know everything about you, questions like a preprogrammed train circling into each stop: *Where are you from? What do you do? Who's your family?* A line of inquiry meant to make sense of things of which there was no sense to be made. Everybody wanting reassuring stories, happy stories, stories that made you feel good about life. Not the truth of what each decision had cost. Slipping into dark waters and breathing in. Nobody wanted to talk about how things *didn't* work out, even though that was life's reality.

Outside, despite what she'd told Becky, Silva decided she wouldn't unload until everyone was gone for the night. Who knew what kind of questions Eamon's trees would precipitate—things so ancient that to look at them was to see your own mortality, your life as a blip in universal time. Instead, she walked to a tiny real estate office already closed for the day and looked at property photos taped to the front window. Acres and acres of emptiness—places where you could hide yourself away so well you might never be found. Even by your own family members.

Farther down the street, a small log building's carved wooden sign declared itself the Two Rivers Museum. A teenage girl wearing too much makeup and not enough clothes sat inside the propped-open door, reading just out of the sun's reach, hardly glancing up as Silva went in. The log space contained some historical heirlooms but was mostly filled with pictures—old black-and-whites of stiff and solemn-faced ranchers and miners. Men with wide foreheads, piercing eyes, and rounded upper backs. Men who looked as if they'd grown around carrying too much weight.

Silva hoped perhaps she might find some trace of Isabelle, or at least what thing or place she'd thought profound enough a "truth" to disappear into, but none in the sea of faces was familiar—certainly nobody resembling Isabelle with her redheaded wild-artist look. A woman Silva had always imagined belonged in expat Paris, drinking, smoking, and painting nudes.

Like the hardware store, the museum's back wall was covered with dead animals, captured in photographs instead of mounted. Men crouched over their kills, holding up animal heads proudly in display: cougar, elk, deer, mountain goats, bighorn sheep, clutches of sage grouse, and blood-streaked wolves stung upright to demonstrate their length and girth against the men who'd shot them as a trophy.

Several of the kill photos featured the same big, stiff-faced, dark-haired, camo-wearing man, captions naming him Len Dietz. Seemingly the town's most successful killer. He was there in an older display, as well, this time in a Vietnam uniform, hair shaved, rifle slung over his shoulder, baby-faced but holding the same stiff, threatening posture. One of those men who'd never been able to leave combat behind.

Already this place was somewhere Silva didn't want to be. Maybe that was what had driven Isabelle, too. A need to escape the inescapable.

When Silva braved Build It Best's cowbells again, hoping Rick had done whatever needed doing for her room to be ready, Becky was in the back helping someone else. While she waited, Silva glanced at a stack of newspapers on the counter featuring a front-page picture of a snarling wolf and the bolded headline PREDATOR AT LARGE. The picture matched the wolf in the front window, the same threatening expression taxidermied onto its face. A plaque underneath the mounted wolf read, *Canadian Gray Wolf. Shot by Len Dietz*. It seemed the locals weren't fond of any predator besides themselves. She'd heard about the wolf wars being waged in the interior west, an old fury reignited with the animal's successful reintroduction, but it had always felt far removed from the island.

When she heard Becky coming, Silva readied herself for the friendly onslaught, but this time Becky's face was serious, preoccupied. She went behind the counter to ring up a bundle of wire and two dozen boxes of ammunition, which she pulled out of a locked cabinet beside her.

The man who'd followed her to the counter pulled a wad of cash from his wallet and counted out stacks of twenties. He was dressed for combat: Vietnam-era camo pants tucked into military-style boots and a large pistol in a tactical holster. Everything was part of a uniform except the pristine white shirt he wore—so clean and starched it looked as if it'd just come from the ironing board, sharp creases running down each sleeve, its collar stiff and open. His long hair hung loose, silver streaked and carefully manicured, a leather-strung pendant around his neck—a pyramid with a circle and an eye engraved in its center. Everything about him a strange mix of military and dandy.

"Is that all you have?" he asked, gesturing to the ammo, his voice commanding, his posture upright, his hair rippling on his white shirt like the pelt of an animal.

Silva looked away. *Another open-carry asshole.* Even if he was just a flamboyantly dressed rancher or hunter, even if this was just another small, bloodthirsty western town in a parched wilderness where guns probably outnumbered people a hundred to one, the man seemed like someone with way too much to prove. Someone who liked attention and intimidation.

"Might be able to get another shipment in next week, but I wouldn't be surprised if they shut that down, too," Becky said, giving the man a guarded look before glancing over at Silva.

On Becky's cue, the man looked at Silva, too, staring at her as if he'd recognized a ghost, his gaze at first startled, then sharp and focused—forceful enough that she wanted to step away, as disconcerted by his response to her as she was by her own recognition. A half hour in this place and she already knew who he was. The museum's photographs a prelude to the real thing: a self-fashioned Samsonite who killed wolves instead of lions. She wondered if along with his pistol he kept the jawbone of an ass handy for all his slaying purposes.

"This is Sylvia from Trawler Island," Becky said.

"Silva," she corrected automatically, before she thought better of it, her name out there in between them. To make up for it, she squared herself off, radiating unfriendliness. The last thing she wanted was an introduction to a man like him.

"*Silva*," Becky said, as if it were something foreign and unsavory. Then Becky turned to him and said, "She's staying here with us a while, renting the room upstairs." No regard whatsoever to Silva's right to privacy or safety. A woman on her own in strange territory. A woman with nothing and nobody but herself for protection.

Len Dietz stepped closer to her, and Silva again fought the urge to back away, her adrenaline pumping for fight or flight no matter how calm she willed herself to be. Something in the way he looked at her—as if he already knew who she was and why she'd come. She'd seen that look in men's eyes before. She understood what it meant, what kind of darkness it could lead to.

"Nice to meet you, Silva," he said, drawing out her name, studying her carefully.

Deep instinct told her to retreat, to gain distance as quickly as possible, but she wouldn't give into it. She held herself steady, meeting his gaze, challenging whatever question he was asking of her, whatever recognition he thought he'd had, whatever power he thought he wielded.

But then he looked down and studied her abdomen, his eyes flickering with a kind of interest—a sudden intimate knowledge that took her breath away.

She crossed her arms quickly over her stomach and stepped backward with a protective instinct she couldn't override. There was no way he could know. She wasn't even close to showing yet, and she'd told no one.

Everything turned silent. Becky's eyes darted back and forth between Len and Silva. The surrounding animal eyes looked on, as though they were all aware something was happening.

Len took a step closer and held his hand out to Silva as if she were a skittish animal in need of his help. "'Lo, children are a heritage of the Lord and the fruit of the womb a reward,'" he said, and Silva's body froze in place, her breath like a solid thing inside her lungs.

"You are alone and with child. You don't know if you will keep it, or yourself. Don't know if you'll keep anything," he said, quiet and sure—a tone of divine proclamation, of a wilderness prophet, casting Silva's darkest secrets out to the world as if they were nothing, his knowledge of what she carried as evident as the pistol on his hip.

And as if in direct response to his words, Silva's uterus cramped so sudden and hard that the pain nearly buckled her to her knees. She grabbed the counter, knocking over the newspapers, snarling wolves sent scattering on the floor under her feet in warning: *Predator at Large*, Len Dietz next to her, grabbing her arm guiding her to a nearby plastic chair she crumpled into as her uterus cramped hard enough that she couldn't help crying out.

Len leaned down and stroked her back as if she were a woman in labor, and perhaps she was—her own body already rejecting itself, trying to expel the new shape forming inside of it.

"You need to take care of yourself—there's more to consider now," he said, his words heavy with implied meaning, as if Silva had submitted to his care, as if she were a child he was guiding along the right path. Someone used to being obeyed. Someone used to giving rules meant for others to follow. Someone who knew things about her *nobody* could possibly know.

He was close enough that she could feel his body heat as he bent over and spoke softly into her ear. "'Come to me and find refuge. Seek and ye shall find.'" Then he walked to the counter and gathered his bags, his gun hanging heavy on his hip, his arms full of enough ammo to supply a war. He turned and pushed through the doors, cowbells left ringing behind him.

As soon as she was sure he was gone, Silva slumped forward, the chair tipping. She wanted to throw something, yell, cry, scream, but she was stricken mute. Being handled by this stranger, this man with impossible intimate knowledge of her.

Becky hurried to her side. "You poor thing. Len was right. You look just terrible. We need to get you upstairs to rest"—as if all of it, Len's impossible knowledge of Silva and her own dramatic bodily reaction, were something she could recover from by taking a quick nap.

Silva wanted to get up and run, escape what she'd so foolishly thought she'd come to find, but her hands and legs were shaking so badly it was all she could do to get herself upright. Being exposed like that—left as crumpled and wilted as a trodden flower.

Outside, the apartment steps swayed and creaked as if they, too, were coming undone, and Silva was afraid she was going to crumple again before she made it up—her body quaking, her ears whooshing as if stopped up with water, her abdomen pulsing and raw with pain.

Becky unlocked the door and helped her into the small, bleak room. Silva sank onto a narrow single bed on the far wall under a dirty window, a tiny bathroom no bigger than a closet to the right and a kitchenette to the left. A prisoner's dorm. A place she never should have come.

Becky hesitated at Silva's side, fiddling with her name tag, touching the tattoo again as if to reassure herself. "You can trust Len," she said, a hard look passing over her face. "He takes care of all the mothers. He's only trying to take back what's rightfully ours—give us what we need to survive."

This town, these people—everything they said disjointed and full of threat.

Silva was too stricken to respond, to say that trusting someone like Len Dietz was like being held underwater, staring at the light above you as you fought your own end.

When Becky finally closed the door, the stairs groaning with her depar-ture, Silva curled into a fetal position and buried herself under the covers, her insides radiating pain, her limbs loose in their sockets, her thoughts crowded and thick. Who spoke to someone that way? Who said those kinds of things? Casting her secrets to the air as if they were nothing more than drifting seeds driven by the vagrancies of the wind.

CHAPTER FOUR

— ◆→✦←◆ —

You who are without blame, you who are pure, you who are we—
these our bodies, our flesh, our holiness made into words, our fingers
grasping at his hem as he chooses one, as he chooses you and you
rise to your feet, your flesh unto his flesh, your body unto his body,
your eyes unto his eyes. You, the chosen one, you the promise, you the
blessed, you who follow his path in the dark, two made into one,
two made into you. And he tells you what he tells the others, whis-
pering into your ear as he takes hold of you, his words fluttering
like swarming winged creatures you can't catch a hold of as his body
becomes the flesh of your flesh, flesh cleaved in two, the echoes of his
words swirling your head like a swarm of bees intent on driving
you away—over the cliff, they say, but you must keep them beaten
back so that he might stay, keep yourself still until he pulls away,
holding your loose hair in his hands, grasping your chin so as to
look into your eyes and remind you of your promises coming like
shelter from the rushing swarm of his words, your promises like the
walls that surround you, that keep you safe from the outside, from
a world made evil, your body seeping in the seeds of his holiness, his
flesh made into word.

CHAPTER FIVE

Silva awoke gulping for air, the sheets tangled around her legs. A sorrow like suffocation, like drowning. She wasn't sure which had awakened her—her still-pulsing insides, or her nightmare of a woman, wet and desolate, swimming underwater with a slick gray fish body, mouth gaped open in a cry so full of desperation that Silva had awakened crying, too, awash in the fresh emotion of a child who'd lost her mother to the water. She felt it in her own blood—felt the moment her mother had breathed the river in and let it flow through her veins like an icy current.

Outside, morning activities came through Build It Best's thin walls: a diesel truck idling somewhere close by, a child squealing in the distance, and conversations drifting up from the lumberyard below—a high-pitched peal of laughter Silva recognized as Becky's.

Remembering everything from the night before in a sudden rush, Silva sat up quickly, imagining Len Dietz climbing the stairs to her room, Becky close on his heels. She held her breath and waited, but first the diesel truck pulled out of the lumberyard, and then everything else turned quiet, too.

The night before, her brain and body had been too overloaded to fight back, unable to process everything that had happened, but now, in the clear light of morning, the grief she'd awakened with was burned away by a deep, blinding fury. A stranger speaking to her like that. As if he controlled her. As if she were his to command.

She replayed the encounter in her head, a revision in which she yelled at him to get the fuck away from her, yelled at him that everything he said was wrong: god had never been a part of anything, and he certainly wasn't now.

She wished she had been able to deliver the kind of equalizing someone like Len Dietz deserved—threatening instead of being threatened.

She put a hand to her stomach, shuddering to think of what might happen to any woman ill-fated enough to be in his care. A town brimming with its own kind of infection.

She carefully palpitated the soft space under her ribs until she reached the hard rise of her hipbones, the bruised reminder of the night before buried deep. Under her fingers, her guts gurgled, protesting their emptiness. The basic need to survive trumping everything else.

Still dressed in the same clothes she'd driven and slept in, she pulled on her boots, lacing them tight before yanking her hair into a ponytail, twisting a rubber band over it until it stuck out from the base of her skull like an oversize barber brush. She splashed water on her face and then looked out the window to make sure the sidewalk was empty before going out to her truck, its windows fogged over with the trees' night breathing.

Working as quickly as she could, she hauled the trees and boxes to her room. She kept her back turned toward Build It Best as she made each trip, hoping Becky was busy inside and wouldn't notice her carrying the bonsai up. She arranged the trees around the kitchen table, and they overtook the room, each bonsai bearing its own powerful personality, its own timeless sense of being, its own spirituality. Sitka spruce—protection from death and illness. Western red cedar—vivid dreams, warding away evil spirits, and purification from death. Needle juniper—protection, love, cleansing from the spread of poisons or disease. Western larch—protection against evil and to induce visions. Bristlecone pine—longevity and strength, alleviation of guilt.

Eamon had taught her each tree's spiritual and symbolic significance along with the science of their shaping and care, trees throughout centuries and cultures thought to be the houses of gods, entrances to higher realms. And his bonsai looked it. As if they held all the answers for which she was searching. An embodiment of the divine. Her favorite story had been the hamadryads—female spirits presiding over the forests, born bonded to a certain tree. Should their tree perish, the hamadryad would die, too. Should their tree or forest be threatened by a mortal, the dryads and the gods would punish the mortal. Silva just wondered if there was a tree left to sustain her.

Arranged in a circle on the small round table, the bonsai reminded her of westward settlers who'd circled their wagon trains for the night, turning their strongest side outward in defense against attack and protecting the vulnerable inner circle. She wished she could shrink herself and hide inside, find shelter.

Instead, she misted each tree, checking every branch and nodule, every whorl of root, patting their moss-covered soil back into place, watering them carefully, worried that, like her, they, too, would be misshapen and damaged by their adaptation to failure.

Turning sideways to eye her body's profile in the bathroom mirror, she tried to see what had tipped off Len Dietz, but her stomach was sunken, her complexion wan. In a young memory, she stood next to her mother, holding her own small, pasty-white arm up to her mother's darkly tanned arm. Her mother had told her that when she was born, the full moon had claimed her as its own. Silva had loved thinking about it when she was a child—her kinship with the moon—even if it frightened her a bit. The remote coolness. The unreachability. The latent power. Power enough to command the tides, direct the earth's axis. Reflect and redirect the frenetic energy of the sun. She'd been born outside on the night of the full Sturgeon Moon, everything earth-centered, everything full of meaning and portent. They'd celebrated with a moon dance, named her Silvania August Moonbeam Merigal. She had been wanted, treasured, part of a family.

Six weeks. Enough time for anyone to know what to do with themselves. Nerve cells branching and connecting, forming primitive neural pathways. Forming the makings of memory.

She locked the room and tucked the green key fob in her pocket. Len and Becky were right—she was in Two Rivers for a reason, except that reason had *nothing* to do with any divine predestination. No matter what Len said he knew, he had no idea what Silva needed to find.

Armed with directions to McGregor's Healthy Hive-Fresh Honey, she spread out the atlas on the truck seat again. Two Rivers was just a small dot at the junction of topography lines. Outside of town, the Salmon River bent inward, a curve that on the map looked haphazardly drawn, accidental. But her plan was straightforward enough: she would follow the road, find McGregor's, and then she would find out what happened to Isabelle. It didn't matter what Len Dietz thought or what kind of twisted history this town held. All that mattered was that she found out what she needed to know—wherever and whatever that meant. It was a measure of her own mortality.

She'd half expected Becky to show up ushering Len Dietz, both of them ready to guide her on god's chosen path, spouting deific secrets they didn't know, but everything remained still as she started the Dodge, the town itself seeming to wait to see what direction she would take.

She drove to the outskirts of Two Rivers past the Yellow-Pine Motel— the place full of the "idiot feds" the receptionist had griped about, a grouping of white government vehicles parked outside the motel in an orderly line. She wondered if they called it the Piss-Pine Motel. Yellow, piss, bull—each alternative ponderosa name casting a social meaning beyond itself.

Growing up on Trawler, kids had called Silva Tree Girl. Every school project she completed from first grade on had something to do with trees. How they communicated. How they reproduced—her classmates tittering when they realized she was talking about tree sex. How they could survive everything from floods to fire, thriving under hardship. She'd liked the nickname, even if it wasn't always meant as a compliment. She'd imagined herself as a dryad superhero whose powers changed according to the type of tree she happened to be most attached to at the time. When she walked to and from school, she imagined the papery discs floating down from the elms following her just like the tumbling leaves, attracted to her with magnetic force. Imagined that she could direct them, raising them into a whirlwind of her own making.

As a teen, she had carried Eamon's old college dendrology textbook with her wherever they went, matching leaf margins and cones, learning the world through trees, naming their favorites: "Newton," an ancient heirloom apple tree on the island's south side; "Montezuma," a wide-girthed western red cedar Eamon named after the 119-foot-circumference cypress that grew in Oaxaca, Mexico; "Kodama," a Japanese yew, home to tree spirits; and "Pando," a giant quaking aspen on the island's point they named after the Utah Pando Clone—a grove of 47,000 genetically identical trees forming a single organism that covered over a hundred acres and weighed thirteen million pounds. The oldest living organism on earth, tree after tree resprouting and growing anew century after century, functioning as a single whole made up of thousands of individuals. A family of interconnected roots.

Outside the grocery store—a squat cinderblock building painted bright orange, its plate-glass windows boarded up—a sheriff in a mud-spattered SUV pulled out, a news van following closely behind him. Whatever "action" Becky had been referring to had garnered both the government's and the news's attention. Something, according to Becky's intimations, that involved Len Dietz, although it seemed there wasn't anything in town that *didn't* involve him.

Silva pulled in and parked. Her body had made its demands clear even if she didn't want to stop now any more than she had on the way over. Wandering the aisles, she quickly gathered enough items to pass for a few meals and went to the only checker—a woman who peered at her from behind purple glasses, her fingers agile on the ten-key despite their girding, flesh bubbled up around rings of varying patterns of leaves and rosettes and grape clusters, fingernails clicking in sharp little taps, and there on her wrist, the same circular tattoo Becky had. Silva found herself staring, unable to look away, wondering if everyone in town had matching tattoos.

Mistaking Silva's interest, the woman proudly held out her hand. "Black Hills gold, every one of them," she said, leaning toward Silva and pulling her hair back, exposing an earlobe studded with multiple matching earrings. "Them long ones," she said, shaking her head to show off the dangles that hung against her downy-haired neck, "my Charlie gave me for Christmas." She gestured. "That's him there."

Tacked to the partition wall next to an ad for $3.99/lb. rib roast was a photo of a bearded man in full camouflage crouched behind a prone elk, holding up its head by the antlers, its pink tongue lolling out of its mouth. Another of the town's proud hunters.

The woman looked around as if making sure not to be overheard. "Won the Paradise elk raffle last fall. Got him a six-point. Good folks, those, standing up for our rights. Calling it an *occupation*. Nobody cares the government took all the land illegally in the first place. They think they can tell us what to do when we've got a God-given right to hunt, mine, log, fish, drill, whatever. It's called *do-min-ion*." She shook her head in disgust and pulled out a brochure from under the counter. "Paradise gives free jerky to visitors. Coupon's in the back. Them folks are the real patriots," she said, hastily tucking in the brochure with Silva's groceries as a middle-aged man wearing a red store apron approached the check-stand, his name, *Charu Cheema*, stitched on the front.

The man stopped at the end of the counter, his attention directed at the checker. "Sherry, I believe we have discussed this before," he said, each word enunciated with musical cadence. His dark hair was parted neatly to the side and combed back, everything about him tidy and tucked and careful. He tipped his head at Silva. "So sorry for the inconvenience, ma'am," he said, his brow furrowed in genuine apology and concern, as if Silva had been somehow terribly mistreated.

"It's no problem," she said, although she could see how much everything *was* a problem here. She tried not to show her surprise at an Indian man owning a grocery store in the middle-of-nowhere, white-antigovernment Idaho.

"We at C&C Foods wish only to offer the best products at the best prices." He tried a smile, but it was thin, his eyes wary behind his glasses. "Nothing here but good food. Everybody needs food," he said, but there was a hesitation to his voice, as if he were trying to convince himself, too.

For the first time, Silva realized the store was empty of customers except her, the windows boarded over as if there had been a looting. She wished she could go back and load her cart heaping with items. She already knew what it meant to be so clearly an outsider in this town.

"Have a good day," Mr. Cheema said, stepping back courteously as Silva left, waiting to further address the recalcitrant Sherry. One small skirmish of the battle clearly being waged.

Silva stashed the groceries on the Dodge's passenger floorboards. Sheets of paper fluttered from a bulletin board next to the store's front doors—trucks and dogs for sale, a misspelled ad for handyman work and house-cleaning, and several of the same glossy-fronted brochures Sherry had tucked into Silva's groceries, *Paradise Elk Ranch* in bright blue with a picture of a bugling bull elk on the front. Eating quickly, Silva pulled out the bro-chure, reading descriptions of guided hunts and meat products. The last page featured a fireball sun over a dark, smoking world with the text, *Don't Wait Until The End To Think About Your Fate*, accompanied by an address for "Almost Paradise." An oddly sarcastic name for an empty, dry-baked land that seemed more concerned with self-destruction than paradise. She crumpled the flyer and threw it on the floor. She'd already had plenty of this town talking about her fate.

Other than the new-age beliefs expressed in her mother's commune, and Eamon's tree stories, Silva had never paid much attention to religion. A few clients slipped church invitations in with their tree-trimming payments, but religion—even of the ordinary, standard variety—held the tang of foreign-ness to her, never mind the brand Len Dietz and Becky seemed to be a part of. Becky, then Len Dietz, then Sherry all speaking to Silva as if she were a free agent they could convert just by luring her with something: threats, divination, or elk jerky—whatever worked.

Past the grocery store, the town ended, a gas station on the corner marking a converging hub of roads. As Silva pulled up to the stop sign, an old military deuce-and-a-half turned into one of the pumps. Dark green camo with two tall aluminum stacks on either side of the passenger and driver's doors and tires almost as tall as Silva, the truck looked like something out of a postapocalyptic movie set—some mechanized expression of a disturbing antigovernment, religious, militant identity of which this town seemed to be brimming full.

As she pulled out quickly, following one of the roads, a man climbed out of the deuce-and-a-half. The way he held himself was unmistakable, even if this time, like his truck, he was decked out in full camo, his long hair tucked out of sight. Silva sucked in her breath and took the upcoming corner too fast. Narrow and supered the wrong way, the blacktop felt as if it had been laid to lead vehicles from the road into the river. She had to brake hard, yanking the steering wheel until the play was gone, her grocery bags spewing their contents across the floorboards. An apple caught in the gearshift along with the crumpled brochure that tied the fate of humankind and the end of the world to hunting fenced elk.

As she straightened the wheel, she checked her rearview mirror and pinned the gas pedal, each vehicle on the road behind her making her heart thump in alarm. She was afraid Len Dietz would suddenly appear behind her, and what would she do if he did? Get out and tell him to fuck off? A paltry response to what he really deserved.

The road wound for miles into uninhabited land, nobody else around. Silva fought her sense of unease, being in a place like this on her own. Then, after climbing a steep series of corners and dropping lower again, suddenly the land flattened and opened up, and there, right off the highway, was a large field filled with news vans, government vehicles, and sheriff 4x4s. A small, unassuming visitor center with a slanted roof was perched back from them all, overlooking Hells Canyon. Silva hit the brakes hard and pulled off the side of the highway, the Dodge shuddering to a stop. So this is what Becky had been talking about, the place stirred up like a beehive.

Outside the visitor center, a line of heavily armed, camouflaged men clad in military gear stood posted along what looked like a hastily erected fence, its lines jagged and incomplete. Law enforcement officers and newspeople paced in the field, their cameras, microphones, and faces warily pointed the men's way. And then, just as Silva had feared, looming in her rearview mirror, the deuce-and-a-half came roaring up behind her, rocking the Dodge as it passed, its engine screaming in low gear when it turned onto the visitor center driveway.

The reaction was like something out of a movie—sheriffs running to hunker behind their vehicles, firearms drawn and aimed, everyone scattering and taking cover except a few gutsy cameramen, who kept filming as Len Dietz drove past them, his men at full attention now, their own weapons drawn. While the rest of them stood guard, two of the men opened a barb-wire gate and then closed it behind Len after he drove in. He parked the oversize war truck in the visitor center parking lot like it was a regular passenger vehicle, then got out and stretched luxuriously, as if he'd just been on a long family road trip and had stopped for a moment to take in the landmarks. But then, when he reached inside the truck, all the law enforcement officers went into full threat-response mode, yelling over their opened vehicle doors as they crouched behind them like shields, preparing for the onslaught. Instead, Len pulled out a white bullhorn. Smiling sardonically, he lifted it to his mouth to speak, his voice echoing out.

"Oh ye of little faith, we are here to stay," he said, striding forward until he was standing at the fence with his men in armed-and-aimed formation on either side of him, the police yelling for him to stop, for his men to put down their weapons.

Len walked over to the gate. "We understand that you do not wish to do your duty for the free God-fearing people of these United States," he said, his voice crackly over the loudspeaker. "We understand that you are content in acting in negligence toward your obligations to defend the rights and liberties of these people. Therefore, we are here to take our rights back from you. From the government. From all who would stand in our way."

Silva felt herself shrinking down behind the steering wheel as Len turned and seemed to glance her way, even though she'd stopped far enough back on the highway to be inconspicuous.

Finally, he quit speaking—baiting the police, putting on a show for the cameras—and walked back to the visitor center, disappearing inside. His men returned to their original posts, their weapons ready at their sides.

Silva reversed quickly, pulling out and driving back the way she'd come as fast as she could on the winding road, watching her rearview mirror so much she was afraid she would wreck.

When she reached the gas station on the outskirts of Two Rivers, she realized her mistake: in her earlier haste to get away from Len Dietz, she had taken the wrong road out of town. Instead of avoiding him, she'd driven right into his hornet's nest.

This time she was more careful, stopping to consult the atlas before taking the highway along the Salmon River, away from the visitor center, away from all of them.

Many miles downriver, she found the turn to McGregor's Healthy Hive-Fresh Honey—a gravel road, thickets of blackberry bramble forming dusty hedges, thistle-encroached gullies breaking line with a spattering of fir and pine. Dust rose behind her, and gravel pinged against the undercarriage as she navigated washboards. A doe high-stepped across the road and down the bank, but otherwise the road was empty. It paralleled a dry creek bed—a snaking gully of silt-caked rocks subsumed by a mat of overgrown brush. An unlikely escape for Silva and Isabelle both.

Silva wondered what kind of life Isabelle had lived in Two Rivers—if she'd longed for all she'd left behind, or if Trawler and Eamon had just been spots of green in the rearview dust, part of the retreating scenery, indistinguishable after enough time had passed by. Perhaps Two Rivers had just been a regular town when Isabelle arrived, secluded enough that she'd found herself at home, free to make her art, painting a dozen haunted pregnant girls along with Eamon's bonsai.

The Dodge jounced rhythmically, ratcheted enough by the washboards that she was forced to creep along or be pitched off the side of the road, and it was a good thing, or she would have driven past the turn to McGregor's, overgrown as it was, even with its colorful mailbox on the road's shoulder—a standard-issue front-hinge, red-flagged version, but painted turquoise with a two-tone yellow sun wrapping from one side to the other, the same words as the package's return address painted in orange on each sun ray: *McGregor's Healthy Hive-Fresh Honey.*

She'd made it. She took a deep breath and turned in, imagining Isabelle doing the same thing not long ago.

A dozen chickens scattered from a weed-heavy yard, clucking and flying up to perch on a porch rail that looked as if it might give way under them. There was an old log house, dilapidated in that particular turn-of-the-century charm. But it was a tree next to the house that caught Silva's attention. An ancient lilac—masterfully pruned, elegant, trunk-like branches gracefully reaching outward, no suckers or sprouts or offshoots. She could tell it had recently been in magnificent bloom even though most of the purple blossoms had dropped. Someone with a touch you rarely saw—the kind of tree-vision Eamon had had.

She got out of the truck and went to examine the tree up close. Bees hummed the crown in a steady drone, searching out the last nectar.

She walked across the front porch, a host of scolding clucks behind her. Then, as she lifted her hand to knock, a grizzle-bearded man suddenly came around the side of the house and charged up the porch steps, further dithering the hens.

"Sorry about that—these ladies here think they own the place," he said as he wiped his hands on the baggy apron he wore over his cutoffs, his hair frizzed into a gray nimbus, his bare feet so dirt-blackened it looked as if he'd been working in tar. "Eli McGregor, at your service." He clasped her hand between both of his own and looked her over, shaking his shaggy head in disbelief. "You're the spitting image of someone I knew once," he said in soft wonder, his voice wistful. "She loved that lilac, too. Painted it over and over again . . ."

Silva's arms prickled into goose bumps. She wanted to say Isabelle's name, but Eli held the front door open and gestured her inside.

"Come, come, my dear. It's a fine day for the bees," he said, navigating a zigzagging footpath through a maze of books, boxes, Mason jars, and heaps of newspapers that had sloughed off into small avalanches of print, everything covered in layers of dust. Silva looked around for signs of Isabelle, but the house was devoid of a woman's touch. A bachelor's pad gone to seed.

Ducking under dried herb bunches hanging from the kitchen's entrance, Eli motioned for her to sit at a table next to a claw-foot tub, a bottle of peppermint soap and a stack of grayed washcloths on the windowsill behind. A newspaper lay dissected on the table, the snarling wolf from the day before replaced by a photo of a group of militarily armed, camo-clad men standing behind a fence. The article was titled, THE U.S. GOVERNMENT VS. THE OCCUPATION. WHO WINS?

"Bees," Eli said, waving his hands. "Bees are more than just makers of honey. They're the royalty of insects, the monarchy of order, the matriarchs of nature." He scowled in concentration as he filled a teakettle with water and shoved a few pieces of kindling under the burner of a wood cookstove until flames licked up. "You have to respect them, or they won't respect you. They'll leave you scorned and alone. You've got to treat them right. . . . They don't just take to anybody, you know. They have fine taste, high standards."

As the kettle started to hiss, he pulled down one of the dried herb bunches and crumbled its leaves into two heavy ceramic mugs. The smell of peppermint filled the kitchen.

Silva rubbed her hands across the table, imagining Isabelle's prints under her own—a trace of DNA she might sense, like a honeybee locating the source of nectar.

"Everything I know, they taught me," Eli said, thrusting a steaming mug into her hands before grabbing two spoons. "Come—we must go upstairs for the most important ingredient."

Silva didn't hesitate, eager to be every place Isabelle had been. The traveling art show Isabelle's honeysuckle painting had been in had had its final showing in Port Townsend—only a short boat trip from Trawler. Silva wondered if Isabelle had known that was where it would end. So close to Eamon. Sending her paintings to him before the exhibition arrived like sending a message in a bottle, hoping it would eventually wash up on shore and find its intended recipient.

They climbed a winding set of wooden stairs, the staircase low-ceilinged and narrow enough that Silva's shoulders brushed the walls as she climbed. She was careful not to tip the sodden stew of leaves in her cup, the peppermint fumes so strong her eyes watered. A low hum filled the space, the walls themselves vibrating. Two five-panel doors off the landing were closed, each painted dark green with light green panels. Silva looked around, wondering what other items Isabelle might have left behind.

Eli thrust his mug into Silva's hand, nudged a rolled-up towel away from the bottom of the closest door, and tapped on the door with his knuckles before opening it.

The hum became louder even though the room seemed empty: bare log walls, bare floor, and, at the far end, a small window that let in the afternoon's bright light.

Eli motioned for Silva to stay at the doorway as he walked to the corner of the room, a spoon in each hand. He crouched to lift a floorboard, exposing the active comb beneath it. Bees were suddenly everywhere, landing on Eli's exposed hands and the back of his neck, the space alive with buzzing. He stuck a spoon down and scooped honey off a section of comb attached to the underside of the plank, then repeated it with the second spoon, twirling them as he stood, keeping the amber thread wrapped upon itself. He came out, closed the door, and plunked the spoons in their mugs of tea. Bees were in the hallway now, fifteen or more crawling all over his head and face, but he only nodded and said, "This, my dear, is hive-fresh honey."

"To the bees," Silva said, lifting her mug in toast before she took a drink, careful to avoid the sodden peppermint leaves and bee parts floating on the surface.

She'd always thought of honey as the plastic bears lined up next to peanut butter and jelly, honey that tasted dusty, as if left exposed in a musty room. But Eli's honey was robust and hearty, not only delicately floral but bursting with the tang of earth and sun. Clover, honeysuckle, thistle—she could taste them all.

"I knew when the time was right someone would come," Eli said. "And now here you are. The one we've been waiting for. They won't abandon you as they have the others. . . ."

The reverberation those words had: *they won't abandon you*, the bees waggling their way through Eli's thick beard, circling around his head as if crowning him. Something regal, something gilded and otherworldly about all of it—Eli's floral apron and dirty feet, his wild hair crawling with bees. She felt as though she were receiving a benediction. Something she hadn't known she'd been looking for, but something that felt so true she wanted to kneel and bow her head, let Eli grant her all he was offering. But Silva wasn't who Eli thought she was—someone coming to get his bees, everything just some terrible mix-up.

"I came here hoping to find someone," she said, the sudden emotion she felt welling up so powerfully she had to look away, focus on anything besides Eli's questioning face. Everything leading to this moment.

"I believe you knew her. Isabelle Fullbrook, my grandmother," she finally said, her throat gone tight around the words. A name uttered, the universe taking notice, the momentum set.

And just like that, Eli's face transformed, going from surprise to pained sorrow in one quick sweep. A gut-punched mime acting out his pain. "Isabelle," he said with quiet, wondering sadness. Love and loss and all that lay in between. A family of ghosts gone to roost. "I didn't know she had family," he said, his awe soft. Full of tenderness. He had loved her, Isabelle. Perhaps had even loved her as much as Eamon had.

"I don't think she did either," Silva said, trying to give Isabelle's desertion room for the unknowns life was always full of, even if in this case the unknown was Silva herself.

She had the urge to hold out her arms, say, *Here I am, in all my tattered glory.* A scarecrow husk left out to weather until it disintegrated into empty rags of mourning. But Eli turned away abruptly, going down the stairs to the front door. At first, Silva thought he was going to usher her out the same as he'd invited her in, but he just stood in the threshold, gently brushing away the bees still crawling on him. Little yellow bodies tumbled and flew from his hair and joined the others already airborne in a steady activity of motion above the hens who had perched back on the porch rail, feathers fluffed contentedly. A small, peaceable kingdom.

"The scientists don't know what it is, you know," he said, walking to the kitchen. "Mites, pesticides, radio waves, genetically modified crops, neonicotinoids, viruses, fungus, bacteria. But it's all right there in their name for it: colony collapse disorder. You have to keep your colonies strong, protect them, nurture them, give them everything they need to thrive, or they will leave, collapse. Disappear. It's always been the rule of the universe—perhaps more so now than ever. Our world is dying from all the ills we've subjected it to, one poison after another."

Silva thought of the embryo growing inside her, of Eamon and her mother dying, of Isabelle leaving, time and time again. The pathogens of place, of family. All the things that outside pestilence could jeopardize. Men in the dark, a baby in utero, a colony of honeybees, a family of bonsai trees. She stared at the wilted peppermint leaves in the bottom of her mug, wishing they might offer some kind of answer to everything she'd come find, to ask.

"Where did she go?" she asked finally. A trail of crumbs. A journey down the rabbit hole, Alice frightening the mouse by asking, "Where's my cat?" when she just wanted to know who she was, where she'd gone, and what would happen next.

"She found something she needed more," Eli said simply. A bee he'd missed crawled up his arm, high-stepping over wiry arm hair, its hair as fuzzed as his, its eyes as big and round as a baby's. He reached down and carefully pinched it between his finger and thumb, looked at it thoughtfully a moment, then opened the kitchen window and released it to join the others.

Old childhood fantasies played out again in Silva's head: Isabelle hopping from island to tropical island, wild and free, Silva tracking her from one place to the next until she finally pinned her down and demanded she become the woman, the family, she needed her to be.

"Almost Paradise," Eli said, frowning as he looked at the newspaper spread on the table.

"I'm sorry?" Silva asked, her mind skipping as she tried to put the name in context.

"A place nobody should go," Eli said. He gestured vehemently, the sudden anger coming off him visceral enough that Silva's heart clenched. "Dietz ought to be hung for what he's done. People looking to him for safety, for security, but he's not offering anything but a damn cult—taking over the visitor center now, convincing everyone he's the chosen one come to lead them."

"Is she still . . . ," Silva began, unable to finish the sentence. Unable to voice even the word *there*. She felt light-headed. Each fact repelled the other like magnets held face-to-face. Isabelle a part of something so vile Silva couldn't even name it.

"Once they enter, all ties are cut. There's no way of knowing. It's been a long time now."

Everything breaking along the old fault lines of familiar sorrow, frac-turing anew. As surreal as waking from a nightmare—the wailing woman swimming underwater with her gray fish body—only this one didn't recede. Instead Silva saw Isabelle on her knees, worshipfully washing Len Dietz's feet before moving upward.

He had known who she was, Silva realized, her heart thudding heavy. He had recognized her, looking at her as if he'd seen a ghost. Isabelle's ghost. He hadn't been divining at all, had just made a connection handed to him by a freak of genetic code cloning grandmother to granddaughter. Nothing more than a lucky guess. *All the mothers*, whom he supposedly cared for—except Isabelle had never been a mother to anyone. And despite the steady march of her own body's growth, Silva didn't know if she could be either.

She wanted to lie down and weep, but there was no escaping it, nowhere left for her to run. She was trapped in this moment, the irrefutable fact of Isabelle's last act. *Almost Paradise.* A mockery of all Silva had let herself imagine her life might be.

Seeming to recognize her distress, Eli laid a gnarled hand over hers. "I'm sorry, lass," he said. "Isabelle came and left and took this old man's heart with her. It looks like she did the same to you."

CHAPTER SIX

Date: September 15, 1999
Title(s): Maiden 1–Maiden 12
Subject: Maidens before marriage
Setting: Almost Paradise Grounds
Medium: Watercolor and graphite on cold-press
Size(s): 8×8

Dearest Eamon,

The Baptism of the Virgins done, they prepare now for the main event—the Wedding Ceremony, a series of synchronized proceedings, each of the maidens going through the same preparation:

1) Baptism of the Virgins 2) Servant-heart Ceremony 3) Religious-training Ceremony 4) Childbearing Ceremony 5) Dowry Ceremony 6) Conjoining Ceremony 7) Cleansing Ceremony. Then, the wedding, and, of course, the subsequent births. The main goal seems to be for Len to not only have his twelve virgin-child concubines, but also for them to bear his fruit, prolifically.

I have gotten myself here, but I don't know if I can make it through this project's completion—even though I keep telling myself that's all it is: a project, work, a commissioned series. But I sit in my small, windowless, concrete-block bunker room in the compound each night, alone with my paints, questioning myself. What it is that I think I can accomplish, taking part in this, even if my part is to play witness to the atrocity? The war correspondent, sending back images that tell more of the true story than any words can. But you know how much this could be anything but detached and objective "work" to me. How setting myself at this means nothing more than a protracted battle between self-preservation and self-flagellation. Perhaps penance and recompense are just lies that we tell ourselves. Perhaps they can never be achieved, no matter how hard and long we try. Perhaps I, too, will be swallowed (again) by the darkness.

I have spent the last weeks painting each child bride's portrait before she is taken, before she is gone forever to Dietz, which won't be long now—a pendulum tick, tick, ticking. Each of them has already been given over, trapped in his well-spun web, encased and immobilized by him before they realize their final outcome has already been determined. They don't need the end of the world, the millennium, Y2K, to bring about their own ending. It's already here.

Faith has been my guide—Faith, a woman, not a pattern of belief. I have none of that left, no belief in a higher power, in some guiding force that can direct our lives, give reason for our existence. Faith is the one who authorized my presence and work within the compound, invited me in. Not that I didn't know ahead of time what I was getting into. I knew (I've always known) exactly what that means—being a woman, a girl, conscribed to a man, a "father," who takes your body and your mind and your spirit as his own. But how can you really be prepared for that reality, even if you've already known it yourself? Even if your own body has born the results of it?

Faith arranges the girls for me to paint. She attends to them, prepares them, moves them, tilts their faces for me, as though they were wooden art models, the figure of a body meant to be manipulated. Meant to be traced into lines and then filled in, fleshed into imitation. Shadows of light and dark. Twelve paintings in replicate. Blues and grays and browns. The color of mourning. The color of heaviness. The color of my impossibly weighty but still beating heart.

I sit here, pouring out my soul, wishing for the comfort of you. Of the time before I left, water washing on shore, pebbles tinking against themselves in its ebb and flow. Where have I been? Where did I go?

Maybe the only way out of the dark is to descend all the way into it.

My love,
Isabelle

CHAPTER SEVEN

MARCH 2001

At the sound of a rumbling engine downshifting, its low-gear rev approaching Eli's house, Silva panicked, thinking Len Dietz had followed her after all, had come to take her captive just as he had somehow taken Isabelle. Silva looked wildly around Eli's kitchen for a place of exit, but instead of Len's war truck, a rusty patchwork of a pickup in primer-gray and turquoise drove up and parked next to her Dodge, a cloud of dust drifting and settling as a tall, lanky man jumped out, walking purposefully toward Eli's front porch. A few strides and he was at the door, knocking in sharp announcement he didn't need, the hens clucking their displeasure at being disturbed again, Eli bracing both hands on the table and pushing himself up to answer.

Silva tensed, ready to spring up and run away, hide herself from any other Two Rivers men, but Eli ushered the man through the living-room maze and into the kitchen with her. There was nowhere she could go to escape.

"Nick Larkins," the man said, holding out his hand, close enough Silva could smell weeds and leather and something warm—sunbaked denim, fresh cotton. A smell that reminded her with startling force of Eamon.

"Didn't mean to break in on you," he said, hesitating, looking at her as if worried she might be the one to break.

"Silva Merigal," she said, letting go of his hand quickly, the warmth of his palm disconcerting—the sudden connection of physicality a jolt that put her whole body on edge.

"*Silva.* Unusual name," he said. There was a pale scar on the side of his face that connected dimple to chin. Sun-streaked hair, tanned face, and light blue eyes, he looked like the men in the museum's oldest black-and-white photographs, their work-worn bodies and faces forever marked by hard physical labor.

She was surprised he'd gotten it right the first try. Everyone always called her Sylvia no matter how much she corrected them. Sometimes she recited her whole hippie earth name—*Silvania August Moonbeam Merigal*—just to throw people off-balance. She wished she would have now, if only for a brief distraction, her seemingly the only one discomposed.

"I've come to convince Eli to part with his field bees," Nick said, smiling. The person Eli had been expecting instead of her.

Eli glanced back and forth between them and seemed to arrive at some sort of conclusion. "First, we must eat," he declared, pointing to a dusty wall clock as if it had just issued a mandate. "'One cannot think well, love well, sleep well, if one has not dined well.'" The same quote Eamon had used. Something Isabelle must have said. A mantra she'd probably recited for Len Dietz, too.

"I don't want to intrude," Nick said in question, looking at Silva.

"I'm not hungry," Silva said, her stomach twisting at the mental image of Isabelle with Len, but Eli was deaf to their objections, rummaging around inside his tiny, ancient fridge.

"Honeybee soufflé," Eli announced, pulling out a dish and cutting thick yellow wedges.

He served each of them a plate, and when Silva hesitated, her fork hovering, he scowled and motioned impatiently, commanding, "Eat, eat."

She could tell there was no choice in the matter, even if Nick was close enough their elbows were hitting. Even if the last thing she wanted was honeybee soufflé.

She took a small, careful bite, hoping she could stomach it, especially after Eli started naming off ingredients that included "marinated bees"—bee larvae he'd marinated in whiskey, garlic, hot pepper, and ginger. At first, she thought he was kidding, and she chewed cautiously, expecting something caustic and juicy to pop in her mouth, trying not to imagine the softened bodies of bee larvae floating in eggs, but instead it was delicious—a gustatory delight, spicy and rich with a deep complexity of flavors. She thought she could even taste a hint of honey. She ate the whole piece, finishing before Nick, who kept up a steady conversation like a child adept at distracting an overbearing adult bent on force-feeding.

"You've got to keep the colony healthy and strong, keep them together as a family," Eli was saying—the same thing he'd told Silva earlier when she'd wondered if he was really talking about Isabelle, "colony collapse" a code for everything that had ever happened in her life.

"I plan on it," Nick said, but Eli shook his head.

"Lad, there is no *planning*. There is only doing. But I think maybe you already know that." He regarded Nick, the two of them sharing some kind of understanding.

"What do you do?" Nick asked, turning to Silva with a smile.

"I'm an arborist—have a business on Trawler Island," she answered quickly. "So you're from Two Rivers?"

She hoped to change the subject, make polite conversation through the buzzing in her mind: Isabelle painting pregnant girls in a wedding dress, living in a walled city, like something out of the Dark Ages. It was everything she could do not to grab the newspaper and start reading the article on the occupation that she had just seen in person. She needed to know everything about them—these people Isabelle had joined. No matter that the Isabelle Silva had in her head would have never joined a group—*a cult*—run by someone like Len Dietz. Silva realized that she'd been wrong all along. Despite their shared DNA, their clone-like resemblance, Isabelle wasn't anyone she would be able to recognize.

"Grew up not far from here, really, as the crow flies. Down in the canyon on the Snake, a ranch my great-great-grandfather Eldridge homesteaded in the early 1900s," Nick said, pointing somewhere behind their heads. "Two Rivers is the closest town, though. Have to either boat, hike, or ride to get to the ranch. Big, rugged, wild country, what's left of it."

"Prettiest country there is," Eli said.

Silva hadn't thought of it that way. Austere, yes. Isolated and harsh and unforgiving. Threatening. Nothing as soft as what "pretty" connoted—swells of silver water shapeshifting like mercury under her outstretched palm, lapping on the shore like the breath after a first kiss.

But Nick was off, talking about his family's place, where he'd grown up, describing every ravine, every outcropping. He used the table's plank top to delineate the once-expansive property: a knot as the house site, a whorl the pasture ground, the narrow grain lines as the property's far reaches, and the wide swath of lighter grain as the river. He described how the summer grasses rolled and heaved like an ocean, the way the pines grew gnarled and mammoth on the tops of the hills, the way the land was full of hidden life. Then he glanced at the newspaper Eli had pushed away, his face changing enough that Silva could see the headline and photo had bothered him, too.

"But that's all in the past," Nick said. "Things are different now. They've been different for a long time." His voice was tinged with anger and regret.

"You still live there?" Silva asked. "At the ranch?"

"Not since I was twelve," Nick said, fiddling with his fork. "But I will again soon. Once the outfitting lease expires and I pay off the back taxes. Only fifteen acres left out of twenty-five hundred, but it's enough. It'll have to be." His face changed. Something sorrowful yet hopeful. Something Silva recognized—an outline of her own emotion. The doomed and their sinking.

"The outfitters still using the cabin?" Eli asked.

"Jet boaters, mostly. I'm meeting a group in a few days, pack-stringing them into the Seven Devils. Hopefully the last time I'll be a boarder on my own place. Then it'll be just me and the bees, starting fresh, reclaiming the homestead." He was trying to be glib, but his body belied him. Silva could feel the tension radiating off him. It was clear how much stake he'd put into the plan, a kind of desperation she knew too well.

"Has the drought hit hard down there?" Eli asked, gesturing outside even though everything was still green, trees leafed so heavily you couldn't see through them to the hills.

"Record low snowpack, record low water levels, record high temperatures. Worst fire danger in a century—all the dry years adding up. It's only green by the river, even this time of year." Nick looked out the window. "It's just a matter of time before the whole place ignites."

Silva hadn't considered this risk. Fire, too, along with everything else. She imagined trees sapped of moisture, flames climbing limb to limb, crown to crown. In Trawler, the moss was like a sponge, everything dripping with moisture. She'd never needed to trim the ladder fuels on the island, surrounded by enough moisture and water to drown out the rest of the world's woes and leave enough for the end of the world, too.

"Does it burn here often?" she asked.

"We're due," Nick said, as if wildfire were a scheduled event. "The last summer I lived in the canyon, everything downriver burned. There was a plague of grasshoppers that year, too. They popped like popcorn when the fire came. Everything—houses, barns, fences—gone in minutes, nothing left of entire ranches but a few smoldering heaps. You can still find old pieces of charred tin if you know where to look—bedframes grown up with weeds, old plows left standing in the fields, rock foundations with nothing left on top. The Larkins Ranch is well situated, though. Creek on the side, river on the front. Others aren't so lucky. Almost Paradise, the property above, nearly burned a few years ago. Would have been fitting, too. *Almost Hell . . .*" He glanced at Silva. "People you don't want to ever meet," he added, as if she needed the warning. Somebody yelling *fire* after the flames had already consumed everything.

"So I've been told."

"Your ranch's river access is a hot commodity," Eli said. "Dietz will bid high at the tax auction when it comes up, you can be sure of that. He has the funds to go as high as he needs. He was nearly successful with a land-grab above Pittsburg Landing, too, where the field bees are."

"I'm prepared for that," Nick said, his posture stiff with hostility. Jaw muscles clenched, hands curled into fists on his lap, enough threat in his voice and body, Silva believed him. A person backed into a corner was a dangerous enemy, even if only to themselves.

"Why does Len Dietz want your land?" Silva asked, trying to shake the memory of Len standing over her, saying he knew why she'd come. He was omnipresent, something that couldn't be purged from the air, a handprint she couldn't wash off. Had that been a warning, too?

"Already has most of it. My mother signed everything over to him before she died. Would have given him all of it, but the house, barn, and fifteen acres were protected by the outfitting lease that's just going back up for auction. He wants the last piece."

"So, they're a religious group?" Silva asked carefully, trying not to show any emotion—Len's hand on her as he whispered scripture like pillow talk. There was bad blood between him and Nick, that much was clear. Nick's mother involved with Len Dietz, too, along with Isabelle. Nick and Eli and Mr. Cheema seemingly the only ones on the other side of the town's alliance.

"More like a cult," Nick replied, using Eli's exact word. "You can spot them a mile away—bearded men in camo and long-haired women in pilgrim dresses, a dozen children apiece. Proselytizing, procreating, and preparing for the apocalypse. The three *p*'s. It's no accident that Dietz owns more property in the canyon than anyone else and has claimed more women for himself than any polygamist ever dreamed of. A while back, they started an elk ranch to fund their enterprise. When the rut's on, elk bugling reverberates down-canyon like a blood call."

Silva's skin prickled in goose bumps, all of it something otherworldly, something as old as the beginning. A man taking dominion over women and beasts alike. The town's secret. *All the mothers.* Nick's mother. Isabelle's pregnant girls. Bonsai roots cradling the unborn. Everything had been about Almost Paradise and Len Dietz from the moment she'd found Isabelle's packet.

"Last week they rallied into full mobilization," Nick continued. "Shot at a government plane flying over the compound, broke out C&C's windows, and took over the visitor center. There've been enough other things. Len's already been suspected of poisoning Ted's dogs and lighting the Updahls' place on fire when they wouldn't sell to him. Nothing's been proven of course, but it's all been ratcheting up for a long time—especially going into Y2K, although that seemed like a big disappointment to them all. With all the media attention now, though, it's bound to get worse. Everyone knows how these things end. Waco. Ruby Ridge. The Lenites won't go down easily."

"Why did they target the grocery store?"

"They think it's a terrorist front, a sleeper cell, part of the Islamic State. They aren't big fans of any outsiders, especially brown ones," Nick answered. "The Lenites think they're the only true patriots and Christians, guarding the Constitution for god and from the government."

It would have seemed like a joke, had Silva not seen it herself—Len and his armed men, handkerchiefs covering their faces and semiautomatic rifles and ammo bandoliers strung across their torsos, looking more like the Islamic State fighters they feared than a small-town cult.

The newspaper photographs showed them holding two signs that read: *FBI—Another Intrusive Tyranical Goverment Entity Doing What The Feds Do Best, Abusing Power & Oppressing the Backbone of America.* And, *Tyran-ny: is cruel, unreasonable, arbitrary use of Power or Control.* People who couldn't spell-check their own self-benefitting propaganda, but who readily took up arms over it. A tiny Idaho backwoods town a guerrilla war zone.

Silva had heard of the northwest's doomsday, antigovernment preppers—people preparing for the coming apocalypse however they envisioned it: computing systems crashing, dirty bombs, EMPs taking out the power grid, financial collapse, looting, raids, disease, pestilence, terrorism, the government taking away everyone's guns, assault on religious freedom, etc. A mass of chaos. People who believed the only way to make it through the end was to move to the hills, build compounds, and take up arms against anyone who opposed their brand of survivalist, gun-toting religion. But she'd never expected to be face-to-face with it all.

"All downtown was just refaced to look 'authentic,' so Two Rivers would draw in more tourism money—people banking on rich Lewis-Clark Trail tourists flooding the town, even though Two Rivers isn't on the actual trail route," Nick said. "The bank had a Sacagawea mural painted on its side, pointing the way, they hope, right into their accounts. The real estate ads show nothing but burbling-brook mountain scenes, no matter the drought or the fact that to get power and water to the properties costs more than the land itself. This place has never been able to sustain more than bunch grass and thistle and the kind of fanaticism that worries even fundamentalists."

"How far is Almost Paradise from your ranch?" Silva asked Nick suddenly, everything forming in her head as she spoke.

"Not far enough. I used to ride up and explore there as a kid. That's why Dietz wants the ranch. With the overland routes so heavily monitored now, the river's the only access without checkpoints. The upriver trail ends just past the visitor center."

"There's a wall?" she asked, looking to Eli for clarification, trying to calculate the physical difficulties of reaching the compound, ignoring the complete unknown of what she would do once she was there. Walk up and knock on the compound's drawbridge gate, ask if Isabelle Fullbrook was in? She felt as if she were in some superhero movie: a woman on her own, planning her own takeover, rescuing a harem of lost women who happened to include her runaway hippie-artist grandmother. Women who, it seemed, had gone willingly to Len Dietz.

"Oh, there have been big plans," Nick said, answering for Eli. "Blueprints for a walled-in city complete with a firearms museum, munitions factory, reflecting pool, amphitheater, and market—just as soon as more followers are willing to pony up the cash. But it's just a run-down ranch like any other around here. Don't even need fences except to keep their elk in. Got their own private Idaho dystopia, but that's about it. What they really need is a wall to keep their own people captive, not to stop the nonexistent hordes of outsiders from invading."

Silva tried to imagine Isabelle living in such a place, nobody but Eli aware of her disappearance. What if she'd wanted to leave but couldn't, a prisoner to Len Dietz's captivity? What if she were still there now, looking for a way out, waiting for escape? Silva thought of her dream the night before she'd left Trawler—a trio of woman dancing on a hilltop. Three versions of herself looking back at her. Past. Present. Future. A pool of shared genes. The division of cells reshaping the DNA that might redefine them all.

She turned to Nick. "You said they were looking for a temporary caretaker for your ranch—until you get it back?"

Nick lifted his eyebrows in surprise. "You know someone who might be interested?"

Seeming to anticipate the trajectory of her thoughts, Eli watched her face. He leaned over and put his hand on hers. "Are you sure?" he asked quietly, his real question clear.

She met his eyes. This was what it'd always been coming to. She'd thought she was making the journey for herself, for her own life, but she wasn't the only one who needed saving.

"You want the job?" Nick glanced back and forth between Silva and Eli in confusion.

"I can do grounds work," she said. "I have referrals you can check."

Nick leaned back. "Mack would be thrilled to have someone handed up so easily. . . ."

As if Silva were a willing sacrifice. And perhaps she was. Perhaps that's what it'd been about all along—surrendering herself to the will of a fate she had thought was intent on her destruction, when in fact it was leading her to this moment all along. Hadn't she, too, in her weakest moments, wished for something bigger than herself to take charge, offer her shelter and protection from herself, from all her life had become? Someone to give her security—even if it was a promise she knew couldn't be kept?

She and Nick settled the job details quickly, Nick all seriousness, delivering grave-toned warnings about the situation she would be facing in the
canyon—the visitor center occupation going on only fifteen miles upriver
from his ranch, everything a powder keg of tension. He said she was about
to enter into enemy territory, nobody in the canyon for miles in every direction, no way to contact anyone except by radio, no easy access for help. Told
her not to underestimate Len Dietz, what he was capable of doing. Said he,
Nick, didn't want her going in blind, without being prepared, but she already
knew what she was up against. She'd already been face-to-face with Len
Dietz and his followers, had seen firsthand what kind of danger they posed.
She was just surprised that Nick didn't question her reasons for wanting to
go to the canyon in the first place—Almost Paradise within striking distance of his family's homestead. Instead they made arrangements for her to
come down to the Larkins Ranch in time to get things in order before the
first outfitting group arrived.

Eli stood when they were done. "Come. It's time we consulted with the
bees," he said, as if the bees could offer all the answers they sought. All Silva
really wanted to do now was race down each mile to Isabelle, all her pain
and sorrow redirected at this one thing, this one goal.

Eli took them outside to a clearing tucked between pines and an open
shed stacked full of hay in an irregular crosshatch, a calico cat stretched out
on a shelf of bales. "Thought the coyotes found you out," Eli said as the cat
rolled to her back, yawning long teeth, Eli ruffling her belly fur before she
had a chance to kick.

In the clearing, Eli's rainbow-colored hive boxes looked like oversize
children's play-blocks. Clouds had moved in, the air layered heavy, filled
with the sonorous humming of thousands of bees—a disciplined and
orderly rank of nectar crusaders going from one clover blossom to the next
so fast Silva wondered how they were gathering anything at all. When she
held out her hand, one crawled on her finger. Tiny and golden, it was the
color of pollen and honey, its hair fuzzed like baby hair, its globe eyes black

and inscrutable. She could feel the touch of its proboscis long after it had flown.

Eli walked over to a shed full of dusty tarps and stacks of empty hive boxes as Nick backed up his truck, the two of them talking about how Eli's field colonies were a strong, hearty breed, well-acclimated to the harshness of the canyon.

Silva was glad to have a moment to think through all the implications— going down to live in the canyon, seeking out Len Dietz's cult on purpose as if she were one of his converts, as if their shared experience in Build It Best had convinced her of the error of her ways. She felt like a chain smoker, lighting a fresh cigarette from the one still hanging off her lips. Tied to this thing until the end, no matter what happened, no matter where it took her. That was the deal she'd made with herself after all. *Six weeks and counting.*

Eli walked over to her as Nick started loading hive boxes. "You liked the honey, the soufflé?" he asked her, the question somehow too personal.

Heat rose up her neck even as she tried to will it away. "Yes. I liked them," she said.

Eli fished around in his pocket and handed her a piece of paper. The soufflé recipe. "You carry the pheromones of a queen. The bees already see you as one of them, part of the colony."

"Nick's the one getting your bees, not me," she said, fighting back a well of unbidden emotion, like a contrary child self-declaring she couldn't have the very thing she'd been offered.

Standing in the back of his pickup, the bed already stacked with hives, Nick saw them look his way and smiled, held his arms out wide. "The future of the Larkins Ranch. There's a sweet irony to it, don't you think? The future all wrapped up in bees."

CHAPTER EIGHT

———•◆•———

You can feel it coming—a whisper in the air above you, a wind that takes hold of the trees and sends them shivering. You stop and lift your arms, close your eyes, and wait as it swirls around you, rushing by with its whispering voices, so many calling so fast from so far away that you can't understand them whirling closer and closer, faster and faster, shivering down your back, pulling at your skirts, wrapping around you so tight you open your mouth to cry out and that's when it enters you, rushing down your throat, pouring itself into you. It's cold, a feeling like choking, but then it warms inside you, swelling and filling you until you tingle with a pressure that sends the words cascading out of your mouth like silver water spilling from a fountain into the air, lifting from your outstretched palms, from your mouth, from deep within your dark insides, and you call out, singing in voices of the lost, your words coming faster and faster as it flows through you in languages you can't understand. You try to give it all it wants, try to hold on as it takes you, but then you feel it leaving you again, leaving you right when you feel it deeper than you've ever felt it before, right when you think it's going to take you all the way with it as it has the others, leaving them collapsed and shaking on the floor, their eyes rolled back in their heads in ecstasy, their tongues spilling limp from the dark cavity of their mouths, their dresses pulled damp against their own flesh. You want to be filled as they have been filled, but it's leaving you, rising in a great swirling mass like the river's mist as you sank below the surface, the gray water over-taking each of you as he lowered you one by one, sinking farther and farther until you felt as if you were drowning, as if you would never breathe again, until finally he lifted you from the depths of your submersion and claimed you as his own. And as it leaves you, it takes your song with it, leaves your voice cracked and torn, your words falling back to you like white feathers drifting slowly back down from the sky into your empty, outstretched palms.

CHAPTER NINE

MARCH 2001

As Silva wandered from booth to booth at the Two Rivers farmers market—the fragrance of flower bouquets wrapping the air along with the smell of trodden grass and fried elephant ears—she could feel people staring. A dozen faces turned her way as she stopped at a table full of dream catchers, their feathers meant to hold the good, their webs meant to dissipate the bad. She wished it was as easy as hanging one like a charm, as easy as believing in its magical powers of protection, directing your dreams to safe places.

The first time Eamon had taken Silva to a big mainland farmers market as a child, she had been overwhelmed by the crowding smells of sawdust and fried food and hundreds of strangers. Lost in the sea of striped awnings and flapping tents, she'd felt as if she were in a circus and any minute a flap-eared elephant would come trumpeting by, but somewhere between the gourd bowls, driftwood birdhouses, and lavender oil, she'd fallen in love. After that, going to farmers markets had become part of their routine together, their monthly outing away from the island.

She fought the urge to run away and escape all the deliberate perusal. She had the feeling that if she let down her guard, everyone in Two Rivers would be all over her, pawing through her personal business like shoppers eager to find some treasure—*look what I found!*—seeming to intuit what juicy tidbits she might provide. She wondered if Isabelle had faced the same kind of close scrutiny, living with Eli, the two of them falling so far outside the area's social norms.

Eamon had valued his privacy, had lectured Silva once about gossiping, told her that the US's original 1790 one-cent coin had been engraved with the slogan "mind your business" before it was changed to "in god we trust." Told her that minding your own business had been a good idea then and was a good idea now. But it seemed as if there was no such thing as minding your own business here, people openly discussing Silva as she walked by. She wondered if they, too, were connecting her to Isabelle, if they all knew where Isabelle had gone, what she'd willingly taken herself into.

Making her way down the tables, Silva saw a woman minding a booth full of colorful produce. She was dressed in a long-sleeved, high-collared dress that went to her ankles, her blond hair in a thick braid that hung to her hips. A marker of Len Dietz's clan of women.

"May I serve you?" the woman asked, standing up as Silva approached her table. She had an accent from somewhere else, soft and lightly twanged, as if they were in Appalachia instead of the middle of the Idaho wilderness. Her hands clasped carefully in front of her, her oval face smooth and pale—high cheekbones, arched eyebrows, light blue eyes, shapely lips. A delicate beauty, unexpected in a place like this.

A small girl with apple cheeks and wispy blond hair peeked out from behind the woman's skirts, her arms wrapped around the backs of the woman's legs. She glanced shyly at Silva, then ducked her head and fingered the embroidered cuff of the woman's sleeve.

"Momma, may I please have more pie?" she asked, her voice as light as summer wind.

The woman looked down and wiped the hair back from the child's face. "We must not be greedy. We must think of others before ourselves."

The child glanced at Silva suspiciously, as though she were one of the others to whom her mother was referring, and assessed Silva with round baby eyes, a worldly wise soul staring from a cherub's face.

"Your produce is amazing," Silva said, and it was—heads of cabbage like cannonballs, flowered dill bundles standing as tall as her, strawberries as big as her dozens of fresh eggs.

"The Lord blesses us," the woman said, looking at Silva with meaning, something beyond the words, her hand fluttering to her side like a pale night moth. "Are you looking for something in particular?" she asked, her posture perfectly upright, the air suddenly pregnant with meaning, as if she'd been waiting all along for the single question with which Silva had come.

"I'll take these," Silva said. She stepped in closer, picking up a basket of bright strawberries, meeting the woman's eyes, ready to voice Isabelle's name out loud for a second time that day, but the woman glanced past Silva's shoulder and then quickly looked away, bagging the berries and giving Silva back her change without any eye contact or another word.

When Silva turned, she saw what had silenced the woman—two bearded men dressed in camo with pistols on their hips, walking straight toward them.

Heart racing, Silva walked away quickly, keeping her head down, following the flattened path past the tables and away from the market, aware of each piece of gravel, each glob of flattened gum. On the sidewalk, she sidestepped a child's dropped ice-cream cone, ants and bees swarming the coagulated, dirt-covered mass. She fought the urge to look back at the woman and her child—a woman with sad, penetrating eyes. Men dressed like soldiers from a war that had been lost a long time ago, although here the war seemed to be ongoing.

Sitting on the apartment's narrow bed, Silva pulled out Isabelle's packet again. She wondered what Eamon had thought when he'd gotten it in the mail—all those years passing, and then Isabelle dropping right back into his life as though she'd never left.

Since leaving Eli's, Silva had wished she'd asked him more questions when she'd had the chance. Asked him about the life he and Isabelle had lived together, however briefly. What kind of woman Isabelle had been, what kinds of things she'd done and who she'd known, living near Two Rivers, so close to the Lenites. But more than anything, Silva wanted to ask how Isabelle had been seduced into following Len Dietz into the dark, leaving the fullness of her life behind when it seemed as though she'd led an idyllic artist's life with Eli, just as she had with Eamon.

Now, with new context, Silva saw the twelve pregnant girls not as some random, disturbing artist's study but as critical clues to Isabelle's leaving, abandoning not only Eli but Eamon and Silva, too. Why would Isabelle have painted them and sent them to Eamon? Was it a cry for help, an SOS? The only thing she had to speak for them, for herself?

Silva put the paintings back and got the Dodge's keys. She didn't know where she was going, but she couldn't stay holed up in the apartment above Becky and her occupation customers, Len taking care of "all the mothers." Becky voicing it as though Silva were one of them, too, as though Len had already laid claim to her and the fetus inside her.

Keeping her head down past Build It Best's front windows, Silva climbed into the Dodge quickly and tweaked the starter a second too long in her haste to escape, the starter's high whine preceding her quick slam into reverse. She winced, picturing shavings of metal sifting down into the gearbox and gear oil pocketing in pavement dust. Eamon wouldn't have approved.

She drove out the way she'd come into town, going the opposite direction from all the paths that seemed to lead to Len Dietz. She turned onto a dirt road to Heaven's Gate, a seven-thousand-foot mountain-summit viewing spot overlooking Hells Canyon, the Salmon River Canyon, and the Seven Devils. Somewhere she hoped might offer the respite she needed.

The Dodge's back end recoiled over the water bars, the whole truck threatening to come apart on the road's uneven corduroy as she steadily climbed in elevation. The hillsides were tawny with spent grasses, the evening's heat banking along the southern slopes, patches of timber the only spots of green. Then she heard a telltale snap under the floorboards, felt the stutter and clanking, the Dodge's engine revving out with no forward motion. The middle driveline again.

When she was young, Silva had been the one to crawl under the truck and wrap a sheet around the broken shaft, running alongside the truck, holding the driveline up while Eamon pulled off the road. She'd helped him fix the U-joint on the middle driveline again and again, the Dodge just like an old man, he'd said—an old man with a bad back that kept blowing out, faulty discs bulging against the spinal nerves until it could no longer move. He said it marked the truck all the more as their own, *a part of the family*. Now it was the only family left to easily be a part of.

She rolled backward until she was off the road enough, then leaned her head back against the seat and closed her eyes, connected to Eamon and her past by this faulty mechanical thread, heat radiating through the windows, pricking her skin. She licked the salt edging the corners of her mouth, let the sauna-like heat fill her nose and lungs before shoving the door open and jumping out in one quick motion. Her hands and knees planted in the dirt, she peered under the truck, saw the back driveline angled down, lodged between boulders.

She got up, brushed off her hands, and walked to a dry wash cut into the steep hillside, a gully of cracked silt and rocks coated in drab glaze. She started up and then, compelled, kept going, pebbled sand cascading into irregular heaps at her sides, jogged loose from its rock base, the terrain growing steeper, hillsides peaking into sharp, jagged formations devoid of anything but lichen. She could see the road up ahead where it turned to boulders and washouts, Heaven's Gate somewhere she wasn't destined to reach after all. Beyond, the peaks of the Seven Devils rose against the horizon as bare and serrated as teeth, blunted where they'd been worn down by wind and weather. A turkey vulture circled overhead, head tipped sideways, looking for carrion.

Farther up, the slopes had green shadows—small pockets nourished by shade and dew. She stopped at a stream still trickling, a grouse startling her in sudden flight, leaving behind downy feathers pinning slow spirals on the water's surface, tiny pools rife with minnows, algae skins left boulder-bound, like frog hides stretched to cure. Streams shrinking to pools shrinking to puddles shrinking to nothing, minnow clouds drifting in devouring, shimmering hunger.

Finally, angling toward a line of contorted subalpine fir and whitebark pine, she stopped at a heavily branched white fir and sat against its anchored roots, leaning into its coarse bark—the fir a symbol of endurance and determination, resilience and longevity, signifying strength, hope, and renewal. Everything quiet in the evening's solitude, she kept watch until the landscape blurred, her thoughts spinning away from her until all that mattered was the way the tree's roots intertwined underneath her, spreading under the exposed surface, searching for some nutrient ensconced in the rocky earth, until they found new soil and laid themselves down deep.

In Scottish folklore, a friendly tree spirit called the Ghillie Dhu helped lost children find their way home; Silva hoped there was a tree spirit to help a granddaughter find her lost grandmother and bring her home. *Home.* Wherever that might be. Whatever that might mean.

She was chilled, goose bumps creeping up her bare arms as if she'd been swimming in cold water, everything in full shadow, a robin singing its night song—the one that felt like rain, a rack of clouds piled up against the exposed western peaks. She pulled herself up from the pad of roots and rock, grimacing at the needles in her feet. The freckled skin exposed from her V-neck felt flushed, the heat of a sunburn chilling her more. She wrapped her arms around her waist trying to warm herself as she made her way to the cliff edge and looked out, the sky backed by the orange glow of night coming on, quarter moon planted on blue.

When she started back down, knocking rocks loose in her descent, a squirrel squealed and dove back in its burrow with a scattering of pebbles and dried grass as bats swooped low through the hatches of dusky-winged ash aphids bumbling through the warm updrafts—the canyon's nightlife beginning. Nighthawks would be out soon, their dives vibrating the tips of trees.

Back at the truck, she got out the flashlight and tools Eamon had stored behind the seat—new U-joints in greasy boxes and the ancient sledge-hammer with its red-painted handle. She shimmied under the truck in the dust, until she was positioned beneath the broken driveshaft.

Lying on her back, she couldn't get a good angle, her reach cramped, her aim faulty without Eamon's help, the flashlight never shining in the right place. It took her an hour just to get the old U-joints out and replaced, then another forty minutes to get the strap bolts fastened back to the transfer case and transmission. By the time she was done, it was fully dark. She pulled herself out, hands black with grease, hair and clothes coated in dust. She bent over to shake out her hair, everything smelling of gear oil, dust, and grease. Upside down, she saw a wash of lights on the road below, then heard the growl of an engine.

She packed the tools back behind the seat, turned over the engine, shifted into gear, and pulled forward cautiously, trying to get in motion before whoever was coming made it to her. She held her breath, but the drive-shaft held. She thought about continuing up the road, driving the remaining miles to the summit overlook just to be able to say she'd made it, but she didn't want to risk interaction with other people.

As she tried to turn around on the narrow road, a pickup rounded the corner below her, its headlights hitting the Dodge broadside, so bright in her face she had to close her eyes. A dented Toyota covered in mud, its bed filled with a built-in plywood box, holes cut in the sides, each hole filled with a hound's head, the din of their braying so forceful, she had to resist covering her ears to block the assault.

They stopped in the middle of the road as she stalled out, cranking the starter over and over again. She pushed her door lock down as the hound pickup's driver got out. He looked as if he was just out of high school—his team shirt tucked into his jeans, his hair buzzed into a hi-low.

She rolled down her window a few inches. "Give me just a minute here," she said.

He raised his eyebrows when he saw Silva up close. "Won't start?" he asked, glancing at the truck hopefully. "Drove one of these on fire-crew. Persnickety sonsabitches . . ."

"It's just flooded," Silva said.

He nodded with authority his body didn't yet carry. "Happens a lot with these," he said.

A young woman got out of his truck and stood hunched next to the braying hounds, her arms wrapped around her chest, obviously not happy about her man talking to Silva.

"Hush them dogs," he called out before turning back to Silva. "You make it up to the summit? Nice view. We're just heading up. I'm shipping out after the weekend. Going to miss this place," he said, looking around, even though there was nothing to see in the dark.

"I was headed there, but the driveline went out. Just got it back together." She held up her greasy hands as proof then adjusted the choke as she tried the key again. This time the engine fired and popped, chugging as she feathered the gas.

"Well, looks like you don't need no help at all," he said, giving her a thumbs-up as he jogged back to his girlfriend. She climbed into the pickup ahead of him, her bare legs flashing white in Silva's headlights. She snuggled in tight to the boy's side and gave Silva a hard look.

"Good luck to you!" the boy yelled out his window, his arm back around the girl's shoulders, practicing being a man before he went to fight as one, the two of them not realizing where all their hoping and dreaming would likely end—a future they would be lucky to get at all.

"Good luck to you, too," Silva said, choking around her words.

She drove back to town in the dark, the Salmon glinting like oil next to the highway, stars enough to pin the sky wide open—night air that felt enough like Trawler's, Silva could imagine the tide sweeping in. A hebdomadal reckoning of memory.

Nobody had ever warned her that in grieving the ones you've lost, you're really grieving for yourself the most. Your whole world, the story of your life, shaped and defined by your loved ones' experience of it. That without them, you can't ever see or understand yourself fully again.

Though she hadn't been able to stop forgetting little pieces of her mother until she wasn't much more than a shadow-memory of what once was, though everyone said time solved the pain of loss, that forgetting was a balm, Silva had always thought that there was something intrinsically wrong with those failures of memory—a lack of loyalty, a flaw of character that would let you disregard the way you ached in each individual cell, missing someone so badly it felt as if you could never be whole again, the dark watery depths of despairing. A rushing current that had carried her tumbling and half-drowned to this moment, and then dissipated, leaving her suddenly still, questioning where she was and how she'd gotten there. She realized she'd never really had a choice. The only option she'd ever had was to figure out a way to make it through this new reality along with everything else.

CHAPTER TEN

Date: October 1, 1999
Title: Servant-Heart Ceremony
Subject: Maiden Training
Setting: Almost Paradise Sanctuary
Medium: Watercolor and graphite on cold-press
Size: 14×10

Dearest Eamon,

We are—each of us—forgotten to the outside world, captured fully and completely to this place like a nightmare you wake from and then descend back into a month that feels like a lifetime.

We have arrived at the Servant-Heart Ceremony—the culmination of everything a girl needs to know in order to best serve her man. Four weeks of maiden-training sessions led by the Almost Paradise women. This has been the order and theme of each week:

Cleanliness Is Godliness: Learning how to scrub each tile line, each mop-board seam, each sink and faucet and toilet and floor surface with a toothbrush and scouring pad dipped in bleach. Learning how to properly scour piles of dirty pots and pans with steel wool and dip clean dishes in a vinegar rinse for shine. Learning how to dust so not a speck is left, learning how to vacuum perfect lines in the compound's carpet, learning how to mop so the linoleum floors gleam, learning how to wash windows with vinegar and newspaper inside and out, "polishing the eyes of the palace." Learning how to properly launder and dry your master's white shirts, which must always be spotless, bleached, starched, pressed, and hung in perfectly spaced rows, two inches between each hanger, buttons tightened down with extra thread, hems and cuffs and collars extra crisp.

Fueling God's Work: (aka how to please your man's palate). Learning how to cook your master's roasts, chops, ribs, brisket, backstrap, tenderloin. Learning how to prepare and steam his favorite vegetables. Learning how to can his favorite fruit and jelly and pie-filling. Learning how to prepare his favorite legumes and grains and season his jerky. Learning how to bake him bread, pies, muffins, cookies, cakes. Learning how to fry his potatoes, bacon, eggs, chicken, and fresh doughnuts. Learning how to grill his sandwiches and toss his chef's salad. Learning how to set his table and how to serve him plates, platters, and saucers of food. Learning how to eat after he has eaten, keeping your face tucked and your chewing silent so as not to disturb him.

Tending to the Body: Learning how to best work out your master's kinks and knots in full-body massage. Learning how to wash and rub and moisturize his feet and hands after his daily work. Learning how to wash and condition and trim his hair. Learning how to shave his face and neck. Learning how to trim his nose and ear hair. Learning how to trim his cuticles, fingernails, and toenails, and buff his nails to a shine. (The other more intimate "body tending" training will come in a future special session.)

Tending to the Spirit: Learning to speak only when spoken to, learning to sit with hands folded and head bowed, learning to kneel at the feet of your master, waiting for him to bless you. Learning to pray prone in submission each morning out of bed for thirty minutes, each noon for ten minutes, and each evening before bed for sixty minutes—your daily devotions. Learning how to read the scriptures and support your master's sermons. Learning how to speak and sing in your heavenly, angelic voices. Learning how to beg god daily for forgiveness of your sinful womanly nature.

Twelve hours a day for four weeks the maidens have been taught their master's every need and desire, and they are nothing but devout. Delores—Holy Mother of Len Dietz and maiden trainer—makes sure of that. She, not Faith, was the one to arrange the girls for the Servant-Heart Ceremony painting at the end of the training sessions. A wooden line of girls, six on either side of the altar, a sickly yellowed side light shining in through the stained glass, casting deep shadows. I wanted to paint it all black: the pews, the sanctuary, their dresses, their faces. A frozen flock of funereal birds. A mourning mass crying ballads for the lost. Except I know it only gets worse from here.

May my soul be as sheltered and strong as yours always has been. May we each of us find our way through the coming darkness.

My love & despair,
Isabelle

PART TWO

....

There we see before us, in miniature, the large and simple lines of

our own disproportionate sphere. . . . Spirit and matter are there,

the race and the individual, evolution and permanence,

life and death, the past and the future.

Who shall say where the wisdom resides that can thus balance

present and future, and prefer what is not yet visible to that

which already is seen? . . . Each man makes his own choice,

or rather, perhaps, has it thrust upon him; and this choice,

whether it be thrust upon him, or whether, as is often the case,

he have made it without due reflection, this choice, to which he clings,

will determine the form and the conduct of all that enters within him.

-THE LIFE OF THE BEE

CHAPTER ELEVEN

APRIL 2001

Hells Canyon was in the full of its counterfeit spring, that single month of lushness—the bushes and lower hills green, even the river green in a headlong rush of growth, a frenzy of moisture. Silva found everything full of portent: the slap of river against shore, the arrangement of bunch grass on barren slope, the way the canyon swallowed the sun. In the hard, dry air of Two Rivers, it had been impossible for her to remember what it'd felt like to be subsumed with moisture, everything damp.

The Larkins Ranch was on several acres of flat land adjoining the Snake River. A tidy cabin and old barn sat surrounded by century-old black locusts, curl-leaf mountain mahoganies, and tall ponderosas, a rushing creek off to the side lined in serviceberry brush and hackberries. The vegetation softened the raw harshness of the basalt bluffs climbing nearly ten thousand feet into distant peaks—the Seven Devils. Even the names of the place some version of menace. She pushed back the trepidation that welled in her gut—being so close to everything now. A line separating what would be from what had always been.

By the time the jet-boat driver, Mack, powered down into an idle, aiming for the tumble of boulders that made up the ranch's docking, the sun was low in the sky. A day spent bucking rapids, skirting cliffs, and parting bends of smooth water—the presence of water the only soothing thing about this place. Each beach crescent they'd passed had been graced with a stunted hackberry tree sculpted into a wild bonsai. Reminded Silva of long days spent with Eamon rowing the Sound, studying trees.

Eamon's nighttime stories had been stories of the world's trees, each connecting somehow to the other. He made Silva feel a part of it—a family formed out of roots that stretched across the continents, across what could be known of human existence and beyond.

Once, when Silva was eleven, they'd taken a road trip to see the giant sequoias in Northern California. They'd walked around their god-size trunks in hushed awe. It was like traveling to another world and communing with ancient beings full of deep, reverberating power. Their thrumming treeness overtook you, reshaped you into something new and better.

As Mack secured the boat, Silva pulled her wind-knotted hair into a ponytail and gathered her belongings. Wind-chaffed and raw, she was as numbed by the hours spent jet-boating through the rushing canyon air as much as she was by the reality of what she'd done, transporting herself this close to the lion's den, armed with nothing but a pebble in her slingshot.

A tall mailbox perched a few yards up the slope along a path leading to the lawn above—mail delivered by jet boat, like everything else in the canyon, the Larkins Ranch the last stop of a seventy-mile stretch of nearly uninhabited canyon, the end of boatable river, leaving fifteen miles of wild water above until the dam and the visitor center. No roads, no access other than trails miles away from anything, the canyon well suited for people either running away or running toward something bigger than themselves.

Mack helped Silva unload her boxes and then the five bonsai, their trays spilling pebbles from Trawler's beach onto this new shore, each move a further realignment, an uprooting of the very molecules that made up the air and water and soil of their existence. He took Silva on a tour of the grounds, told her to keep watch for snakes, and recited a stream of clipped instructions. He knew the Larkins Ranch well—the sickly poplars, the overgrowth of ivy on the pump house, where the porch boards had warped and come loose. He left Silva a list of grounds duties and the outfitting schedule—the groups dropped off by boat to meet with Nick and pack into the Seven

Devils' alpine lakes—then showed Silva how to light the cantankerous stove and prime the pump that ran water from the creek to the house, and how to operate the water-generated power and short-wave radio—the only means of communication besides the mail he would boat up once a week along with any supplies Silva would need.

Climbing into the jet boat to leave, he glanced up at the hills behind the house, hesitating a moment before saying, "Watch out for trespassers."

As the jet boat roared off, Silva scanned the hillsides behind her, but they were an uninhabited barrenness just like everything else she'd seen of the canyon so far, the land offering the kind of distance and isolation that left her at the mercy of only herself.

She watched the jet boat leave. Boats were a part of her passage, the roll and chop of metal on water, engines churning against the spray. She knelt at the river and submerged her hands, sifting her fingers in silt. The water lapped in steady surges, every seventh swell a little stronger. A tidal flow. Heavy and cold. It felt as if it could hold her there forever, anchored against bottom.

She put a cold hand to her stomach, wondering how her body could foster any life at all. *Six and a half weeks.* Later than she'd planned to wait. Later than she'd planned to live through. A tryptic of women circling one another on the way down the drain.

The afternoon was already turning into early evening—she could feel it in the air, that subtle change in temperature, a soft coolness. In Trawler, the evenings had come in on cat's feet.

She stood, wiping her hands against her jeans. A lifetime ago. Another age.

She walked up the slope that led to the house, keeping an eye out for snakes as Mack had instructed, but the lawn was short and sparse. No good for hiding.

Inside the house, it was cool and damp and smelled of musty propane. The windowsills were lined with old metal boxes full of arrowheads. On the way up the river, Mack had told her about the canyon's early history, Nez Perce women gathering wild carrots and camas bulbs while their men fished salmon and hunted deer and mountain sheep grown fat on summer grass.

Silva picked up a couple of arrowheads, marveling at the perfect triangles chipped out of stone, impressed with their weightiness, the dark glint of their facets, wondering at the stories behind them: the hunt and the kill, the filling of hungry stomachs. Family and tribe living as one, supporting one another, nobody left to fend for themselves.

Old photographs hung on the walls: rugged Larkins men standing at a barn surrounded by hundreds of sheep or posed by some piece of heavy farming equipment Silva couldn't imagine having gotten upriver, no roads other than the water's treacherous path. The homesteaders looked as if they could survive just about anything this place dished out—drought and heat as well as Almost Paradise—even if she already knew the outcome of that assumption, Len Dietz having taken over the place they thought could sustain them.

One more recent photo, softly colored instead of gray scale, showed a tousle-headed boy on the verge of manhood standing next to a woman who looked too young to be his mother, although there was no denying the genetic evidence—the way they both held their bodies side by side, their solemn expressions as they gazed back at the camera. A boy too young to be old and too old to be young, already carrying the weight of the world on his shoulders. Nick.

She walked into the tiny kitchen, the doorway trim marked with horizontal lines and spidery writing: *Nick 8 mths*, all the way to *Nick 12 yrs*, each line drawn a year and two inches apart, the tallest ending at Silva's height of five and a half feet.

She tried to imagine Nick as a boy her size, a boy who was about to lose everything: his father, his mother, his home, his inheritance. Left as drifting and alone as Silva was. She'd wanted to ask what had happened to his family, his mother, why he didn't caretake the ranch himself, but there hadn't been time, everything a rush of details and action after they'd made the arrangements: meeting Mack at Pittsburg Landing, loading her things in the boat, and leaving the Dodge parked alone in a gravel parking lot—the last point of road entry into the canyon besides the visitor center just below the dam. She hadn't looked back at Two Rivers; she'd already seen enough of it to last a lifetime.

Now she looked at the flyer collection Mack had given her, created for canyon tourists: *Native American History*; *Hells Canyon Geology*; *The History of Sternwheelers*: *Mining, Sheep, and the Delivery of the US Mail*. Seven miles below the Larkins Ranch, they had passed the Kirkwood Museum—a tourist hot spot made up of an old sheep rancher's log bunkhouse filled with ranching artifacts, along with Chinese miners' tools and antique bottles, photos of early canyon ranching, and ancient artifacts from the Nez Perce and Shoshone tribes, the remains of their pit houses still dotting the land. A conglomeration depicting the evolution of Hells Canyon.

Gregarious and well-informed about the canyon's history, Mack had told her of the last Larkins Ranch summer caretaker, Jim Waters, who'd battled a family of skunks. He'd trapped them, built a driftwood raft, and sent them downriver in a flotilla, but some "hippie hikers" had found them drowned in the trap and called in complaints—the reason Jim wasn't coming back.

As the jet boat roared steadily upriver, its din echoing off the canyon walls, Silva had pumped Mack for more information about the Larkins Ranch, asking what had happened to Nick's family. He'd told her that Nick's father, Otto Larkins, had "just up and disappeared one day, left wife and kid behind," and then Meg, Nick's mother, had moved with Nick to town.

"So, they never came back?" she'd asked, trying to get beyond what she already knew.

"Dad never came back. Mom got caught up with the Lenites. Pretty one, Meg Larkins. Len Dietz always did like the pretty ones. Signed over all her land to him before she died. Kid just drifted about afterward, doing odd jobs. Sad story, really."

Mack had frowned then in mock seriousness. "Did you know it's the End Times? Look out—people 'round here like to grow religious prepper psychosis along with their vegetables and kids."

"So I've been warned," Silva replied, trying to keep her voice even.

"Those Lenite women sure know how to make some pies, though," he'd added, grinning. "That's all it takes, you know. Godliness through sugar. Some good sweets to eat and people'll overlook just about anything." He'd turned to her then, his seriousness returned and real. "No offense, but this country ain't much fit for a woman alone. History repeats itself, you know. Pretty girl like you staying in the canyon by yourself . . . better keep an eye out. The Lenites get a good look at you, they'll try and keep you." He'd smiled as if he were making a joke, but his eyes were troubled.

"I don't think that'll be a problem," she'd replied, more sharply than she'd intended. She was accustomed to people's discomfort with her solitariness and independence, but this time she understood what was at stake. Enough that she fell silent, tracing the hills as they powered through rapid after rapid, water spray atomizing around them. She took in the dark maws of hillside caves, a prey animal scoping its surroundings for the musky, warning sign of predators.

———————

Other than a few feminine kitchen items, there weren't traces of a woman ever having lived at the Larkins house—a mother whose writing had charted her son's growth. All that existed were a few unexpected touches of domesticity: Fostoria stacked in the cupboards along with fluted pie plates and teacups with matching saucers. Not what Silva had anticipated this far upriver. Not this cabin, with its unlikely Depression-era dishes meant for an unachievable kind of civility—no power, no real running water, an outhouse behind the barn. The winters harsh, the summers even harsher. An emptiness that seemed complete, even if Silva knew it wasn't. She wondered what kind of future Nick believed he could have, reinstating himself at the ranch, Almost Paradise looming above.

She went down the short, narrow hallway at the back of the kitchen and found two tiny bedrooms across from each other, just like Eamon's cabin. She picked the west-facing room so she could see the striated bluffs across the river, rumpled and lined as if squeezed together. She carried the bonsai into the small room one by one, situating them on the nightstand and desk, keeping them in for the night as a kind of comfort she didn't want to admit she needed—alone in this place, so close to everything she'd come to find, all the warnings echoing in her head.

She stored her seed collection, situated Eamon's bonsai tools, angled a lamp for good lighting, and stacked Eamon's mildewed journals. On her way out, she paused to study a picture hanging in the hallway, a high-school photo of a young woman with blue eyes and a dimpled smile. A woman who'd tried to feed her family on fancy glassware before she gave over the family inheritance to Len Dietz and died, leaving Nick behind. She, too, had left—left her child, left her things, left the future unmarked. Maybe you had to. Maybe that was just how it worked. Isabelle had. Silva's mother and Eamon, too.

She walked the Larkins property, wondering where the lines met Almost Paradise's. She paused at the old sheep shed filled with an assortment of castoffs. An old boot, stiff and curled up at the toe, sole loose and hanging, was perched on a glassless window ledge as if, like everyone and everything else in the canyon, it, too, had tried and failed to escape.

Next to the barn, the rectangular outline of an old garden plot was still visible. The canyon offered plenty of sun and an early growing season. The spring frosts having receded, it would have been time to till and plant, hope for a good season, a good harvest.

Silva wondered if Nick's mother, Meg, had been the gardener, too, if she'd grown heirloom vegetables she sliced and arranged on her fancy teatime dishes. If, like Silva's mother at the New Community, Meg Larkins had canned, pickled, dried, and "put up," until the Larkins house pantry was stacked with colorful jars like presents waiting to be opened.

Inside the barn, the chewed-up stalls were heaped with dried manure, a rusted barrel spilling tangled orange twine like intestines. The back room so full of junk the door wouldn't open beyond a crack, the acrid stink of mice-habitat wafting out. Silva went out and sat on the corral's three-rail fence. A deer skull hung on the barn, a bird nest built in the cranium, tailings of grass blowing from eye sockets. A canyon wren flitted in and out, scolding Silva's presence. Somewhere in the distance a meadowlark trilled—that lonely, solitary call of the grasslands.

Night wafted from the barn's dark entryway—dry-molded hay and dust—and Silva imagined Eamon's cabin, boarded up and thick with moss, abandoned just as this place was. She wished she could just forget about the island. Go on with life as if none of it had happened, as if it didn't exist. These people had. Everyone in her family had. She pressed her fists against her stomach. There were good reasons for leaving things behind.

• • •

She stayed up late that night with the bonsai's watchful outlines in the dark as she read the canyon history books laid out by the Larkins Ranch visitors' log with its assortment of names and dates—a reminder she wouldn't be alone for long. A week until the first group's arrival. Hopefully time enough to sort through and figure out everything she'd come to do.

First, she would recon the trail behind the Larkins house that led to Almost Paradise, and then, after getting the lay of the land, she would try to hike there. Even if she didn't know what she would do once she arrived, each step closer—even just in planning—was like releasing a breath she was only now realizing she'd been holding her whole life.

The history books were as dark as Silva's thoughts, full of drownings, murders, droughts, disease-ridden sheep, and ill-fated riverboats. As North America's deepest river gorge, Hells Canyon, despite its navigational and logistical difficulties, had been inhabited by some of the first people in North America. Ancient rock shelters, Clovis points, and pictographs found within the canyon dated back at least 13,000 years. For centuries, the Nez Perce, Shoshone-Bannock, Northern Paiute, and Cayuse tribes had all been drawn to the canyon's depths by mild winters and productive foraging and fishing. And then after them came the white settlers, pushing upriver in the late 1800s and early 1900s, going to great lengths in order to make a go of it, despite what the land could tell them in one look: dreams were frivolous in a place like this.

To get water to parched bunch-grass plateaus, homesteaders had dug miles of ditches, navigating through rock, stringing miles of pipe to creeks along cliffs they scaled and hung from on thin ropes, often falling to their deaths. They tilled the ground one painstaking foot at a time, removing boulders that studded the fields like a crop growing of their own accord. Plying basalt into fences and foundations for their one-room cabins, they'd imagined the land transformed into lush orchards and fields of rich alfalfa and timothy, but after a century of their sweating labor the only thing that remained were the same basalt boulders stacked in new human configurations.

Chinese miners had come to the canyon to mine the rivers and creeks and were brutally murdered over scant bits of gold. In the 1887 Deep Creek Massacre alone, thirty-four people were ambushed and slaughtered by a gang of horse thieves and schoolboys, the crime not discovered until the miners' tortured bodies, thrown by the killers into the Snake, were spotted near Lewiston, Idaho, sixty-five miles away. The site was named Chinese Massacre Cove and marked with a memorial stone inscribed in Chinese, English, and Nez Perce that overlooked the river.

The canyon took back what it had never consented to give in the first place, its landscape defined by the names given to it: *gorge, snake, devil, hell*.

Rotting shacks, rock piles, rusted implements, and caving-in mine shafts now home to rattlesnakes, packrats, and bats. A place of unsurpassed hardship. A place that demanded everything. A place where failure was a definition, not an exception. The canyon bewitching people, century after century, calling them like a Siren to its slopes, its riverbank, its great austere expanse of sky and mountaintops, its hidden shoals and rocky outcrops. Pulling them toward the very things meant to take them under.

Eldridge Larkins, great-great-grandfather of the Larkins Ranch—the man in the oldest photos hanging on the wall—was in the canyon books, homesteading the original Larkins property, thousands of acres. He was successful for a while. It wasn't until Nick's father, Otto Larkins, that the decline began. Otto tried wheat, then rapeseed, then cows, but seed went sky-high and the price of beef through the floor and he, too, like nearly all the others, failed.

Silva tried to find more on the family, but other than a quick mention of Otto marrying Meg Ehrlich in his later years—him fifty and her twenty—and having an only son, Nick, the three of them living for a little over a decade in the canyon as a family of three, there wasn't much. The more recent the canyon's human history, the sparser it was, as if along with the homesteaders' failure to sustain themselves, there was a failure in story, a failure in words.

Silva was left wondering about the Larkinses' life in the place she now inhabited—if they'd been happy in the beginning, sustained by one another and by the land, or if like everyone else in the canyon, they'd been overcome by loss. Enough to leave behind the things that had once mattered. Enough to stay gone forever. The kind of existence that brooked no self-pity. The kind of existence where survival was a matter of definition nobody could make except for themselves.

She studied the photo of the two of them—Meg and Nick, mother and son, twin expressions of sorrow and hardship on their faces and in their posture—and felt as if she were standing there with them, gazing out at the chilling unknown.

CHAPTER TWELVE

What does the river say as it speaks its tongues into your listening ear, her paint dripping wet like water entering into the secret recesses of your flesh? Colors upon you like the newness of light shining on your pale skin, anointing your forehead, there and there and there. You hold your head down, listen to the gurgling popping rushing burbling glug-glug-glugging flow into your ears, filling you with liquid like blessings, flowing down your chest, over your stomach, in between your legs. You are birth and born, you are afire, flaming in clear water, your skin streaming colors of pink light— wash ov'r me Holy Holy, wash ov'r me Holiness—a wink into night, into arms that hold you tight, blessed of virgins, blessed are thee, blessed are we.

CHAPTER THIRTEEN

APRIL 2001

At the sound of crows cawing, Silva awoke transported back to childhood—a small girl hiding behind damp-pinned clothes hung on the clothesline to dry, the smell of beaten cotton billowing around her as her mother battled the crows that flocked each morning to feast in the New Community garden. Outside, mist rose off the Snake, wreathing and twisting like wraiths set free.

Determined to make quick progress of her work, she transferred the bonsai to a makeshift table on the porch that she'd patched together out of weathered plywood propped on top of rickety sawhorses. She checked each tree over, worried how they would fare in the heat and aridity, the drastic alteration to everything they were acclimated to. The only things to survive the canyon had to foster themselves in a continual environment of elemental abuse.

Looking for fasteners to better secure the table, she found a topo map buried in the back of a kitchen drawer. Grease-stained and tattered, the map looked as if it'd been consulted often, its creases ripped, a man's tidy block print edging its perimeters in bled ink. She spread out the map on the table and oriented herself at the flat representing the Larkins homestead, a spidery trail winding up the elevation lines behind the house and then splitting off in two directions. The map was old—predating the mark of what was to come, Almost Paradise laying claim to all the surrounding land, all the Larkins land—but it gave her what she needed: a distinct, marked route.

She shook dust off an old rucksack hanging on the porch, packed a water bottle and a sandwich along with the map, left the bonsai in the porch shade, and started. Up the draw behind the house, she found the trail, pushing cautiously through brush and climbing steep switchbacks, expecting to find some marker to indicate where she was headed, but there was nothing but rocks and brush and more switchbacks. Nothing to say what really loomed ahead. Nothing to say what kind of disease the land had contracted—spaces vast enough to swallow something so vile.

She hiked the several miles up to the fork, but the map didn't show which path would lead her the right way, so she went up both spurs, timing herself for a few miles in either direction, hoping for something, anything, to let her know she was getting closer, but she found nothing but more switchbacks leading her farther up.

Finally, sweaty and tired, she stopped at an overlook, the canyon opened up below her, the river looking like what it'd been named for: a snake undulating through the steep-walled gorge—a dark, liquid swath in the canyon's austere emptiness. She knew she had to turn around in order to make it back before evening, but the thought of having to give up without making it anywhere left her more deflated than she'd expected—miles that had told her next to nothing, except to prove how infinite the land actually was and how little she could accomplish on her own, on foot. Each plan she made resulting in the same empty-handed outcome. What did she think she was going to accomplish, trying to find a place that kept captive all who entered?

In the next days, the outfitting group nearly on its way, Silva had no choice but to dig into the ranch work—pruning, pulling, and digging. Trying to rechart each possibility, trying to read into the future, just as Eamon had said he could. See what she might make out of things wholly outside her control, outside of what she could touch with her hand and trace with her fingers, intuiting each movement of growth.

She labored from dawn until dusk, until she was too tired to think, too tired to do anything but eat and sleep and work again the next day. Her stubborn white skin finally succumbed to the canyon sun, growing if not tan, apricot, each day warmer than the last. Nick's drought in action, marching toward the flames he warned of—fire, air, earth, water. Each element calling you to its treacherous banks.

To stay cool in the canyon's unrelenting heat as she worked, she took to wetting a handkerchief in the icy creek and tying it around her head, rivulets of water flowing down the sides of her face, edging into the corners of her mouth—water sated with mineral wash and decomposition that left a tackish coating on the back of her tongue, a taste like rotting leaves.

At the end of the week, she went down to the creek, pant legs scrunched up to her thighs, shirt unbuttoned, ready to wash the sweat from her skin and hair. It'd been an especially hot day, and at first that was what she thought she was smelling—heat that brought with it the smell of summer decay— but then the stink became full-bodied and moist, the air imbued with rot.

She followed the creek to the river, where a dead mountain sheep floated, so inflated with gasses it seemed to bob in the grasses in which it was moored. Bits of ragged flesh exposed, it looked ready to explode, and she was afraid it would, sending bits of putrid flesh like shrapnel, the smell of its rot on her skin, in her hair, in the back of her throat. She crushed some sage and rolled it in the handkerchief, pulling it up over her nose as though she were warding off evil, then searched out a piece of wood, long and smooth and as light as balsa. She poled the sheep out as far as she could reach, turning her head as its feet rolled up, stiff and pointed as it drifted on the river's surface—a slow, bloodstained churl.

The canyon was quiet, the last jet boats gone from their fishing holes, the owls starting to call their hunts. The creek's current created whirlpools of flotsam at her submerged feet—leaves, rafts of small sticks, a dead beetle— everything in this place in some flux, transitioning from life to death and back again.

She went back to her washing pool and scrubbed her hands with the grit from the creek bottom, but no matter how much she scoured, dirt pleated her palms and rimmed her nails. She'd never been able to wear gloves. Without the intimacy of a seed's smooth hull, a leaf stalk's rough bur, the soft crumbling of casting-rich dirt, it was as though she had lost the ability to see.

As she finished washing up, she noticed something lodged against the opposite bank. She waded in and fished it out—a jagged piece of plywood, most of a NO TRESPASSING sign still attached. She threw it into her growing burn pile heaped with brush, pruning clippings, and wood scraps. A few nights before, a storm had surged the creeks full of mountain runoff, and the next day, a wooden door had washed up on shore along with driftwood and wads of tangled fishing line. The door lay flat, moored on the beach as if it were a secret passageway, as though all she had to do was pull it open and walk into a whole new world. She had dragged it to the burn pile and leaned it upright against a tree where it still stood—an entryway to another land. She wished she might cross space and time that easily, transport herself entirely.

She walked down to the beach where she could see the moon rising, heavy and low, nestled like an egg on the still-blue evening sky between the peaks. She'd started to wonder if there was something fatalistic, something cursed and restless to her birth story. All that unreachable, latent power— power to command the tides, direct the earth's axis, and modulate the frenetic energy of the sun threatening to pull her under.

Underwater boulders shifted in the current, sending up otherworldly echoes, as if the river were slowly purling loose, pulling up the stakes that held it earthbound to join with the air. She breathed in the smell of fecund dirt, wet sand, and algae, and when a particularly warm gust lifted the hem of her shirt, she let it, her skin contracting at its touch. She felt the night's movement against the sharp spine of the canyon.

In the moonlit dark, she peeled off her shirt, then her pants, stripping until her skin was fully exposed. She looked down and studied the nearly imperceptible swelling beneath her flesh. Who would choose a life defined by never-ending heartbreak? A life of aloneness. She walked along the water's edge and kept going, first toward the mailbox, then past the trailhead. Finally, she took off running, following the river, legs lifting, arms pumping, the wind kicking her hair up behind her, lifting and falling in rhythm to her stride. She let the pounding enter her and carry her, running over this hill and the next, finding that the farther she went, the less there was left behind, the less there was to feel—the familiar pain, the ache deep inside that never left.

She didn't stop until her muscles combusted, until she had to bend over and grab her knees to breathe, her pulse roaring, her bare skin flushed and mottled, her nerves tingling as if she'd been electrocuted, every muscle twitching, every cell of her body lit on fire.

The moon had climbed high over the hills, everything silvering under its touch, the striated sky bright with raked clouds. She felt the lunar weight pulling at her. She let her hands rest against her bare stomach, imagining what the first quickening would feel like—a bump, a nudge outward, a movement like bird wings under the surface of flesh fluttering again her palms? The thought left her shaken. She already knew that the best you could often hope for was to be overlooked by fate's dark attentions. That maybe if you kept your head down, if you worked hard enough to make yourself invisible, it might pass you over when it came around, rattling at the doors, knocking at the windows, looking for entry.

Clumps of brush surrounded her, a game trail leading down to the water's edge. As she made her way down it, she almost stepped on a snake, its dark shape stretched across the trail. She was close enough to see its opaque, segmented tail-tip, its wedged head and black-bead eyes. It tightened the muscle of its body, flicked its tongue out to test the air, and a rush of adrenaline jellied her knees. She knew she should back away, but its beauty and danger transfixed her. She wanted to reach down, run a finger over its diamond-stitched scales, but it was gone as suddenly as it had appeared—a dry scrape of belly, a whisper in the dirt, rattles shaking loosely in warning.

The heat of her run had worn off and left her chilled, her feet raw. She lowered herself into the water, wincing at its bite. As the water reached her waist, she imagined letting go, the small weight of her stomach pulling her under like an anchor until she, too, disappeared into the dark—a full circle traced wide. Why fight the inevitable? Why not let go like everyone else had? But when she looked up, she saw a brown lump bobbing on the water's dark expanse, bumping against shore rocks. Something fleshy, a wet shifting of hair and bloated gut. Another mountain sheep.

It rolled in the water, and she saw a distinct pattern of exploded flesh. With the extent of the first sheep's bloating decay and her lack of expertise, she'd thought perhaps it was just the normal process of decomposition. But this time it was clear, evident in the symmetry of the wounds. She'd thought she'd heard shots in the hills, had imagined with cold dread what they might mean. Her fears translated into reality, this place deadly to anything that ventured too close. Full of enough threat and violence she'd wondered at her own foolishness in coming, in thinking she could do anything to save anybody, including herself, submerged in cold, dark water flowing swift enough to take you under and keep you there forever. She imagined her body floating to the river's surface, rolling bloated like the sheep's—exposed, vulnerable. A physical betrayal of a private act meant for nobody but herself.

She pulled herself out of the river, climbing through the rocks until she found the trail again, her wet feet coating in its soft dust as she walked back. She glanced uneasily at the empty hills, her arms wrapped over her chest, her teeth chattering, her skin wet and exposed.

She'd come farther than she realized, and it took a long time to reach the ranch, tree trunks standing out ghostly in the dark, her clothes a heap on the beach. She tried to dress quickly, grit grinding against her damp skin as she struggled with her pants and shirt. Then she froze in place, clothes half on, as she heard a weak but distinct splashing over the lap of water on the shore.

Shivering in the night air, she tried to tell herself the noise was just another river murmur, the night making each noise new and strange, but the splashing moved closer, became rhythmic. She couldn't breathe, couldn't move to hide herself. What if someone had been watching her all along? Someone who gunned down mountain sheep off river bluffs. A man in the dark.

The splashing was closer, just up the shore but even with the full moon, the night was dark enough that, at first, she couldn't make out anything other than a wheezing pant. Then, finally, she saw it. A waterlogged dog clawing shore boulders, trying to find purchase. It slipped and disappeared underwater, and Silva ran, stumbling past the boulders, wading into the water, her wet clothes and the current pulling her in deeper, as if the river were trying to get back its chance to keep her. She grabbed the dog by the neck and hauled it out of the water, wincing as it yelped.

When Silva got it to shore, the dog tried to stand, but its legs went wobbly and it collapsed at her feet. She carefully ran her hands along its legs, shoulders, and hips, feeling for any broken bones, any evidence of it, too, being shot, but everything seemed intact.

Scanning the dark for things she couldn't see, she asked in a shaky voice, "Are you okay?" and at her words, the dog's tail thumped weakly. It was a male husky mix, cream and gray, a black stripe up his nose and a mask over the top of his brown eyes that made him seem thoughtful, as if he, too, were assessing the situation. The tops of his ears were blunted and torn, as if they had been shot off, edges of skin tattered where bits of fur had grown back. She wondered if he'd escaped whoever was massacring mountain sheep.

He didn't protest when she scooped him up and carried him like a baby, even though he was big enough that he dwarfed her, filling her arms.

Inside the house, she built a fire even though the night was still warm, situating the dog next to the stove. She fed him out of her hands, and he licked her palms clean over and over again. His brown eyes followed her whenever she got up. Finally, she lay down next to him, snuggling close and stroking his side as much for her comfort as his own. She'd determined she would stay up all night, keeping guard, but the fire's heat was flush on her skin, a slow radiating prickle, and she fell asleep breathing in the dog's wet leather smell, her hand buried in his fur, finding reassurance and comfort in each of his breaths.

———•••———

When she woke, the dog was standing quietly at the screen door, looking out.

"Ready to leave already?" she asked, heart in her throat. She pushed open the door, expecting the dog to dart out and run away, but he just stood there looking at her expectantly. She went out and sat on the porch steps in the sun, and as if in reply, the dog sat next to her and leaned up against her side. She put her arm around him and stroked the soft fur on his chest. They sat this way a long time, gazing out at the river reflecting the morning light, pondering everything the waters had carried.

Later that morning, she called in an order for dog food and to report the shot-up mountain sheep. The dispatcher told her to keep an eye out, *keep watch*. As if she could prevent anything bad from happening—to herself or anyone else. The river and creek had already delivered their own messages of warning. Shot-up mountain sheep, a no-trespassing sign, a nearly drowned dog.

She named him Juniper after the twin-trunk bonsai Eamon had given her—child and parent always together. As a child, the closest thing to a pet that Silva had were the island seagulls that followed her, mawing and mewling as they begged for scraps. But all Juniper cared about was her. He slept next to her bed at night, and stayed at her side all day as she worked. On her daily hikes—surveying the canyon as far as she could on foot—Juniper stayed on alert next to her as he, too, listened and watched for things up in the hills, even though no other warnings had floated down. Silva didn't know if Juniper's original owner might eventually show up, or who that owner might prove to be, but she knew that no matter what she wouldn't be able to give Juniper back if someone did come for him. It was as if, in Juniper, she'd discovered a lost soulmate—a part of her that had always been missing. She fell asleep each night with her hand in his fur and woke each morning to him licking her face, his own face an expression of devoted love. They had found each other, and that was enough.

Silva brought back pieces of the canyon from their hikes until the house was a naturalist's arrangement of feathers, bones, and pieces of rock that were once wood—metamorphosis into an indestructible mass she wished she, too, might achieve. She found a dusty, desiccated frog resting in a corner of the kitchen, its long-toed feet arranged in repose, small snout of a nose, bony-ridged back, eyes dried shiny black. Succumbed to this land of contradiction: a place baked harsh enough to suck your bodily fluids dry, leave you husked and drifting, as insubstantial as air. A place that tore everything down until all that remained was its essence—life in sharp relief.

She misted the bonsai each evening, checking for stress, but despite the unwavering heat, they, too, were sprouting new growth, the deadwood larch covered in lacy needles, and even the bristlecone pine cautiously budding, recovered from the shock of transport. She'll come to understand that the canyon was thrumming with life despite its barrenness at first glance.

On an early-morning hike, several miles upriver, she found what she hadn't known she'd been looking for: two small hackberry trees growing in a boulder pile, their small, twisted forms stunted and warped. Thick, bent trunks, strong branches, healthy arrowhead-shaped leaves. The only trees she'd ever seen that mimicked Eamon's honeysuckle. She carefully dug them up, severing their roots and wrapping them in wet burlap before taking them back to the house.

At her desk, she flipped Eamon's honeysuckle notebook open to diagrams of trimming, the process of charted and deliberate growth. She sat the trees next to the notebook and examined the corresponding lines of the bodies she would re-create, reading Eamon's words: *Initial wiring is the foundational stage of creating a bonsai from a raw piece of plant material, re-creating nature's elegant balance. This is the most important step as it lays the foundation of all future growth.*

Silva loosened the hackberry's roots and made the trims Eamon had sketched decades earlier. She ran her fingers over the trunks and branches, tracing future lines of bark and bud—the only thing that reassured her, the only thing that made any real sense, formed any kind of unity. The similarity between the new sketch and the beginnings of her trees provided the kind of certainty she needed. The only kind she could count on. Meticulous planning, things in order—these were things Eamon had taught her. The things on which she'd depended. First one tiny move, then another. A trim, a twist of wire, a new shape. Each centimeter of growth charted.

She flipped the pages as she wired branches until her hands were numb and rank with copper, trying to see the shapes she needed to create, repruning what she'd already gone over until she'd reached the vision that'd led her there. She felt the connection in her fingers—knowledge of the form the trees would become. She, too, could see into the trees' future.

Forty years before, Eamon had written, *The larger trunk has been trained into the informal, upright style and the smaller trunk trained into the semi-cascade style, giving the composition a feeling of motion and drama, suggesting a tree blown by the wind, clinging tenaciously to a steep cliff, stretching horizontally to find the sun. This is the result of not only the directional flow of the two trunks but the alternating spirals of live and dead tissue in the larger trunk, the crown of "jin," or dead wood, and the strongly defined and layered branching.*

She examined the wires she'd twined up the hackberry's branches and read more: *First the foundation is laid, then the structure is built, then the painting and decorating is done. Each stage has a different goal and therefore a different technique. . . . One must never stop looking at the larger picture—a lifetime of reenvisioning.*

Hundreds of years' worth of reenvisioning and reshaping. Losing the honeysuckle along with Eamon had been like losing a conjoined twin, the presence of it torn violently from Silva's body, leaving her mortally wounded, without equilibrium just when she'd needed the stability of her roots the most, weighted with all the possibility of future growth.

Finally, she planted the wired hackberry trees together and examined her work. Although they were stripped and bound tight, she could see the way they would grow together—the grace they could achieve with the right constraint. They, too, would learn to survive with trimmed and cramped roots, branches wired and bent. She peered at them, reading their destiny in each nodule and bud, the bodies they would create when woven together. Two shapes grown into one.

This she could understand. This she could control. Roots, branches, trunks. Through containment she would set them loose.

CHAPTER FOURTEEN

Date: October 15, 1999
Title: Religious-training Ceremony
Subject: Twelve Maidens
Setting: Almost Paradise Sanctuary
Medium: Watercolor and graphite on cold-press
Size: 10×12

Dearest Eamon,

We have moved on to the next stage of preparation: the maidens' religious training undertaken by Mother Delores. Len's sermons each Wednesday night and Sunday morning bookend the training sessions, highlighting god's holy will toward a woman's place with her husband-master. The scriptures they cite and compel the maidens to memorize would take pages to document, handpicked bits they string together into their own self-fashioned edicts. I'm only surprised they aren't more militant in their requirements, adding more subjugation, more covering, more retreat to the list. As it is, the maidens have withdrawn into near full silence, speaking only when spoken to, and even that predesigned—scriptures spoken back and forth like some kind of riddle they might solve with enough devotion, enough erasure of self. A thorough brainwashing of the order we know is possible with any religiously motivated radical regime. Each morning they process through their chanting/singing, on their knees in the sanctuary, rice scattered beneath them on the wood floor in mimicry of Christ's suffering. They end each evening the same, heads draped in veils. Their voices echo in my head all night long, haunting my dreams. That is something I cannot capture in this painting—the sound of their retreat, the sound of their internment, the sound of their pain and belief.

They are kept separate from the rest of the compound, dwelling in their own walled-off harem space that nobody is allowed to enter. I am given access to them only in their training sessions, and then only when it is something Delores deems open to outside observation, important enough that it might be visually rendered and thus remembered. And so I paint them—again and again. They treat me like one of their many ruling matrons, but with more fear, deference, and even a tinge of amazement. What I can capture, what I can reproduce of them—even they understand that power. They look at me with eyes that cry out, eyes that I'll never be able to forget.

This composition is much like the last, a sanctuary scene, except here the maidens are kneeling in a half circle around the altar, Len Dietz standing as their deity behind it. Their heads are bowed and covered, their faces hidden. As is pleasing to their master. As is pleasing to their god.

I find my own retreat only in their garden—a space run by Faith, who allows me the quiet, the solitude. A space that brings me back home once again to you, where I can believe in reality again. Where I can find relief in growth, in greenness, in soil and insect and root. I picture your trees, I picture you. I find some measure of succor.

All my love,
Isabelle

CHAPTER FIFTEEN

APRIL 2001

Juniper slept on the porch, shaded from the afternoon heat while Silva made pass after pass with the ancient lawnmower, getting everything ready for the outfitters' arrival. As she finished the lawn's back perimeter, she caught movement up the trail. She'd seen animals use the path and thought at first that was what she'd spotted—deer drawn to the smell of fresh-cut grass—but then she saw a rider, horses.

She killed the mower and quickly pushed it to the house, Juniper still asleep on the porch, having completely failed his guarding duties. The exact scenario she'd been worried about: her alone at the Larkins house and a stranger showing up—whether Juniper's old owner or one of the Lenites, if there was even a distinction between the two.

It didn't take long for the man to appear from where the trail dropped down to creek—close enough that she could see him now, loose and solitary, lanky limbs and wide shoulders, sun-faded clothes, face shadowed under his hat. Nick, two days early.

He rode in slowly, a pack string behind him, and glanced at everything: the newly cleared water intake, the patch of bushes she'd thinned and mulched, the wire she'd put around a sapling to keep the deer from chewing its bark, the conifer ladder-fuel trimming she'd finished.

Finally alert to the intrusion, Juniper woke and jumped up, let out a series of deep warning barks that echoed off the canyon walls.

Nick pulled up his horse hard, the gangly gray gelding behind him rearing and dancing sideways, eyes white-rimmed and wild. Working the reins, Nick called out, "Whoa, whoa," trying to keep the pack string in line.

Silva ran to hush Juniper. "You're going to cause a rodeo," she scolded as Nick circled the stock, trying to keep them from rioting, the wild-eyed gelding behind him snorting and throwing his head.

"We weren't expecting you yet," she called out, trying not to make it sound like an accusation. Nick was the Larkins Ranch owner, after all—sort of, maybe, whatever that meant.

"Sorry about that. Thought I could maybe get some things wrapped up here early, before the group arrives. But don't worry, I've got my own supplies. I'll stay in the barn, keep out of your hair," Nick said, his voice calm, seemingly at ease despite the animal ruckus.

But of course he would be. He'd grown up there, memorizing each clump of bunchgrass, each rock bluff.

"Didn't know you had a dog," he said, reining his horse from the side.

"I didn't. He showed up a while ago," she said, thinking about the dead sheep. What else the river had delivered.

As Nick took the stock to the corral, Silva led Juniper into the house where he couldn't charge anyone and hastily assessed things with an owner's eyes. She checked her reflection quickly in the wavery mirror that hung next to the door. When she opened the screen, Juniper darted past her and went straight for Nick's legs. At first, she thought he was going to latch on, but instead, he nosed Nick's hand enthusiastically, wagging his whole back end in greeting.

Nick leaned over and ruffled his tattered ears. "Hello there, handsome. Thought we were going to have a little Wild West action for a minute," he said, grinning disarmingly at Silva—the same smile as his mother's portrait in the house. "What's his name? Looks like a little Yoda—those brown eyes. Like some kind of wise sage . . ."

"Juniper," she said, and the dog's ears pricked forward, his thoughtful eyes meeting hers. Some kind of sage indeed. "Found him in the river, half-drowned. Nobody came to claim him," she said, relief flooding her again over this fact—Nick instead of an unknown previous owner.

"Lucky for him," Nick said looking at Silva. "There's sets of class-IV rapids up above. It's rough country for people and dogs—especially one that looks so much like a wolf."

Silva pictured the dog bobbing and banking over whitecaps, taking on water. She knew the feeling. "Two shot-up mountain sheep carcasses washed downriver, too," she added.

Nick frowned, a dark expression passing over his face. "'Shot up'?"

"Like someone used them for target practice. I called it in, but they said there was nothing to do about it except keep an eye out. I thought I heard shooting up above when I got here."

"It's good you have a dog. It's not always safe, being down here by yourself," Nick said, communicating more than his words. Why he'd come early—checking in on her. Nobody comfortable with her being alone in the canyon. All she'd risked in coming here, seemingly no closer to finding Isabelle than she'd been before.

He glanced around. "You've been busy. The place looks great." He walked over to the bonsai sitting on the table in the porch shade and touched the larch's branches carefully. "This a tamarack?" he asked.

"A deadwood larch, yes," she said, surprised. The tree, bent and shaped for decades into something other than itself, wouldn't have been easy for most to identify by either of its names.

"A firewood tree, although this one wouldn't provide much warmth I'm afraid," he said, touching the silvered streak of deadwood grown into the trunk, twined perfectly with the live wood, anchoring branches and leader.

She shuddered at the thought of it—a hundred years of meticulously trained growth gone in one quick spit of flames. She had the quick urge to run over and soak all of them down, to drench every tree in sight.

Nick looked at her quizzically. "Where did you come from, anyway? There aren't many bonsai masters in these parts."

She wiped hair away from her sweaty forehead, feeling as out of place as Eamon's gnarled trees. "A long way from here," she said. She offered Nick a drink and went in to get it, glad he stayed outside even though he had every right to come in. It was his place to claim. All those wall markings, *Nick 12 yrs*. She wondered who he'd been—a boy who tamed snakes, a boy who rode the river like Huck Finn?

She sat next to him on the front steps. "Your name's in the kitchen, on the wall," she said, holding a hand up in measurement.

He shook his head and smiled. "My mother always did love to keep a record of things."

"That's her in the house pictures? Brown hair, your same smile?"

Nick glanced over at Silva, surprised.

"There's a lot of family pictures. You look like her."

"Yeah, I guess so, although as a kid I hated that, people saying I took after my mother. Thought that was a bad thing somehow." He shrugged. "You know, as a boy."

"There are worse things than having your mom's smile."

"Ah, but a boy's ego is a very delicate thing," he said with a grin.

Silva tried to imagine Nick as a child, possessor of a delicate ego, but it seemed as farfetched as herself as a small girl, carefree and happy in her mother's New Community garden.

"So, how do you like it here?" he asked, squinting out at the fresh-mown lawn, but the question seemed personal somehow—her staying in his house, on his property.

"It's nice," she said, trying to figure out what kind of terms they were on. Sweat prickled her scalp, the sun beating down with late-afternoon intensity, a harbinger of the flames he had warned of. She had to resist fanning herself like an overdressed church lady. "I wasn't sure if I was supposed to clean the barn, too? Mack didn't leave any instructions. . . ."

Nick shook his head. "It's my father's mess. I just haven't been able to get to it yet."

She turned to him before she could change her mind. "You don't need to stay in the barn. It isn't fit for a horse, much less a person. There's an empty bedroom in the house—no reason for you not to use it. It is your place, after all," she said, no matter how awkward it would be—two tiny bedrooms so close together they seemed practically connected.

"Not yet," Nick said, looking out. "But thank you. If you're sure you don't mind. . . ."

"Of course," she said, but suddenly she realized she didn't know which bedroom had been Nick's. She might have been sleeping in his childhood bed all along. He'd learned to walk on the cabin's uneven floors, eaten his first meals inside its walls, said his first words. She was living among the details of his beginnings, sharing his family intimacy.

She swiped at a sweat fly hovering around her face, but it knew its calling. Despite the breeze that had kicked up, she could feel sweat breaking under her breasts, sticking her shirt to her stomach's translucent skin—skin grown pliant in preparation for its upcoming stretching.

Nick stood. "Guess I better tend the crew. Would you like to meet them? They don't bite—well, at least most of them." The scar on his face moved like a fault line when he smiled.

They went to the corral, Juniper sniffing noses with the chestnut mare Nick had ridden.

"This is Sage," he said. "She's a good one. Tiko, on the other hand . . ."

As if on cue, the gelding came skidding up to the fence, blowing at Juniper.

"The rest belong to friends I work for," Nick went on. "Mule One, Mule Two, Mule Three, and the horses—Savage, Nit, and Killer. Their names, not mine."

Silva offered her palm to Tiko, who snorted and looked at her from under long eyelashes, his eyes rimmed as black as a showgirl's. He lipped her palm before Nick pushed his head back.

"Look out," he said. "You can't trust this one."

She dropped her hand. There were certain lines to be maintained. Even if she was already calculating in her head, remaking her plans. A fit horse could average five miles an hour, easily covering the distance to Almost Paradise and back in a day's ride—even carrying two people.

She'd learned to ride on Trawler. One of Eamon's wealthy customers had an arena and a barn full of papered Arabians not much bigger than ponies. They had traded tree work for riding lessons, and Silva had bonded with a fourteen-hand dapple-gray named Sunchero Siete Cielo, who at twenty-five years old had hardly mellowed enough for pleasure riding, always tossing his arched neck and high-stepping as if he were adorned with tassels and bells. For a year, Silva had imagined herself an Arabian princess, always galloping about, whether on the horse or not. But then Sunchero had died suddenly. Silva had insisted on going to see him one last time; she still remembered the morning glory twined around a post, and light through the barn's battens, the Bobcat's lugged tires driving through the talcum-powder dirt, its bucket levered out, metal teeth biting into dry grass, dust throbbing up, wrinkling into the texture of her skin. The sharp odor of earth and pine—roots peeled flesh white and slick, poking out of the dark earth like broken ribs. The driver wrapping a rope behind the horse's front legs and withers, hitching it tight to the bucket, the Bobcat's tires spinning, spraying up bits of straw and dirt as they gained purchase against the gelding's weight, his slick gray neck stretched out, his head twisting behind him. Sloughing horsehair and abraded hide, the smell of dirt and wet flesh. Dust-caked eyes and nostrils and flesh. Eamon had tried to make Silva look away, but she'd refused, the air thick and gray with fog, blowing damply against her face.

Nick stayed at the barn taking care of the stock, and Silva tidied up, sweeping grass from the porch. It was a small thing, she told herself, Nick spending a few nights while she was there. Although it didn't feel small, any of it. She checked the room she'd offered him: bed, side table, window. Feet away from her door. So close they would be able to hear each other sleep.

Finally, she went back to work, thinning the overgrown alder brush behind the house, out of sight of the barn, the sun setting behind the hills, shadows grown long. When Nick came back to the house, arms loaded with pack bags, he didn't see her at first. Silva could hear him unpacking inside through the open windows as dusk settled outside.

When he passed the bedroom window, he looked out and spotted her. "Working in the dark?" he asked, smiling through the window screen.

She felt herself blush. "Just finishing up," she lied. She washed in the creek, the canyon transforming into its night self, everything already altered in Nick's presence.

When she went back inside, she wasn't sure what she should do. Was she supposed to feed him, too? Instead, she joined him in the living room, where he was reading a newspaper. She sat on the floor next to Juniper, trying not to act as awkward as she felt, a houseguest who wasn't really a guest.

"Anything new going on with the occupation?" she asked.

"Well, the latest demand is that the government hand over control of the Hells Canyon Wilderness Area. Two hundred thousand acres or so. The Lenites videoed themselves burning the visitor center's Native American displays. Just your friendly neighborhood bullies playing G.I. Joe and destroying priceless cultural and historical artifacts. So, no, nothing new, really."

"Why isn't anyone stopping them—the cops, the feds?"

"The Lenites would love nothing more than a Ruby Ridge–style siege— give them a chance to go full-out, play the martyr, especially after Y2K came and went, and The End along with it. People are coming in to support them, readying to make something happen this time."

"Is Len going to be staying there?" She tried not to show her hope—the occupation keeping him busy long enough that she might be able to find Isabelle without having to confront him again.

"Long enough to get some more press attention. Struts around in his occupation outfit acting important whenever there's a photo op, gives reporters sound bites, then goes home to be served a warm meal and a bed with one of his acolyte girls so he can make more little Lenites for his growing army."

Silva felt the bile rise in her throat and wished she hadn't said anything, the image of Len so strong she had to shut her eyes a moment to rid herself of it.

"Listen, I'm going to get out of your way, go work on the barn," Nick said, seemingly as wary of talking about Len Dietz as she was now that both of them were within riding distance of Almost Paradise.

After he left, Silva fixed herself a quick salad and took the newspaper to her room. Juniper sniffed at Nick's open doorway without crossing in, seemingly aware that the space wasn't theirs alone anymore. Bags sagged in the middle of the guest bed, shirts and jeans in tidy folds, a pair of boots heeled against the wall. Books and a bathroom kit sat on the side table, along with a quart jar of what looked like honey. Nick had packed in more than she'd thought—as if he were settling in for the long haul, as if he planned on staying. She tipped her head and read the book titles sideways: *Apiary Science, The Bee Reader, Colony Health and Wellness.*

She closed her door, sat on her bed, and speared forkfuls of salad, trying not to think about Nick sleeping right there, a dozen feet away. What that might mean, her whole body responding to him against her will each time they were together. She kept telling herself that she already had too many life complexities and complications going on without adding romance into the mix.

She distracted herself with newspaper photos of the Lenite men patrolling the visitor center, armed with AKs and covered in face paint as if they were at a desert outpost in a war-torn land. Len's quote was front and center: "Mark my words: We will never return this land to the government, but if they want to take the situation to violence, we're ready for it. And if they want a war, we'll give them a conflagration so great it'll be unstoppable."

Silva laid down the newspaper. She could see now why Mack hadn't been more specific in his warning, why Nick had come down early to check on her. Who would want to come stay for months in an isolated place that was home to a man like Len Dietz—a man who lurked with his followers up in the hills, planning for the end times, who kept women held captive, who spoke of things he couldn't possibly know? Only someone gone mad. Only someone desperate themselves.

It was late when Nick finally came in, light edging under his door. She wondered what it felt like, staying in his old childhood home after all these years. She tried not to think about what he was doing. Undressing, reading bee books in bed?

She tossed and turned, sitting up to listen throughout the night, thinking she'd heard him moving around, but the house was quiet, a pair of owls somewhere far off crying distant mating calls to one another. She wanted to get up, but she felt trapped to her room like a curfewed dorm.

She was still awake when the first early-morning birds started singing. Barely light out, she heard Nick's door open, then the creak of floorboards as he walked to the kitchen. Late to bed and an early riser. Like Eamon.

Juniper got up and stared at the bedroom door, everyone up early, ready to go, but Silva waited until she heard the screen door squeak and shut, the house go silent, before she finally got out of bed.

Nick's door was open, his bed tautly made, looking as though nobody had slept in it. In the kitchen, a washed cup and bowl were tipped upside down next to the sink. Taking care of himself like he said he would.

The morning brought heat like a punishment, the canyon already moving to summer. Silva thought she was prepared, acclimated, but the days' stilled swelter worried her. This heat was something more—an intensity of air and sun that felt more like a presence than temperature.

She walked out to the barn and paused in the entryway, Nick's back to her as he cleaned out the room she hadn't been able to see into before, its corners and floor heaped with sloughing stacks of old magazines: *Ferrier's Digest*,

Sheep Guide, Farm and Ranch. His T-shirt stuck to the corded muscles next to his spine, his shoulder blades shifting in tempo to his movements: *fork, lift, plop, fork, lift, plop,* a rusted wheelbarrow heaped full, things already looking orderly.

Noticing her, he stopped and leaned against his pitchfork, his face dripping sweat. "It's hot. Should've worn my long johns."

"What?" she asked, laughing in confusion, distracted by his physicality.

"When I was a kid, there were these old-timers called the Bull-Gang. Wore their wool long underwear year-round under jeans and flannels. Swore it kept them cooler in the heat. Can you image the *sweat*? The *smell*? It's no wonder they were all bachelors."

He leaned over and picked up a rotting seed bag and threw it in the wheelbarrow. There was a sudden scurry of movement, mice scampering from a nest of thimble-size, pink, writhing babies.

Silva shuddered as Nick scooped them into the wheelbarrow along with the rest of the room's offal. *Seven weeks.* A countdown that seemed detonated—a fuse already lit.

"Sorry about that. Never know what you'll uncover. Found a watch in a packrat's nest once. Still works." He held out an old, ornately scrolled silver pocket watch on a chain, its ticking audible from feet away. Silva could picture him dressed like James Dean: jeans and motorcycle boots, T-shirt sleeves cuffed over a pack of smokes. Muscle cars and curvy dates sliding across a slick bench seat as he cornered fast, double-clutching, smoking the tires.

"It's nice to get something done. I hope it's not too much of an imposition," he said, employing his good manners again. He didn't know he'd already offered her a solution to her access problem—for the second time. "Let me make it up to you. Mind if I use the kitchen, cook us dinner tonight? My mom was a good cook, taught me a few things in the kitchen."

Silva tried not to show her surprise. She hadn't pictured Nick cooking with his mother, but he hadn't yet fit in any of the prepackaged categories she'd tried to sort him into.

"I'm thinking of going downriver to gather pitch for fire starters," he said. "You're welcome to come, if you'd like—you could ride Sage. She's about as surefooted as they come. I've been trying to get her out more, make her forget. Bred her last fall, but it didn't go so well. Little stillborn filly, perfect replica of her mama." He looked at Sage and lowered his voice as if she might overhear. "She wouldn't eat, just kept whinnying, trying to bring back her baby."

Silva looked away, hiding her sharp stab of emotion. What she'd been trying so hard to keep at bay, even from herself. She resisted reaching down and touching her own stomach, reminding herself of the reality of her condition. What decisions she'd come here to make.

Out in the pasture, Sage flopped down and rolled in a dustbowl, coating herself gray until it looked as if she'd been dipped in ashes. A horse in mourning. Nick was offering the opening Silva had been waiting and hoping for. She refrained from looking up at the hills behind the house. There were plenty enough reasons for being duplicitous, for having a self-serving agenda.

"Tiko reminds me of the horse I used to ride on the island, a headstrong Arabian named Sunchero. I miss him. I'd love to ride Tiko, get my sea legs back," she said.

"Okay, but don't say I didn't warn you," Nick said, joking, but nobody could claim Silva hadn't been warned, everything a flashing red light since she'd arrived in Two Rivers.

CHAPTER SIXTEEN

———◆※◆———

Your face a veil, your body a wash of white, your finger ringed in gold, his seeing eye upon you in blessing, his hand covering your hand in godship. Say these vows, speak these words, remember not your own will, your own life. You look in his eyes, and you see specks of dark and light, planetary orbs of the all-seeing-eye, liquid and night. They sing your praises, sing you both into your right: man and wife, man and life, man and woman, ceremony of light, a new-crowned glory of wifeliness, of womanliness, of life. You are clean and fresh and bright. You are God's holiest maiden of paradise, your womb a fertile harbinger of life. You will never waver, you will never doubt, you will give of this over and over again, your will always and never made of flight.

Leaves like a covering, a hidden garden of Eve, find your way through to the other side, the tree of life and death among this garden of delight, fruits like globes, fruits like honey, fruits like your womb, growing and swelling with the seeds of life. Bees sipping sweet nectar at this tree of life, growing and growing into something new, a body like a soul made fresh, this world made of holiness, full of your song reaching heavenward, singing that what you will have is this, is you.

CHAPTER SEVENTEEN

APRIL 2001

Silva got herself ready as Nick bridled and saddled the horses. A western-riding setup instead of the English setup she'd used as a child. She swung herself into the saddle and directed Tiko forward, the horse responding to each shift of her body. She rode a few yard loops and then pulled up next to Nick. Tiko stood still, his ears flicking back toward her.

"Huh," Nick said, regarding the horse with bemusement.

"What?" Silva said, concerned she'd done something wrong.

"He wants to do your bidding. It's a new one, that's all."

She patted the horse's neck, surprised how comfortable she was. "We understand each other," she said, hoping it were true, everything possible from a new angle.

The horses rode easily, the sandy trail muffling the sound of their hooves as they brushed through hackberry thickets and rock tumbles studded with prickly pear and coyote scat, crickets chirring in dry grass, poison ivy growing riotous in dry creek beds, drought-starved trees like skeletal sentinels. Along the flats, the remnants of ranches: a tumble of rocks alongside rusted farm implements and windrows of piled boulders, everything declarative of collective failure.

Juniper ran ahead as they followed the trail past an old mine, winding down into a still-damp slurry. Suddenly he stopped, staring warily into the brush, his hackles up. Tiko snorted and tossed his head, and Silva worried he would rear up, throw her off. Nick pointed to a coyote carcass lying tufted in the shadows, the stink swelling into the warm air.

"Was it shot?" Silva asked, thinking of the dead sheep.

"People kill them anyway they can. Ranchers have M44s planted all over the place. . . ."

"M44s?" Silva asked, picturing landmines set to blow up anything that touched them, the human-made war zone of this place at odds with the land's deep quietude.

"Torture devices. Look like a sprinkler stake, but with a spring-powered ejector loaded with sodium cyanide capsules and bait. My dog died from one when I was young—breathed out blood-froth and writhed in pain all the way to the end. Nothing the locals like about top predators—especially the wolves coming back after nearly a century of peaceful eradication. 'Blood-thirsty sport-killers, don't eat what they kill.' Putting human morals on a wild animal. Better start condemning all of nature, if that's the case. I say better wolves kill elk and deer like nature intended than some overfed hicks taking potshots at a thousand yards, but being a coyote or wolf supporter around here is about as sacrilegious as being a Democrat, even though wolves and coyotes will probably be the ones to survive the end of the world if it does come. Get the last laugh when they have this place back to themselves, just as it was in the beginning." Nick looked back at Juniper. "He's not safe around here. People shoot first and ask questions later."

It didn't seem to Silva anything in the canyon was safe to just *be*. Just having a presence was enough of a threat to warrant violence.

The trail dropped to a ponderosa-studded flat carved in half by a dry-wash gully full of debris washed down in spring flash floods. The ground beneath the trees was carpeted with long needles, the air imbued with their warm-pine scent and the dry mineral smell of heated scree.

Nick pulled Sage up, dismounted, and went to help Silva. He held her arm as she jumped down. "Bones like a bird," he said.

"Don't worry. I won't break," she said, but she had already been broken— shattered into pieces and then hastily put back together, edges all out of alignment.

They led the horses to a patch of shade under the trees and tied them off. The wind blew placid and warm—the touch of lips against bare skin. The taste of sweet water, the taste of fruit warmed in the sun. Silva sat on a beached log, throwing sticks for Juniper into the river. He swam hard into the current, his shoulders lifting out of the water, unafraid, having already forgotten his journey downriver, his near demise. She wished it were as easy as that—forgetting your destiny. A body not your own. A life that cast you loose and left you to sink.

Nick sat down next to her. "Beautiful out." He glanced over at her.

"It is," she said, watching the river, keeping her tone neutral, as though she'd missed his meaning. She pushed back her real response—wanting to meet his eyes, communicate what she really felt. "I saw a sturgeon for the first time a few days ago. Strangest thing I've seen—even if I was born under the Sturgeon Moon."

"I caught my first when I was just a kid. Bigger than I was, jaws full of teeth. This place is full of strangeness," Nick said, his voice suddenly changed. Winsome, she realized.

She almost touched her stomach again before catching herself. Instead, she planted her hands on the log's hieroglyphics, her fingers worrying the riddled scorings of beetles as though working to decipher some strange cuneiform, the past's collision course with the present.

The river's murmuring at their feet, she leaned over and picked up a flat stone, winging her wrist and releasing it in one quick, smooth motion. It skipped cross-current in fast, evenly spaced dips.

Nick whistled. "Winner take all?" he asked, lifting his eyebrows and smiling at her.

Silva laughed, then stood without waiting and winged another stone. It kissed the river's surface over and over again with increasing speed until it finally clattered against the boulders on the other side.

Nick let out another appreciative whistle. "Ah, I see how it's gonna be," he said, pursing his lips and frowning in concentration as he bent over and carefully selected a flat rock from the beach. At the water's edge, he made a big show of setting up his skip, standing sideways and whipping his arm back and forth through the air, making Silva laugh. Then he finally muscled a hard throw, his stone gracelessly plunking six ringed pools before disappearing mid-current. He shook his head in defeat. "Should've known better than to challenge an island girl."

He hadn't missed a thing.

Silva brushed off her hands and glanced over at the horses. "So, what do I win?"

<hr />

The ponderosas had what they'd come for: crystalized amber globs of pitch that smelled like fungus and tree sap. They used a small hatchet to chunk off pieces into a paper bag, their fingers sticky and covered with bits of bark and lichen when they were done, the bag full. Silva didn't wait for Nick's help to remount, launching herself into Tiko's saddle with ease. She needed to show Nick she could handle herself, that she knew enough of what she was doing to be trusted, even if she was making things up as she went along.

When they started off, she leaned over Tiko's neck and said, "You'll do just fine, won't you?" His ears swiveled back toward the sound of her voice, each thing leading to the next, leading to the next.

When they got back to the barn, she stayed to brush Tiko, slicking metal tines over croup, withers, and stifle, smoothing away saddle-sweat lines, everything like some muscle memory—the earthy muskiness of horse and hay and leather, the texture of horsehair under her hands. She brushed her hands over Tiko's coat. Even without an ulterior motive, she would have loved him.

Back at the house, she carried the bonsai into her room. The only way she'd ever been able to work through problems, puzzles of geometry or planting or grafting, was to work with her hands—touching the bark of a tree, tracing the tender veining of a leaf, delicately dividing a tangle of hair-roots, the world suddenly opening up like a seed casing sprouting open underneath the warm embrace of spring soil.

When she was young, Eamon had had a ginkgo bonsai he called the Child-Giver—a representation of the ginkgo tree that grew in Tokyo's Zoshigaya Kishimojin Temple that was thought to bring fertility to worshippers. The goddess Kishimojin was the guardian deity of children, even though Kishimojin had first fed her own thousands of offspring by devouring the children of others, until Buddha hid one of her own children in an alms bowl to teach her a lesson, admonishing her for the suffering she had caused. Distraught and chastised, she finally repented, vowing to protect all children from thereon. Eamon had left the tree in Silva's room each night as a banishment of her nightmares, and it'd worked. Instead of drowning, she'd started dreaming of floating—her body riding the top of the water as the current swept her gently underneath a reaching canopy of trees, leaves extended toward her in embrace.

She got out Isabelle's paintings and propped them up on her desk. "What are you trying to tell me?" she asked, her hands resting on the driftwood cedar's enameled turquoise tray, looking at the girls' enigmatic gazes staring inscrutably out to the unknown.

She didn't hear Nick come to her doorway. He knocked quietly, standing just outside, hands braced on either side of her door, face scrubbed, hair wet, clothes changed. The same vague scent of evergreen she'd smelled earlier.

Silva grabbed the paintings and laid them facedown on the desk next to the bonsai.

"Sorry, I didn't want to disturb your work. Just wanted to tell you dinner is on its way," Nick said, careful in his assessment.

She tucked her hair behind her ear, realizing how she must look, hunched over her table, surrounded by twisted and stunted trees as strange and exotic as hothouse flowers, relevant to some foreign setting. The hackberry next to her, stripped and wired. Eamon's journals open, Isabelle's paintings next to them. Silva was dressed in the same shorts and T-shirt she'd worn since coming to the canyon, her body caught in the folds. Despite her body's steady march of growth, the canyon had honed her, too, wearing away any excess until only essential structure was left—bones and muscle and sinew not unlike the river canyon's spines and ridges.

Nick fingered a sliver on the doorjamb. "Are they very old?" He nodded to the Sitka spruce with its ankle-thick trunk. A cluster of wizened foreigners, unaware of their otherness.

"Some of them are," she said.

He hesitated, then took a step through the threshold, going to examine the trees up close—the bristlecone pine first, its trunk bent into a fused *U*. "This one looks old," he said.

"Trained two hundred years or so," she said, and Nick pulled his hand back. "Don't worry, they aren't fragile. My grandfather valued hardiness," she said.

"So you learned this from him, your grandfather?"

"Everything I know," she said. A statement devoid of a lifetime's worth of context.

"Latin?" Nick asked, glancing down. "*Lonicera nat. Elegens*?" His pronunciation close.

"It means honeysuckle." *Honeysuckle.* What that word carried. Silva shifted in the chair, hoping Nick wouldn't notice the bodies that revealed so clearly her own story of sorrow and loss.

He pointed to Eamon's journal sketch. "Is that what the hackberries are going to become?"

"Hopefully."

He didn't know all he was asking, both of them still trying to gauge the other's woundedness. She'd said the bonsai weren't fragile, but it wasn't true. It was as simple as making the cuts, pulling roots from soil.

She joined Nick in the kitchen after putting away Eamon's notebooks and Isabelle's paintings, leaving the bonsai in for the night. The smell of warm yeast filled the kitchen, a floury mass pliant under Nick's hands, his shoulders working under his shirt as he moved, spreading the dough with butter, sugar, cinnamon, and raisins that looked as if they'd been stored for a decade.

"You know what you're doing." She sat watching as he rolled dough, as at home in the kitchen as he was in the barn. It had taken her days to even remember where the silverware was.

"I hated living in town. Flowered curtains and picket fences. All I wanted to do was run away. Tried it a time or two. My mother thought I needed to stay busy, so she took to making me help her in the kitchen. Pies, cakes, cookies, rolls—any sweet to keep me busy. I still remember how to make a few things. Breakfast for dinner, for instance," he said, rolling the dough into a log and cutting it into pinwheeled pieces before scrubbing potatoes and skinning onions.

Silva's stomach rumbled. She hadn't realized how hungry she was. She thought of Eli's soufflé recipe. *Honeybees Honeymoon*. Everything somehow connected.

As if reading her mind, Nick looked over at her. "Have you spent much time around honeybees? They have these intricate ways of communication— dances, the ways they fly—that tell the whole hive where a good batch of flowers are," he said, each word punctuated by the *chock chock chock* of the knife on the board. "Work together for the whole hive's good. Take care of the queen, the eggs, each other, better than people do. Never leave each other out in the cold. Treat them well, protect them, give them houses, feed them in the winter, and they do everything else—locate the nectar, make honey and beebread, fill their pollen baskets full. Pure simplicity."

He lit the stove, oil sizzling in a cast-iron pan as he scraped in a heap of diced onions and potatoes and seasoned them with unlabeled things on the stove's upper shelf Silva had been too afraid to try. The noise and smell of frying overtook the kitchen. He worked with his back to her, talking about hive production, honey quality, bee species—how Hells Canyon and bees were a perfect match. Yellow star thistle finally good for something. Nick was lean, almost sinewy, but he had a certain bulk to him, an energy that filled the room. The land seemed to be a part of him, evidenced in his body—brown and earthy, as if he'd been formed and baked out of the very dirt.

The onion and pepper made Silva's eyes stream. She wiped her face, not wanting Nick to think she was weak to a little spice, but he was distracted, saying that all he had to do was pick up Eli's hives and bring them back to the ranch, get the barn room set up for extraction. Bees the only thing nobody in the canyon had ever tried.

"Give them a home, and they do the rest," he said. "No property lines to worry about, no equipment to break down, no need for thousands of acres. No stock to take care of, no fluctuating seed prices, no heavy machinery. Just bees. What could be easier than that? One good season can gross over fifteen thousand, and it only goes up from there." He glanced out the window. "A gamble, but it's time. It's already been too long."

But he didn't need to convince her. Eli and his bees already had, even if bees weren't something she'd been prepared for—that intimacy—but there was beauty to it. Something so small the answer all along, accomplishing what everything else in the canyon had failed to do.

Nick stopped for a moment and took a long swallow of water, then stirred cloudy blocks of paraffin into clear liquid in a coffee can he had heating on a back burner, a stack of stained egg cartons along with the paper bag full of pitch ready on the counter.

An early-evening breeze blew high cirrus clouds into furrowed rows outside while he fried strips of bacon and whisked eggs into a froth, the kitchen filling with the smell of browning things. He kept up a steady stream of conversation while he worked, talking about bees, pollination, honey, propolis, wax products. The steady tenor of his voice and the language he used—hive boxes, apiaries, flower crops, honey quality—comforting and somehow familiar.

Silva kept telling herself that this was not what she'd come here to find, not what she wanted, but she couldn't stop herself from watching Nick move effortlessly through the space they now shared, couldn't help herself from feeling the current of electricity that flowed between them, as real as anything she'd ever known.

When he was finished at the stove, Nick brought out the jar of honey she had seen on his bed stand. "Yellow star thistle makes the best, but people like the sound of clover better. One taste is all it takes, though. . . ."

He waited as she swirled a spoonful, picking out a distinct beelike leg and specks of unidentifiable things before sticking the spoon in her mouth.

He nodded, satisfied. "Good, isn't it?"

"It's good," she said, the honey on her tongue, on her lips. She chewed the softened wax in between her front teeth until it dissolved. She wanted to scoop out spoonful after spoonful, wanted to cover herself in it, let Nick lick it off her skin.

Nick got the bag of pitch they'd gathered for fire starters and started putting chunks of it in the empty paper egg cartons, arranging the pieces of pitch carefully in each egg compartment. Then he got the coffee can of hot, melted paraffin and poured it over the pitch, the carton paper turning dark with saturation.

"There, all we have to do is let it cool and harden, and then cut into pieces, and voilà—the best fire starters you'll ever use," he said. He started singing the *Jungle Book* movie's "I Wan'na Be Like You"—fire as the red flower of men's power that all the animals sought. He laughed at the look on Silva's face. "What? You didn't want to be like Mowgli, swinging through the vines, living wild in the jungle, sleeping in trees, drinking water from their leaves? And making fire, of course, too. . . ."

Silva smiled. "I just always wanted to be a dryad in her forest."

Both of them with some childhood version of magical woods.

They went out to sit on the porch and eat, leaving the hot kitchen to cool down. Swallows swept the air currents, their fighter-plane silhouettes dark against pale sky. On the river, trout leapt after insect quarry, their bodies wetly slapping the river's surface. Dust devils blew up in the corral; a flock of sparrows surged like minnows. Earth, air, fire, water. Silva imagined Trawler, the cabin, the trees. The waters and the salt air. The smell of seaweed and old shells.

Eamon had always said that caring for the bonsai made you a part of something bigger than yourself. Brought on new growth—something so unfamiliar Silva didn't yet have the name for it.

Once she tasted Nick's food, she had to stop herself from shoveling it in as if she were starving. There was something about his penchant for spices, a heat that went deep inside, that she couldn't resist. All his talk of bees and childhood. Find a different angle, a different vantage point, and a scene could change entirely. Out of the dark you might see yourself—a woman alone, an embryo formed by an unknown body—but you might see other things, too.

She had become used to keeping herself like the bonsai—clipping and wiring, holding herself in—but now, despite everything, despite all the bad that had already happened, despite all the challenges still to come, she felt the stirrings of something new. Something like creation. It was as if a floral, southerly wind had blown in overnight, hot and buzzing with insect and bird calls, everything responding to its touch. All she had to do was find the source of its movement.

She put her hands on her stomach and let herself for a moment imagine a child playing in tree-dappled light, running through the summer sun, dragging her hands through the seeded tops of grasses, finding delight in the world.

CHAPTER EIGHTEEN

Date: November 1, 1999
Title: Childbearing Ceremony
Subject: The Twelve Maidens, Almost Paradise's pregnant and
  nursing mothers, and Faith the midwife
Setting: Almost Paradise Greenhouse & Garden
Medium: Watercolor and graphite on cold-press
Size: 14×20

Dearest Eamon,

We've come nearly to winter now. The river's rising fog always
brings me home to you, to the island, and I am thankful each time it
swallows the canyon and transports me out of it.

We have just finished the Childbearing Ceremony, following
training sessions led this time by Faith. At least there's that, instead of
the choking suffocation of Delores and her son. He has been working
to draw me in, so sure of his own power, speaking words he thinks I
would like to hear, as if I am one of his cowed and caved women, born
into silence and submission. He has had many "wives"—his concubine women, along with the virgins he has married. More than I have
been allowed to know. They come here willingly to be with him, to be
given over to him. To believe in him and bear his children. I wonder
how many there are? How many there have been over the years.
Because that's the thing—this has been forming for years now, Len
and his followers, this compound, these beliefs. The twelve maidens,

his virgin child brides, are just the newest addition—a way to build his holy family and army for the coming war of the millennium.

The pregnant and nursing mothers have come for the childbearing training sessions, but I think it's more of an excuse for the women to gather together and speak freely than anything else. There's a lot of coffee and pie, a lot of stomach stroking, a lot of birth-story sharing and quiet laughter. It's the only time I've seen the women and girls smile, much less laugh. Delores leaves us alone. She is uncomfortable with this part of the training, it would seem. But Faith is a good midwife, a good leader. Quiet, sure, calming. I am glad for the girls to at least be in Faith's care this way. One woman making a positive impact in this wretched place. Someone I wish could have attended me when I was a frightened girl giving birth instead of the man, the doctor, who handled me like a psych patient, strapping my feet wide and painting my inner legs brown with iodine, as though my thigh skin posed the most significant risk to my baby.

I asked Faith for a change in venue for this ceremony's painting: the Almost Paradise garden—a giant greenhouse still humid with fall's late coaxed growth, plants heavy with cabbage and cauliflower, broccoli and Brussels sprouts. When the men were gone, she gathered them there for me—the maidens and the pregnant or nursing mothers. I painted them all, Faith in their center flanked by green. Breathing in that air, just for a moment I felt it all could have been something else. Something bright with filtered light. Something with the promise of new life.

Only it isn't. And it never will be. Instead, I reach again for you, this fog like my coming home.

When did we ever see anything but each other? When did I turn my face away? Forgive me for that inward turn, for not seeing what was right in front of me all along.

All my love,
Isabelle

CHAPTER NINETEEN

MAY 2001

One of the stories Eamon had told Silva as a child was about the holy neem tree—curer of all ailments, manifestation of the Hindu mother-figure goddess Shitala. It grew up through a Nanghan Bir Baba Temple room and its worshippers dressed its trunk in red cloth, adorning it with scarves and flowers and a golden Shitala mask, finding healing and hope by praying to it. She had found such comfort in the story she'd made Eamon promise to help her find their own holy tree on the island that they might adorn and pray to.

As a girl, Silva had devoured anything concerning holy or magical trees. The May Tree, used as a psychic shield for the innocent and vulnerable, particularly children at puberty, sensitive to change; the Tree of Enchantment, at whose roots worshippers sat to gain eloquence, inspiration, and prophecies; the Wish Tree, tied with prayer cloth, its crevices filled with change left by the hopeful. And just like then, she wished now, lying in her bed in the Larkins cabin, that she had a tree she might adorn and pray to, finding direction.

When she finally got up and opened her door to let Juniper out, her hair loose and tangled around her shoulders, Nick was dressed and sitting on his bed with his door open, as though he'd been waiting for her. She reached up subconsciously to smooth her wild hair. She understood what the sudden darkening of his eyes meant as he regarded her. She felt it, too, looking at him.

Juniper pushed past her and gave each of them a quick glance, as if he, too, were assessing this new thing.

"Juniper can come outside with me if you want. I'll be careful, keep an eye on him," Nick said, as if that's what he'd been doing—waiting to be of service to her.

She met his gaze. He had been nothing but careful. Nothing but conscientious and polite.

When they left, she closed her bedroom door and leaned against it. What was she doing? She told herself again that this wasn't what she'd come for. That she needed to be clearheaded in forming the terms of her decisions—even if she didn't know yet what those terms would be, even if every decision was a part of Nick's life, too, whether he knew it yet or not. Even if around him, her body was constantly warring with her mind, each of them after different things.

She got dressed and went out to sit on the porch steps. A robin fluttered into the nearest locust and chirp-clucked, its three hatchlings' wobbly heads rising with frantic peeping. After stuffing beaks, the robin flew to the birdbath Silva had fashioned out of rusted implement scraps gathered from around the ranch—a shallow-cupped harrowing disc on the top of a rusted camshaft, anchored to the ground by an empty-toothed gear the size of a fifty-pound weight-lifting plate. She'd wrangled an old machine brake drum over to the house, sat it on some other rusted machine parts for a base, and made it into a barbecue. Nick had been impressed with her industry, examining each thing as if they were pieces of art.

The air held portent; she could feel it stirring the ground around her. A perfect growing season. Sun every day, no frosts, the air fragrant with warmth. As a child, the New Community garden had seemed enormous, a place where she'd happily lost herself in the plants. Suddenly all Silva wanted to do was expose black soil, plant, and grow. She pictured clematis winding up porch timbers and wisteria over the well house. The old Larkins garden was nothing but a patch of overgrown weeds, but it had perfect exposure and was shaded from the afternoon heat, the creek nearby for plentiful water. She could already picture it: a riotous mix of flowers and vegetables, Nick gathering the fruits of her labor long after she was gone, finding his way back to all he'd lost. At least one of them ought to be able to claim their inheritance.

She rubber-banded her hair and pulled on her cutoffs and the olive-green Wellies she'd been wearing for years, then walked quickly to the barn, Nick still working in the empty room, Juniper lying by his side, happily chewing on a horse hoof trimming.

"I have seeds," she announced, smiling at the look of confusion on Nick's face. "The garden could be tilled and planted."

He wiped his face with the back of a gloved hand and looking out the window toward the overgrown, inextirpable plot. "It's grown nothing but weeds for too long now, that's for sure."

"Do you have a tiller?"

He wrinkled his brow and nodded. "Yes, although it hasn't been run in years."

"Can I use it?"

"Right now?" he asked, lifting his eyebrows in surprise, a grin stretched across his face. He went to the shed and came out wheeling an ancient, battered tiller, filled it with fresh gas and oil, changed the spark plug, and then pulled the rope until Silva thought either his arm or the rope would break, sweat dripping from his face. Finally, the motor turned over and roared to life, smoking and shaking with indignation like a beast disrupted from hibernation.

"Amazing the thing still runs after all this time." He throttled it over to the edge of the garden plot and got it positioned, tines whirring. "You sure you're up for this?"

Silva let the clutch lever out carefully, but the tiller still jerked and surged ahead, yanking her behind it. She leaned back, throwing her weight against its bucking rush, but it was all she could do to hold on. It felt as if she were wrestling a wild animal.

Nick, looking concerned, yelled over the engine noise, "Do you need some help?"

She shook her head and held on tight, the tines sinking into the weeds and pulling up rich black soil—the kind of soil that would grow anything. She breathed in the smell of exposed dirt and thought of the salsa she could make—a punch of hot alongside the cool zing of tomato and cilantro. Under her feet, the dark loam looked as if it were already a crop, ripe and ready to eat. She had to restrain herself from bending down to try it. Something hungry had awakened inside her, something insatiable. She felt a part of a bigger, symbiotic thing—bigger than the sum of her experiences, bigger than what she'd thought she'd come to understand about herself.

When she was done, tracks of deep steps behind her, the whole garden turned over, she turned off the tiller and dug her fingers into the soil, cupping a palmful, inhaling its rich humus smell before letting it trickle through her open fingers back to the ground already buzzing with insects interested in the newly exposed territory of earth. As she wheeled the tiller back to the barn, the robin flew down from its locust nest, plucked a fat earthworm out of the garden soil, and took it back to its nest full of wide-open beaks.

Nick grinned when he saw her—dirt-streaked legs, dirt-caked boots, dirt all over her face. "Quite the combination—bonsai, bees, and now a garden," he said, as if they were indeed together in this, and perhaps they were.

In the mirror, she'd noticed the new curving of her waist, her stomach, her breasts—her body already growing softer, fuller, as if she, too, were a fruit ripening under the sun. But she wasn't ready yet to face it all aloud, in the light. She would rather focus on the growth outside her instead of the growth inside.

She raked a ridge between the tilled soil and the grass, then worked until she'd smoothed the garden into a flat, brown expanse, like prepping a canvas for paint. Then, sorting through her seed collection until she found what she wanted, she started sowing, trying to account for the canyon's aridity, this new ecosystem. All the seeds she'd saved over the years, devoted to finding the best blooms and fruits. She'd inherited her mother's touch as well as Eamon's.

She planted the perimeter first: poppies and columbine, cosmos and wild geranium, asters and lupine. Then the interior: rows of corn, peppers, tomatoes, carrots, radishes, and chives. She planted the herbs last: cilantro, basil, thyme, lemon balm, peppermint. Hundreds of her heirloom seeds planted in Hells Canyon. An incongruent pairing she hoped would take root and flourish.

She washed up at the river, watched the trout's shimmering swim upstream, the water-skipper's surface-skimming dance, the periwinkle's laborious crawl, tracing its tracks into the sand. Up in the hills behind the house, a family of coyotes began their nightly howling, their wavering calls rising like a mourning song. She imagined them running in a phosphorescent afterworld, surviving—thriving—as Nick predicted they would.

Juniper laid a stick at her side like an offered gift. She threw it out into the river for him, but it sank before he reached it. He swam circles around where it had gone under, refusing to give up. Something lost was always something lost. She'd always hated things left unfinished—houses sheathed in Tyvek, cars painted primer gray, trees full of untrimmed suckers—but she didn't know quite how to finish what she'd started now. Eamon had taught her that often all you had to do was leave things to sort themselves out on their own, see what new shape emerged. Then you would know what you had to work with. Even a cicatrix scar formed something new—fibrous tissue forming and contracting, filling in the empty wound after a branch was severed. Sealing the damage, protection from outside threats: rot and infection and predation.

Once, working a job on the island, Silva had found an old revolver grown into an oak—a loaded Remington new-model Army as brown as the wood surrounding it, encased in over 150 years of scarred growth rings like a piece of art. There had been others found throughout the years: a black-powder rifle in a Montana hickory packed with bear fat to keep the metal from rusting; an ancient flintlock in a Missouri weeping willow; a Spanish conquistador sword grown into a sprawling Texas walnut.

Weapons hidden in trees, relics of the past forming a new thing together, just as Eamon had said.

———※———

Nick cooked dinner again, said it was a small thank-you for all of Silva's work, getting everything in better shape than it'd been in for decades. After she'd finished planting and had gone inside, she'd noticed Nick looking the garden over and wondered if he, too, had envisioned all it could become, all its promise still hidden, seeds furrowed into dark soil. *Sowing. Germinating. Growing. Harvesting.* The kind of future she'd thought wouldn't be hers again.

"Did you get the barn room finished, ready for the extraction equipment?" she asked as she flopped down in a living-room chair. When they'd stood looking around the room together before, Nick had explained to Silva how he would set it up for his coming honey harvest—where the nectar-laden hives and frame hanger and uncapper and extractor would go, where the finish table would sit, full of all the freshly filled honey jars. She had been able to imagine it all—the room permeated with golden light, with all that sticky sweetness.

"As ready as it'll ever be." Nick stood at the window, staring outside, everything about him quietly on edge, although Silva didn't understand why. He'd seemed happy and relaxed before—her working in the garden, him working in the barn, as if they were just another canyon couple bent on shaping their mutual dreams, their destiny, out of the labor of their own hands.

"Will you bring the bees soon?" she asked, trying to gauge the ribbons of tension coming from him, undercurrents of something she couldn't name. Anger, yes, but something else, too.

"As soon as I can," he said, his back stiff. He leaned hard enough on the windowsill that she thought it might break under the pressure. Outside, the river was steel-gray, the sky a bruised purple-brown, ominous with cumulonimbus brewing up behind the hills, wind gusting through the trees and along the shore in short, fierce bursts. The horses trotted nervously in the pasture, the evening air hanging heavy and thick. She, too, felt threat coming like a storm.

This wasn't how she'd expected things to go. In any other circumstance, she could have politely taken leave, left Nick to sort through his bad mood on his own, but she had her own pressing need that she'd left until now, hoping to lay good groundwork ahead of time, prove herself worthy. The outfitting group would arrive in the morning. She'd planned to edge around to the horses, to her using Tiko. Now she realized she might have waited too long.

Finally, Nick sat down, wearing an expression of sorrow and bare longing she recognized from some other place and time. Something intimate and vulnerable—a letting down of the masculine guard, an interior landscape of raw, gripping helplessness. He hesitated a moment as if deciding something, then said, "I found something today I never expected to see again." His jaw muscles clenched and unclenched as if he were gnawing on boot leather

"What?" Silva asked, hoping it had nothing to do with her, what she was trying to find herself.

"Proof of my failure," he said simply, both of them gauging in each other all that had been left unspoken. "I blamed my mother for a long time, but I was the one who convinced her. The first to believe. We went into it together, like the buddy system. Got saved and baptized, took communion, joined Dietz." He looked down at his hands. "I was so proud to join, so proud when he proclaimed us part of his Divine Family, so proud when he 'chose' my mother as one of his women, so proud when she got pregnant with my brother. The Chosen Ones."

Silva pressed back against the tormenting heartbreak and surprise of it. Nick a child-Lenite, his mother one of Len Dietz's women, pregnant with his child before she died, forever biologically tying Nick to Dietz. The kind of thing from which you could never escape.

"He gave me a gift at the end of my 'journey,' after I was sworn into the covenant," Nick said, his expression tormented, his hands hanging limp in between his legs, and finally she could see what she hadn't been able to before. *Shame.* Anger like a skin covering shame's raw, fleshy, pulsing vulnerability. She wanted to cry out, *I know, I know.*

"My Ascension Pendant, buried beneath a pile of junk, engraved with my name and the date of my *ascension,*" Nick said, holding it up: a circle with a pyramid and an eye in its middle.

The Eye of Providence—the all-seeing eye. The pendant Len had been wearing in the hardware store. She couldn't tell him what the all-seeing eye had told her, what Len Dietz had known just by looking at her. What he'd whispered to her, laying claim, pinning her in place just as surely as he'd done with Isabelle, with Nick's mother, too. Ownership along with god's will.

"What happened to you and your mom?" she asked quietly, crossing her arms and clutching her own torso, shielding herself against what she feared was coming next.

"We went in just like the rest, looking for family, looking for the relief and security of belonging," Nick said, his voice flattened, his confession pressing on him as physically as a weight. "I thought everything Len did was god's will. His 'Family of God,' his 'godly love,' his 'righteous anger.' We all thought we were god's holy family, serving each other in a life of divinity—no doctors for our illnesses or injuries, no schools for our learning, no government for our laws. No tenets besides Len's."

Silva felt faint, nauseated, at the thought of Nick for a time calling Len Dietz *Father.*

"You were a child. You wanted a family. A father, a mother, a sibling. People to love you and for you to love back. We all have the same needs. We do what we do, for better or worse."

"Well, a family isn't what I got," Nick said.

Nor I, she wanted to say.

"'Birth complications,' they called it, but I saw what Len did to her." Nick's face twisted, the agony and anger coming off him visceral enough that Silva braced herself for the rest. There was only one way things like this ever ended.

"She was his flagellant. All of them were—all the women and girls. Mortification of the flesh and spirit in action. But even though it was right there in front of me, in front of us all, we kept our eyes closed tight, refusing to see it until it was too late."

Goose bumps prickled Silva's limbs. The way Len had looked at her. All-knowing. All-seeing. Reaching for her, disguising her vulnerability as his own. Disguising his dark appetite with soft words. She'd known the insatiability of his lust the minute she'd looked at him.

"What happened to the baby?" she asked quietly, afraid of the answer.

"They buried him next to my mother. Said it was SIDS. I can't forgive myself for leaving him," Nick said, his voice breaking. He touched the scar on his cheek, and Silva imagined a knife fight, bloodshed. A feud stretched through time. So much left behind. Pie plates. A child's growth marks. The sins of the father. The sins of the mother. Sins enough to bury them all.

"I'm so sorry," she said. The most worthless words there were. She put a hand on Nick's.

His eyes full of sorrow, he met her gaze. "So am I," he said.

"You still want to be here, after all that?" she asked quietly. She'd seen the power of Len Dietz's desire. His need for control. The kind of need that would never be satisfied.

"Once I get things cleaned up, pay off the taxes, I'll get this place put to rights again. Make up for what was lost. Dietz will eventually go the way of all fanatics, of everything else that has flown through this country. The canyon will go on like it always has, this millennium and the next, no matter what kind of end they all think is coming."

He wiped his face with a handkerchief, stuffed it back in his pocket, and looked away.

People needed to believe in something, no matter what inherent futility there was to it, no matter what destruction came in its wake, no matter what forces were set against the believing.

Unlike Nick, Isabelle hadn't been too young to know better, hadn't been broken into that kind of vulnerability; the only things she'd lost, she'd willingly tossed out. Silva considered telling Nick her own story—Isabelle's story—but darkness was sweeping up the river valley, the sky thick and brown, the wind steadily picking up, filming the river's surface with dust. Silva remembered storms that had blown in when she was a child—the call of the crows huddled up in trees, the whistling of branches, the lightning that split the sky into fissures, and the thunder that sounded like mountains tearing loose.

The air breathed inward in a gasp, and then let loose with a simultaneous peal of lightning and thunder that percussed overhead like canon shots.

Nick stood in concern as Silva tried to calm Juniper, who cowered into her, his body quaking hard enough against hers that it felt as though she were shaking loose, too.

"This wasn't supposed to hit us here—was forecasted north of the canyon," Nick said, scowling out the window as if the weather were another foe he could exact his own revenge on.

"I think it missed its mark," she said, although perhaps the storm hadn't missed anything at all. An external reflection of the internal. A sign she couldn't help worrying about.

"I need to get the horses to shelter." Nick threw on a coat and rushed outside.

Silva locked Juniper in her bedroom and sprinted outside to help Nick with the stock as more flashes of pitched light strobed the sky, fingers of lightning so bright the jagged lines branded into her retinas, repeating as she blinked—white lines sketched like fire against the dark. In the black-blue storm glow, everything looked like ship wreckage drifting on shadowy swells.

When she was just off the porch, there came the thundering fall of a lightning-struck tree somewhere close by, the shock of its impact translating through the ground into her bones. A smell of torn and seared wood, uprooted bareness. A taste like punk-rot in the back of her throat.

Hail pelted the house's tin roof, pinging off and bouncing like popcorn kernels bursting open. Such late-spring heat, thermals of hot air rising against cold downdrafts, opposing layers bashing against each other like tectonic plates shifting under the earth's crust. Natural powers far outside anyone's control. Hail growing from pellets to marble-size balls that hit with enough force to break windows and injure flesh, the ground white and alive with movement.

She could feel the bruises rising as she ran to the barn, hail pummeling her back and shoulders, hitting her head like rocks. The horses and mules had bunched against the fence in panic, the whites of their eyes showing as they whinnied and jerked, flinching as if they were being beaten. Nick was trying to throw on halters as she ran in to help, both of them dragging one head of stock after another into safety, each of them holding onto a nervously shifting horse as hail blew in through the barn door. Everyone would be sore for the pack-ride in the morning—if the storm subsided enough for the group to even go.

Silva patted Tiko's neck, trying to soothe him and herself as round, red welts rose on her arms and torso and Tiko's hide twitched with his own discomfort. The storm's din was loud enough that it was useless to try to talk, each word hammered away before it was fully formed.

Knowing she couldn't, with the hail and thunder raining down, she wanted now, more than ever, to tell Nick about Isabelle, about the paintings, about her own pregnancy, about her own woundedness. But where would she start in the botany of grief?

The hail finally receded, leaving a maimed landscape behind: the yard blanketed white, tender spring leaves shredded to tatters, bark and branches scattered everywhere. Still, they waited, the wind howling around the barn as if it were searching for entry, lifting the corners of tin on the roof and then slapping them back into place.

"I lost my grandfather five months ago," Silva said, finally braving at least a part of it. The least she could do was let Nick know he wasn't alone. "My mother died in a car accident when I was five, and he raised me. I don't have anyone else. . . ."

See? she told herself. *It doesn't take more than a breath to say it all.* Almost all.

Nick looked at her with compassion. "I'm sorry to hear that. We're pretty young to have outlived both our families. Len Dietz has been the longest-lasting person in my life." His voice was resonant with pain, fury, shame—things he still hadn't yet fully named. But how could you name such things? Things interwoven inside you so tightly it seemed they could never be unwound without destroying you in the process.

She looked at his scar and wondered what else he hadn't told her, what else had happened between him and Dietz. What kind of unseen scars his young faith had left him with. She resisted asking him more, asking what he'd seen, what Len Dietz had done to his mother, what had happened to the others. He'd told her much more than he had to, and she'd shared nothing except the barest facts of her own loss. She wanted to be able to tell him all she'd lost. All she hoped to find, too, even if she didn't yet know what that meant. She wanted to tell him all Len had said to her, what he'd insinuated, but she was wary of the look she'd seen in Nick's eyes—what he, too, might be capable of. What he might do with such clear provocation, itching for a first punch to be thrown, everything escalating with the kind of momentum that couldn't be stopped. She didn't want to be a reason for any further violence.

CHAPTER TWENTY

You are one of many, one more of many to come, one more of many before, one of many more, many of one more taking another and another and another's place, her skin like clay, like the floured Play-Doh you make for the little ones, their dirty hands always grasping at you for more, squeezing fleshy globs through their fingers until, shuddering, you make them stop, but now you want to squeeze it, take her gray clay flesh in your hands and warm it back into being, grasp great handfuls and mold it back into life, something so soft you couldn't help touch it then just as you touch it now, there, where her sleeve pulls away from her wrist, the hair as soft and downy as the secret reaches of your own flesh. You undress her and wash her and wash her. You try to wash the gray away, but the clay won't warm, won't pink into what you remember touching before, won't respond to your pliant pleading fingers, so instead, you brush her hair smooth, coil it into a thick golden coronet around her still face, her eyes forever now closed to you, her body formed and shaped into this new silent state of truth.

CHAPTER TWENTY-ONE
MAY 2001

Silva awoke with the smell of acrid char in her nose and checked out the window for fresh-burned ground, but it was still damp and green, the burning only in her dreams—flames like a torrent raining down on the tops of their heads. She couldn't bring herself to look out at the garden plot, her mother's seeds hail-hammered in Nick's mother's old garden.

Nick had left a note on the kitchen table, the same tidy block print as the writing on the map she'd found: *Off to Sheep Lake. Left you Tiko in case you need to leave. I hope you find everything you've been looking for. —N*

Her heart beat like a startled bird in her chest. Had he guessed what she was looking for? Did he know what she meant to do? Reading her like a horoscope, all her stars in disarray. She wondered what he'd think if he came back and found Isabelle staying in the Larkins cabin, too.

She went out to the barn, nails holding the tack Nick had left for her, a smell like sulfur still in the air. She picked up a halter, inhaling its horse scent as she looked in at the empty extraction room, striated with hay dust and light, the day's budding heat.

Mack was due up with the mail, and then she would be alone, nobody to question her, to stop her when she saddled Tiko and followed the Larkins Ranch trail to its end. But already the ranch seemed altered in Nick's absence—lesser than what it'd become with him there, weed heads already rising above the lawn she'd mown as he'd ridden in.

She took Tiko grain, Juniper eating grass alongside them. "It's just the three of us now," she said, trying to reassure herself as well as the twitchy horse. The morning was bright and muggy, the sky turned from its warning crimson to brilliant blue, the only thing left of the storm a rim of darkened clouds hovering at the canyon's edge, the same shifting colors as melted lead. She wondered if the storm would regather on Nick in the mountains, wind and hail battering against thin tent walls.

She walked to the trailhead, following the storm's path. An elm lay broken across the creek, split halfway down the middle, its splintered shock of wood white as bone. Below it, the creek trickled dark, its rank mud banks teeming with insects. She bent to splash her face, then followed the creek's mineral-whitened boulders that shifted and clanked under her feet like bones. She dared not look up for more than a fraction of a second for fear of falling face-first into the creek's memory. She pushed through brush and stooped into a hidden void, toeing the flotsam that'd washed up like a child's junk treasure collection: old dirt-crusted bottles, a rusted hoe head, a glistening tangle of fishing line. Then, beneath a heap of sticks, she saw pink skin.

She held her breath as she uncovered it: a naked baby missing one arm, one blue eye askew, the other a black hole. A child's doll. For a moment, she'd thought it was real. She backed out of the brush quickly, bile rising in her throat.

As a child, she and Eamon had driven past a Trawler funeral—a black-clad mother keening over her lost child in a high, thin, wavering sound held aloft by the wind. Silva had plugged her ears and closed her eyes against it, but it had carried forth, becoming the sound of Silva's mother calling to her from underneath the waters. In desperation to escape it, Silva had tried to open the Dodge's door and jump from the moving truck. Eamon had swerved to a stop and held onto her until the keening was finally silenced. That night, he'd told her stories of baobab trees, the cavernous space inside their massive trunks used throughout the centuries for burial crypts, offering solace and strength to those entering into the afterlife. He'd brought his oldest bonsai—the bristlecone pine—into her room and left it with her overnight, saying that such ancient wisdom would always watch over her, that both bristlecones and baobabs had magical abilities to survive adverse growing conditions—that their secret to longevity was in fact the harsh environment in which they grew, making them true survivors. Just as she was.

Finally, she braved the garden, walking its soft perimeter, the soil pocked and covered in debris, her carefully sown seeds battered and displaced. They would be lucky to sprout and take root at all, lucky to escape a slow rotting.

She raked piles of leaves and sticks onto a tarp she dragged by the corners, emptying load after load into the burn-pile heaps. Come fall, the Larkins Ranch would look like some medieval village, surrounded by burning pyres. An appropriate representation of the coming battle—Nick's fight to reclaim his rights.

She leaned her rake against a tree as the mail-boat surged into sight, navigating the last rapids and then slowing into the docking. Juniper ran ahead as they walked down to meet Mack.

"Last stop is always the best," Mack said, climbing stiffly out of the boat to hand Silva an assortment of junk mail strangely juxtaposed with the canyon's isolation: movie rental coupons, discount pizza, and two-for-one manicures. Things of another world, of no use in hers. "The crew already head out?" he asked, glancing up toward the house and barn.

"Bright and early," she said. The cheerful caretaker. Not a worry in the world.

He bent down and patted Juniper's head roughly. "Well, at least you've got this fella's company," he said, wincing as he straightened. "I'm getting too old for all this river running. Speaking of, did you know you've got company on the way? The Hells Canyon River Runners. Why anybody would *run* in this canyon is beyond me. Miles of hills, not to mention the snakes. Dens full of dozens slithering out, all hungry and testy. Can you imagine running into *that*?"

She thought of her own run down the canyon, the rattlesnake stretched across the trail. "When will they be here?" she asked, frowning and scanning downriver, translating how much she didn't welcome the intrusion, even if she was being paid for it.

"Anytime now. The speedy ones are just a few miles down. Started out from Pittsburg Landing this morning. Tents and tarps all battened down. I bet they had a good time riding out the storm. Never know what the canyon's going to dish out, especially this time of year. In fact, I better get going—don't want to have to take on any snake-bitten hitchhikers unless I have to!"

She helped him get out a few bags of groceries, wishing it had kept storming, kept the runners from being able to make it to the ranch at all. But after he left, it took her only a moment to spot the blobs of color bobbing along the shore trail. He'd been right to leave quickly. The canyon's distances took her by surprise—things so much closer than she realized and others far enough it seemed the land stretched forever, covering centuries, eons.

In this case, she didn't have to wait long. In a half hour the Larkins' lawn was replete with dozens of people clad in high-tech sneakers and brightly colored nylon and spandex, stretching and bouncing as if their legs were full of springs. An invasion of colors and sounds, as though a flock of migrating tropical birds had blown off course to alight on the ranch's storm-bruised ground, squawking and fluttering in their confused and exhausted amazement.

Several of the runners wore snake chaps over their running tights—a good precaution in theory but overkill with all the racket of vibrations they'd already set off, thundering along in their vivid throngs. Any self-respecting snake would have taken cover as fast as its cold-blooded body could. She wanted to take cover, too, but she went to greet them instead, shaking hands and welcoming them to the Larkins Ranch as if she were a B&B host. Unlike her, Juniper greeted each new person enthusiastically as they came in, all dog smiles and friendly licks, his white tail wagging like a welcome flag, making up for Silva's reticence.

A mother-daughter duo stood apart from the rest of the group, both long-legged in their black running tights, the daughter a rangy teen who moved with surprising assurance and grace. They bent over Juniper, gushing and sweet-talking him, asking Silva if he was a wolf hybrid. Silva tried to imagine a world where you grew up with a mother who ran alongside you, encouraging you onward with each stride. What kind of difference that might make.

A last straggler jogged in, sweaty and panting—a man in his sixties, dressed in camo cargo shorts with a tucked-in work shirt and white tube socks and hiking boots, a pistol in a hard-plastic case strapped on top of his daypack.

"Have to show these people how it's done," he said, winking at Silva as he heaved into a cooldown walk around the ranch yard, his pistol rattling on his back. She kept a wary eye on him, wondering if he were a part of the Lenites or a paramilitary survivalist of a different breed.

But it was one of the first runners to arrive—not the survivalist man or the mother-daughter duo—who shook Silva. A tall pregnant woman, near-term but running in an effortless lope that looked as if it would eat up the miles, her legs and arms sporting defined muscles their whole length. She smiled at Silva as she stretched, lifting her arms over her head, her belly a taut round ball seemingly grafted onto the long pole of her body, like a burl growing out of the middle of a sapling. Not even breathing hard, she looked as if she would finish the remaining fifteen miles back at the lead of the pack, a fully developed fetus sloshing around inside her.

"Have you seen any snakes out?" the pregnant woman asked, looking serene as she ran her hand around the perfect orb of her stomach.

"One, a week ago. Downcanyon," Silva answered, speaking in staccato. How fooled she'd been, thinking how alone she was. She made herself breathe deep and exhale slowly, filling her lungs with oxygen as if she were the one who'd been running, the one out of breath, trying to create distance between herself and her own future.

Seven and a half weeks. Heart divided into four chambers, eyes fused shut.

The hubbub was brief, all the runners heading out again within the hour.

Silva climbed to a spot where she could see downriver, watching as the bright neon dotting the trail dispersed, the pregnant woman and the mother-daughter duo in the front ranks, the camo man bringing up the rear. Silva wondered if the pregnant woman would keep the pace she'd set, the rhythm of her feet entering the baby's blood, wondered if they would still be together years from now like the mother-daughter duo, running as if they'd never been apart.

The weight of the thought was the same as the undertow of current hidden beneath the surface. "Keepers," Eamon called them—rapids that curled backward onto themselves, so full of tumultuous power that if you got caught in them, you might never make it out, kept churning in their death hold. Rip currents, shore breaks, broaching, strainers, sweeping you in and pinning you, trapping you in unrelenting pressure until you gave in.

Finally, Silva went inside to put away groceries and read the week's worth of newspapers Mack had brought up, each with their own occupation headline. She read each article carefully, assessing between the lines where Len and Isabelle might be—analyses of laws and criminal charges along with the pandering to local politicians. Members of the Nez Perce tribe, fearing that the occupiers would further damage important spiritual artifacts at the visitor center, had asked law officials to clamp down on the occupiers, but so far there was no real enforcement, the Lenites coming and going whenever they wanted. The county sheriff had organized a meeting with the occupiers, urging them to leave peacefully, but Dietz publicly declined, putting out a video of his men dismantling fences. Idaho Fish and Game condemned "the fence removal by militants occupying the public's property," while the FBI continued to take no action, saying that if the occupiers couldn't get the standoff they wanted, they would eventually get worn out and hungry, and disperse on their own.

There'd been a small protest outside the FBI's makeshift headquarters in the Yellow-Pine Motel in town, a handful of people advocating for the occupiers. Silva pictured Sherry and Becky marching around with their matching tattoos, had feared she might even see Isabelle marching, too, but the only picture of the protest published was of a scruffy, heavyset man in a baseball cap and camo shirt sitting in the back of his pickup with two full-size American flags and chip-board signs that read, in spray-painted, red-white-and-blue letters, *Go Home FBI* and *Two Rivers will not be run by the FEDS.*

Suddenly exhausted and left with the clinging nausea that came whenever she thought of Len Dietz, Silva put the newspapers aside and sank into the living room chair. Juniper curled at her feet, and Tiko paced the fence line as if he were plotting his own escape, the ranch reverted to its previous wild loneliness. She fell asleep, everything so quiet it seemed as if the runners had been a figment, Nick somewhere deep in the mountains, camp set up, waiting for nightfall.

⁕

When she woke, it was early evening. She walked to Nick's open bedroom door and reached in fast, flicking on the light, hesitating a moment before walking in. She stood looking at his folded clothes, then went to the nightstand, picked up the jar, and turned it in her hands. What kind of man packed around a jar of honey? She examined the wrinkled label decorated with bees, careful to put the jar back in the same position as she'd found it before paging through a beekeeping book until she got to the center photo insert: piñata-size swarms hanging from tree branches and close-ups of hive interiors. Diagrams of bee anatomy; differences of wing pattern, body size, and antennae placement; bees classified according to type: *Apis mellifera ligustica*, the Italian honeybee, or *Apis mellifera carnica*, the Carniolan honeybee. Pictures of the queen and the drones and the workers, pictures of the eggs, the pollen cells and wax caps. Illustrations and captions on nectar collection, propolis storage, egg rearing, honey production, and hive health.

Flipping to a chapter titled "The Trials and Tribulations of Beekeeping," she stopped to read. It said the beekeeper must be patient. Building the hives was slow, painstaking work—battling diseases, mites and viruses, frosts, wax moths, mice, skunks, bears, yellow jackets. Unknown pestilence. Colony collapse. Keeping bees was a way of life, a lost art. She read terms common to her—order, family, tribe, genus, species—immersing herself in the world of bees: nectar and honey, breeding and rearing, broods and queens. The queen's calls of sovereignty, of mating, everything somehow imbued with sex, full and pulsating.

The author was photographed in front of flowering honeysuckle, serenely bearded with bees. Bees clustered on his cheeks, on his neck, on his lips. Beads of bees dangling from his ears. She imagined exposing herself like that—bees all over her body, buzzing her skin.

The house creaked, and she jumped. She closed the books hastily and put them back in place, then walked quickly out and shut the door behind her.

Safely in her own bedroom, she opened the window, warm night air gusting in, the river a murmuring backdrop, a family of coyotes singing to one another. Silva pulled off her clothes and lay on her bed in the dark, the bonsai silhouetted against the bedroom walls. Nick's lingering presence just across the hall. Close enough almost to reach. She imagined the heavy portent of all those swarming wings—her body entombed with crawling insects and dripping with honey. The words of beekeeping a litany running through her subconscious: *brood nest, beemilk, deep super, nurse bees, virgin queen, royal jelly.* She imagined herself with delicate hands breaking open a honeycomb's seal and sucking honey from chambers of wax, her skin and mouth sticky and ripe.

When she reached for herself, she sucked in her breath at the shock of it, her hands on her skin, on her stomach, on her breasts, her body alive with a kind of longing that took her by surprise. She ran her hands over the bones of her hips, the smooth skin of her upper thighs, found the soft receiving warmth of her center, each thing more demanding and ravenous than the last. The softness of her hidden body, her transformed flesh. An aching release encompassed her, cresting swells that broke and overtook her completely, radiating in electric waves, pulsing from her center outward. She arched her back and buried her face into the folds of wool blanket, crying out into its wet-animal smell, her breath as ragged as if she'd been sobbing. And perhaps she had been—the first time she'd allowed herself to be touched since the night on the mainland.

She rolled to her back and placed her hands on her stomach, felt it raise and lower, felt the place of growth just under the skin. A part of her that felt as if it had been there forever—a rising tide pushing her to the surface, gasping for air.

<hr />

She awoke lying on top of her bedcovers, the windows still open, night-cool air coming in. It took her several minutes to become aware that something besides her dream—bees covering her body like a mantle—had pulled her to consciousness. At first, she couldn't make sense out of anything—it was as if she'd come to in the sea's dark, caught in its depths. But next to her, Juniper was alert and listening, too, staring out the window.

When she finally recognized unfamiliar sounds outside, she sat up, the stir in the air pricking her arms in alarm. She hushed Juniper from his growling and listened, finally making out the quiet idle of a boat motor farther up the shore than she'd ever heard Mack's boat. Her heart picked up its pace. The time in the canyon had already taught her to differentiate the sounds of the few boats that made it this far upriver, and it wasn't one she recognized—all the warnings she'd gotten taking shape.

She wrapped herself in the blanket and got up carefully, peering out the dark window, but she could see nothing. She heard other faint noises—a horse's snort, a man's voice—and for a moment she thought perhaps Nick had come home early, pushed back to the canyon by an accident or a storm, but then the noises became jumbled into things she wasn't sure she was imagining or actually hearing. A bright beam swept up from shore before dissipating somewhere below, and finally she could clearly hear men's voices—voices that didn't belong to Nick. There was no doubt now.

She pulled her clothes on quickly, wishing she'd taken the shotgun Mack had offered to bring to her—"The Equalizer," he'd called it. Instead, she armed herself with her tiny pocketknife and went to the kitchen, where she could see farther down shore. From the different vantage point, the lights shone bright enough to blind her night vision for a moment, but when her eyes adjusted, she could make out dark figures—several people moving objects from a boat to shore and then transferring the bulk to horses tethered to the side.

Juniper growled at the door, his torn ears cocked. She was glad she hadn't used any lights herself, glad Juniper, too, seemed to understand the importance of maintaining quiet. She hoped the trespassers would think the Larkins house was still empty. It was far less sinister to imagine someone conducting business in the middle of the night, in the middle of this isolated place, ignorant of her presence, than someone who didn't care that she was there. She thought again of the no-trespassing sign washed downstream. This time it was the Larkins Ranch trespassed upon.

Done transferring their cargo, the boat accelerated out, its lights illuminating everything clearly for a moment—several men and horses with bulky packs. Definitely not Nick or his outfitting group. Then the lights went to the river, and she couldn't see anything but black.

Through the open window, she heard the sounds of horses moving toward the house along with men's low voices. She could make out only a few snatches of conversation—"ghost guns," "never too late," "high-velocity shells," "they want war, they can have it"—and then suddenly they were right in front of the house. She saw a flashlight's quick blink, and one of them said, "Won't know what hit them," close enough it seemed he was inside the kitchen with her.

She shrank back into the shadows, afraid they would see the open windows and understand her presence, but before she could stop him Juniper started barking with such ferocity she couldn't quiet him, and it was too late anyway, lights already swinging to the house.

"Who's there?" a voice outside commanded—deep and sonorous. A voice already a part of Silva's subconscious. She could feel him there, his presence filling the space in between them.

Lights shone through the windows, illuminating the kitchen's interior. Braced against the counter, Silva wished she could slip outside, hide herself in the darkness, but no matter how much she called Juniper, he wouldn't budge from the door, his mouth frothing with the fervor of his barking. Everyone's warnings taking shape—the river's dead sheep, the creek's broken sign and eyeless doll, even the sky that morning shading its own ominous colors of threat.

She knew what men in the dark could do to a woman on her own. What kind of violence Len Dietz was capable of—Nick's mother and brother gone to an early Almost Paradise grave, Isabelle gone silent and missing. But this wasn't how her story would end. She stepped into the powerful flashlight beam and stood behind the screen gazing blindly out at them in defiance even though she couldn't see anything past the light's glare.

"This is private property. What are you doing here?" she demanded, relieved her voice was steady despite her shaking, the pocketknife with its tiny, useless blade clutched in her palm.

She could sense their surprise. Their sudden assessment. The hair on her neck prickled with electricity. There was no way to hide her aloneness, her vulnerability, no way to take it back. It was a quivering line stretched tight between them all, her hands still suffused with the intimate smell of herself, her body's soft pliancy.

Next to her, Juniper growled deeply, primed for attack, his body rigid with tension, his tail stiff, his hackles raised high, the rusted screen the only thing in between them and the men.

She reached over and flipped on the porch light. Len Dietz stood a few feet from the porch, the others behind him holding onto a heavily loaded pack string. They were armed—holsters on their hips and what she could only assume was a load of illegal weapons in the packs.

"Silva—" Len said, tilting his head and speaking her name slowly, as though it were a secret hanging in the air between them. A slow drawing out. A savoring. He was only a few feet from her, dressed in a military uniform, his pistol and pendant glinting in the porchlight, his hair loose on his shoulders. An older, long-haired version of his Vietnam picture hanging in the Two Rivers Museum.

She held herself still, a cold wash of fear snaking her spine, her skin prickling in alarm.

He looked at her a moment more before turning to his men. "I'll catch up, go ahead," he commanded.

His men mounted, casting backward glances at her as if she were a new creature altogether—one they'd just discovered and wished to further explore.

She expected them to ride to the trail behind the house that led to Almost Paradise—the same trail Nick had taken hours before—but instead they rode to the upriver trail. The visitor center and their occupation site were fifteen miles upcanyon.

Len waited until they were gone before he turned back to her, his eyes deep hollows. "I didn't know you were our neighbor," he said, his tone amused, as if she were a child whose antics had entertained him.

"I'm the Larkins' caretaker," she said stiffly. She stood still, head up, now angry more than anything. He didn't belong here. Didn't have any right. Slinking like a coward in the dark. Trespassing against her, against Nick's family land. Against Isabelle and Nick's mother. Against them all. She would not cower in fear, would not allow her body to be overtaken again—no matter what kind of threat Len Dietz might pose, no matter what kind of damage she might incur.

"What do you want here?" she demanded, her heart beating hard, despite her bravado.

He stepped closer, and Juniper lunged into action, barking so ferociously it seemed as if he would barrel through the flimsy screen and latch on to Len's throat.

Len held up his hands in a posture of surrender, looking at Silva with pity, as though he were trying to calm a child. "Don't fear," he said. "It is His voice you hear calling you forth. 'Come unto me, all ye who labor and are heavy laden, and I will give you rest.'" He regarded her through the screen. "Your burdens have not been light, have they, Silva of the fire-hair? But the Lord has chosen His people. Will you find shelter before the coming storm?" He looked at her, his eyes dark with meaning.

"You have no right to be here. This is private property," she said again, her adrenaline surging. A narrowing of vision, her lungs lifting and falling in fast inhalations. She was afraid her uterus would cramp again, send her to her knees as it had in Build It Best, Becky and all the slain animals witness to her impotence. But this time standing in front of Len Dietz, her limbs felt leaden, as if her flesh had been melted down, poured into a mold, and left to harden into this new, immobilized form— as cold and metallic and lifeless as one of Len's silver Ascension Pendants.

Speaking quietly, he said, "'Behold, thou art fair; thou hast doves' eyes within thy locks: thy hair is as a flock of goats that appear from mount Gilead. . . . Come into my garden, my sister, my bride; I have gathered my myrrh with my spice. I have eaten my honeycomb and my honey.'" He regarded her a moment in silence, then turned, mounted his horse, and trotted away, following the others upriver into the dark.

CHAPTER TWENTY-TWO

Date: November 15, 1999
Title: Dowry Ceremony
Subject: The Twelve Maidens
Setting: Almost Paradise Dining Hall
Medium: Watercolor and graphite on cold-press
Size: 12×36

Dearest Eamon,

They gather in force now. We have entered the final stretch, three more ceremonies leading up to the New Year's Wedding of the Maidens. The families have brought all their goods to give Len Dietz for their daughters' dowries—a kind of Almost Paradise early Thanksgiving. Two of the original maidens were lost to illness or regret, ushered quickly and quietly back to their now-shunned families, but not to worry—they have been swiftly replaced by others even more eager to prove themselves worthy, their families heaping their gifts even higher than the others, trying to outdo each other in demonstrating their devotion to the cause, to Len Dietz, to their god.

This celebration has been reminiscent of an aristocratic Renaissance feast: candlelit tables heaped with roast pheasant; whole suckling pigs, mouths stuffed with apples; quail and endangered sage grouse; platters of roasted vegetables and breads and cheeses; bowls of grapes and plums; every baked good you can imagine—all of it either grown, harvested, or made by one of the Almost Paradise faithful, self-sufficiency their creed. All of it only a small part of the dowry offerings, gifts that have filled a large room to overflowing. Every piece of handmade, old-fashioned finery that this place would never usher or use. Heaps and piles of fine goods, as if they all imagine themselves a part of a golden castle instead of this hardscrabble canyonland. I wanted to paint the maidens buried alive in it all—as they are—but as always they have been arranged for me: twelve girls in matching, hand-sewn "modesty veils" and dresses, every part of them covered, their families standing in the background, stacks of their dowry gifts spread all around.

What can they believe is going to happen when this is all over? These girls, their bodies not their own. These families feast to their deaths—their own daughters. To their utter and full destruction. The men, the fathers, toast each other as if they've accomplished divinity, as if this is a fantasy fulfilled. They—the girls—are to be kept isolated in their under-construction maiden quarters at all times now, "protected" from outside pestilence. I see them only when I am summoned from my own quarters with my paints. But I don't need to see their faces, don't need to see them at all to be haunted forever by their shuttered eyes—a disappearance happening right in front of us. A slow and steady diminishment.

I spend hours staring at my own limbs, the reality of myself, feeling as if I, too, am disappearing, sinking into the dark. I reach for you in my sleep—imagine your body there next to me, solid. Real. Lasting. If only I can make my way through. If only I can find my way out, back to you.

All my love,
Isabelle

PART THREE

*They are not without prescience, therefore, of what is to befall them
on this, the most dangerous day of all their existence. Absorbed by
the cares, the prodigious perils of this mighty adventure, they will
have no time now to visit the gardens and meadows; and tomorrow,
and after tomorrow, it may happen that rain may fall, or there may
be wind; that their wings may be frozen or the flowers refuse to open.*

*Some succumb to their wounds and are at once borne away to distant
cemeteries by two or three of their executioners. Others, whose
injuries are less, succeed in sheltering themselves in some corner.
For it is evident that these daughters of secluded darkness shrink
from the vault of blue, from the infinite loneliness of the light. . . .
Their joy is halting and woven of terror. They cross the threshold
and pause; they depart, they return. . . . They hover aloft in the air,
their head persistently turned to home; they describe great soaring
circles that suddenly sink beneath the weight of regret . . . till at last
the aerial course of their return shall become as indelibly stamped in
their memory as though it were marked in space by two lines of steel.*

—THE LIFE OF THE BEE

CHAPTER TWENTY-THREE

MAY 2001

Silva tried to replicate Nick's saddling steps, but everything was tense and bungled, Tiko dancing in circles as she tried to tighten all the various straps. She was sweaty and disheveled by the time she finished, her guts clamped tight, seething as they had been lately—intermittently cramping and gurgling, as if she'd eaten or drunk something tainted.

Juniper watched her from a safe distance with concerned eyes.

"It's okay, we're going for a ride, that's all," she said, trying to ease all their anxiety, even if it were a lie, nothing okay about any of it.

She'd radioed in immediately to report the trespassing incident, the dispatcher asking her to repeat exactly what she'd heard. She'd said that the men had said something like, "They want war, they can have it," that they'd picked up arms and ammunition and were headed upriver, probably to further arm their occupation, but she didn't say the rest of what Len Dietz had said, attempting to woo her, draw her into the fold, just like Isabelle, just like Nick's mother. Len didn't know who she was. What kind of woman her experiences had shaped her into. A woman who already knew with great intimacy the face of the monster under her own bed. Len had helped her see *that* clearly at least.

The dispatcher said they would look into the situation, notify the proper authorities. The same as when she'd reported the shot-up mountain sheep. Len continuing to do what he pleased.

She led Tiko to the corral, climbed the outside rail, and jumped on his back, barely making her landing as he took off. She went sideways, her weight tipping so that she almost lost her balance entirely before she grabbed the saddle horn, recovering enough to yank the reins, trying to force him to stop or at least slow. Instead, he danced sideways and then surged forward, breaking into a punishing trot, every bone in Silva's body feeling as if it were knocking against the other, her stomach cramping as if Len's visit had poisoned her body.

As they climbed the trail, Tiko threw his head, threatening to rear up on the steep incline. It was as though he could still smell Nick's pack-string and was trying to catch up, even though it'd been forty-eight hours since they'd left, their tracks already softened into dust.

Silva used her legs to pogo herself in tandem with the bone-jarring trot, but she'd learned to post in an arena, not climbing a narrow mountainside trail littered with loose rock, sides steep enough that a person would rag doll for hundreds of feet.

She wouldn't let herself consider beyond her arrival—beyond the point of no return. The bonsai and all her belongings stowed safely in Nick's cabin, Len and his men heading back to the visitor center occupation with their load of ghost guns, leaving Almost Paradise to the women and children—a group of Lenites that might still include Isabelle. Women who maybe didn't want to be rescued, gone somewhere Silva couldn't follow.

Nick thought his mother duped by Len Dietz, but Silva imagined that, by the end, Meg Larkins had understood only too well what she'd gotten herself into. Just how deep and dark those waters were. Silva, too, had needed rescue.

When they reached a plateau, the steep cliffsides safely yards away, Silva reined Tiko in tight circles, forcefully spinning him around and around until they were both dizzy and panting, trying to disorient him enough that he would finally slow down, pay attention to her lead.

It worked. When she let the reins go slack, he stood still, breathing hard through distended nostrils, the smell of warm pine needles drifting up. When they reached the fork, Nick's pack-string tracks were barely notice-able on the left spur. Silva reined right, entering new territory. She heeled

Juniper in close, alert to any sign of movement or habitation as they climbed, coyote scat littering the ground in furry tufts. Another mile and she finally spotted something man-made—a weathered square of wood on a T-post anchored in a heap of basalt. A no-trespassing sign, like the one washed down the creek, this one's lettered warning complete.

Silva laced her fingers through the reins as if to anchor herself against gale-force winds as movement along a hillside caught her eye. At first it just looked like a clump of bunch grass blowing, but then she made out the tawny form of a coyote, the wheat-grass gold of its fur blending in perfectly with the surroundings. It stood motionless, head tipped; then without warning, it sprang straight up and landed in a forceful, front-footed pounce. It came up shaking its head, a small furry body clutched in its mouth, then trotted into the trees, taking its quarry back to the clan she'd heard every night, its pack living like specters in Almost Paradise territory.

Juniper watched, his torn ears alert, looking like the coyote's cousin. Silva hadn't wanted to bring him so close to danger, wanted to leave him locked safely in the house with the bonsai, but she wasn't sure how long she would be gone, wasn't sure what might happen—no way for him to escape, no one to check on him for days if she didn't make it back. She just hoped he had enough survival instincts to know when to run and hide.

They rounded a corner to a three-strand barbwire fence stretched across the trail, each T-post painted orange, a sign declaring, *Private Property, Keep Out*, a group of whitewashed buildings clustered a quarter-mile ahead. *Almost Paradise.*

From a distance, the compound looked innocuous. The arch of a Quonset hut sheathed in opaque corrugated plastic, several white bunk-houses spoking out from a large central building, and a scattering of sheds and other outbuildings. Off to the left, tall wire fences encircled dozens of clustered elk grazing placidly on short-cropped pasture grass, orange tags hanging off their ears like price tags. Gray and thin and antlerless, the elk looked more like domesticated cattle than the wild bull elk pictured in the brochure Sherry had given Silva at the grocery store. She pictured hunters like Sherry's raffle-winning husband crouched in camouflage among the grazing herd, picking out their kill.

Silva had imagined some kind of disturbing, salacious scene: a religious paramilitary compound housing a harem full of women and acolyte-girls surrounded by razor-wire-topped fences and armed guards. Something more alarming, something that fit more closely with Len Dietz's exploits, but other than the pastured elk, the compound looked like any other isolated western ranch, no one in sight, the pastoral scene at odds with everything Silva knew to be true about it, including Nick's description of the blueprints of future plans—a self-sustaining, walled-off militia city in the wilderness complete with a gazing pool and a firearms museum.

She loosened the reins and dismounted. She led Tiko through the gate and called Juniper as she stepped on the compound's grounds. Jittery with nerves, she kept to the perimeter, where she might escape quickly, aiming for the back of the rough buildings, keeping watch for Lenites, waiting for someone to suddenly appear. Everything was quiet and still, as if the place had been abandoned like all the other canyon ranches, a narrow road leading her past a shed full of farming implements and toward the next building, an *Office* placard in its front window.

Off to the right, tucked along the border of the brush-tangled draw that marked the steep drop into the canyon, rows and rows of wooden crosses sprouted out of the ground, a single towering ponderosa standing sentry. The Almost Paradise cemetery, where Nick's mother and baby brother were buried. Women and babies unable or unwilling to carry forth. *Isabelle, maybe, too.*

Warily, Silva walked to the office building and looped Tiko's reins around the front porch rail, tying Juniper to it as well and telling him to stay as she tried to push away her fear. The dog refused, stood starting at her in appeal with his brown eyes, as ill at ease as she was.

A small herd of elk stood clustered nearby behind a tall double-wire fence, their smell a powerful wild musk even though they looked tame, sedately chewing their cud, lifting their heads to stare. They were surprisingly large up close, their hair twitching against biting flies, their eyes watching with aplomb. Animals meant to roam wild, to run free. Tiko snorted and eyed them warily. She was afraid he would shy, pull back against his reins and injure himself, but instead he let out a low nicker and the elks' fawn-colored ears tipped toward him.

"Have you come for a tour?" a woman's voice asked.

Startled, Juniper let out an alarmed bark, and Silva turned, her heart thudding in her chest.

The woman stood to the side of the office, a child next to her, the soft lines of her face undermining the boldness Silva had tried to work up as she'd ridden in. The farmers market woman—a Lenite whose beauty likely marked her as one of Len's wives, her child likely another of Len's fated progeny. Not the kind of woman who belonged in a militant cult in a dried-out patch of nowhere surrounded by herds of fenced elk and a cemetery laid full.

"The tour? Yes," Silva said, her breath coming in shallow bursts.

"My name is Faith," she said, then looked over at Tiko and Juniper. "I will have Isaac bring water, keep an eye on them."

Faith spun on her heels, her long skirt swirling and her child scampering behind, casting wary looks at Silva. Silva followed them, trying to act as if nothing out of the ordinary was happening, while all the stories of this place rang as one loud alarm in her head.

The office was cool and smelled of meat and musk. Faith radioed in a call for water for Tiko and Juniper and came back with a small gilded book. "Tours are free. You just need to sign our guestbook. We like to keep track of who we've served," she said, looking at Silva with an examination that felt uncomfortably intimate—as if Silva was someone she'd been expecting.

Pen in hand, Silva hesitated, Faith's anticipation making her uneasy. Finally, under the listing of dozens of names, she signed *Isabelle Fullbrook*, surprised by the immediate effect it had on her. The softly voweled name seemed to always be a part of her—a twin identity as familiar as her own.

Faith took the book, glancing down at Isabelle's name quickly before closing it. "Calving finished a month ago. The calves are with their mothers, too young for viewing. The main herd is above the river for grazing, but we have one of the big bulls here out back," she said, gesturing toward another two-layered wire fence outside. She held the little girl's hand as they went out, the two of them different-size versions of the same. Just as Silva and Isabelle had been. An inheritance of powerful genes marking appearance and temperament, drawing them together like a mime's invisible mirrored reflection. She wondered if Faith had recognized her, too.

When they approached a fenced pen, Silva spotted a magnificent bull elk, blond with age, lying peacefully in his sawdust enclosure, the orange tag hanging off his ear moving to the rhythm of his ruminating. His enormity and musky scent betrayed the docile nature of the scene—antlers as wide-stretching and thick as tree limbs. Even lying down, his head hanging lazily, his rack was as tall as Silva. A placard hung on the wire above him, a name carved into it.

"This is Nehemiah," Faith said. "The other trophy bulls, Ezekiel, Mordecai, and Zachariah, are out to pasture."

Silva looked at Faith quickly, thinking perhaps the Old Testament names were some kind of joke, but Faith was all seriousness. This place wasn't meant for joking, for taking things at more than face value.

Faith pointed to a group of spike elk pacing the back perimeter like prisoners looking for release. "We keep the young bulls separate from the others," she said in her practiced tour-guide voice. "Up there is our order-processing center—everything from jerky to antler velvet." She looked at Silva again and then turned to walk to the new building.

One of Silva's gregarious mainland clients had once remarked how you could tell inbred, rural people by their eyes, miming a slack-jawed, cross-eyed stare, but Faith's eyes were lovely—wide-spaced and oceanic blue. She looked like someone Isabelle would have painted.

Inside the order center, wide tables and shelves were stacked high with hides and antlers. "We ship all over the country," Faith said, sitting the little girl down and walking to a chest freezer. She retrieved a small plastic packet out of its depths and handed it to Silva. "Paradise pepper jerky. The Lord has blessed us. May His blessings be upon you as well," she said.

Silva thanked her and put the jerky in her pack, her stomach revolting at the smell of it.

"So this is all a part of Almost Paradise?" she asked, as if she didn't already know about Len Dietz, about Meg Larkins and Isabelle.

"It is," Faith said, holding Silva's eyes for a long moment, assessing her as if she were someone of interest. "We are all one family. God's Family." She gazed at Silva with meaning, her little girl playing with a scrap of elk hide she'd picked up off the floor.

As they turned to leave, a tall, clean-cut boy hobbled in through a back door hidden behind a stack of hides, his leg encased in some kind of brace, a bulky mechanical apparatus that looked homemade.

He stopped uncomfortably when he saw Silva. No more than fifteen, a scattering of freckles on his otherwise smooth face, he was hovering on the brink of manhood—chin squaring with the definition of testosterone, shoulders beginning to widen, lanky and ill at ease in his own skin, like the young bulls pacing behind the fence.

"Isaac, this is our visitor," Faith said, tipping her head slightly, looking at the boy with some kind of meaning Silva couldn't decipher, some communication translating between them.

"Isabelle," Silva said, reaching out to shake the boy's hand, the same three-lined tattoo inked inside his wrist.

"Nice to meet you," he said with a voice deeper than his body, his blue-eyed gaze questioning the world. He looked like she felt—a caged animal looking for escape. A boy neck-deep in this place, in these people. He reminded her so much of Nick, she had to look away.

"*Isabelle*. A lovely name," Faith said, studying Silva.

"My grandmother's name," Silva said, watching for recognition—a confirmation that she'd known Isabelle, but Faith just nodded, her expression carefully veiled.

"To the greenhouse next?" she asked, giving nothing away. She turned to Isaac. "It's time for Ruth's rest. Will you take her, please?" she asked.

Silva felt as if she'd walked into a trap, flummoxed by Faith's strange expectation and formality coupled with her softly accented voice, Isabelle's paintings resting in her pack—a host of troubled girls waiting for the end.

Isaac hobbled over to the girl and scooped her up. "Nap time," he said, the firmness of his tone quelling the child's protest. He glanced at Silva as the child's lower lip quivered. "Hush now," he said to the little girl, all tender brusqueness, more at ease with handling a child than Silva had ever been.

She was unable to keep herself from watching as he carried the child back to whatever was hidden behind the door from which he'd come, something about the boy pulling at her like a word she couldn't remember, like a question she couldn't define.

Outside, as Faith led Silva to the greenhouse, she tried to see where he'd gone, but all was as empty as when Silva had ridden in. Everyone tucked out of sight from the intruder, holed up in some bunker along with stockpiles of weapons and food. She wondered if the house was Len's, if that was where Nick and his mother had once lived, where Isabelle might be, hidden away with the rest of his women.

Inside the greenhouse, the heavy warmth and humidity and the smell of compost were an overwhelming presence, row after row of heavy-leafed plants in raised beds separated by wood-chipped walkways. For the first time since arriving, Silva breathed in deeply, trying to settle her stomach, the smell of humus and soil and green growth like a memory before time.

Faith walked the rows, talking of harvest, the tomato and pepper plants' immature fruits hanging like ornaments—months earlier than they would be producing if grown traditionally, outside. Silva imagined the Almost Paradise women working the plants and then "putting up," like her mother had. Not much different than the New Community women working their gardens together, joined by belief and structure, hard work and kinship. Trust in a bigger whole.

Maybe that was how they converted people, how they'd drawn Isabelle in, and before her, Nick and his mother. All that concerted attentiveness, all that unrestrained growth. Everyone looking for belonging. Everyone wanting to be seen, to be loved and cherished. None of them any different from anyone else trying to find a place in the world.

Faith guided her alongside the grow-boxes overflowing with produce: chives, cilantro, parsley, leeks, lemon balm. Silva bent to touch the oversize heads of purple tipped lettuce.

"We've been blessed with plenty," Faith said, fixing her eyes on Silva with a veiled mix of sorrow and resignation. The same look Isabelle had captured in her paintings of the girls.

Silva wanted to ask her where Isabelle was, but instead she asked, "Do you think it's too late to plant in the canyon?" Trying to speak in the only common language she shared with Faith, hoping she wasn't giving away too much—marking herself from the canyon, from the Larkins Ranch, although they probably already knew all of it, already knew about the garden she'd planted. They seemed to know everything else.

Faith calculated. "The river has a long season. Harvest would be later, but the lower elevation is more forgiving. More access to water. More protected from storms."

Silva couldn't help wondering if there was more context to Faith's comment. If she, too, were trying to communicate in code. She could still feel the little girl's eyes like holes into her soul, Isaac looking at her with a hidden wild fervor. She imagined Nick as an indoctrinated teen not much younger than Isaac, convincing himself and Len Dietz what a good convert he was, what a good Lenite he was and would forever be.

Nick had been Len's real conversion prize, bringing with him thousands of acres of land and a beautiful mother who'd borne Len a son—even if they had both died. No wonder Len wouldn't leave Nick alone. Nick was his unfinished business, a repudiation of his power—an opponent who knew too many secrets. And now Silva was connected to Nick and the ranch, as well as Isabelle.

"You belong to the Larkins Ranch?" Faith asked, her expression carefully indistinct. As if she could hear Silva's thoughts, as if belonging could be mapped by mere presence.

Silva nodded carefully, Isabelle's paintings in the rucksack like a weighted entity.

"The garden there has long been fallow. It's good someone is working the grounds again," Faith said, studying Silva. She ran her hand through a patch of fennel, releasing the deep earthy fragrance of its stalks. "We had an Isabelle, too. She loved painting in the garden, the greenhouse. She was very gifted in her talents." Everything was past tense, as Faith watched Silva closely. She'd known the reason for Silva's visit all along.

Hands shaking, Silva shrugged off the rucksack and pulled out the pregnant girls.

Her porcelain mask slipping, Faith took the paintings carefully, studying them with an equally matched sorrow.

Silva tried to steady herself, her emotions rising like a storm. She looked at Faith, squaring herself against all that was about to come. "I've come for Isabelle," she said.

And you, and you, and you, she wanted to add.

"You shouldn't have," Faith said quietly, handing the paintings back to Silva.

CHAPTER TWENTY-FOUR

Where have you gone? You, and you, and you, and me. I am here, she says, but where are you? You are me, you say, but where am I? Are you me? No, you are you, I am me, she is you, and I am she.

CHAPTER TWENTY-FIVE

The air was thin and harsh, the waves of heat like a physical force. Silva's face felt stretched tight as she rode away from Almost Paradise, as if the skin were pinned back behind her ears, as if pulled anymore she would crack, fissures opening up like canyons in her flesh.

By the time she reached the ranch, she was weak with nausea and pain. When she pulled Tiko up at the corral and dismounted, she nearly fell over, her knees gone wobbly, her insides roiling. Her guts clamped down so hard this time that she had to run for the outhouse, leaving Tiko lathered with sweat. She unsaddled him after, her whole body tilting and on edge, as if she were locked in a ship's hold on a storm-tossed sea, preparing for her own sinking.

Juniper on her heels, she hobbled to the cabin, her nerves jumping as though she were short-circuiting, her body and mind both in equal distress. All the agony she'd pushed away making up for lost time, flooding in like a tidal wave that pulled her out into the deep.

At first she thought her body's distress was a direct reaction to the Almost Paradise visit—but as it grew worse, she realized that it was something more, something with teeth. A bright-white cramping pain, tearing her from the inside out. She ran, stumbling, from the house to the outhouse over and over again, until she couldn't leave the outhouse at all, glad nobody was there to witness her guttural cries, grim with the fact of her own body's purging, its instinct to empty itself with such violence that soon there was nothing more to expel.

She curled in a fetal position on the board floor, her guts twisting, each cramp seeming to build in strength and intensity, her mind whirling with fragmented scenes, nightmares and reality blending together until there was no distinction from the other, each event shadowed with the weight of presentiment, as if she were indeed the product of a twisted prophecy, a foretelling that left no way open except the one leading to her own end. Living a preordained life that left her to sink into the fate of her own inescapable destiny, all of it some kind of surreal nightmare: searching for Isabelle among the fenced elk and greenhouse, Faith ushering her out, saying that she must leave, saying that there was nothing for her there.

Nick had been right. Silva didn't belong here. She didn't belong anywhere.

Her guts seizing with each systolic movement, her stomach a tight ball of pain between her ribs, she felt as if her whole existence was unraveling—a tapestry pulled apart thread by thread until nothing was left but a scrap heap of disconnected endings. Rows of headstones beneath a palaver tree marking the place where the Lenites buried their dead instead of a place to celebrate weddings or harvest, a place to pray for protection and gather for storytelling.

Silva imagined Isabelle's grave there, too—her final act of defiance, documenting a dozen pregnant girls who would never be able to speak in her defense. They clamored against Silva's consciousness demanding, *What will you do?*, calling out for retribution, recompense. Isabelle's last word and testament. A woman who was already gone, who had been gone forever.

————

When the next wave of cramps hit, this time there was blood. A lot of it, not just some spotting. A warm, wet seep from between her legs that wouldn't stop.

She didn't need a doctor to tell her. She knew that it was over. She could feel the absence inside her, wave after wave of expelling spasms, different than all the others. What her body had been trying to tell her all along, recognizing the outcome of its own certain destiny.

As the bloody, clotted tissue purged from her body, she bent forward, sobbing, her forehead on her knees, the sounds coming from her animalistic, her voice as raw and torn as her insides. She felt as if she had been bleeding out for months now, as if when she closed her eyes the darkness would completely engulf her, just as it had before. A beginning in darkness and an ending in darkness. Her body shedding anything beyond its own driving need for survival.

She told herself that this was the outcome she'd wanted in the beginning, anyway. On the island, running and running, trying to jar her body loose. Wanting to slip forever into the sea's dark depths. She'd been headed to the same place all along. Nothing left to keep her.

———

When it was finally over, when her body had shed the last of what she had thought might be able to sustain her, she pushed herself up on shaking hands and knees and stuffed a wad of toilet paper in her underwear, the outhouse full of the heavy mineral smell of blood and shit.

Juniper was waiting for her outside, circling her with concern, following her as she crawled to the bonsai on the porch. She labored to transport each tree out to the yard, the center of her being radiating with pain, her limbs like rubber, mucous and tears dripping off her face, her heart beating a crescendo, a pulsing agony as relentless as her own blood.

She set the trees in a rough circle and curled up in the middle of them, the grass's fresh dampness seeping into her clothes, sunlit droplets of water hanging on the blade tips like prisms. Juniper sat next to her and whined quietly, nosing her. Silva's mind jumped from one disconnected detail to another: a pot of congealed stew, cold and fat-scrimmed, that she'd found after coming home from the hospital, Eamon's last supper. The perfumed, dusty smell of Isabelle's old wool coat that Eamon had kept in the back of his closet. The feel of her mother's work-strong hands weaving field daisies into her hair.

She wanted to rend her clothes, cover herself in ashes, mourn until there was nothing more to give. She craved the early numbness that had come in the days after Eamon's death—an unfeeling blankness that'd felt deeper than sleep or waking. The kind of reverberating silence she'd hoped her own death might deliver.

She lay there, her legs bent as though she'd been struck down, as though she'd fallen from a great height, her eyes closed against the sky's bright glare, her brain refusing to budge from its iteration: *Isabelle is gone, everyone is gone, and you are gone, too.* A subconscious incantation she couldn't undo. A family that had never been meant to exist in the first place.

CHAPTER TWENTY-SIX

Date: December 1, 1999
Title: Conjoining Ceremony
Subject: The Twelve Maidens & Len Dietz
Setting: Almost Paradise Maidens' Quarters
Medium: Watercolor and graphite on cold-press
Size: 12×14

Dearest Eamon,

We are one month away, a feeling like pending doom. Perhaps they have gotten in my head with all their End Times talk. I try to keep to myself, try to keep grounded in reality as they spin their dark-world prophecies. My bunker room has become the only way I can survive here—that and my few private moments in the greenhouse, listening to the elk moan and call from their pens. It feels like the end of something, although I'm not sure what. Perhaps it's the end of me. I remember tossing in our shared sheets, crying out in my sleep from the dreams of the past that never left me—guttural whimpers full of both remembered panic and a lifetime of mourning.

The conjoining training has been a private matter, and for that I am grateful, if only for my own selfish need to hide from the reality of it. There are moments, out of sheer self-preservation, when I hold my breath and stick my head in the sand, close my eyes and plug my ears, pretend I can't see or hear or feel what is happening all around me, pretend I'm not here, stuck in the middle of this compound, paying witness to it all.

Only Delores and a few other senior Almost Paradise women have been allowed with the maidens for this stage of preparation. I shudder to think of it—these acolyte women teaching Dietz's child brides what's expected of them in bed, how to serve their master's most intimate carnal desires. You know how we always said that you can be sure whenever you hear a preacher or politician rail on one particular subject over and over again that that subject is a personal problem for them? How surprising is it, then, that Len Dietz is obsessed with preaching about "the carnality of the flesh," the "sins of the body," the "traps of impurity," the requirement that "a woman bow to a man's will?" There is one goal here with the maidens, with the upcoming wedding, and it doesn't have anything to do with the "End Times."

The maidens' communal living quarters have been completed, off-limits to everyone else, walled off like any proper concubine compound. The Conjoining Ceremony painting was the only exception, and that only allowed in one sitting, "for posterity's sake." Len positioned in the middle of the maidens' communal center, all of them kneeling around him like fallen petals, the openings to their surrounding bedrooms covered in thick, heavy drapes meant only for Len to part. I shook so much as I painted them there that their shapes blurred into indistinct forms, and maybe that's as it should be—the overtaking of each of them, their bodies, their very being.

I'm afraid I, too, have been lost, sucked under by all the trauma of the past flooding back. What did I think I could achieve, coming here, trying to face down my own demons, make something new of the past? Did I think that I alone could save them? That I alone might be able to make a difference, break through into the light? I have always known the depths of this darkness, the power of this particular chokehold. I have always known what this place has proven over and over again: we the girls, we the women, we the females, are the prey, and all it takes is for one man to be the predator. It is clear who that man is, who that man always has been.

The night has come in as heavy as my heart and mind and spirit. I lay down my pen. I lay down my brush. I cover my head. I am buried alive in this place. I reach for you, imagining your body real next to mine. What that used to feel like, lying next to you, listening to the hum of insects moving through the night, the lap of tide on beach, nighthawks calling, herons leaving the imprints of tracks behind in the dark, your name in my mouth like water.

Forgive me, Eamon. Forgive me.

                              All my love,
                              Isabelle

CHAPTER TWENTY-SEVEN

When Nick and his outfitting group rode in—dust streaked and disheveled, looking as if they'd been doing hard labor instead of on a mountain-lake fly-fishing trip—Silva wondered if he had noticed the tracks coming from the Almost Paradise trail, Len's presence still lingering along with her bodily failure. She wondered if her pain and loss were palpable in the canyon's harsh air, her body and mind and spirit emptied shells, scraped raw and wounded. Everything she'd thought she had now gone blank. A wiped slate.

Nick sent the men to rest in the shade, where they wilted into wrinkled lumps as he unsaddled the stock and refilled the water trough. The unfettered stock rolled up clouds of dust that settled into saddle shadows on their sweaty backs, Tiko the only one that looked fresh for a change. He ran, whinnying, as if to tell everything that had happened while they'd been gone.

Silva waited until the outfitting boat had picked up the men and left, growling a deep, underwater rumble, before walking out slowly to the barn where Nick was cleaning dirty tack. Her tender insides jarred with each step, blood still seeping from inside her, the intestinal and uterine cramps still a near-constant presence despite all the time she'd spent in bed, her nightmares fueled by fevered sleep, something gone wrong inside her, something that wouldn't let go, gnawing and gnawing until it went all the way through her, until it consumed her wholly.

It'd been all she could do to force herself out of bed that afternoon, knowing that Nick would be coming back to the ranch. Knowing that all she'd come to find was irrevocably lost—Isabelle and the baby inextricably wound together, as if they had just been different versions of each other. Just like her dream: the three of them as one. The three of them now gone.

"Hello there," Nick said when he saw Silva, his smile white against the dusty tan of his face. "Babysitting duty's finally over. I just wish the Bull-Gang was still around. Would have taught that lazy group a thing or two."

So that's what it'd been about—Nick versus the town softies. An uneven matchup in every way. He and the Larkins men before him looked as if they could survive just about anything nature dished out. Unlike Silva, seemingly as susceptible to colony collapse as the bees.

He glanced around the grounds, looking pleased. "You got the storm mess cleaned up fast. Too bad you haven't always been the caretaker, whipping things into shape while I get my sorry ass in gear." He rubbed a hand over his face, his beard a lighter shade than his hair, golden whiskers that made him look younger, more vulnerable. "It's about time I got going, maybe bring the bees down early, in between outfitting trips—if you don't mind hanging out with us a little more. I have an order coming in any day now—a new extractor, along with everything else we should need to get the honey flowing," he said.

We. As if they were a team. Sharing the same isolated space together, bent on rebuilding what they'd lost. Banishing their combined host of familial ghosts. But Nick didn't know what Silva had just lost.

He was cheerful, optimistic. Different than before he'd left, the night he'd found the pendant. Before Len and his men had come to pick up their load of guns and ammo. Before her ride to Almost Paradise, everything spiraling out of control. She'd gone out to tell him about Len, about Faith and Isabelle, but instead her guts cramped again, the nausea rising so fast she fought to hold herself still, to not let her anguish show on her face, to act as though her body hadn't already violently voided itself.

Nick frowned in concern, looking at her closely. "Is everything okay?" he asked.

Her throat tight, she nodded. "I'm just tired." Her voice and emotions both threatening to break, her intestines roiling, as distended as the dead sheep's.

"Well, that makes two of us," Nick said. "Let me just get this dirt washed off and then I'll make us dinner and we can call it an early night?" he asked, watching her face closely, trying to pick up the same routine they'd had before, as though nothing had happened in the in-between.

The night she'd gone into his room and looked through his bee books hadn't been that long ago, but the space between then and now was filled with so much she could hardly find her way back to the memory, the emotions she'd felt, studying the photographs of the bee-bearded man and the brood chamber, the diagramed intricacies of the queen's mating dance.

She let Juniper go with Nick to the river to wash up, waiting until they came back, both happily dripping wet, before she told Nick she was too tired to eat, to stay up. Since he'd left, she hadn't eaten anything more than a few bites, her body reverting to its previous, grief-stricken despair: bones sharp enough to sever her from the inside out, her stomach a sunken valley below her ribs, everything grown strangely distinct—bones and sinew, muscles twining tight to bone, like choke-weeds grown desperate for water.

She crawled into bed, but she couldn't sleep any better than she had the nights before, her guts' rumbling movements keeping her awake well after Nick had gone to bed himself, the house silent and dark. When she finally fell asleep, she had another nightmare—a mother keening like the one in Trawler's graveyard, but then the mourning cry became a pregnant girl calling out, clutching her swollen stomach before she suddenly burst open, blooming red, the flesh of her stomach pealing back like flower petals in the sun, exposing her red, pulsing center—a lifeless baby, its limbs like sticks, its face shriveled and gray.

She woke herself crying out, cramping pangs like jaws eating her from the inside out. She got up and walked like a drunken sleepwalker for the kitchen, disoriented and nauseated. She splashed icy water on her face at the sink, trying to shock the nausea and stomach cramps away. Then she pawed through the back of the pantry where she'd seen a bottle of ancient pink liquid antacid and took a long, gulping guzzle, hoping maybe that would help her stomach's distress, but as soon as it hit, her guts let out a series of foreboding squeals and gurgles. Trying to hold herself up, she knocked a jar over on the kitchen counter, sending it clattering, and Juniper let out a startled bark from the bedroom, both he and Nick coming to the kitchen alarmed.

"What's wrong?" Nick asked. Bed-rumpled, he looked like a child who'd been awakened by a fire alarm—all guileless, sleep-blurred worry.

"Just a bad dream," she said, clutching her stomach, filled with foreboding, a taste like metal in the back of her throat.

"I used to have terrible dreams after we moved to town," he said. "Woke up yelling night after night. My mother was convinced it was a sign of parasites. Used this thick, yellow wormer she got in syringes from our vet, who insisted it was safe—that he used it regularly himself. I can still remember the sickly sweet aftertaste. I've always wondered what kind of damage that might have done."

Silva's guts lurched at the thought, and she grimaced at the pain of another cramp.

"Is your stomach bothering you?" Nick asked.

There was no use in trying to hide it, her guts seething in audible distress.

His brow creased, Nick got up and went to his room, came back with the honey jar. "Another of my mother's remedies—a good one, though. Worth trying. Helps calm things down sometimes," he said, scooping out a thick, granulated spoonful of honey and handing it to her.

She took the spoon from him and put it in her mouth as he filled the kettle and put tea in mugs. Eamon had always cared for her when she was sick—brought her crackers and cool washcloths. She hadn't realized how much she'd missed that, too, along with everything else. If only she could lie down, his hands resting on her forehead, stroking her hair back from her face.

"Did your nightmares ever stop?" she asked as Nick handed her a steaming mug.

He shook his head. "Len's mother, Delores, prayed over me for a year, castigating the weakness of my flesh, demanding deliverance from familiar spirits, speaking in tongues and then exclaiming, 'The hand of God on this child, yes Jesus, the hand of God,' but the nightmares only got worse. Finally, she gave up, said it marked me as a suffering prophet, which I thought made me sound like Jesus, sort of." He smiled wryly. "Even though I don't believe in anything anymore besides the ground under my feet, I'll admit I've wondered if the bees were indeed a gift of vision. I sure hope so. I could use one about now."

Silva pictured Nick as a boy locked in a house full of nightmares and praying women. She could imagine it too well now. She'd already seen enough that she was afraid she'd never be able to purge the real nightmare from her mind.

"I ordered some new queens, a new strain. They should be arriving soon," Nick said.

"The bees will be okay with that—stranger-queens coming in?" Silva asked.

"They come in little boxes with candy plugs. You put the box in the hive, and if the bees like the new queen's smell, they eat through the candy plug to free her," Nick said.

"What if they don't like her?" Silva asked, looking over at him.

"Then she stays trapped. Or they cuddle her to death—surround her in a ball of workers until she overheats and dies. But new blood is always a good thing. Otherwise they stagnate, become less viable. Queens from some of the newer strains will lay better workers. The bees know that instinctively. They do what it takes to survive, just like us," Nick said.

His words seized her breath. Both of them trying to fight their way forward, make progress toward some future that wasn't predicated on the strata of trauma.

"I've already arranged things with Mack. I'll drive the hives down to Pittsburg Landing, load everything in the jet boat, and come upriver. A lot easier than trying to get ranch equipment up. The extractor is the only sizable thing, but even that's a lot smaller than farm implements . . . and then we'll begin." He smiled at Silva. "Honeybees in Hells Canyon. It's a nice fit, don't you think?" But everything had changed, even if he didn't know that yet.

"I think I need some fresh air," Silva said, putting a hand to her stomach.

Nick deserved to know what had happened, but even more than that, she *wanted* to tell him what had happened—Len's visit to the ranch, her own visit to Almost Paradise, the miscarriage—but she couldn't see a way to tell him one thing without telling him everything else, all of it like a weight hanging around her neck, pulling her down into the depths. She struggled against the powerful urge to free herself from it, tell Nick everything, from the beginning. She and Eamon had always shared every part of their lives with each other, but since he'd been gone, she'd felt locked within herself with no way out, paralyzed by her inability to say what was really going on, trapped in her aloneness and the wreckage of her life.

Nick made her want to empty herself the same way Eamon had—all his concern, all his quiet care. But she told herself that her burdens weren't for Nick to share. That he had plenty enough of his own. That they were just cabinmates, anyway—although she knew it was already much more than that. Each of them riding the same waters, floating downriver just as Juniper had, rapids and current sweeping them toward their own demise.

"Are you sure you shouldn't just rest?" Nick asked, frowning as she pushed herself up.

"My guts and stomach have been bothering me for the last few weeks, but they've gotten worse. Maybe getting out and moving a little will help?"

she said, trying not to show her real physical weakness any more than she already had. And it was true—her gut troubles had started not long after she'd arrived at the ranch; she was just leaving out that in the time in between then and now, she'd also lost an embryo that she'd thought was a part of her future.

Nick's face remained troubled as she and Juniper left. He walked to the porch and watched them cross the creek bridge, Juniper running ahead of Silva, happy to be on the move.

A half mile up, they took a fork away from the main trail and angled into the hillsides, following the narrow game trail Silva had found the first days she was there, a mining cave nestled in the hills above with an overlook of the river. When she'd first discovered the cave, she'd wondered if the miner who'd dug it out of the cliffside had had an eye for aesthetics or if such lovely placement was just an accident of design. It was farther than she wanted to go, but she needed the expanse of its view to give her distance from her own suffering.

She hiked the steep path, climbing in elevation. Even though it was early enough that the sun wasn't yet scorching, she had to stop several times, sweating with the pain of the unrelenting cramps. Below her, the river receded into a winding line—a tracing at the bottom of the canyon.

By the time she got to the top of the hill, her hair was hanging heavy and wet on the back of her neck. The morning was clear, both the river and the hills glinting with golden light. She pushed the ten extra minutes up to where the mining cave lay, where she might sit and reshape her own direction—although if she left the canyon now, escaping everything she'd come to find, she had nowhere to go but Trawler, and she already knew what kind of future lay there.

She scanned the grass ahead, hoping the rattlesnakes would be holed up in their morning-cool dens. She'd come across another one the other day at the creek. It wasn't big, but there was no reassurance in that—the young ones could be all the deadlier with their unpracticed injections. In the canyon books, there were pictures of dead coyotes, their muzzles swollen with the "death-tattoo," working to paralyze and rot the flesh from the inside out.

On the hillside below her, Juniper was distracted, sniffing something out. He gave no warning as Silva rounded the knob and came face-to-face with a man dressed in desert camo, the same color as the hills. There was no mistaking his look: a rifle slung over his shoulder, a pistol and long knife snug at his hip, a silver pendant hanging from his neck. The Lenite uniform.

He was moving a box into the cave's dark but stood when he saw her, tension strung between his arms like a cat's cradle. She couldn't do anything more than suck in her breath, the loudly ringing alarm bell only in her head. She took a quick step backward, but the trail was too steep for hasty retreat, and she didn't dare turn away with only a few strides between them.

He cocked his head sideways. "You must be the Larkins caretaker," he said, his expression shifting subtly as he ran his eyes over her. "Shouldn't wander so far from home. It's not safe out here," he said mockingly, but a sudden bark shifted his attention—Juniper on the hill below, looking up at them, his body on alert.

The man swung into instant action, raising his rifle and sighting down the scope.

Silva yelled just as the shot rang out—a deafening percussion followed by a rebounding report. The dirt behind Juniper's head leapt and fell back into place as if the sound itself had stirred it. Juniper yelped and tucked his tail, sprinting out of sight as Silva yelled his name, her heart thundering in her chest, her stomach twisting.

"That your dog?" the man asked, his voice casual and cool. "Looked like a coyote to me. Like I said, can't take any chances. It's not safe out here."

"They know what you're doing—the shot-up mountain sheep, the illegal weapons, the girls. They know about all of it—" Silva said, trying to keep her voice from climbing, match threat with threat as her heart hammered in her chest and tears stung her eyes. *Juniper.*

"That right?" the man said, his expression amused. "Well, thanks for letting us know. We'll be sure to keep a lookout. You, too," he said, smiling tightly at her, his eyes full of threat.

Silva edged back down the slope, making sure each step was solid before taking it, not turning her back until the hill dropped her out of sight. She looked everywhere, but Juniper was gone. She tried to run and her stomach hit again, the harsh movement turning into wrenching cramps that crumpled her to the ground, hands and knees in the dirt. She pushed herself up, forcing herself to breathe, light-headed and dizzy with pain and adrenaline. By the time she made it to the gentler inclines, she couldn't stop her legs from wobbling, her joints and guts both strung loose. She was glad for the anchoring clumps of bunch grass that kept her from losing her footing altogether and sliding into the river.

When she finally stumbled into the yard, Nick came out of the barn, his face turning instantly serious as he ran to her side and helped her up to the porch.

"What happened?" he demanded, his voice stern in alarm.

But she couldn't answer, the cramps coming hard and fast, a cold panic seizing up what was left of her pulverized insides as she pushed herself up and ran for the outhouse, her body turning itself inside out.

When she came back out, Nick was waiting. He gestured to the water ditch leading to the cabin from the creek as he helped her back to the house. "Could be giardia. You can never be sure what's going on in the water, what kind of pathogens might have been introduced from up above. It's not something you want to mess around with, especially a severe case," he said.

She'd never considered the water, but she should have. The rotten sheep, bloated and bobbing in the water. A wave of nausea rushed over her. "Did Juniper come back?" she choked out, clenching her guts, the man's face flashing in her mind, his rifle held to his shoulder.

Nick shook his head slowly, his brows furrowed. "Is he lost?"

"We ran into a Lenite. He shot at Juniper—I tried to find him, but he ran away," she blurted, everything crashing in around her head, burying her in the violence of its wake.

Nick's jaw muscles clenched, his body suddenly going still. "Where?"

"At the old mine shaft—I don't know if he hit him or not," she said, crying.

Nick went inside and came back out with a pistol strapped to his waist.

"What are you doing?" she asked, panicking, her body folding in on itself.

His face was white, his arms as tense as coiled snakes. "Going to find him," he said, but Silva wasn't sure if he meant Juniper or the man. "Stay in the house. Don't open the door for anyone." Anger was evident in his every move as he left, retracing her steps.

Her intestinal distress matched her emotions, trading punch for punch, everything coming together in one mass that felled her under its weight. Isabelle and the baby, and now Juniper, too. She feared the worst—Nick taking the fight where it'd been threatening to go all along. She wanted to run out, stop him, but her body wasn't her own to command anymore.

She gripped her middle, listening for gunshots from inside the locked-up house, unable to prevent anything from happening. It'd all been set in motion long before her.

When she heard footfalls on the porch an hour later, her first thought was that the man had come to finish what he'd started, but it was Nick, his face grim, Juniper clutched in his arms. She rushed out, looking for bullet-torn flesh as Nick laid Juniper on the porch, but both dog and man seemed intact. It was only when she took Juniper's head in her hands that she saw the clean-edged hole shot through his ear, noticed the frantic rhythm to his panting, the drool running from his muzzle, his ears pinned back, his eyes glazed in distress.

Silva's agony was like a chokehold. This was her punishment for not listening to her own strangling gut, for thinking she could fix anything.

"I have a med kit. We'll get some water down him, do what we can," Nick said.

Juniper whimpered as Nick settled him on a blanket on the living room floor, just as Silva had the night he'd washed up. He yelped when Silva touched his side, his heart beating so fast under her hands, it seemed it would burst. Silva couldn't stop herself from sobbing.

"It's going to be okay. We'll get you both taken care of. Juniper's tough, he's already proven that," Nick said, but she knew there were no assurances she could count on, however desperate she might try. Life took what it wanted. Left you to pick up the remains.

"I'll get a call into Mack, then ride upstream, try to locate the source of the giardia, if there is one," Nick said, turning his face away, but he wasn't fast enough. Silva saw the dark trace of his thoughts. "I need to boil some more water—don't want to take any more chances."

He got up, but it seemed she'd already used up the chances she'd been given. She wondered if Nick's mother's belief had been right all along: that parasites and nightmares went together.

Before leaving, Nick brought Silva cool washcloths and tea, thoroughly cleaned and dressed Juniper's wounded ear, and administered several syringes of water to Juniper, making sure they were both well-hydrated, the two of them on the same trajectory.

Silva kept vigil at Juniper's side the rest of the morning, running her hands through his soft fur and murmuring words of comfort, soothing herself as much as him as she tried to convince herself that everything would be okay, even though it felt as if everything were ending. Her world tipping on its axis, throwing her overboard to sink into the abyss.

———

By the time Nick got back hours later, Silva could hear a jet boat engine coming upriver fast. Nick went out to meet Mack and when they came in the house, Mack's face was lined deep with worry. "I was prepared for the worst," he said, looking grimly back and forth from Silva to Juniper as though he'd expected both of them to be gone. But how could you prepare yourself for that—the worst—when it seemed to shift into darker and darker territory with each breath?

Mack had brought antibiotics for both her and the dog—his "Canada supplies," he called them, no prescription needed. He quizzed Silva on her symptoms and the timeframe of her illness, and then nodded seriously, agreeing with Nick's giardia conclusion. All the people in the canyon had had a round or two of it, he said, and they'd all become pretty familiar with the treatment, the recovery methods. Since testing for giardia was so faulty and often took weeks to complete, they had all just learned to diagnose and treat it themselves. He said he'd be happy to boat Silva back so she could go to the clinic in Two Rivers, but that they'd most likely send her back with the same meds he'd brought.

Mack and Nick knew only part of what ailed her body, but the last thing Silva wanted to do was leave the canyon—leave Juniper and Isabelle, too—in order to seek medical care, even if she needed it. She realized for the first time that the giardia itself might have been the cause of her miscarriage. Willing to do anything that might help calm her body—both guts and uterus—she swallowed the antibiotics with a tepid glass of boiled water that tasted like blood, dry-heaving when the taste hit the back of her throat, her guts and womb both pulsing with referred pain, her mind blurred with the familiar sinking weight of lament.

"Did you figure out where the giardia might have come from?" Mack asked Nick.

Nick nodded. "I rode up the creek. There was a heap of decaying elk several miles up, hidden behind a brush pile. They didn't get there by chance."

"Dietz's?" Silva asked, fearing the answer. What it would mean, Len poisoning the creek that led to the Larkins place, the same water she'd been drinking for weeks now.

He nodded, his face inscrutable. "Skinned and left to rot."

Her stomach flip-flopped. Len, the cause of her body's distress—the water as poisoned and ominous as her nightmare.

"So, what happens now?" Mack asked.

"I notified Ted, the game warden. Len wouldn't let Ted on his property to examine the elk for disease when he brought them in. Captive elk are often full of stress-related diseases. Not something to take lightly, especially when all that separates them from the wild herds is a bit of wire. The creek runs close by Almost Paradise's pastures. These were dumped. Ted's going to have to get a court order to do it, but with this now, there's plenty to warrant it, especially with the occupation going on, too. They're getting ready for something. War, it would seem." Nick's jaw was set, the scar stretched tight across it. "If he wants a battle, he can have it."

"A group came by when you were gone," Silva finally said, all of it seeming like a betrayal now, speaking with Len and Faith, going to Almost Paradise, even though she hadn't meant it that way.

Nick sat still, considering her carefully, waiting for her to explain. She could see his struggle with it—a new thread, unraveling something she wasn't sure should be unraveled.

"Several men, along with Len Dietz, met a boat in the middle of the night, picked up a load of weapons and ammo, and rode upriver. I called it in the next morning," she said quickly.

"They're gearing up for something, that's for sure," Mack said. "And it ain't good. . . ."

Nick walked to the window, his back to them like a wall. She'd seen him like this before.

Silva regretted speaking the Lenites into existence. She pictured Len standing above her, his hand on her shoulder, marking his territory. She wished she'd been able to say what she'd known immediately upon meeting him: that he was a man who took everything captive.

In the window's reflection, her face was pale and gaunt. Again, she fought the urge to tell Nick everything she hadn't yet been able to say, but all the conclusions had already been finalized. What more did she need to go through before she accepted what the universe seemed intent on telling her? What more would it take for her to understand all that was not meant to be hers? What more would it take for her to stop wishing for things she couldn't have? Going back to the boarded-up cabin, nothing remaining but herself, everything stopped before it had even had a chance to begin.

She looked down, fighting the sting of tears behind her eyes. After being able to suppress outward emotion for so long, why did it come to this now? She blinked hard. She wouldn't cry, not here, not now, with Mack and Nick watching. She looked at her hands mutely, worrying her torn cuticles, tucking her misery and grief back where she hoped they couldn't see it.

After Mack left, Nick said she should go to bed, get some rest, but she refused to leave Juniper's side. Just as Nick couldn't forgive himself for leaving his baby brother behind, she couldn't forgive herself for going to the mainland and leaving Eamon, alone and dying. She wouldn't do the same ever again.

Nick dozed off late in the evening, sitting slumped in the chair. Silva watched him sleep, the long scar highlighted along the contours of his face, until she, too, dozed off.

When she awoke, Nick was standing and looking out the window, the sound of the river amplified in the still air as light advanced along the canyon's rim, the sky shifting and rolling—the same as her insides, despite Mack's pills. A blanket Nick had laid over her fell from her shoulders when she got up. On the floor, Juniper didn't move and she panicked, dropping to her knees beside him, but when she touched his side, his eyes shifted under his lids.

"Made it through the night," Nick said. "Sleep has a way of healing everything."

She studied his face. "My grandfather used to say that. You remind me of him," she said.

Nick glanced at her questioningly. "He was a good guy, right?"

She looked out the window. "The best there was."

"How are you feeling?" Nick asked, his voice soft with concern.

She smoothed her wrinkled shirt to give herself time to lie, say she was fine, but it seemed in one fell swoop she'd lost the ability to pretend she was okay when she wasn't.

"You're nothing but skin and bones—look like you'd blow away if the wind came up," he said, walking over and circling her wrist between his thumb and index finger to illustrate his point, his hand warm on her skin. "The giardia hit you hard. You've got a lot of ground to make up," he said, but he didn't know how hard she'd been hit, what kind of ending she'd reached.

"Don't we all?" She pushed herself up, willing her legs to obey.

"I hope you'll give the canyon a second chance," he said, and she could hear it buried in his voice—the sincerity and hope, along with notes of hidden anger and desperation. He, too, had staked everything on this one final thing, this one last way to make it.

They were standing close enough she could sense his body heat, and it was all she could do not to lean into the shelf of it, find stillness there, as if taking shelter from a battering wind.

"I don't have anywhere else to go," she said, even if it weren't exactly true—Fallon's cabin boarded up and waiting. His ashes drifting on its shore. She was pretty certain if Nick knew everything she'd done, he wouldn't be so eager to have her stay.

CHAPTER TWENTY-EIGHT

Babies like dust, like powder, their skin like paper, like ash, babies like cordwood, stacked. Babies like you, babies like her, babies like them, babies like him—a new likeness, a vision projected, a cluster of wavering hearts. Her lips pulling at your breasts, her milk streaming from your chest, her whorled nest of hair that you breathe in like light, this holiness made manifest, this heavenly angelic earth. You hold her tight, keep her close, touch her smooth, plump skin, lowering her into the water that breaks like glass beneath her, covering her as it covered you once, too, this reminder of air, of lungs and blood, of crystalline sunlight shot through. She cries and your breasts release, a soaking for both of you, washing away the sins of the fathers, the sins of the flesh, the sins of your inner being made manifest. She will live afresh, she will breathe, she will rise up in holiness.

CHAPTER TWENTY-NINE

Mack brought something up for you. I almost forgot," Nick said, knocking on the bedroom door before handing Silva a large, stiffly padded brown envelope, addressed to her at the Larkins Ranch in unfamiliar handwriting, no return address. "A secret admirer?" he said, lifting his eyebrows at her before closing the door behind him, leaving her alone to open it.

She was glad he had. When she tore the envelope open, she found a raw-edged twelve-by-twelve watercolor inside—another of Isabelle's paintings, this one both larger and more detailed than the pregnant girls. "Baptism of the Virgin Maidens" was written on the back in Isabelle's looping cursive, and Silva recognized the scene with a start. It was at the Larkins Ranch's small beach, Sheep Creek surging into confluence with the Snake, a line of girls standing thigh-deep in the river, flanked by Faith at one end and Len Dietz on the other. Faith's gaze was as grave as Dorothea Lange's "Migrant Mother," looking out into the unknown as if she were waiting for some foretold disaster to unfold. As if she were carrying the world's burdens on her shoulders.

It was the same look Isabelle had captured before. The same brushstrokes, the same color palette, the same mood and tone. Dressed from head to toe in white, the girls had their heads covered with lace veils. Water streaming from their outstretched arms, long white dresses wet against their child bodies, they looked like repeating replicas of Christ the Redeemer at the summit of Mount Corcovado. Off to the right, Len Dietz was bent over, submerging the last maiden, her deific child's face visible just under the water's silvery surface, her veil floating like a shroud behind her, her eyes closed, her hands clasped to her chest in worship.

Len on Nick's family land, baptizing his child brides in the Snake River of Hells Canyon, its waters bringing one kind of death or another over and over again. Isabelle serving as witness to the virgin maidens' baptism— before Len took the girls as his concubines. Before his seed grew in their wombs. Before they were shrouded in birthing blood instead of lace.

Silva went over every detail, the dusty smell of watercolor like some kind of direct communication from Isabelle, as though she'd meant for Silva to come find her. A trail of crumbs, one painting at a time. It wasn't until Silva looked in the envelope again that she saw the small slip of torn paper, five words written above Faith's signature: *Seek and ye shall find.*

Silva stood up so fast, her head swam. A warning? A sign—the only one Faith could give—that Isabelle was still there, still on the compound, still waiting to be found?

She hastily got out the other paintings she kept buried under Eamon's journals and studied each one for further clues on Isabelle's journey and disappearance into the abyss of Almost Paradise, but there was nothing there to give her any more than she already understood: Isabelle had painted things so intimate to the Lenites it took Silva's breath away. A part of the inside circle, it would seem. Faith and Isabelle and Len—all connected in one scene, even if Isabelle was an invisible observer.

Silva put the new painting with the others. Faith's cryptic words were a puzzle for Silva to solve, even if Isabelle was just another grave dug under their palaver tree, even if it felt as if Silva had been doing nothing but seeking Isabelle her whole life.

———

"Come get the bees with me," Nick said, the two of them sitting on the shore later that afternoon, Nick throwing sticks for Juniper, Mack's contraband antibiotics finally having helped both of them after all, even if Silva's guts still rumbled threateningly every time she ate.

Juniper's ear had crusted over the bullet hole's raw edges, the wound healing itself closed like bark growing over a severed limb. Her uterus shrinking, its seep drying, her stomach a shrunken plane under her ribs as if nothing had occupied it. *It just takes time.* A presence come and gone.

"It'll just be a quick trip downriver once I'm back from the next outfitting trip. I'd like you to be a part of it," Nick said, his voice sincere, as though summer were still stretched out peacefully in front of them instead of everything being turned upside down, shaken, and spun.

Silva felt like she was reeling, trying to understand what other sacrifices might be demanded of her before it was all over.

Nick planned out loud, said he'd leave Sage and Tiko at the ranch, ride the pack-string back up to his truck after the outfitting trip, then pick up the beekeeping equipment and drive it down to the landing where they could meet, get the bees, and then boat up Hells Canyon to the ranch—a new piece of the canyon's history. Another hope for survival, everyone bent on demonstrating their own measures of self-sufficiency. Her stomach rumbled loudly and she pressed her hand against it.

Warm air rushed down the slopes to the river, its silvery surface flowing like molten metal. In the wake of her failures, Silva was glad for Nick's order—a checklist to mark off, one thing at a time. She felt as if she were a passenger in a boat without a rudder, without paddles, spinning dizzying circles on the surface, nothing to direct her other than the vagrancies of wind or current. *Was. Is. Past. Present. Future.* The whole world changing with each designation, each repetition, each difference of categorization.

"Okay," she said finally. A giving in, a giving up. A surrender. She was exhausted by her own pain and sorrow. Tired of her own head, her own wash of emotions and unanswerable questions. She needed to mark a passage, find a clear line, a new sense of direction—one that didn't end in disaster, even if the canyon were always threatening otherwise.

"Great," Nick said, smiling widely.

———•◦•———

He spent the following days getting ready, clearing a spot for the apiary behind the house, sheltered in the lee of the hills, and completing all the extraction-room preparations. Each evening he cooked dinner after patrolling the ranch's perimeters, keeping watch for trespassers just as Mack had warned Silva to do, even if it had always been too late to stop Len's trespasses.

The night before Nick was to ride the pack-string out, he was in the kitchen for hours, making a feast to celebrate the bees' coming arrival, he said, as well as get some meat back on Silva's bones.

"I'd like to take you to the Morgans', meet Dean and Kay—my surrogate family," he said as he laid out their plates, the tiny kitchen table already heaped with food. "Show you where I live when I'm not with you in the canyon. Kay's got the best barn and arena around. Used to be a barrel racer. Doesn't compete anymore, but in her early days she ran pro. All the girls in the area still look up to her, bring her their horses to train." His pride was clear, everything that had defined his life, right there within reach.

Silva fiddled with her fork, smoothed the napkin on her lap. She wasn't sure how to navigate her own expectations, let alone others'—especially Nick's surrogate family's. When she was young, Silva's quiet introversion had always made people think she was judging them, adding up their deficiencies, noting their failures. *She just thinks she's better than everyone else.* But the irony was that her own failures muted her more keenly than anyone knew.

"What's happening with the occupation?" she asked, trying to separate the known from the unknown. Figure out her next steps.

"The FBI has started putting more pressure on—set up a perimeter around the visitor center, blocking road access so the Lenites can't come and go. In retaliation, Len released footage of him and his men shooting the big, wooden welcome sign to splinters with a fully automatic machine gun. It was supposed to be a warning, but they just look like petty bullies," Nick said. "Charges are in motion to try to shut them down, but we don't know when yet."

"What *are* the charges for that—for all of it?" Silva asked. Holding a place captive, claiming one woman and girl after another, calling himself the chosen one.

"There are plenty to choose from: possession of firearms and dangerous weapons in federal facilities, depredation, theft, destruction of government property, felony conspiracy to impede officers of the US from discharging their official duties through the use of force, intimidation, or threats—just to name a few. But if Len fights the feds, which he promises to do, it could get ugly really fast," Nick said. "Nobody wants that outcome."

"It seems like that's exactly what they want," Silva said, then asked carefully, "Are the same people you knew at the compound still living there?"

She was thinking of Faith and Isaac in particular, Faith somewhere around Nick's same age. Silva imagined them as early teens before Nick escaped. They would have made a pretty couple. Silva could imagine them finding comfort in each other's arms, even if they'd only been children; obviously being a child on the Almost Paradise compound had spared no one from anything. The boy, Isaac, was a crippled captive. He would have just been born when Nick escaped the compound, Silva realized, time like a vise pressing in, compressing reality into something else, endings and beginnings blended together.

"Some, yes, but there's been a new surge of people joining in the last few years, everyone stocking up on guns and conspiracy theories along with their religion," he said. "They've gotten more militant since I was there, more extreme. Always in combat gear, running around playing soldier, 'training' by blowing human-shaped targets to smithereens."

"Like the guy who shot Juniper."

"Yes," Nick said, looking at her, the frown on his face joining the old scar tissue.

"Is that what happened to your face—that scar?" Silva finally asked.

He kept his eyes on his plate. "I was angry for a long time when I was young, fought a lot," he said, as if he weren't still, rage bubbling there under his calm-willed surface. Silva imagined blood and blades. A lifetime of being locked in battle, Nick and Len circling each other like dogs readying for the kill.

"I'm glad you found a surrogate family," she said, and he looked over at her quickly.

"They must have done something right," she went on. "You seem to have turned out all right. . . ." She smiled and put her hand on his for a quick moment.

"Well, we'll see what the bees think about that. The proof's in the pudding . . . or, in this case, the honey, I guess," Nick said, smiling back at her.

Silva imagined Eli's rainbow-colored hive boxes in the canyon, his worker bees deciding the fate of Nick's new queens as they all moved into their new home, fraught as it might be.

Outside, a flicker winged by the window, the orange-red of its undertail flashing. It landed on a ponderosa and scuttled to the backside, where it hammered against a dead branch, the ringing knocks echoing in the quiet air. Deadwood and live wood. Bonsai and bees. Like twin skins, like a mother tongue, like home—wherever and whatever that proved to be.

She'd been reading Eamon's notes about talking trees—their symbiotic relationship with fungi a kind of deep, hidden intelligence. *Mycorrhizae*—a vast network nobody had known existed until now, even if for millennia people like Eamon, like Silva, had understood trees' communication, each one a speaking entity to itself. Each one a lost DNA connection when it was gone. The forest's hub trees sharing their resources with the under-story nursery, using the network—the "wood-wide web"—to identify and nurture seedlings as well as trees in distress, communicating need and excess through a mass of fungal threads. The mycelium fed the hub tree soil nutrients in exchange for the photosynthesis sugar it lacked. Each thing worked together to sustain the whole, each thing affected when the other was gone. Everything a part of a larger, unseen rhythm.

Silva just hoped that like the bristlecones, she might be able to outsurvive herself, find rootedness on the other side of her own calamity—Nick's garden that she'd planted leafing into tidy green rows, Eamon's bonsai sprouting new buds, even her newly formed hackberry bonsai unfurling tender new leaves toward the sun, transforming itself into the new shape she hoped it would take. Isabelle sending her honeysuckle bonsai painting out into the world but leaving Len's pregnant girls tucked away—bellies taut and round with new life, their faces too young for their bodies' biological maturity, each thing contradicting the other. The sins of loving and leaving, of enacting your own fate.

"I lived on a commune when I was young, before my mother died," she said suddenly, looking out the window. "I don't remember much about that time except the giant community garden and always being with my mother. I played in the dirt and ran barefoot through the fields, listening to her sing as she gardened." She glanced over at Nick. "I've never been able to stop thinking about her or the life we had then. Do you think it ever goes away—those previous things we've lived, the people who once made up our whole world? Sometimes I wish it'd all just disappear, so I could stop always trying to figure out what went wrong and dreaming up alternate realities with new, better outcomes."

Nick's face flashed with compassion as he reached out and put his hand on Silva's. "I think maybe everyone's always just searching for answers no matter what. No matter what's happened to them. I'm sorry about your mom, and your grandfather. I'm sorry you were left alone. I know what that feels like."

She wrapped her fingers into his. "I know you do."

She looked at their hands, intertwined together, the warmth of his touch like a balm.

"What was she like, your mother?" Nick asked.

It was a question most people usually steered clear of, not wanting to cause pain, but the real pain came from not being able to talk about your loved one after they were gone—a disappearance more agonizing than the first. Though she'd just said she wished all the memories would disappear, it was the remembering that held everything together.

"She was beautiful and strong," Silva said. "She loved being outside, loved her plants. Everyone always asked her how to do everything. I remember thinking she was the smartest person alive, that she could do anything. Maybe because that's what she always told me about myself. With her, I was never afraid. I think that's what I noticed the most when I finally understood she was gone—how frightening the world was without her."

"It doesn't ever leave, does it? All that maternal love and security," Nick said. "My mom was everything to me, too. We were friends—coconspirators, really. We did everything together. Sometimes I still feel like I could just call her up, tell her what's happened. She's still the only person I want to tell a lot of things to. I wish I could tell her about you. . . ."

Silva shook her head. "I'm nothing but a mess. But I wish we could both tell our moms about each other, too. Tell them about our lives. It sounds like they would have known all the right things to do."

"It seems like you're doing okay to me." Nick squeezed Silva's hand in his. "You just have to give it a little more time. Things always make more sense after a while. Or at least, life seems to find its own path, whether we try or not."

"I hope that's true," Silva said, thinking about Isabelle, thinking about the lost baby, thinking about what her life would be now, but she couldn't see beyond it, beyond this moment.

"So your life on the island with your grandfather, it was good?" Nick asked.

Silva relaxed a little, leaned back in her chair. That past, she could handle.

"Yes, it was good," she said. "We were like partners in crime, living out in our little cabin in the woods, tending trees, rowing on the Sound, keeping to ourselves. Everyone called us 'the Tree People.' I always liked that—being a tree person. Still do, obviously," she said as Nick laughed.

"I can see you like that, as a little tree girl."

"I was convinced it was my superpower—being able to talk to trees and have them talk back. You can imagine what the other kids thought about that."

"I don't know—seems like a pretty good superpower to me," Nick said. "I just thought I should be able to fly like Superman, and we all know how *that* goes. Jumping off the barn roof with a red polyester cape on and landing in the manure pile with a giant splat. My mom had to scrub me down with the hose outside after that one. She sent me to bed early, said the smell alone should teach me a lesson."

"I guess we've both had to learn a few lessons about the limitations of our superpowers," Silva said, smiling.

Nick nodded toward the bonsai sitting out on the porch. "Looks like you've done a pretty good job of keeping yours intact."

RTY

press

as before the End of the
en Dietz. We have held
k, marking this end time,
his virgin birth, preparing
edding of the Maidens
he End, the apocalypse.
ct, have been lowered to
luding mine—have been
c lights used, no singing,
s of scriptures and prayers
rt from one of his wives
my full-covering veil, my
all—all these trappings of
whirling with grief and
pale. I have become now

Today the maidens have been ga

the Cleansing Ceremony, where M

the other wives will ceremonially l

their private parts, brushing and

powdering their skin white, and o

wedding tomorrow. I have been su

pre-wedding night—this last nigh

glowing dark against their pallid ch

society, to each other, to themselves

What have I been doing these

been? How have I disappeared so f

the island, it both feels as though

though a whole lifetime has come a

drifting years. A haze of memories r

I thought I was finding myself, but

and more lost. Going further and fu

from the life I was meant to live.

You remember how much I was

realities—those branching momen

leading one way or another, changi

It feels that way now—if only I wou

choice, the choice to stay with you,

our life together last forever, everythi

resolved, healed, made whole. Inste

own ending. This place, these peopl

trapped by my own naive beliefs tha

this life's losses by descending into th

I have done this to myself. Just li

worst enemy. Handing over my own

Dietz, someone like Mother Delores

by recording what they have done an

able to change anything. I have realized the full, unending futility of my own life. Nothing kept. Not my child from so long ago. Not you. Not the island or my life on it. Nothing that has ever mattered. I wish I had let you come for me, bring me back. Even now I wish for rescue. How pathetic is that?

Someday—perhaps in another life—I will learn to rescue myself. Learn what it means to make my way in a world bereft of anything but death and loss and lostness. I only hope that I can make my way to you again someday. In this life, or another. Find what it means to lay down my burdens from the past and make something new. Something with meaning that lasts.

I hope you make it through the end. I hope we all do.

All my love,
Isabelle

CHAPTER THIRTY-ONE

JULY 2001

After Nick left for his outfitting trip, Silva locked Juniper in the house, saddled Tiko, and rode back up the trail to Almost Paradise. This time it was Sage who was left pacing the fence, whinnying at them. It seemed to calm Tiko, being the one doing the leaving instead of the one left behind.

This time Silva knew where she was going, what to expect. What she knew she could fight back against. What she understood couldn't wreck her—at least that's what she hoped.

When they got to Almost Paradise's wire gate, she left it open, Tiko tethered in the shade where they might escape quickly. She walked to the main structure, cautiously scanning the surroundings, trying to analyze each detail and sort each possibility of where Isabelle might be.

When she heard music coming from the main building, she stopped abruptly. The high quaver of a woman's voice was joined by a few faltering piano notes, and then other women's voices joined in until the singing swelled into form.

The front door burst open, a pale-faced girl looking out past Silva, then, startled, right at her. "Oh!" the girl said, shock clear on her face. Then she cried out, "Mother Delores!"

An older, heavy-bosomed woman, her gray hair pulled into a low bun, came to the door, appraising Silva, her expression inscrutable. "Sister Faith isn't available for tours right now, but she will be back as soon as she can," she said, her words devoid of any real meaning, her tone as stiff and rehearsed as a prerecorded phone message.

Behind her, the building had fallen ominously quiet. Silva pictured Lenite women huddled behind the doors, clutching each other protectively, shielding themselves against the intruder.

Then, unexpectedly, the older woman held the door open. "Please, come in," she said, attempting a smile that didn't move past her mouth. But Silva didn't feel welcome, didn't feel anything but a sense of building dread—alone with these people, at their house of worship. Finally this close to finding what she'd left Trawler for.

Silva's soul recoiled at the idea of submitting herself to the Lenites, a "guest" on their compound. The oppression of their faith was like weeds nothing could kill, each repudiation, each assault against them only serving for further growth—a spreading that overtook everything within its reach. But there was no choice. She stepped up the stairs and entered the sanctuary.

Inside, a few high, yellow-glass windows let in light, but after the brightness outside, the central room's interior was dim enough that Silva's eyes had to adjust. The space was Spartan, a large wooden cross hanging at the far end, folding chairs lined up behind a sermon podium, an upright piano to the right. The singers—a cluster of women and teen girls—stood in front. Dressed in floor-length, long-sleeved, cuffed and collared dresses, their long hair either in braids or an anchoring of barrettes, they stared at Silva without reserve. There was a pall of concern hanging in the air, feeling of impending trauma, Silva's visit part of something that hadn't been rehearsed—though she'd obviously been expected. Everyone looking at her with a kind of knowingness that left her cold. She reached up instinctively to smooth her loose-blown hair.

The older woman, obviously the one in charge, said, "I'm Mother Delores Dietz, and this is Sister Esther, Twelfth Maiden." She held the pale-faced girl in front of her by the shoulders, as if squaring her off against an adversary. "Sister Esther, please welcome our guest," she ordered.

A Dietz family affair, Len's mother a part of the compound, too, commanding the same subservience as her son, training up girls meant to serve her son's needs, calling them by the number of their conquering, enforcer of Len's patriarchy.

Esther's face blanched whiter than before. She stood very straight in her long dress, and that's when Silva saw it—a perfectly round orb extending from underneath her apron.

"Would you care for some coffee or tea?" she asked Silva stiffly, matching Faith's formality of manners, though Esther couldn't have been more than fourteen. A pregnant child-Lenite, her expression waxen and panicked—a girl far too young to carry a child, far too young for childbirth.

Silva's insides tightened with remembered cramps, a sorrow that overtook her so fast she didn't have time to prepare for it. She wanted to reach out and pull the girl in close enough that they couldn't grab her back, scream, *What have you done to her?* Fight back for all of them—Isabelle, Meg Larkins and her baby, and now Esther, too—all the ones who'd been lost, who'd been taken, captured alive, until they were formed into Len's receptacles, emptied out and reshaped in the image of his making.

Delores held out her arm. "Let us serve you. Won't you please join us?" she said, walking to a set of linoleum-covered stairs, disguising her commands in the language of generosity, demanding that everyone in her purview follow a strictly prescribed protocol.

"I came here to find someone," Silva said, scanning the women's shuttered faces, all of them watching her, her urgency and agitation juxtaposed against their watchful, careful reserve.

"Yes," Delores said simply, ushering everyone downstairs.

The others didn't speak as they descended, following Delores with a quiet rustling of skirts into an open kitchen space arranged with more folding chairs and tables. It smelled of cleaner wax and coffee, the sugary scent of fruit baking. Open shelves from ceiling to floor were stacked with colorful jars of home-canned goods—apples, pears, peaches, cherries, and green beans. Against the back wall, bags of wheat and powdered milk were piled waist-high around a back door like a bomb-shelter trench. Silva wondered if the door led to bunkers with more stockpiles—enough food to last years, even with a compound full of consuming Lenites.

Esther ushered Silva to a seat at the end of a table and stood with her hands clasped behind her back, glancing quickly at Delores before asking if Silva took anything in her coffee.

Folding her own hands in front of her, Silva said, "Cream, please," her nerves roiling. She, too, could play the part—all polite manners and murmuring consent—even if all she wanted to do was jump up and run, pull Esther out along with her. She looked around to see how many more of the women and girls were pregnant, wondering again where Isaac had taken Faith's child, where all the other young children were, where Faith was in the maze of this place.

The women broke into choreographed action as though they'd rehearsed this, too—serving Isabelle's granddaughter pie and coffee. Like Faith and Delores, they all seemed to know exactly who Silva was and why she'd come. They got out white ceramic mugs and plates and pulled pans of warm pie out of the oven, working in unison, the younger ones taking plates of pie and mugs of coffee to the tables where the older women were already sitting.

Silva wondered if they'd all known Isabelle, if they all knew what had happened to her. If Isabelle—and, over a decade before her, Meg Larkins—had sat in the same basement kitchen, serving or being served as Silva was, eating pie off the same plates, drinking coffee out of the same mugs. If Meg Larkins, pregnant with Len's son, had been served as a holy woman of the faith, under Delores's thumb, servile and obedient all the way to her death.

Esther brought Silva a piece of cherry pie and a mug of caramel-colored coffee, the cream already stirred in. Delores sat next to Silva and took a sip of her black coffee, studying Silva over the rim of her cup. When she set down her cup, the room suddenly went quiet.

"You are here for Isabelle," she said, each syllable laden with implied meaning. She had known what Silva was looking for all along.

"Yes," Silva said, glancing around, working to keep the emotion out of her voice, to act as calm as they all were, their faces and eyes as carefully veiled as if they were shrouded in cloth.

Delores paused, tilting her head and regarding Silva the same way Len Dietz had in the hardware store—a look of muted challenge, asking something of her, expecting something of her. "I'm afraid she's no longer with us," she finally said.

Silva tried to stiffen herself against the words, but it was too late, her body sagging under the familiar crushing weight. *No longer with us.* Everything she'd feared, what deep down she'd already suspected: there might not ever be any redemption. She thought of Isabelle's mound in the cross-studded graveyard and was overcome by a wave of nausea, the uneaten pie in front of her oozing thick red syrup out its sides as if it were bleeding out.

Delores pushed her chair back and stood. "Come. I have something to show you." She didn't wait to see if Silva was following as she got up and walked to the bunker door.

Silva hoped it would lead back outside where she might find escape— both from this place and the emotions overtaking her, building like a dam ready to break. Instead, Delores went down a short hallway and opened a door to a small, dark room illuminated with a million tiny blinking lights, the whole space filled with radio equipment: wires, boxes, switches, microphones, speakers.

She flipped a few switches and the air came alive, a humming feed, disembodied voices crackling the speakers. She adjusted the squelch and turned up the volume, concentrating on one feed—a deep male voice, modulated and clear.

"Why? you ask. I'll tell you why. The world has become greedy. Greedy for wealth. Greedy for power. Greedy for everything that is temporal. It is up to us, my sisters and brothers. We must stop the darkness before it consumes us all. Before there is nothing left but husks after the plague of locusts has come—the

world's carnal appetites consuming, consuming, consuming. It is up to us, the Chosen Ones, to heed His call, who, in this evil world, can still recognize His voice. 'Come,' He says. 'Come and bring to me your children, the fruit of your womb, and together we will build God's Army.' Do you hear His call? Will you heed His voice? The time is here. Be strong and rejoice. The Lord's Army is marching forward—an unstoppable force."

Delores reached over, clicking the knobs off, and the sudden silence was deafening.

Silva felt electricity spool and spark along the back of her neck. "Why have you brought me here?" she asked, stepping backward. There was nowhere to run, buried in the bowels of this place, no route of escape. Rising panic threatened to overtake her.

"It is the Lord directing your path," Delores said, walking to the last doorway in the narrow hall before stopping again. "The Dowry Room," she announced as she opened the door, exposing a room full of thick woven rugs and large wooden chests, a commanding armoire on the back wall along with a tall, spindled wooden crib and high-backed high chair, lacy blankets and baby clothes stacked inside the open chests—hand-stitched Victorian items in soft cream hues, looking as if they'd been transported hundreds of years forward to Almost Paradise's bunker.

"What is all of this?" Silva asked, her heart speeding, her mouth gone dry.

Delores walked over and opened the armoire's doors.

At first all Silva could see was yards and yards of white spilling out, and then, finally, she understood what it was. The same wedding dress Isabelle had painted all the maidens in, yards of white satin covered in hand-stitched lace embroidery and studded with pearls.

Silva held herself very still, swallowing hard, trying to stop herself from shaking.

"The wives of the Chosen One shall cleave unto the House of the Lord, their offspring forming the Nation of God," Delores said, her eyes flitting to Silva's stomach and back up again as though Silva were already destined

to become one of them—a succubus to Len Dietz's desires. Isabelle's abandoned, grieving granddaughter, looking for answers to her own lost faith,
come to be Len's wife, taking up where Meg Larkins had left off.

Silva choked back the waves of fear threatening to overtake her, tried
to calculate a way to bolt past Delores and the others awaiting her in the
church kitchen. She imagined being locked in the bunker dowry room, left
with the baby crib and wedding dress until Len Dietz came calling for her.

Delores placed the wedding dress back into the armoire and turned to
face Silva. "Your grandmother didn't heed God's will. Will you?"

Someone was walking down the hall toward them, and Silva's nerves
jumped with the wild hope that it was Nick coming for her, even if there
was no way he could know where she was, in this place meant somehow to
convince her, to pull her in among them, another of Len's women. A woman
who'd been carrying "the fruit of the holy union"—her body to be given over
to Len, destined for his "holy family."

Instead, Faith rushed in, her face ashen, her eyes wide with alarm, her
sleeves rolled up past her elbows to expose her thin, pale-skinned arms and
raw-scrubbed hands, her apron and dress soaked with enough fresh blood
that it looked as if she'd just sustained a fatal injury.

"There's a situation. The birth—" she said breathlessly, her voice as shaken
as her expression.

Delores stepped between her and Silva. "The Lord's will be done," she
stated, her voice low and commanding, a silencing reprimand.

Faith dropped her head as if she'd been slapped. "The Lord's will be
done," she repeated, all the color drained from her face as she left, rushing
back to the bloody scene from which she'd come. A birthing gone terribly
wrong. A girl bleeding out according to god's will.

Silva's insides responded, twisting and heaving until she felt as if she were
about to be sick—the close air of the buttressed dowry room, the sight of so
much fresh blood on Faith's dress, the overpowering presence of Delores
Dietz. Len's mother seemed as bent on holding Silva captive as her son was.

She could hear the women in the kitchen, the sound of their voices rising after Faith's sudden appearance and departure—a swelling of volume, urgent, fast-blended syllables coupled with discordant, guttural moans rounded with vowels and the hiss of consonants so that it sounded as if dozens of people were chanting in a medieval language Silva had never heard before. The hair on Silva's arms stood as Delores paused, looking out toward the voices as if she were translating the unintelligible moans into meaning—the all-seeing, all-knowing cult mother-figure.

Delores addressed Silva. "Abigail needs my assistance," she said, the words hanging heavy with dark meaning. She walked out of the room quickly, past the radio equipment, and to the kitchen where the women were assembled in a circle, their heads thrown back, their eyes closed and hands uplifted, swaying in rhythm to their guttural praying. They didn't stop, didn't open their eyes, as Delores walked past them. Silva followed her up the stairs.

"There's a storm brewing," Delores said, stopping abruptly at the front door, holding Silva captive with her gaze. "And the second angel poured out his vial upon the sea; and it became as the blood of the dead and every living soul died in the sea. And the third angel poured out his vial upon the rivers and fountains of waters; and they became blood. . . .'" She paused, her hand on the doorknob. "'There shall be signs in the sun, and in the moon, and in the stars; and upon the earth distress of nations . . . the sea and the waves roaring in great tribulation, such as was not since the beginning of the world to this time, no, nor ever shall be.'"

Delores opened the door and stepped away to attend the birth-gone-wrong, releasing Silva.

Silva made herself keep pace as she walked across the lawn toward the fence, every fiber of her being acutely alert. It was everything she could do to restrain herself from sprinting away so fast she kicked up clods of dirt and gravel, everything scattering in her wake.

The sun beat down on the back of her neck, and the wind blew small cyclones of dust, the sky an eerie shade of purple-blue above the cemetery.

Perhaps the canyon books were right after all. Perhaps this place was cursed. A place meant to eat you up and spit you out—your existence nothing more than a pile of bones. Almost Paradise's grounds were filled with the remains of the lost, women and girls crying out from underneath the earth. A graveyard full of supplicants—shells sucked empty, husks left to drift. Isabelle's honeysuckle nurse tree.

Silva pictured the Snake's waters running red, dead sheep floating down. Her nightmare of the gray woman swimming upcurrent, her agonized scream. Everyone always trying to warn Silva, not realizing it was too late for anything but mourning, everything put into motion long before she could do anything to stop it, before she could right any wrong, before she could enact any different outcome, everything over before it'd even begun. Storms raging around her, propelling her to her own annihilation.

Tiko saw her coming and whinnied, tossing his head in impatience, as ready for flight as she was. She ran the last several yards to him, rushing to loosen the reins and rope from the fence rail. A bucket of water sat in the shade next to him. *Isaac.*

She looked around quickly for him, the wild, trapped boy who reminded her of Nick—Nick, a boy who, in other circumstances, could have been another Lenite trained to harness his own destructive powers, abusing those beneath him. She wondered how fast Isaac, too, might run away if he were set loose, his leg made whole. Faith, too—Almost Paradise's midwife, a woman who'd seen the direct results of Len's preying, his pedophilia all a part of being "god's family," it seemed—another fresh grave coming soon, or perhaps two: one for the birthing child-mother, and one for her doomed fetus. *Another and another and another.* Enough to call out from the grave in voices meant to be silenced. Enough to haunt anyone all the way to their own tomb.

She wondered what kind of warnings Isabelle had gotten before joining Len, conscripting herself to his "care." Everything some form of recurrent injury she hadn't been able to escape, a maiming that stretched a lifetime, a family line, no escape from the reality of her own personal fate—searching for something that could never be recovered, each loss renewing the devastation of all the previous losses until they built into a mountainous mass that sat atop her, pressing her into the unrelenting depths that had finally claimed her as their own.

Silva leapt on Tiko and let him have his head, his hooves skidding against the trail's loose rocks and dust, everything a blur of speed as they careened away from the compound. She imagined cartwheeling off the side of the trail, her body airborne as she fell hundreds of feet before smashing into the ravine that led to dark waters. She could feel the loss of traction, the ground suddenly gone from under her, leaving her plummeting, gasping for breath. The same as her nightmares, except she had already tumbled down, had already found what was waiting below in that abyss, rushing her own hasty escape.

CHAPTER THIRTY-TWO

⬦✴⬦

Your fingers are five and ten, your toes are ten and five; twenty nails and nailbeds; teeth: twenty-eight, like appendage knuckles of the hands and feet; the big joints: twelve; ribs: twenty-four; and all the two-by-twos: eyes, eyebrows, cheeks, nostrils, ears, shoulders, clavicles, breasts, elbows, wrists, hands, hips, knees, ankles, heels, arches, balls of feet. Your spine, thirty-three. Your skull, twenty-two. Your hands, twenty-seven. Your feet, twenty-six. Your legs, thirty. Two hundred and six bones. You are mine body, mine self, mine skeleton, and mine flesh. Bone of my bone, blood of my blood, skin of my skin, flesh of my flesh. You are mine, and I am yours. You are me, and I am you. We are thee we are me we are you we are I we are bones and flesh and spirit and life and death.

CHAPTER THIRTY-THREE

JULY 2001

Silva spent the next days in a haze, doing nothing but the stumbling motions of living: sleeping, getting dressed, trying to eat and then pushing the food away, her stomach rejecting everything she put in it. A place deep in her abdomen pulsed like a smashed hand, and she wondered how much damage a body could sustain before it was broken beyond repair.

One evening, she took Juniper to the river to cool down and clambered onto a boulder above the water. She sat, her eyes unfocused, startled by the strange luminescence of the moment: cool pebbles pressed into palms, dust motes dancing in light, inches of surface water rendered clear, her hands clutching the boulder's bulk in anchoring entreaty as the mountains redeemed themselves, the river turning into the sea, rivulets of sand and rock baked hard as earthenware, ribbed like roots leading down to the Straights. In her mind, she slipped and fell, washboarding down, funneled into the cold, cobalt water.

The river swirling below her, she tried to press back her own rising emotion. She wanted to raise her fists, cry out, *Why did you leave me?* But she knew there would be only silence in reply, everyone gone now but her. Everything some version of lost—a darkness that stretched all the way though the layers of grieving.

She'd kept Isabelle's paintings boxed up, but the girls were always there, beseeching her, calling for recognition. The girls, Faith, Isabelle. How had she thought it was going to end—taking herself to Almost Paradise? She had already seen too much, been through too much, to believe there was any way for any of them to escape the life they'd been born into. Isabelle hadn't been able to save them or herself either. How could Silva hope for any different outcome?

Gnats swarmed in the dusk, bats swooping in for the kill, darkness pooling and shifting in the shape of people no longer there.

And perhaps it really was that simple—things just ending up this way. Her mother gone, Eamon gone, Isabelle gone, the baby gone. Acts of happenstance. Silva's life a seed blown by the wind, ending up wherever and however the breeze dropped her, when all she'd ever wanted was to set roots that resisted the forces intent on shaping her into something else. This terrain she'd tread into, everything some version of trespass.

◦—◦◦◦—◦

Mack came for her midweek, before the sun was up, boating her downriver the way she'd come only a few months ago, the trip down twice as fast as the trip up, no rushing currents to force their way through, carried along by the water's flow like just another piece of flotsam.

Nick was at the landing waiting for them when they docked, the hills shifting in shadow underneath a bright patchwork of clouds. He told Mack they'd be no more than a couple of hours; then, all pertinacious energy, he turned to Silva and asked, "You ready for this?" smiling as if they were about to embark on some wild adventure. And in a way, she supposed they were. Nothing now but this.

Juniper ran up the dock ahead of them, Nick's enthusiasm catching. When they got to the parking area, Nick pointed to the Dodge and said, "That yours? A '70, right? I've never seen one like it—the oak flatbed and all. Fire-engine red. It's a beauty."

But coated in a thick layer of dust, the pickup looked as though it'd been parked at the landing a year instead of a few months, time both compressed and extended until there was no beginning or ending, just a continual loop.

"My grandfather and I overhauled it together," Silva said. She could still remember the grit under her fingernails as they finished, Eamon donning his paint mask and miming Darth Vader—"*Silva, I am your grandfather*"—the two of them sparring with brooms as lightsabers until they'd collapsed, breathless with laughter.

"He must have meant a lot to you," Nick said.

Her throat tightened. "He did."

Nick's truck, despite its patchwork appearance, was tidy inside and smelled of leather and oats. He loaded Juniper in the back and shifted into granny gear to power up the steep incline out of the canyon, winding the switchbacks just as she'd done on the trail to Almost Paradise.

Halfway up, they turned and drove to an open field where Eli's field hives stood, sunrise pinking the pale blue sky, the clouds casting dappled light, the morning a soft wash of pastels. The boxes were shaded enough that the foragers would still be inside. Any later and they would head out for nectar gathering and come back to find themselves displaced—no colony, no brood, no queen.

They left Juniper in the cab and leaned against the truck's grille, listening to the bees' quiet humming, heat from the ticking engine against their backs. Silva closed her eyes and tipped her head back, breathed in deeply. When she opened her eyes, Nick was looking at her.

"Are you okay?" he asked, his tone quiet, full of something beyond concern.

"I hope so. I'm trying to be," she said, meeting his eyes, the words she wanted to tell him forming in her.

But he went around to the back of the truck and came back with a bulky package.

"What's this?" she asked, turning it over in her hands.

"Open it—you'll see," he said, his face eager with anticipation, everything washed fresh with a new day, a new start.

She tore the bag and shook out a length of white material and immediately thought of Len's maidens' shared wedding dress stored waiting in the Almost Paradise dowry room.

She held it to her shoulders, kicked her feet out beneath the too-long legs. "A bee suit?"

"I know Eli said we could work naked with his bees, but I don't think that's a good idea. For one, I'd be way too distracted to get anything done," Nick said, his grin crooked.

She pulled it on, and he taped up her wrists and ankles before adjusting the helmet and veil. She felt ridiculous, the helmet flopping over her eyes or bobbing to the side whenever she moved, threatening to tumble off and drag her veil with it; she had to constantly readjust in order to see where she was going. Heat built underneath the suit despite the cool air, her skin crawling with moisture, her face flushed under the veil—a blushing bee bride. Claustrophobic, she wanted to strip everything off, no matter what Nick thought.

The steady drone of buzzing built as they walked to the hives. A few foragers were positioned on the hive entrances, testing the early-morning air for new scents of nectar, their front legs held out, bodies swaying as they memorized their surroundings—the pattern of hive boxes, the rise of the hills, the dark swath of trees. They didn't seem alarmed by the sudden human presence. A few flew without notice around Silva's head, but when Nick lifted a hive cover, exposing the frames inside, a small cloud of bodies buzzed around their faces, landing on the mesh in front of her eyes, walking the nylon, their abdomens throbbing. Instead of fear, Silva felt herself pulsing with them—a deep, musical kind of answering that she let herself enter into. She wanted to feel what it would be like to have the bees humming against her skin. Perhaps Eli had been right—perhaps she did carry the pheromones of a queen.

Nick packed the smoker with straw and lit it, drifting smoke in front of a hive entrance. He waited for a moment, then removed the roof board, smoked the inside, and lifted out one of the nine frames filled with hexagons of wax-capped honey and larvae cells, the brood nestled in the middle of the frames surrounded by cells full of deposited nectar, fast becoming honey. He pulled each frame, examining them closely. He held one out for Silva to see, pointed out the honey cells, the elongated queen cells, and the copper patterns of pollen. One frame had a dozen elongated pods like tiny elephant trunks, the colony already raising new queens of their own.

As they moved through the supers, Nick smoking the bees into a stupor, Silva helped staple covers and place screens over the entrances, all Nick's dreams wrapped up in each hive full of brood and honey chambers, each frame of wax and pollen. They carried the supers together, each on an end of the hive lifter, the boxes heavy with ripening honey. They stacked them in the back of Nick's truck until the leaf springs flattened, the bed only an inch or two from the tires. It was slow work, the morning fully in by the time they finished loading.

With all the hives secured in Nick's truck, they stripped down to their regular clothes, wadding the bee suits, helmets, veils, and gloves on the floorboards, Juniper asleep on the passenger seat. They drove back down the landing thigh to thigh, Silva straddling the stick shift, close enough she could smell Nick's skin—baked leather, sand, and salt. She snuck a glance at the smooth stretch of tanned neck below his ear, and as they eased over ruts and washboards she thought of the queens huddled in the center of the hives, attended by the guards, the drones, the workers—all of them making this journey together. Honey and nectar, candy cages and queens, everything some version of sweetness.

Mack was waiting for them at the dock, the "fishing sled" cleared and ready. Nick backed the truck down, and they all worked to load. By the time they were done—all the hives secured, Juniper loaded in the prow—they were sweating and exhausted.

"It's no wonder nobody lasted long in this damn canyon," Mack said, arching his back. "Everything's twice as hard as it should be."

They powered upriver, heading back to the Larkins Ranch—a jet boat loaded full of bee boxes and bee-keeping equipment, a wolf-dog perched in the prow, the canyon walls rising sharply at their sides, the Snake winding ahead of them like its namesake—and everything felt suddenly different, new, even if they had to brace themselves for the jar of whitewater.

As the boat slammed over the rapids, pitching from the tops of the whitecaps, sprays of water shooting up, Silva worried about the colonies, what kind of havoc the move could wreak upon them, exposed as they were to the river, the baking sun. Still, with the water and wind, the canyon air reminded her of Trawler's damp permeation. With her own acclimation to the canyons' temperatures and aridity, the island weather would probably now chill her to the bone, each point of change marking the next in a line until where she'd started seemed like another lifetime so far removed, she didn't recognize her own beginnings anymore.

<hr />

Hours later, when the Larkins house finally came into view, it looked insignificant—a small brown blot, barely noticeable. Not at all how it figured in her mind. At last she'd found something in the canyon: the spiny leaves of coyote mint, the fresh earth tang of sage, the newborn sweet of willow scrub, the yellow blooms of rabbit brush, the surprise red scatter of rosehips, the rattler's black diamonds, the lone canyon wren's grace note, the cliffside eagle cave's smoke-dark maw, the murder of crows rustling by, cawing their dry-feather calls—and now, the bees.

Isabelle had flown from one lover to the next, always craving more light, more air, until they'd both been extinguished. A woman disquieted by her own restless need, trying to find everything she thought she'd been missing when it was right within her grasp all along. Silva shuddered at the thought of how close she herself had come to an alternate future—her body drifting downriver, carried by the currents.

After they got the boat secured and the hives unloaded to shore, Mack looked around and shook his head. "Look at you two—like Adam and Eve in your little Eden."

Getting the bees finally up the canyon to the ranch seemed to have released something in Nick, a long-held breath. He winked at Silva, his boyish impishness coming out. There was something appealing about the thought of their own Eden, even if it was one obfuscated and thorny. Even if it hadn't been what she'd come there to find.

Mack left as the sun sank behind the hills, everything in sudden shadow. A few escaped worker bees flew around the hives, their bodies dark against the boxes, everything cast golden. Silva and Nick suited up again and wheeled and stacked the bee boxes in the lee of the hill behind the house, pulling staples and unscreening the colonies in the quiet of the evening's gloaming, the last of the day's heat dissipating, the bees humming with their own expectations of this new place. They came out of the hive entrances and crawled along the boxes, scenting the canyon air, the sky turning golden over the new horseshoe of hives, as if in benediction.

When Nick went inside the house to wash up and change, Silva stayed outside, wanting to trace the evening's movements, watch the bees explore their new home. She dumped off her helmet and veil, stripped her gloves, and massaged the hardened lump of her neck muscles. Her body pulsed with heat. Swallows swooped and dove in evening flight and the crickets were in full song. The ground was dry, soft with needles that stuck to her feet. She sifted through them and brought a handful to her nose, breathing in the smell of resin—something that reminded her of her early years, that golden time of memory, her mother as lithe and sinuous and alive as the plants with which she'd surrounded herself.

Silva walked over to the hives and stood watching the bees for several moments before she shed her sweaty shirt and pants, draped her bra and underwear over the old plow.

She sat down among the hives naked, knees to chest, waiting. The buzzing reverberated in her ears until it became the sound of quiet, bees moving around her without noise, without motion. They waggled in the air in front of her face, crawled down her forehead, her neck, her shoulders, like an anointing, like the fingers of a lover tracing over her skin. She closed her eyes and felt the probing electricity from their bodies, the pulse of them like her own.

When she rose, the bees flew away from her hands, her arms, her breasts, like pieces of confetti. She was breathless, full of something she couldn't name. The air covered her like a mantle. She held her breath as if she were underwater, her arms floating at her sides. She felt weightless, drifting without touching anything but air, at one with the bees—a part of this new colony just as Eli said she would be.

The sky ignited where the sun dropped over the horizon, burnished from pink to orange until everything was dyed some tint of crimson, the hills reflecting the color, sky meeting earth in intimate touch. She followed the path of a blinking satellite and watched clouds move in, covering the moon just rising over the hills.

When Nick came out, called her name, she stepped from the hives, waited for him to see her. When he fell silent and still, she knew he had.

Electricity ran along her body as he came to her, stopping just before he got to her, taking in her naked body. She sniffed the air like an animal, scenting him as he covered the rest of the distance between them.

"What are you doing?" he asked, his voice husky.

She reached out and let her hand trail down his chest. "It's a nice night for a swim," she said, momentum charging the air. There would be no going back. Whatever it was, whatever it came to.

She walked to the river, and at the shore, she knelt and cupped water over her arms and chest, the copper of her hair reflected on the river's surface, drifting about her shoulders like a wild thing, the same color as the sky and her sunburned skin. She felt febrile. A wild, alive being. She stood, her skin damp, the air a warm touch against her, reminding her of the intimacy of her own flesh, the way her skin had turned electric at her own caress.

On the beach, Nick shed his clothes and stood before her naked, his arms and neck shades darker than anywhere else, the exposed skin of his torso washed pale in the soft evening light.

So this was how it began.

He came to her, pulled her into him. She put her face to his neck and started licking the smooth skin just below his ear, humming her lips against his neck, tasting his salt skin. She ran her tongue along the stubbly line of his jaw, held his earlobes between her front teeth and bit down, his breath a hitch in her ear. She kissed him, running her hands along the planes of his body until he tipped back his head in agony, and then she ran for the water, diving in, the cold embrace of it contracting her skin, streaming from her face as she surfaced, her breath rippling in front of her. As she smoothed back her hair, Nick dove in next to her, coming up several feet away, his arms and feet scissoring white underwater.

"The water's nice," he said, his voice close and musical.

Gnats touched down delicately on the surface of the water between them, flirting with the skin of the river until the water caught their infinitesimal wings and seized them in a wet embrace. They flailed, then submitted, a part of the river's offerings, swirling down current, catching in pools where fish jumped, their bodies taut with muscle and hunger

The side eddy drifted them toward the shore, the river's green washing pale against Silva's chest and shoulders, lapping against her collarbone, cupping in the hollow place behind it.

Nick's feet edged the bottom first. He reached for her, and she let him pull her to him again, her body floating through the water without resistance. He wrapped his fingers in her hair, kissed her, the taste of river on his mouth, his skin cool and wet against hers. He cupped his hands behind her, pulling her tight against his body. She wrapped her legs around his hips and held on to his neck as he stepped streaming from the water, carrying her to shore.

They fell tangled to the ground, their hunger matching each other's, their wet bodies sticking to the sand nested soft beneath them. Silva rolled and straddled his waist, pinning him by the wrists, bearing down all her weight upon him—a woman leaned into a man, her body flowing from root to branch tip, shaping the whole, his body forming the bulk of the trunk, a mass anchoring them against hard winds. A shared grace with no ending and no beginning. She was surprised at her own body, surprised by what she felt—a sense of security, of self-willed power. Taking what had been given.

She let the air and the river inform her movements—two bodies interwoven, succumbing to their own remaking. A slow, warm melting into sweetness, the breath of water everywhere, the air full of the river's gurgling, headlong rush.

A coyote's wavering howl lifted up in the hills above them, a call of commemoration. This place, this moment. A small piece of belonging—as new and fraught as that belonging might be. Something opening up in her soul that had been sealed off for so long that the hinges had rusted shut and she'd forgotten what possibilities there were left inside her.

Nick trailed his hand along the sharp bone of her hips, the soft curves of her breasts, tracing the lines of her body, the knowledge of his hand on her like knowledge of herself. Water and salt, sand and algae—the taste of him, the smell of him, something she'd always known. He kissed her stomach, stroked her back, and she pressed her body close, hungry for the radiant heat of his skin, the feel of the beat of his heart against her own. She was still there, whittled down and battered as she might be.

She stroked a finger over his forehead and cheek, let it hover just over his lips where she could feel his breath against her skin, tracing the contours of his face, taking each detail in, memorizing this moment so she might hold it again—his mussed hair, his stubbly growth of beard, the line of his scar. She turned his hand palm up and marked his calluses, all the scars of his body like a map she could learn to follow.

A breeze gusted up the canyon, bringing with it the sounds of the night: crickets chirring, the wash of the creek, tree branches touching the house. She imagined the bees tucked in their hives, tasting new air full of the secret wash of pollen dust, the wafting drift of hidden blooms full of nectar, divining the movement of current and wind, learning their new home with each inhalation, with each surge of breath.

"It would seem we've finally begun," she said, her fingers trailing over the delineations of Nick's body.

He rolled onto her. "So we have," he said, his muffled voice resonant against her. *So we have....*

CHAPTER THIRTY-FOUR

Date: January 1, 2000
Title: Wedding of the Maidens
Subject: The Twelve Maidens & Len Dietz
Setting: Almost Paradise Sanctuary
Medium: Watercolor and graphite on cold-press
Size: 14×24

Dearest Eamon,

It is the day: Y2K. The new millennium. The End of the World. The Wedding of the Maidens. The Apocalypse.

The sun rose. The birds sang. The sky was blue. The wind blew down the canyon. The trees rustled their dead leaves. The elk chewed their cud and nuzzled one another, calling out for fresh hay. There was no great sweeping darkness, no heavenly trumpets blowing, no horsemen of the apocalypse riding in on clouds of doom.

They have a boy, Isaac, posted in the ham radio room as monitor of the airwaves. Headphones on, he scans and scans, skipping through counties, regions, countries. They wait and they listen, prepared for full failure. Their generators are filled with fuel, their compound is wired for a shift in the power grid, their food coffers are stacked full, their well is primed, their cash is stocked and stored, their guns oiled and their ammo boxes overflowing. They stand at the ready, for the financial world's collapse, for all computers to fail, for all of humanity to crash, for everything to burn in wreck and ruin, for murderous hordes of the desperate and the damned to charge their compound borders.

But so far, life goes on, just as before. The radio deejays chat, the worldly songs of ruin play through, the computers compute, Wall Street trades, the banks and malls open, the gas stations pump fuel, the power stays on, babies are born in warm hospital rooms, and people the world over tip back champagne and celebrate this new year, this new century, this new millennium.

We instead lift our hands in praise of Len Dietz and his successful takeover of the virgin brides—these girls who should be in middle school, passing notes and studying evolution.

The wedding was held in the candlelit dark, a rustling hush of dresses and veils, a quiet hum of women's voices lifting in the night, Faith and the others singing their holy songs. The maidens came in a line, walking down the aisle one by one, their fathers clutching their arms to lead them to Len Dietz, leading them to slaughter. The maidens lined up on either side of Len, centered in the sanctuary beneath the cross, his eyes closed, his arms raised. He is the pastor, the groom, the executioner. When they had assembled, each dressed and veiled in white, he dropped his arms and began the proceedings, speaking words of his own making—this fable of destiny, of holiness, of divine will cloaking the baldness of his raw and insatiable desire. They are his now, each one of them eradicated, burned, and buried to themselves. Disassociated. Fragmented. Lost. Doomed to forever seek what was taken from them, their own selves cast aside and trodden upon until there is nothing more to recognize.

I painted each of them individually in their wedding attire, adding to the private collection I have kept secreted away. A body of work that has kept me from falling completely away into the dark chasm and losing what tiny bit I have left of myself to this voracious black hole.

The main "Wedding of the Maidens" painting is the largest one yet—all the maidens in white gathered around Len beneath the cross, the candles burning around them the only light. The gowns took the wives a year to create, hand-sewn, hand-embroidered, pearl studded. Twelve identical gowns on twelve individual girls, each of them standing stair-stepped up to Len's tall-man height. The veils a full covering, blurring any separate features, blending them into repeating versions of themselves—like cutout dolls accordioned out, hollow stamps for their hearts.

The feast is larger than that of the Dowry Ceremony, all the Almost Paradise people gathered—a hundred or more—to eat and drink to the end of the world and the beginning of their new reign. Except there has been no end other than for the maidens, all these people complicit in their collective violation, their loss of self, their overtaking.

I have hidden myself away, my door barred, the sound of their celebrating a trespass creeping through the cracks. I'm afraid I have gotten myself in too deep. I'm afraid I won't ever be able to make my way back out. I'm afraid I, too, might be lost. I am consumed with what might have been. I replay each island day, each day with you. I remember them so well, it would seem that no time has passed—the way the oars creaked on your dinghy, the water like unending glass; orcas blowing and breaching down the Straight; spotted harbor seals slipping by, their liquid-eyed sea-dog faces wet and slick; shore-bound gulls and bald eagles fighting over a feast of crabs and fish; the steep, sloughing slopes blooming with wild rose and thimbleberry.

I remember our "wedding" day, standing outside the courthouse, a gust of wind blowing against the earrings you carved me. An inter-weaving of our lives I never wanted to end, even if I was the one who made sure it did, unraveling each thread until I—until we—became a loose, shapeless fray. It feels too late now to rewind, respool, restitch. Are you still there? Will I ever find you again? My Eamon. My heart. Oh, how I love you. How I have always loved you. Stay a little while longer, will you? Stay until I can again come find you.

All my love,
Isabelle

CHAPTER THIRTY-FIVE

Nick's rhythmic sleep-breathing was a steady presence beside her, as it'd been for the last weeks. Silva woke early, light breaking against the western hills out Nick's bedroom window, her eyes taking in the world before her brain could transmit. Nick rolled over in his sleep and slung his arm across her middle, as if to make sure she wouldn't leave, as if he were trying to pull her back into his own slumbering reaches.

She lifted his arm in increments, timing her movements to his breathing as she crawled out of bed, trying to avoid the creakiest floorboards, but her weight set off a series of pops and snaps across the whole house as if she were awakening it, too. She held still, trying to let everything settle back into place, but Juniper got up and shook from where he'd slept beneath them on the floor and put his ears back and wagged his tail in morning greeting.

She leaned over to pet him and looked out at the river. A jet boat surged over rapids and then disappeared, the water left empty and rippling in its wake. The canyon felt as it had when Silva had first come: full of quiet promise, buzzing with possibility, with change. She realized it had delivered—change pretty much all she'd had since she'd first set foot on the Larkins Ranch.

Over the months she'd been there, Hells Canyon had fully transitioned into its national-recreation-area self. Another of its strange juxtapositions—the empty, rugged isolation coupled with casual outdoorsmen: jet boaters fishing from early morning until night; groups of weekend rafters lazily drifting by, armed with water guns and coolers laden with beer; sweating Boy Scouts hiking in from Pittsburg Landing, along with groups of backpackers—the last, three tall, lanky brothers from Moscow, where Isabelle's honeysuckle bonsai painting had hung. Silva wondered if any of them had seen it—this one final thing connecting her to Isabelle. Two women who'd never known anything of the other except through Eamon and his trees.

The three brothers had pitched their orange tents on the bouldered flat across the creek near the river. They fly-fished at the convergence, hooting and hollering at their catch of jacks and steelhead grown spring-greedy and too incautious for their own good. Jet-boaters with setups that cost tens of thousands of dollars couldn't compete, one of the brothers landing a thirty-pounder from shore with his undersize backpacking rod, blind to his own good luck.

Nick was a gracious Larkins Ranch host—far better than Silva was, even though it was the job she'd been hired to do. Each day he went out and chatted for hours with jet boaters and Boy Scouts alike. The night before, he'd taken the three brothers lemon and fresh garlic for their catch. She had seen him from the window, casting their rods, talking flies and line weights and reels. When he'd come back in, he'd smelled of fish and smoke and skunkweed, and Silva had asked him why he hadn't just applied for the caretaking job himself—gotten paid to be the host of his own property? In answer, he'd kissed her neck, her collarbone, nuzzled her ears, told her what a good pair they were as he'd ticked each item off his fingers: he took care of the bees and the barn, she took care of the trees and garden; he studied bee books, and she studied bonsai journals; he slept uncovered, she slept with the blanket over her head; he was brown and white and she was gold and copper. He teased her until she relented, letting him reach under her shirt and unbutton her pants, slide his hand against her smooth skin, his movements stirring the ripe sweet of her own body.

"Tell me again," he'd said, his voice like heat against her skin, insistent on rousing her. "Tell me again about all those peaches we're going to eat. . . ."

She'd told him about the dream she'd had—a good one, for once, the two of them surrounded by rows of fresh-churned dirt that they walked along, throwing seeds like confetti, seeds that immediately sprouted and grew into vines and bushes and trees, a jungle full of fruit so ripe and tender the juice ran off their fingers like syrup.

Movin' to the country, gonna eat me a lot of peaches. Her mother's back-to-the-earth dream. After Eamon, Silva had promised herself she wouldn't let herself get attached again, but now she remembered what it felt like to have someone to belong to, what it felt like to give so freely of yourself. Nick's skin was like Trawler in July after the tide—beach sand, sunbaked grass, and salt-tinged rocks dried in the afternoon sun. Sometimes she couldn't help licking him, just as, when she was a child, she'd licked tidal rocks in order to restore their shiny-flecked depth.

Each day they moved around each other like a synchronized team, as if they'd been doing so their whole lives, the work written into them—arms, necks, and faces baked dark, hands callused, hair bleached from the sun. Nick spent his days checking the bees, repairing fences, and beating back the yellow star thistle that sprouted in the cracked and hardened dirt like an army of invaders. He walked the ranch's perimeters every morning and evening, checking for the pale wind of leaves, the small barbed heads, as if they were the trespassing embodiment of Len Dietz.

But there was satisfaction in it, rebuilding the Larkins Ranch until it could finally fulfill its own potential. The garden growing, the bonsai healthy, the bees established in their new colonies, working the land alongside Nick. Everything as it should be, becoming all they'd envisioned. She pushed away the canyon's history, all those who'd come before, working toward the same goal, until, one by one, they had been decimated by their own failure and loss.

Above them in the canyon, the visitor center occupation had settled in as though they planned to stay forever—the land and everyone who cared about it as their hostage.

Behind her, still in bed, Nick's breathing changed. He peered at her, his eyes slitted. "Where are you going?" he asked, his voice thick and sleep soft. He watched her carefully, appraising a creature about to run off. She *had* thought of running, but not away. There was something beckoning about hills, the stillness, the openness, that smelled of tawny grasses. Only in the canyon's silence and isolation did all the trauma of the past dissipate into something better, something without the threat of more loss to come.

Often when she couldn't sleep—when she woke from nightmares of dark rooms or bodies washing downriver—she would get up and walk the house, trailing her hand along the walls in the dark. The first few times Nick had awakened to her empty side of the bed he'd been alarmed, had come out wild-haired, calling her name. He'd grown more accustomed to her wanderings, but still, if she stayed gone long enough, he always came looking for her.

"It's extraction day. The sun's up," she said. Like Eamon, she loved the soft-lighted early morning, everything still possible. "I listened to the birds. Listened to you," she said, studying Nick's sleep-rumpled face. "You said my name in your sleep."

He smiled, a slow-blooming thing that moved up his cheeks and creased around his eyes, edging the scar on his cheek crooked. "That's because I was dreaming about you," he said, pulling back the blankets and beckoning for her to rejoin him in bed.

She shook her head, smiled at him. "Early to bed, early to rise, makes a man healthy, wealthy, and wise," she said. Another of Eamon's sayings. The realization of how much he would have approved of Nick filled her with a sudden rush of sadness.

"There are other things that make a man healthy, wealthy, and wise," Nick said, raising his eyebrows and tilting his head suggestively, his body sprawled across the space she'd left vacant.

She rolled her eyes at him, but couldn't help smiling. "Go back to sleep. I'm not going anywhere."

"Don't know what you're missing," he replied, relaxing back into the covers as she stepped over the heap of clothing that had been mounding in the bedroom for a week. In the passion of their lovemaking, they'd left the bedroom unkempt, their clothes unwashed.

Hot morning air filled the curtains like sails. She closed the window and let the bamboo blinds down, filtering the sun into bars of light on the floor. Outside, even though it was early, the barn roof shimmered as if ready to ignite. It'd taken days just to get the extraction equipment set up in the barn's back room—the extraction room—but everything was ready now, the bees settled in and working steadily, all the empty honey jars waiting.

She went outside, wishing she'd brought Eamon's *Crew Working in Trees* arborist signs—big orange traffic signs she could use to mark where she was for Nick—"working in trees" somehow a good metaphor for all life's quiet, solitary moments. She and Nick the pioneer species, the trees that grew up first after an act of disaster or destruction. The shelterwood—the hardiest mature trees left to propagate, to establish a new generation of strong seed-lings after several forest thinnings took the rest of the mature trees.

Garden dirt crumbled under her bare feet as she let herself in the deer fence they'd put up the weekend before—peeler core posts strung with tall wire, the plants finally growing unmolested behind it. When she'd first planted, Nick had warned her that a few deer might come, but she'd never expected the kind of havoc they could wreak, smelling the fresh dirt and unfurled seeds as keenly as she did. Before the fence, she'd staked out stick scarecrows with floppy plastic bags that snapped in the wind; sprayed the entire garden with deer repellant Mack brought up; tried playing tape recordings of predator calls all night—cougar screams and the resonant howling of wolf packs on the hunt. No matter what method she tried, the next morning she would find entire rows destroyed, tender tips of the delicate new sprouts eaten off. One day, in desperation, she'd gone to the bone pile over the hill and hung skulls on T-posts around the garden's perimeter. She'd thought it would serve as a warning, all those empty sockets staring them down, but it seemed deer weren't too worried about their ancestors' demise.

She'd taken to patrolling the garden at night, sneaking out barefoot until she got close enough she could hear the deer eating, the little snaps and crunches of her demolished plants. She would turn on her flashlight and run at them, hollering and flapping her arms, the light catching the reflection of their eyes until they scattered into the darkness. She would huff around for a minute and then settle back on the porch with her blanket. Despite her efforts, it would often be less than an hour before she would hear them again—whole families pocketed back in the rows, munching away like a herd of lazy cattle.

After days of her nocturnal battling, Nick had surprised her with a boat-load of peeler cores and rolls of wire. They'd put the fence up in a weekend and without the deer eating it, the garden had seemed to grow inches overnight—rows of tall plants from one end to the other that she walked through, dreaming of fresh ears of corn and ripe tomatoes.

She misted the plants as she watched two redtail hawks soar overlapping ellipses, one above the other, coasting on air currents, their undersides gilded in early-morning sun. She imagined the tracings of their flight, a looping gold contrail against her eyelids even when she closed her eyes. This had always been her favorite time of year on Trawler, everything screaming with lush growth and beauty. In the canyon, the heat sucked the breath out of her. She had to water every morning to combat it, but just as she had hoped, the plants were thriving with all the sun and heat. Nick jokingly named her "Granger," said she was growing a Jack-and-the-Beanstalk garden.

She set the sprinkler so it would reach the corners, then took the wheel-barrow to the back to dump her weeds and noticed that the corner wire was rumpled again. A few determined deer still found their way into the garden, the back fence low enough they could leap over. Whenever Juniper saw them, he would charge in barking. The first time that happened, the startled deer had trampled the garden's back section before finding their way back out again. She went back to see what damage they'd managed this time.

She didn't see the doe until she walked all the way to the back. Blond and flawless, white belly taut with a late-term pregnancy, lying askew, neck broken. Her eyes were black and open, still unclouded—not long dead.

Silva stood a long time before bending down. She stroked her hand over the curves of the doe's spine and belly, the velvet of her nose, the delicate boning of slender legs, the tiny, black, polished hooves. Perfect. She tried not to imagine the fawn still enfolded inside.

When Silva tried to lift the doe, its head flopped into the dirt, dust filming the still-open eyes. Silva heaved her into the wheelbarrow, wheeled her to the bone pile, dug a shallow hole, and dumped her in, dirt cascading into the hole, legs askew and pointing, just as Sunchero's had been all those years ago. Silva looked away from the hole as she shoveled the dirt back in.

She coiled the hose, closed up the fence, and called Juniper back inside. As Nick slept, she went to her bedroom and buried herself in Eamon's bonsai journals, trying to push away the aching, keep the past where it had to stay. More than she could ever purge in a lifetime of telling.

When she heard Nick stirring in the bedroom, she wiped her face and put her work away.

"Extraction day," Nick said in a groggy singsong when he came in to greet her.

"And you slept in. What will the bees think?" Silva said, turning and tsking at him.

"All work and no play makes Jack a dull boy. You don't want Jack to turn into a dull boy, do you?" he said as he kissed her collarbone, his hands drifting toward her breasts.

In the yard, robins flitted from the birdbath to the trees, the young fledglings still calling for their mother. "There was a dead doe in the garden," Silva said, broaching it carefully, Nick's concerned eyes on hers. "She was pregnant. I buried her in the bone pile."

"You should have woken me—I would have taken care of it. You didn't need to deal with that," he said. He didn't know that it was too late for her to be spared from much of anything.

"I'm sorry about your brother, your mom," she said, her words rushing out, taking her as much by surprise as they did Nick. "My grandmother gave my mother up when she was born. She had good reasons—she was fifteen, and there was abuse involved—but I always wondered how different life would have turned out if we'd been able to be together, be a family."

Nick bent down and kissed the side of her face. "Sometimes you just have to make your own family," he said.

⸻

When Mack came later, bringing up a week's worth of newspapers and mail, his face was sober. "The occupation has gotten more serious," he said, handing them the papers. "The FBI organized a town-hall meeting, and Len and his men went in unannounced, stood armed in the back of the room. Said there would be no negotiations, said they wouldn't be leaving until the government relinquished control of *all* federal lands to the states, which of course will never happen. . . ."

"So, it's getting worse, not better," Silva said flatly, looking at front-page pictures of Len speaking in front of cameras, his long hair lying loose on his shoulders, his silver all-seeing eye hanging from his neck, his pistol on his side. In these, he looked like some kind of '70s rogue TV cop, not the leader of a militant religious-survivalist cult full of pregnant girls.

"Well, it's not all bad news," Mack said, turning to Nick. "They finally got a court order for the elk ranch. Ted sent word, invited you to come with him when he goes in to examine Len's elk since they're above this place, affect the creek."

"Ted knows what to do. There's no use in me going along. It'd just stir everything back up again," Nick said, and Silva breathed a sigh of relief.

With Nick staying at the ranch and Len staying with the occupation, you could almost forget that they were inextricably joined together, that nothing was resolved.

A few nights before, Nick had come across a rattler stretched along the upriver trail like a root in the grass, its jaws unhinged, a rump and long tail sticking out of its mouth like a tongue, the systolic movement of it working the rodent farther into its throat. Silva had panicked, looking for Juniper behind her, but Nick had picked up a rock the size of a baby's skull and the snake must have sensed danger because it tried to make it to a tumble of boulders, its half-swallowed meal still stuck in its throat, rattles shaking. Nick pounded it with the rock over and over again until he was sweating. By the time he'd stopped, the snake had been smashed into an oozing mass, rattles still twitching. He'd thrown the rock into the bushes, wiped his hands on his pants, and kicked away what had been left of the snake, saying they had to keep their place safe.

"I'm glad you're staying," Silva said, gauging the stress lines in Nick's expression. "I don't want either of us to leave again."

Nick leaned over and kissed her forehead. "Well, then, we won't. We'll just stay here in our little Eden. We've got everything we need right here—all the honey one man could need," he said, turning to Silva and grinning at her quick blush. But she already knew that Edens had a way of disappearing, that most didn't last far beyond conception.

"Come on. I'll show you the setup," Nick said to Mack. "The bees have settled in, made themselves at home."

Silva loved sitting out by the garden and apiary, watching the bees fly back and forth, carrying their loads of pollen and nectar. So industrious. So untiring. So willing to believe in a steady future full of plenty.

Mack whistled appreciatively when they went in the extraction room. "Fancy," he said, and it was—the gleaming extractor a smooth, polished convex of stainless steel, and all the empty jars waiting for their load of honey, gallons and quarts and pints that would soon glow golden.

"Fifty-two-inch diameter, sixteen-gallon tank, sixty-frame reel, and DC motor," Nick recited, his hand on the extractor. "At least yellow star thistle will be good for something. By the end of summer we ought to have quadrupled what's here. Then it'll be time to pay this place off. Settle in."

He looked at Silva, their future prospects growing more believable each day. She'd let herself imagine it, what it would be like to stay in the canyon with Nick, a pantry filled with their own home-canned garden produce and honey, the barn stacked with hay. But there was more to consider, things far outside their control.

"That's good," Mack said. "Real good. The place is looking like a real canyon homestead again instead of an outfitter's stopover spot."

"Well, it's still that, too," Nick said. "I've got a few more horse groups scheduled and we've got a raft group coming down in a couple of days, going to park here, stay overnight."

In preparation, Silva had mowed the flat across the creek, hoping the rafting group would stay there instead of on the backpackers' flat closer to the house, although it wasn't really up to either her or Nick to decide. The outfitters still had the lease of the Larkins Ranch, which meant she and even Nick were there to serve their needs, as much as it seemed it should be the other way around.

"It'll be over soon, with this heat," Mack said. "Set another record-high yesterday. A hundred-plus will run most of the visitors off." He glanced around, then back to them, and said, "I'm happy for you two."

"Why don't you stay overnight?" Silva asked in a sudden rush of tenderness, wanting to offer all they had to give, even if it wasn't really hers for the offering.

He shook his head. "Gotta get back to work, even if this is a little oasis. Nice place to land, that's for sure," he said, tipping his hat.

After she walked down to wave him off, Silva went to help Nick wheel the supers from the apiary to the barn. Although it was still early in the honey season, the hives had plenty for a trial run, and she was glad to get more. Nick said he was going to have to get more hives to keep up with her consumption, devouring all the profits, but she could tell he was happy about it, too.

When she joined him, he gestured at her cutoffs and tank top, asked, "Where's your bee suit?" He frowned as she helped guide his loaded handcart into the extraction room.

She brushed a bee gently out of her face, replied, "Don't worry, the bees and I have our ways of communicating."

The extraction room was stifling, a propane heater running on high along with a fan to circulate the waves of heat. Coupled with the sun streaming through the window, it felt as though they'd walked into a furnace blast that took Silva's breath away. She waved her hand in front of her face, panting, "It's too hot to breathe," sweat running from under her breasts.

"The honey flows better, easier to extract," Nick said.

"Well, it ought to flow like water," she said, her skin flushing as Nick laid out tools like a doctor's surgery table, uncapping knives, scrapers, putty knives.

He pulled off the lid of the top super. "Did you know for a hive to produce eighty-five quarts of honey, the bees have to visit enough wildflowers to gather and carry home 765 quarts, or 2,295 pounds, of nectar?"

"I didn't know that," Silva said, smiling. She liked it when Nick got into his bee-data-reciting mode, his face pulled serious, his voice as formal as any nature-documentary host's.

"A Roman soldier came up with the Honeybee Conjecture two thousand years ago. He thought hexagons would hold more honey than other shapes, or required less building wax. They've proven he was right—mathematically hexagons are the most efficient way of making cells, storing honey," he said, looking into the hive. "It seems that there is almost always a reason for things—a hidden logic putting order to the random."

She wiped sweat from her face and looked into an exposed hive. A few bees flew by, bumping into the ceiling, buzzing against the windows, and one landed on Silva, stiff-walking over her shoulders and chest until it tumbled and flew off.

"I feel like a thief, robbing them blind—all their hard labor," she said, imagining the workers inside walking the empty cells, having to rebuild all they'd lost.

"We'll feed them through the lean times, keep the mites eradicated, protect them from the elements, keep the colony strong. They need us as much as we need them," Nick said.

But the bees didn't seem to need anything, though they all knew what dangers were out there, what could befall them without so much as a warning. Colony collapse was something she understood only too well.

Nick worked the hive tool, loosening the frames and pulling them out one at a time. He held them up for her to see, hexagons full of honey, pounds and pounds of it.

"The food of gods," he said, pulling another frame, this one filled with multicolored hexagons of propolis instead—a metallic rainbow of copper and gold and pink. With a corner prong of his scraper he broke off a small chunk and gave it to Silva. "I guess that means we're immortal now," he said, chewing his own piece. And she wouldn't have minded things staying the way they were, like this, forever.

The fan blew hot, and the air was heavy, sticky, as if already imbued with honey. It smelled of honey, wax, and something else animal and organic, something slightly rotten and sweet at the same time, a smell that clung to their skin and hair like a wet blanket.

Nick set the frames on the parallel rails he'd fashioned, suspending the frames' outer lips on the rails. Avoiding the brood and propolis cells, he used a tool to scratch through the wax caps in the corners of the frames, and then Silva used the heated uncapping knife over the rest of the wax-capped honey cells. With the first swipe of the knife, the wax melted, and the exposed honey dripped golden, running from the frame to the table's steel surface, then to the buckets.

One after another, Nick cracked open the supers and pulled frames full of honey, the two of them working side by side. They worked until they had a surplus of uncapped frames; then Nick loaded them into the extractor. "Here we go," he said, and plugged it in, the whir of the extractor's motor immediate and overpowering. It picked up speed until the centrifugal force pulled out strands of honey, threads that caught and built until there was a thick sludge in the catch basin that slowly moved down to the drain and dripped into a five-gallon bucket.

Both of them stood entranced. They couldn't take their eyes from the honey, spinning load after load, the empty frames hanging from the rails, still dripping, honey everywhere—the very air redolent with it, impregnated with its sweet animal stickiness. Thick umber globs, along with wax, smashed bees, and chunks of propolis stuck to the table, to their fingers, to the floor. With each step, it grabbed their feet like glue.

While the extractor spun out the last load, the honey flow slowing from a steady flow to a trickle, Silva used a wide putty knife to scrape the honey that had dripped onto the uncapping table, not wanting to waste any. Nick shut off the extractor, the fan, and the heater, and the sudden cessation of noise made Silva feel off-balance.

Nick pulled the last bucket from under the extractor and held it out. "Our first harvest. A damn fine thing," he said

Silva nodded, her skin flushed. "A fine thing indeed," she said.

She opened her fingers, and honey stretched between them, threads suspended like spider webs. Nick lifted her hands to his mouth and sucked the honey from her fingers, working over each knuckle, each fingertip. They undressed one another slowly and when they kissed, their mouths were sticky, their skin adhering wherever they touched, as if they were of one skin, one body.

It was late afternoon when they finally pulled away from one another and closed the extraction room, leaving jars full of amber honey lined up on the shelves and table. They washed up at the hand pump in the barn corridor, both of them standing naked, honeyed rivulets of water running down their legs and pooling in the dust.

CHAPTER THIRTY-SIX

Oh Jesus, bless this child, you, bless this, your broken heart, oh Jesus Jesus, deliver this child, you, Lord Jesus, deliver this child, you, from the clutch of the devil, you, from the claws of the flesh, you, the temptations known in your heart, you, your body, your weakness, conquer, you, conquer, oh yes Jesus, if you will just believe, if you will just receive, are you ready to repent, to receive God's punishment? Oh, child of sin, you, child of carnality, you, child of flesh, you, here this is your chance of forgiveness, oh Lord, deliver us from the powers of evil, the darkness that has covered us, rebuke you, this stronghold of deception, of the flesh. Lord, cover us with your holiness, Lord deliver us from this yourself, cast out these spirits of carnality, you, Lord, in your name, command they go— GO! Oh Jesus, you, lift you, lift you this woman out of the pit of carnality, of this, your fleshly desire, oh Jesus, cleanse you with your holy love. Oh Lord, cover you with your grace, your holiness, your beacon of chastity. Oh lord Jesus, oh Jesus, Jesus, oh dear father Jesus, forgive you the sins of your carnality, forgive you the evils of your flesh, forgive you the weakness of your flesh, the wantonness of your flesh, oh Jesus, Jesus, cleanse your flesh in thy holy wrath, cleanse your flesh in the wake of devil's touch, oh lord, thy holy will be done, the fires of your wrath a consuming flame touched to the candle of your flesh.

PART FOUR

....

Prodigious nuptials these, the most fairylike that can be conceived,
azure and tragic, raised high above life by the impetus of desire;
imperishable and terrible, unique and bewildering, solitary and infinite.
An admirable ecstasy, wherein death supervening in all that our sphere
has of most limpid and loveliest, in virginal, limitless space, stamps the
instant of happiness in the sublime transparence of the great sky;
purifying in that immaculate light the something of wretchedness
that always hovers around love, rendering the kiss one that can never
be forgotten; and content this time with moderate tithe, proceeding
herself, with hands that are almost maternal, to introduce and unite,
in one body, for a long and inseparable future, two little fragile lives.

–THE LIFE OF THE BEE

CHAPTER THIRTY-SEVEN

When Mack called in on the radio, his voice was tinny in the small kitchen, Nick standing at the counter, listening with furrowed brows as he spoke.

"Ted sent word about the elk testing," Mack said. "Wanted me to let you know, besides other things, it was conclusive of CWD. Just what you were afraid of. Fish and Game will be handling the situation with high priority."

Perplexed, Silva looked back and forth between Nick and the radio.

"Chronic wasting disease," Nick explained. "A version of mad cow. Spreads easily to wild herds, has a near one hundred percent mortality rate. His elk are probably full of disease—tuberculosis, pneumonia—just like domestic sheep in the canyon. Transfers to everything and wipes out the native herds. With things already so tense, anything coming from Fish and Game will probably be considered a direct attack. It's going to cause a shit-storm. . . ."

"I'll keep you updated. Don't want you caught unawares up there," Mack finished.

It was colony collapse of a different sort. Silva had a sinking feeling in her guts.

"Things can't keep going on like this much longer," Nick said, staring out pensively.

"No, they can't," Silva said, going to him. "Are you okay?"

He paused before answering. "I just don't want any more shit falling on us or this place. . . ." He pulled back for a moment and looked at her with quiet regard, his eyes a clear, potent blue. "We should get out of here—at least for a little while. Take a breather."

At first, her heart sinking, Silva thought he was talking about going back to Two Rivers, choosing to move even closer to all the drama, where they would only get more drawn into it. Len Dietz and his followers had a way of assuring Nick's and Silva's involvement, whether they wanted it or not.

"There's a hidden spot upcanyon, a hackberry growing out of a rock along the river called the Wishing Tree. Like your bonsai. I'd like to take you there. We could ride up, camp out, and then watch the rafters come through the best rapids," he said. His eyes were still troubled even as he tried to get back to where they'd been before the news from Mack.

She was worried he felt it, too—this golden time fleeting. The canyon's reality had come crashing back with resounding force. She glanced outside, imagined the coolness of the river, a root-over-rock hackberry called the Wishing Tree—something Eamon would have loved seeing.

"Only the river and trees this time, I promise," Nick said, looking deep in her eyes.

The river and the trees. The bonsai and the bees. An incantation she had learned to sing.

<hr />

While Nick got the horses ready and packed, Silva went to the house and watered each bonsai thoroughly before placing wet tea bags over their soil for extra moisture. She'd been having to water the bonsai as much as the garden in the new apex of heat. She packed the rucksack, bringing only a small bonsai sketchbook and extra clothes before closing up her workroom, pausing for a moment to look at the evidence of herself left behind: trimming shears, jinning pliers, gravers, root hooks, knob and wire cutters, and coils of different gauged copper wire lined up next to the stack of Eamon's bonsai journals. Everything reimagined, reshaped.

The horses were lazy in the heat, their neck and withers wet, horse smell mixing with leather and sweat as they rode through rolling plateaus of shale and sage. The drought-shrunken trees were spread like an African plain: sky and sun and bleeding rock veins, pink arterial flows. The heat pushed back against them like an invisible hand as the river slipped by, gleaming like metal, the air still, everything dried to dust, grass breaking underfoot like twigs.

The rucksack hung heavy and hot against Silva's back. "So, where is this famous Wishing Tree?" she asked. She felt like a child on a road trip, asking how much farther every five minutes, impatiently waiting for the promised destination.

Nick smiled back at her. "You'll just have to wait and see. Only good secret I have left."

They climbed a steep hillside of bunch grass and then rode under a cluster of huge bull pines that smelled like vanilla. Silva brushed her hand against their rough, orange-veined bark as they rode by, the sky filtered through the trees' long needles, this wild country straddled between two rivers twining their age-old ways, carving out new territory with each pulse.

Nick pointed out the sharp peaks of the Seven Devils shearing above the otherwise smoothly contoured landscape, hills shaped like a woman's body, and told Silva the story of the sky woman who'd run naked and wild, blowing every which way with the wind until finally she'd given into the land's earthward pull, let it claim her as its own. When he pointed out the mounds that formed her hips and thighs and breasts, Silva felt as though he were tracing her own body.

As they finally dropped back down toward the river, he led them off-trail through a burned hackberry thicket, the ghostly shapes of the silvered trunks standing like sentinels on the barren slope. Scrambling down a steep deer trail, the horses shimmied past a basalt bluff that dropped sharply to the water; then the path leveled on a small flat that turned from grass to sand where it met the river, pines encircling the small beach, providing much-needed shade.

Nick leapt off Sage and helped Silva dismount. "Welcome to camp," he said. The water stretched smooth and flat, current swirling with pollen, swallows skimming the surface, winging water loose as a canyon wren sang along the weavings of basalt, syringa sweeting the air, hackberry and mead-owlark tangled together.

"The Wishing Tree is just over the bluff. You can make all the wishes you want," he said.

Silva shucked off the sweaty rucksack and leaned it against a pine. "No limit?" she asked.

"Not for the Tree Girl," he said, grinning.

Juniper paddled around the eddy, his tail extended out behind him like a rudder, as Silva let the horses drink and Nick pitched a tiny, faded green dome tent, frayed at the seams, in a pocket of grass and sand, sweeping out dried bugs from seasons past before unrolling two old Army mummy sleeping bags—more relics from his youth. When he was done, he got the horses hobbled in the shade, contentedly eating the piles of oats he'd poured out for them.

"Come on," he said, pulling Silva up from the river. "The pièce de résis-tance awaits. . . ."

She got the rucksack with her sketchbook and pencils as Nick slung his fishing rod's battered aluminum pack tube over his shoulder. They clambered up the steep bluff, Juniper ahead of them, surefooted on the narrow foot-holds. There were tiny clumps of pink and purple flowering plants nestled in the crevices, the clean, lemon scent of sage blunted by the earthiness of baked dust and the mineral smell of heated scree. The line of past water was a ghost cut against the rock walls around them—a white mark, a sluice of stones swept banking. Pools once filled torrent-high, deep enough you could sink out of sight. A dream of water that once was.

They got to the top and went down the other side, and then, protected and out of view from above, was the Wishing Tree, just as Nick had promised—a gnarled yet elegant hackberry anchored root to rock, growing impossibly out of the sheer basalt outcropping that dropped precipitously to the water. The hackberry's crown was leafed with a streak of deadwood running up its trunk intertwined with the live wood. A bonsai master would work years to achieve that juxtaposition—the living and the dead. The *jin*, the *shari*. The grace of life and death.

"It's perfect," she said with reverence, wishing she could have shown the Wishing Tree to Eamon. Wrapped in the heavy silence, she could feel the force of this otherworldly place winding somewhere below the things we know. She wanted to sit at the rock-anchored roots and wish for everything she had ever wanted: that Eamon had lived, that her mother had lived, that Isabelle had lived, that all of them might be together, here, somehow, in this moment.

Nick put his arm around her shoulder, pulled her into him. "Stay here, do your tree thing, make a hundred wishes," he said. "I brought along my own form of worship."

He pulled out the segmented fishing-rod pieces from the aluminum tube. He fit the pieces together, attached the round reel, and strung the thin, tapered line through the rod eyes before scrabbling up the outcropping and standing where it veered sharply into the water to start his cast—a smooth, sinuous action of line and pole and arm waving in the air until the release, minuscule fly sailing and touching down on the river's surface with a tiny dimpling, then a slow-spinning drift.

Silva started sketching—first the hackberry leaning from the rock, and then Nick standing out on the rocky point over the water, each a complement to the other, Nick and the canyon's Wishing Tree somehow versions of the same thing. A maze of roots holding them onto to the rock. An anchoring they both had learned to trust. Faith in an order that reached beyond them. Eamon had taught her to always embrace the mystery of the unknown, said that when the past and the future met they always created some new shape, one often better-formed than the last.

She could have watched Nick forever—the hypnotic movement of his casting, the quiet drift of the fly on the water, his utter concentration as he read the current, finding the hidden swirls, the secret eddies of desire and release.

He caught the first fish fast, the next soon after. He reeled them in, thrashing, netted them, and held them up triumphantly for Silva to see, their silvery bodies flashing bright in the sun.

"Hungry yet?" Nick called out.

"With you, when am I not?" she said, her voice catching.

After Nick cleaned the fish, wrapped them in damp leaves, and put them in the shade, he scraped a fire line in the sand, brushing away everything organic before assembling a small ring of rocks and starting a fire using one of the egg-carton fire starters they'd made together—wax and pitch and paper melting and catching flame, sparks leaping into the air as the sticks he'd piled in caught fire, everything as dry as tinder. When Silva asked him if it was safe—open flame in drought country after all his warnings of fire—he assured her it was: the flames concentrated, burning only where he directed.

He got a good bed of coals going, then diced the garlic and onion and lemon he'd brought, stuffing the fishes' cavities full before wrapping them in foil and throwing them in the fire along with several large potatoes he'd preseasoned and wrapped in foil as well. She knew by the smell she wouldn't be able to resist it any more than she had anything else he'd cooked.

By the time dinner was done, fragrant and steaming, the river was wafting cool, the sand damp. Nick used green sticks to pull the fish and potatoes out of the coals, their foil wrapping powdery with ash, bits of aluminum flaking away like pieces of mica. When he presented her with a Fostoria plate artfully arranged with fish and potatoes and wedges of lemon, along with a Fostoria glass full of sparkling wine, Silva laughed out loud and shook her head in wonder.

"How?" she asked, turning the clear, star-edged plate around in her hands, its weight sturdy and thick. Fancy, Depression-era glass on a horse camping trip up Hells Canyon—dishes Nick's mother had painstakingly collected and then abandoned in the Larkins house when she'd absconded to Almost Paradise.

"I figured it was the right time to use them—our Wishing Tree trip," Nick said, sitting beside her. The fire crackled as he fed it twigs, building a peak of orange flame that matched the sunset. Across the river, an osprey dove into the water, coming up with a thrashing fish in its talons. "See?" Nick said. "Maybe there's enough here for everybody."

She hoped he was right.

When they were finished eating—tidy skeletons of fish bones and lemon rinds like a still-life Isabelle would have painted—Nick stood and pulled off his clothes. He ran and dove in the river, swimming several strokes out toward the current before turning and blowing the water from his mouth, shaking his hair from his eyes.

"Come on," he said. "What're you waiting for? There's no going slowly . . . but I think you already know that."

She tilted her head at him, her heart beating hard in her chest. He didn't know the half of it. At the shore's edge, Juniper barked and bit at the water, and Silva laughed, picked up a rock, and playfully threw it a few feet from Nick. "Go get it," she said to Juniper, but he just looked, tattered ears perked, smart enough to know a sinking offer.

She stripped down and dove in, Juniper right behind her, the three of them splashing around like a family of otters. She swam over to the basalt bluff and held onto it, its surface teeming with a miniature world of life, insects and rock-clinging plants joining with the darting shadows of fish below. When Nick followed her, she reached out and touched the line etched into his cheek before kissing him long enough that it felt like coming up for air after being held underwater.

"Tell me what happened," she finally said.

He looked at her a moment. "I was eighteen, had been out drinking. Saw Len walking down the sidewalk all slicked up, like he was out on the town. He stopped to talk to a young woman, 'preach the word of god.' He kept touching her, laying his hands on her shoulders, and suddenly it was like I was fourteen all over again, like my mom was still there. . . . I broke a bottle over his head. It was a bad fight."

She reached for his hand and clasped it in her own. "When Eamon died, I had my own version of that same fight," she said. A dark room, her body cast free of itself. "But we're here, in this exact moment, right now. That has to count for something, right?"

"I think so," Nick said, tucking her into his river-wet body, the current swirling pollen, fish muscling into deep water—this their river song, the song of their undoing, the song of their remaking.

The air washed cool, the canyon offering a lovely stretch of black-walled sky view, naked and bragging with stars. Crickets rasped in bunch grass and sage as a breeze sluiced upcanyon like a ghost echo of the river lapping against canyon walls and rushing on into the dark. Silva, too, felt unshackled. Released. She wanted to go back to the Wishing Tree and wish again and again—wishes for the future instead of the past, wishes she wanted to believe could come true.

CHAPTER THIRTY-EIGHT

Date: February 1, 2000
Title: Birth & Death
Subject: Lenite Mother
Setting: Almost Paradise Birthing Room & Cemetery
Medium: Watercolor and graphite on cold-press
Size: 8×10

Dearest Eamon,

There has come a reckoning, as there always eventually is. This isn't the first time it has happened since I've been here—a woman fallen ill in some way and then quickly taken away. Of course it is never the "great leader" who failc. Of course it is the most vulnerable who suffer the dearest consequences of his narcissistic, masochistic rule. Of course it is the women and the children who bear the brunt of all his great wrongs, their lives sacrificed for his self-serving cause over and over again. When has religion ever been anything but a woman's sure way to subjugation and loss?

The birth was to be celebrated as the first of the new millennium. I was allowed into the Birthing Room, a place kept separate and secret, Faith as its guardian—a midwife who has delivered untold numbers of Len's and the Lenites' progeny. It was one of Len's non-maiden wives, a woman named Shoshanna, a woman who laughed and stroked her stomach at the Childbearing Ceremony as she taught the maidens what to expect after their upcoming wedding-night "implanting." I was to paint the mother and child's portrait after the birth—a happy Madonna and babe—but instead, all there was was blood. So much blood. Cord coiled around the tiny neck, slick gray stillborn body, placental separation, maternal hemorrhage. Both mother and child dead within what seemed like moments, then both taken quickly away, buried in a hushed and solemn ceremony under the cemetery tree—a place full of maternal ghosts. Women calling out from the grave as their executioners bend their heads and declare, "The Lord's will be done."

The maidens have been kept separate since the wedding, herded together in waiting suspense until they've missed their first menses, at which point they will be celebrated and waited upon by the rest of the Almost Paradise wives, kept strong and healthy for their upcoming womb growth. A month in, and their time draws nigh.

I must escape this compound. I must leave before it is too late—before I can no longer keep my place. A woman unattached. A woman alone. A woman to be conquered. A woman without a child—even if I once had one, skin pink and flushed, tiny yelling mouth. I have asked Faith for her assistance. Told her my work is done. Told her that I must go to find you—my husband. This they can understand. The bonds that tie us together, even all these years apart. What might I see of myself then? Wrapped in your arms, away from all this, away from all I've become. What might I transform into? A new version of self, a new version of me, a new version of us? You and me and the family we were always meant to be. Is it possible to re-create history, to retrace those lines, to restitch those tapestries? Will you, dear Eamon, still be there, waiting for me?

All my love,
Isabelle

CHAPTER THIRTY-NINE

AUGUST 2001

The next morning, they left the horses hobbled in the shade and hiked to the highest part of the bluff, the trail carved into the sheer rock face, its peak banked around the cliff side—a hundred-foot drop overlooking a frothing set of rapids formed by the confluence of a mountain-fed creek still running high, fed from alpine snowmelt.

The vertical exposed cliffs were riddled with blasting holes where men had forced their way through, setting dynamite. Clusters of tenuous plants grew where the wind had deposited ash and dust enough to hold a few hair roots, but otherwise the bluff was devoid of life—nothing but a weaving of gray basalt rising precipitously above the inky river's depths.

"This isn't suitable for people—only mountain goats or sheep," Silva said, sweat running down her back as they made their way along the hot rock face. She looked down, imagining tumbling through the air to the water, thinking of the two shot-up mountain sheep.

"Nothing good without a little danger," Nick said, grinning, Juniper panting at his heels.

By the time they reached the point, the heat had built to a dizzying height, radiating off the rocks, only the wind sweeping upcanyon offering any relief. Nick sat near the edge, and Silva cautiously settled next to him, hypnotized by the roar of rapids below, surging like a blood-beat. The coiling entryway of this dry-heated underworld—a force so much bigger than everything else, so much more patient.

"My mother used to bring me here when I was young," Nick said, leaning forward, close enough to the edge that it made Silva's stomach tighten with nerves. "Told me the story of the Suicide Point lovers cast out by their tribes—a young warrior and a beautiful woman who fell in love but weren't of the same tribe. They were told they must not be together, that it was against the ways of their people, but they couldn't stop loving one another, so they were thrown out. They had nowhere to go, no family, no protection, only each other. So they went to the highest point they could find, braided their hair together, held each other close, and jumped, perishing in the rapids below, their bodies like the salmon, nestled forever together in the roll of the current."

Silva peeked over the edge, feeling the steep plunge in her gut, the current waving and twisting, bucking into spray. She thought of two bodies in a honeysuckle's trunk, twined around each other in endless embrace. "It wouldn't take much to fall," she said, pulling back.

"Sometimes you don't have a choice," Nick said.

They sat quietly together, waiting for the rafters to appear, Juniper holed up in a pocket of shade, the day too hot and sunny even for snakes. At least there was that much safety—the mammalian acclimation adaptability—the ability to regulate one's core temperature to threat.

Suddenly standing and looking upriver intently, Juniper was the first to spot the rafters. Following his gaze, they saw them, too—two bright blue smudges bobbing along the water.

"Here they come," Nick said, shading his eyes. "And we have the best seats in the house."

The rafts grew more distinct as they drew near—five in each boat along with the oarsman, paddles and helmets gleaming. They were enjoying the ride, hooting and hollering as the current swept them over white-capped swells channeled toward the rapids below the bluff.

As they got closer, one boat drew ahead of the other in order to maneuver the line they needed to take. The oarsman of the first boat looked up, spotted Nick and Silva watching, and yelled for Silva to jump and they would rescue her. A boatload of grinning faces turned up, spray bucking in front of them, but their attention was short-lived, drawn back to the river as the current wrapped sharp, boiling white-peaked, sweeping them into the first slough of real rapids, the raft like a toy bobber, nearly upending in the steep troughs and then rising precipitously to peak again, the river surging and banking in a roil of water around them.

The passengers woo-hooed, gripping the rope strung along the raft's sides while the boatman worked the oars, digging in with his whole body, aiming the raft for the left channel.

The raft followed the water, but instead of sweeping wide like they needed to, they rounded the bend heading directly for the mid-river shallows—a submerged gravel bar clogged with the detritus of spring washout, snags and branches as well as a root wad aimed upriver.

The oarsman leaned back, pulling with all his strength, trying to avoid the mass, but the power of the current swept the raft straight into the root wad and pinned it. The raft upended almost immediately, standing vertical in the middle of the river like some rubber appendage, water boiling around it, passengers and boatman pitched like rag dolls into the river, arms wheeling until they disappeared, bright-colored vests and shorts and helmets subsumed by the water until only the raft was left in its surging stand, the steady sweep of water around it.

First one, then the other rafters surfaced on either side of the tree, swept and dipping through the rapids and rocks, barely able to keep their heads above water. The boatman was pitched close in and grabbed a handful of branches, holding himself to the tree in the middle shallows.

Nick started running back down the trail, and Silva followed. The water was still cold and the undercurrents strong enough to hold on to anything that crossed their path. The river wouldn't offer any forgiveness.

At the bottom of the trail, Nick rushed toward the shore through a maze of boulders that had tumbled down millennia before. The other raft had now entered the channel. They'd come around the bend just as the wreck happened, and that oarsman stood, oaring hard to keep his raft to the left of the root wad. His passengers yelled frantically, and he tried to oar toward the people in the water, but they were swept far out of reach, moving fast. Finally, below the rapid set, he worked hard and made it to two swimmers, hauling them over by their vests. The two they'd missed were swimming toward shore. Those were the ones Nick and Silva aimed for.

Nick got there first and plunged into the water. The second raft beached a hundred yards below, everyone yelling for the swimmers. Nick made it to a rock shelf and grabbed a struggling woman. He pulled her up, helped her stand. She was shaken and weak, thin streams of watery red streaking down her legs where she'd bloodied her shins on rock.

The other swimmer made it to a side eddy that washed him closer to shore. He crawled up the rocks as Nick held the woman's arm and guided her back through the water. Silva met them and took the woman's other arm. On shore, they helped her sit next to the man, who was bent over and heaving, both of them coughing.

They were older than Silva expected—gray hair plastered to their heads, faces haggard with exertion. The woman's skin was as translucent as Eamon's had been in the end. This wasn't the typical college raft party—young kids out for an adrenaline rush. These were retirees, in their late sixties at least, maybe older. Silva took off her shirt and wrapped it around the woman's shoulders, leaving her own exposed to the sun.

At a muffled shout, they all looked to the boatman still in the center shallows, hanging onto the tree that stretched below the upended raft. He was trying to stand, pulling himself along the tree's submerged branches, struggling against the current that tried to take out his legs. He shouted again, a deep, wounded-animal noise, never taking his eyes off a spot in the water just ahead of him, a wash of yellow pinned in the tree's roots.

The woman with the bloodied shins held her hands to her face. "It's Mel, oh my god, it's Mel," she cried out, her voice hoarse and quavering.

The oarsman clawed against the water, but the current kept threatening to sweep him back, and he couldn't get enough purchase to get any farther.

In a final effort, he lunged, grabbing for a thick branch, but his hand missed and the water caught him and spun him down twenty feet before he could dig his feet in again and grab something to stop himself.

Nick took off, running up shore until the bank grew too steeply angled into the water to go any farther. Parallel to the stretch of water pushing headlong into the gravel bar, he rushed in up to his thighs. When he took another step, he lost his footing on the submerged rocks and nearly pitched into the current that swept outward a foot past him.

Silva ran up, stopping just below him. She held out her hand, trying to stay composed. "Nick," she said as carefully as if she were talking him down off a ledge. "Nick. Please, don't." Her hand shook, but otherwise she held completely still.

He looked out, gauging again the water in front of him, tensing his muscles against the current. Twenty feet to bridge the gap between him and the trapped woman. The distance like a chasm. Water strong enough to pull a person in two.

"Please. You can't make it from here," she pleaded. She wouldn't lose him, too, the water taking back anything it might have given.

Water surged past Nick's legs. She remembered the dream she'd had— the gray fish-woman swimming upcurrent, her mouth open in an underwater cry. Silva had thought it a dream of her mother, of what she'd almost become herself, but now it seemed something more. The weight of certainty settled on her chest, a pressure against her lungs like choking. When Nick turned and waded back, she felt as though her legs might give out.

The second boatman and a few passengers portaged the raft upriver, scrambling as fast as they could. The second boatman hollered to the stranded oarsman to stay put, they were coming, but the oarsman was still trying to make his way up the gravel bar, struggling ahead a few inches at a time. The second boatman had called in the accident on his emergency radio, and the radio hung from his side, crackling with coordinates and urgent voices as the rescue effort took shape a hundred miles away from them.

Nick helped hoist the second raft until they were above the upended raft, the sieve of roots and current still holding it there, the spot of yellow undulating in the current below it.

Silva stood, her arms crossed and shivering, watching as the boatman, Nick, and two other passengers oared hard into the current. Nick grappled in the bottom of the raft and found a vest while they angled around the center channel to the left of the other raft. He braced himself by holding the side rope. Silva was glad for at least that much security.

They drew out of the current into a backwash, and when they steadied there, the boatman threw a rope to the other oarsman still struggling in the shallows, yelled for him to take hold. He caught the rope and tried to walk, bracing his weight against it, but he fell facedown, rolling in the water like a log. Nick and the others worked to pull him in against the drag of the current while the boatman backstroked hard.

When they finally got him in the boat, he said, "She's right there," pointing, breathless and choked. Silva could see her—caught in the tree, not a foot under the water. She imagined being held underwater until she sucked in, breathed the river into her lungs. She couldn't look. She made her way back to the group knotted together, pallid faces watching for their friend.

The upended raft was stable in the back current, close to the tree. The boatman gave directions—throw the rope, tie off, hold steady. She was caught in a logjam of roots and current. They worked together, two of them leaning into the water, reaching both hands until they got holds on the vest, clothing, hair, whatever they could reach. Nick heaved with everything he had, but the woman's body wouldn't budge, the suction trapping her there. It took three of them to pull her free. Her helmet was gone, her shoes. She was naked from the waist down. The water had stripped her of everything but her vest.

Silva tried not to look at her pale body slipping over the raft's edge like some fish they'd caught and hauled aboard. Bile rose in Silva's throat.

They put the woman in between the thwarts, and the boatman knelt and unbuckled her vest, exposing her wrinkled breasts, flattened on her chest. He tipped her head to the side, her eyes open and staring, her face pale, her fingers tangled with bits of hairlike roots. The oarsman pushed down in a series of chest compressions, then centered her head, pinched her nose, and breathed into her mouth while the current swept them back out, the oarsman continuing his constant rhythm—pump, pump, pump, breathe, pump, pump, pump, breathe. A rhythm Silva knew well, Eamon swallowed under wires, cords, his knobby hands thin-skinned and utterly still.

Nobody said anything as the boatman strained on the oars, heading for shore. Silva concentrated on the approaching rock shelf, their steady progress toward the bank.

When they cleared the main current and oared into the shallows, Nick jumped out and walked the boat, the river lapping at his shins. Silva didn't want to see the woman, didn't want any of them to see her, but there was no helping it.

The men carried her out of the boat and laid her flat on a rock, and the boatman continued CPR, tipping her on her side every so often. The rest of them stood helpless, hoping for the woman's lungs to work against the water, the miracle cough and choke. But there was nothing but the deadening rhythm of the compressions and breaths, of the river rushing past. The woman's chest made a startling depression with each push, her eyes staring up at nothing, her nakedness a blending of gray. The boatman's sweat dripped down his face as he worked, pumping and breathing under the glaring sun.

Silva went over, put her hand out. "Stop," she said, quiet. She took his clasped hands in her own. "Stop," she said again, holding him still.

He looked at her and shook his head.

"She's not coming back," she said, the woman with her fish body, swimming the current.

There was silence. The man lifted his hands from the woman's chest and stepped backward, almost falling before he sat down heavily.

Silva shaded the woman from the sun. She reached out and stroked the back of her fingers against the woman's cheek until she reached her eyes; she closed them gently, then smoothed back the woman's wet hair. Someone brought towels, and she folded one to put it under the woman's head, then carefully draped the other over the woman's nakedness, covering her.

They were all quiet. Someone gestured toward the river, and they all watched as the pinned raft wobbled and tilted loose, finally shimmying free of the water and root wad. It flipped and floated belly-up, bobbing high over the rapids, skimming fast with no load. One oar was still locked in, and it angled back like a broken arm, making the raft float sideways, bumping into rocks as it swept downriver. They watched until it was gone, the river clear, no evidence left behind of what had just happened.

The first oarsman was sitting with his head in his hands. Juniper sat next to the woman Nick had helped ashore. She buried her face in the dog's neck and started crying, sobs that shook her shoulders. Silva felt a deep choking dread, the woman's sorrow as familiar as her own heartbeat, everything around her always seeming to come undone.

It took another half hour before the helicopter broke the canyon into reverberations. It landed on a bit of shore below them, beach grit blowing out from the wash of its blades.

A young, clean-faced EMT dressed in an orange rescue suit jumped out and ran to the woman. He uncovered her, checked her pulse, listened for breathing, then did a series of deep, violent chest compressions. Between pumps, he asked the boatman what time he'd started CPR, had he fully compressed, had he breathed after fifteen compressions.

Silva turned her head as the pilot brought a spine board and they loaded the woman, stabilizing her head and securing her arms and legs, strapping down her body before lifting her. They said a sheriff boat was on the way up from Kirkwood Ranch, said they would need Nick's and Silva's statement' before they hauled out the crew and passengers.

When the helicopter rose, Nick came to Silva's side and pulled her into him, put his face against her hair.

"You did all you could. There was nothing more you could have done," she said quietly.

He shook his head against her. "There's always more you could've done."

She knew it too well. Each sorrow coming from a set of circumstances that might have been prevented, another choice in one moment.

When the sheriff's jet boat arrived, the deputies handed out drinking water and emergency bags full of supplies: Gatorade, crackers, little red plastic cups of Jell-O—things for people in the hospital, recovering from illness. They took statements—the raft hitting, passengers thrown. A matter of seconds. The sheriff thanked Nick and Silva for their help, gave the number where he could be reached if anything else came to mind, and then helped board the passengers, who were wrapped in blankets, shivering despite the afternoon heat. The river was a dark swath, fish—bug fat and greedy—slapping its surface. Nothing to say a life was lost.

Silva had to sit suddenly, her legs no longer able to hold her up against the familiar weight pressing down. Pain she knew like a second skin.

When they finally got back to the ranch, it was dusk, and across the river, a fishing boat idled, drifting in the current. She wondered if anglers down-river had seen the empty raft float by, if they'd snagged bits of cloth on their hooks, cursed the false weight on their lines.

Nick unpacked and put up the horses, and they went to bed before it was dark, lying curled into each other, Nick trying to whisper comfort to her, but it was as if the woman's death had dredged up everything Silva had packed away. She couldn't shake the feeling of dread, couldn't pull herself from the feeling that she was the one drowning, one breath at a time. She let Nick hold her, tell her it was going to be okay, that he wouldn't let anything bad happen to her. She wanted to believe him, but she knew, as much as he wanted to give, some things weren't there for the offering. Some things were outside of anyone's control.

CHAPTER FORTY

Join hands, join hearts, join minds, fingers intertwined, a circle unbroken, a ring of holy women. Ring around the rosies, pocket full of posies, ashes, ashes, we all fall down. Spinning and spinning, you run, tiger got you by the tail, a churned blur of butter underneath the circling tree. Rise up! Rise up! Their fingers brushing you, wings of light and dust, a garland full of mourning. Be healed! Child of God, be healed of yourself! Their breath like fire, their fingers like gold, your woeful self a sickness, a curse, a dark hole, your tongue seized and swollen, your words like lead inside your head. Be free and rise up! Sing your praises to the Lord! Your new self a blank slate, your purity your veil, your marriage bed your covering, your life not your own. May he find you worthy, may he find you pure, may he find you a vessel he might fill, your breath his breath, your body his body, your soul his soul, your mind his mind. You must die to him in order to rise again. This, your final fall. Circle of women, circle of light, circle of blood, circle of life.

CHAPTER FORTY-ONE

Mack came early the next morning, brought the paper with him. "Front-page news," he said.

WOMAN DIES IN HELLS CANYON was written in huge black letters across the top of the paper. The title on the article read, DEADLY RAFTING ACCIDENT CLAIMS ONE, and was accompanied by a grainy picture of Silva and Nick and a few of the rafters clustered together. Underneath the picture, the caption stated, *Nick Larkins, local outfitter, and Silva Merigal, caretaker of the Larkins Ranch, on scene, helping with rescue attempts.*

Silva couldn't remember anyone taking pictures. She glanced quickly away, scanning the other news as she steadied her breathing. Charts demonstrating record low water tables and the worst drought the area had seen in years; an article detailing a tractor-trailer wreck on Highway 95; a boxed piece giving advice on how to save water in your garden. Only when she'd collected herself did she read the article on the raft wreck, but there was nothing about the woman's body becoming fluid, stripped by the river. Nothing about the knowledge in her gray eyes, the images imprinted into them—a reckoning of her union with the river. Nothing about her swimming upriver, her mouth open in a silent cry. Silva had seen into the woman's eyes. Felt her skin. She couldn't let it go. She folded the paper and put it next to the stove, the news of this place something she wished to burn until it all disintegrated into ash.

"It's got to be taken care of right away," Mack said, Silva catching the end of what he'd been saying to Nick. "The outfitters are worried about getting sued. There's a lot of paperwork to complete." He looked at Silva and shook his head. "That's some hard business you two had."

"They want both of us to come down?" Nick asked.

"No. They said they need Silva to stay here to field anything that might come up. They're going up to blow out the jam today. They may need something or have more questions. I'm sure sorry," he said, looking at Silva as he stood up. "I'll try to get him back to you right away."

"I've got Juniper. I'll be okay," Silva said, trying to reassure Nick as well as Mack, both of them frowning and troubled. She only wished she could believe herself.

Nick gathered his things, then hesitated. "Be careful. Don't go anywhere," he said.

"I won't," she replied, her insides as heavy as lead. Places she'd already been.

She stayed inside as they left, the radio crackling with traffic as leaves on the locust next to the house twisted loose, drifting down the tin roof with a quick slide. Hot air pushed against the heat-weary hills, blowing the pines above the house, needles shaken loose and scattering over the grass in hot dusty gusts. Another layer of drying out, another degree of drought.

She went out to the burn pile she'd made in her first weeks at the ranch: grayed driftwood heaped next to the door she'd found washed up. She pulled the door from where she'd leaned it against the elm and carried it to the river. In the water, the door bobbed and twirled, as if the river was indecisive, settling on which way to carry it. Finally, it caught a bit of current and started downriver, slowly at first, catching in some shallows before gathering speed. Silva walked alongside on the shore, picking up large rocks that she threw until she'd landed several on the door's top. She wanted to sink it, settle it somewhere on the river's bottom—an exit from the world above, entry to some other place, some other life. She wanted to leave it for the woman to find, but it floated just past her reach, heading where she couldn't follow.

She stayed in the house the rest of the day, curled up in bed in the full light like an invalid—a reminder of where she'd been not long ago. She heard a boat surge upriver sometime early midday, heading for the rapids that had taken the woman, going to blast away the jam even though it was too late to do any good now. She paged through the bee books, stopping to read a section about queens. *The queen will not crave for air, or the light of the sun; she will die without even once having tasted a flower. . . . Not even twice, it may be, in her life shall she look on the light . . . and on one occasion only will she make use of her wings . . . to fly to her lover.*

When Juniper woke Silva with his barking the next morning, she jerked upright, thinking of Len and his men, of Nick gone again, but everything was stilled and silent. Then the radio crackled to life in the kitchen. A woman's voice, disembodied and tinny, "Larkins Ranch, repeat, do you read?" followed by a rustling crackle.

Silva got up and rushed to the kitchen, sure that there'd been another accident, another fight, another disaster. She keyed the mic quickly. "This is Larkins Ranch, go on," she said, her heart racing, her breath heaving as she waited for the response, for whatever was coming.

Hesitation, static feed, then, "Larkins Ranch, this is Almost Paradise. We have a large bee swarm on the premises." Static. "Do you copy?" A slight accent lilting over the radio's static—a hesitant voice too close to the microphone. Someone unused to speaking on the radio.

Silva stared at the radio. "Faith?" she finally asked, her own voice thin and questioning.

"This is Faith." Static. "Your bees have come to us."

Silva dropped the mic and sprinted outside.

A few workers flew around the apiary, but when she opened the top boards of the first hives, instead of a buzzing horde, there were only a few forlorn drones crawling along the hexagons of wax. She pulled top after top, her throat tight, her pulse hammering through her limbs. The bees gone. The reality of it took her breath away.

She ran back to the house. "Almost Paradise, do you copy?" she called, trying to control the wavering timbre of her voice, planning as she spoke.

"We copy," Faith said, her sunken voice coming as if from underwater.

"I'm on my way," Silva said.

A hesitation of static, then a reply: "We're expecting you."

Silva ran back to Nick's books, paging through until she found the sections on swarming—what to do, how to gather and transport the swarm—but there was nothing on how to do it in the wild, some burlap bags and a horse your only available tools.

She threw on boots and locked Juniper in the house. She thought about trying to raise Mack on the radio, but it would only cause more agitation. Nick wouldn't be back for hours, and swarms were unpredictable—they might fly farther, fly where she couldn't find them at all. She knew what could happen, what Nick might do if he found the bees absconded to Almost Paradise. Eli had said that the bees wouldn't abandon her as they had the others, but they'd flown to Len Dietz as though he were a Pied Piper singing them forward to their certain death.

She saddled Tiko, grabbed several burlap bags and Nick's smoker, and stuffed them into the knapsack, Juniper barking from inside the house as Tiko took off at a full gallop toward the trail she thought she would never ascend again. This time, she let Tiko go as fast as he wanted, his coat quickly darkening with sweat, his lungs working like bellows underneath her as they climbed. He didn't ease his speed until Silva saw the boundary fence ahead and pulled back. There was someone standing at the wire gate, waiting for her.

When she got close enough, she saw it was Isaac, the bulky leg brace encasing his right leg. Wordlessly, he unhooked the fence and pulled it open for her to ride through, then secured it behind her as she dismounted. She swallowed hard against her fear. It felt like a trap, even if the bees had swarmed to Almost Paradise on their own accord—just as Isabelle had, just as Nick's mother had.

"I've come for the bees, the swarm—" she said to Isaac, glancing around as if she might spot the bees on her own. He looked at her as though she were an apostate, as though she were the one threatening to take everything away when really it was Len who had been robbing everybody, plundering and pilfering, taking what he desired.

Isaac hobbled past her, following the brush line that edged the canyon and backed the Almost Paradise cemetery ahead. The large handheld radio clipped to his front pocket crackled with static as a man's distant voice called out helicopter flight coordinates—a pilot en route somewhere. Silva wondered if the Lenites had been listening in on the raft accident radio correspondence, too, and all her radio correspondence since she'd been in the canyon. No wonder they seemed to know everything.

Isaac led her straight toward the cemetery, dozens of weathered crosses standing solemn in morning shadow, sheltered under the towering palaver tree, its massive roots anchoring all the graves full of women and babies—a meeting spot for conversations of the dead. All the females fallen from paradise. A circle of babies clutched in its roots.

Silva finally saw it—a black, undulating, U-shaped curtain of bees draped from the ponderosa's lower branch, low enough that they almost brushed the graves. Honeybees massed by the thousands, buzzing in unison as though they'd come to speak for the dead.

Isaac stopped at the cemetery's border, and Silva held herself straight, trying to maintain her equanimity, uneasy with the possibilities—this place where Isabelle was likely interred, along with Nick's mother and baby brother. But there was no time to look for them.

Glancing toward the compound and then back to her, his eyes the same startling ice-blue as Nick's, Isaac said, "You should hurry."

She wanted to take his hand, tell him there was more, so much more than this. A future that wasn't shaped by devastation. But his face was as guarded and shuttered as Faith's had been.

"The Larkins Ranch—you're staying there?" he asked as she unbundled the burlap bags.

"Yes. I'm the caretaker," she said, modulating her voice. Some disquieting thing in Isaac's tone started her heart thumping with dread.

"You shouldn't stay—" he blurted, just as his radio squawked to life again. This time the voice was clear and close, a deep, commanding voice Silva knew well.

"Almost Paradise, all hands ready." Len Dietz's voice repeated the phrase twice before the radio went silent.

"You must be fast," Isaac said, before hobbling back toward the white-washed buildings, his bad leg dragging sideways with each step, leaving a skid-line in the path's dust.

Her body alive and pulsing with Isaac's and Len's words—some communication she wasn't a part of, some kind of energy in the air, a feeling of impending disaster—she quickly led Tiko to the brush line and tied him off out of sight from the compound, then gathered the smoker with shaking hands. She lit it and blew on the dry grass until it smoldered, smudging the air with smoke. She walked to the cemetery, stepping cautiously between the graves, scanning for names, but the crosses were blank—nothing to say whose body lay beneath the soil.

When Silva reached the swarm, the sound of buzzing was so loud it took over the air—an electric, humming vibration she could feel in the cavity of her chest. The hair on her arms rose as if she were in a storm, the air charged with current. She sat the smoker on the ground, smoke drifting like graveyard fog around her feet, then offered her hand to the bees. They crawled over and around and under one another, their wings translucent, their antennae waving as they communicated in their unknown language. They swarmed her, shrouding her arm up to the elbow, drawing her into the warmth of their center, humming over her skin with thousands of pulsing abdomens as if she were a part of the swarm herself.

She opened a burlap bag, held it under the swarm, and slowly encased the bottom bees. With gentle movements, she swept in the first tumble of hundreds, tied the top of the bag, and then carefully set it in the tree's shade, where the burlap moved like a shifting shadow. She repeated the same motions again and again, the bees docile, letting themselves be shaken loose. But then those remaining—over half the swarm—suddenly took to the air. They were so thick she couldn't see anything but their bodies hovering around her. They landed on her, covering her head and face, arms, and neck, thousands of wings brushing her skin. They crawled over her lips, along her eyebrows, hung from her earlobes, the weight and warmth of them surprisingly heavy, as if she'd been suddenly anchored. She felt her body respond to theirs—a sonorous humming from deep inside her. Then, one by one, they lifted, the dark mass of them passing overhead, swirling upward until they finally gathered farther up the pine, weighing its upper branches down, massing too high to reach.

A rumble of men's voices came from the compound, and Silva's heart jumped, remembering Isaac's watchful edginess, his warning to hurry. She grabbed the smoker and bags of bees and ran back to Tiko, keeping herself as much out of sight as possible. She looked back and spotted the source of the voices: two dozen or more heavily armed men in head-to-toe camo holding stiff, military poses, a quarter mile away, their backs to her.

Her ears thundering with the rush of her own blood, she led Tiko along the fence back to the gate. Whatever the Lenites were preparing for, she knew Len and his men would stop at nothing. The storm Delores had warned of was coming.

Looking over her shoulder to make sure nobody had spotted her, she mounted Tiko and kicked her heels into his withers until he was streaking downhill, the air rushing past them knife-hot, the sun beating hard into her skin, her sweat running like water. She gripped the bags full of bees, hunkered low as Tiko thundered through the rise and fall of the hills. Flush with heat and surging adrenaline, Silva felt loose limbed, as if she and the bees might take off flying together at any moment, the ground wavering with heat waves until it seemed they weren't running, but floating, gliding through the air without effort.

Backed by sky, the trail swung sharply down and Tiko stumbled, Silva grabbing his mane as he knocked rocks into the abyss, the trail turning to air. He heaved himself to safety at the last minute, skidding through the lower switchbacks, his muscles twitching as finally they broke out onto the Larkins Ranch grounds. A gust of wind hit Silva hard in the face, a hot blast peppering her skin like a swarm of insects as Juniper came sprinting from the house, Nick on his heels.

He grabbed Tiko's reins as she slid off, the burlap sacks clutched in her hands. "The bees," she said breathlessly, still gripping them.

Uncomprehending, Nick looked from the bags back to Silva.

"Faith radioed in early this morning. They swarmed—went to Almost Paradise. I didn't want to lose them. I tried to get as many as I could," she said in a gulping rush.

Nick's face flickered from one emotion to the next as he looked from Silva to the apiary, taking in the weight of the loss. A punch to the gut. She was consumed with shame, as though it'd been her doing—all the things she'd left unsaid, all the things she'd kept from him. He deserved the truth, but it was too late now, everything verging on disaster.

He dropped Tiko's reins, strode quickly to the apiary, and pulled off a hive cover, looking inside in disbelief just as Silva had, going from one hive to the next. She wanted to weep at the look on his face as he took in all the empty interiors—all of his plans gone in one fell swoop.

Her arms quivering, she held out the bags. An offering, a dissolution of her sins.

He took them from her hands, the look in his eyes wild and unseeing. "You shouldn't have risked yourself like that," he said. But he opened the bags as carefully as a lover, pinning open the burlap and releasing the captured bees back to the hives they'd just abandoned. "Where were the rest?" he asked, turning to her.

"At the cemetery, in the ponderosa." She didn't want to say it, make him have to think about his mother, his brother, too, the bees there speaking for them all—all the voices of the lost.

He strode to the house, the screen catching against the porch as he yanked it open. The movement knocked over a vase of flowers Silva had set on the porch railing, shattering it into a mess of water, glass, and petals. She ran to brush the broken pieces into a pile before Juniper could step in them, but a shard lodged in a crack and sliced her palm, a line of blood instantly welling up and dripping from her wrist. She pinched the cut tight, tried to keep from crying, but all of it was right at the surface, threatening to overtake her entirely, everything unraveling at the seams. A deep, gulping pain rose in her chest. She couldn't speak past it, couldn't say or do anything except watch as Nick mounted Sage and rode toward Almost Paradise, where dozens of armed men would be waiting, their anger as sure as his own.

But before he was off the grounds, the sound of a motor reverberated off the canyon walls, and Nick pulled up, watching a helicopter suddenly appear from over the hills downriver, angling up the canyon toward the ranch.

At first Silva thought it was the same search-and-rescue helicopter from the raft wreck, but then she saw it was different—green and white with a Fish and Game emblem, its front a bubble of glass. She remembered Isaac's radio, a pilot calling in flight coordinates.

It flew in low over them and landed on the flat she'd mown for the rafting group; then a man in an olive-green uniform came running from it across the bridge as Nick rode Sage back to the house. Silva could only assume it was Ted, the Fish and Game warden Nick and Mack had discussed.

Over the helicopter's high-pitched whir, the man yelled, "There's been a breach—the Paradise elk have escaped. If we don't get it under control quickly, it could wipe out the whole region's population—elk, deer, and sheep," he said, his voice hoarse. "I could use your aim."

Nick glanced toward the apiary for a split-second, then at Silva.

Ted waved them on, said, "We have room for both of you. There's no time to waste."

Silva locked Juniper back in the house again as Nick stalled Sage and Tiko. They ran together to the helicopter, shielding their faces against the rotor-wash. Salt edged the corners of Silva's mouth. She closed her eyes a moment, breathing through her nose, trying to brace herself for the onslaught of what she'd always feared was coming. A vise pressing in until there was no space left to inhabit.

CHAPTER FORTY-TWO

What comes of love when it is lost, when it circles around you and then flies away, disappearing into the gray sky? What comes of lostness when it is no longer lost, your feet finding their way over and over again to the same spot, resting on ground that was once unbeknownst to you, burial ground of the broken, the sound of wings returning as you look out over the canyon walls into air like breath, rising and dissipating like your own blood? You bury them here, these the lost, these the songs, these the holy buds of life, each like a tiny curled seedpod cradled in the roots of the mother tree. You would save them all if you could—all the words, all the songs, all the lost love winging forever away. You raise your arms, and you cry out into the wind. It takes each word and spreads them until they fall echoing from the cliffsides into the rushing water—birds and leaves and seeds and bees diving and disappearing, following the echoing voices of love lost.

CHAPTER FORTY-THREE

Ted sat up front next to the pilot, Silva and Nick in the back jump-seats, headsets and harnesses on, the inside of the helicopter a sauna despite its open doors. The pilot adjusted knobs and levers, increasing the motor's RPM until it was screaming, blades blurring with speed as they lifted off. He radioed in their location, call numbers, and destination—everything translating to Len's radios as the Lenites prepared for battle. A war that had been coming all along.

"They're monitoring the radio traffic—they can hear everything," Silva said, speaking into her headset. Nick looked over at her. "There was a group of men gathering on the compound this morning. . . ."

"So that's where the occupiers went," Ted replied. "That idiot deputy, Slocum, told me they had it all under control, but the sheriff's office sent word that a group of the Lenites had left the visitor center early this morning."

The Lenites, the bees, the elk—everyone following the instinct to swarm and abscond.

They rose and banked sharply, a dizzying rush of sudden height. As the ground receded under the doors, Silva kept her eyes ahead, staring at the horizon and holding onto her seat.

"How many got out?" Nick asked Ted through the headset, his voice coming from a crackly distance through the earphones even though he was sitting only a foot away.

"Not certain—as many as two dozen," Ted replied. "Enough to cause a disaster. That son of a bitch better have tagged them, is all I can say. They still have their wild instincts—ran north above the river to the thickest

understory, but hopefully we'll still be able to spot them. If we do, you're on."
He gestured to the two rifles secured in between the front seats.

The helicopter fishtailed side to side through air currents in a pause-set
motion that made Silva's stomach feel as if it had flipped over and was
suspended upside down. It felt like her heart was in the same position. Len
Dietz versus Nick—versus them both. More than even Nick understood.

They reached altitude, flying high enough that the spread of the Two
Rivers plateau flattened below, the land losing its contours from the air.
When they reached the back stretch of the elk-ranch acreage a few miles
from the compound, they saw the remaining captive elk bunched together,
their tawny rumps bright against their darker coats. Ted instructed the pilot
to fly to the summer grazing pastures, to follow the fence line. In the back
corner, they found the breach—a mess of boards stacked up against the wire
fence, somebody's attempt at temporarily mending the gap.

The helicopter circled low, flying along the river, then made paths farther
in, but there were no elk—nothing but a few mule deer, who bounded
away in long-distance hops like gazelles when the chopper came near. The
pilot angled toward the foothills.

They flew a few miles, the mountains rising from the rolling plateaus
studded with pine, when the pilot pointed to what looked like brown boulders in a bunch of shrubby growth—several elk bedded down in the day's
heat. The pilot circled in close, and with the chopper's disturbance the elk
took off running, dark necks stretched long, yellow rumps tucking under
as they picked up speed. A dozen cows, eight bulls, and ten calves. More
than they'd expected to find. Nick looked through a spotting scope and said,
"Ears tagged," and that was enough.

The pilot maneuvered the helicopter lower, following the herd as they ran
a loose-fanned line. He passed and banked back, and they scattered, shifting
direction as if pushed by the wind.

Ted indicated a large cow in the rear of the herd, running a few yards
behind. "Think you can take that one?" he asked.

Nick swung his leg out into the empty space outside his door, the harness snug against his chest as he held the rifle low, following the cow over the top of the scope, lining up the sights. When he pulled the trigger, the cow's front knees buckled and she fell, skidding and tumbling to a stop, her body in a twitching heap.

Back around, the remaining elk close below, Nick lined up his next shot, but it went high, a spine shot, and the cow bellowed in pain. She stopped running, circling drunkenly. One of the calves stopped and looked back at her, bleating.

Nick cursed, waiting for the pilot to swing back around so he could take another shot, and as the helicopter tipped, he took the cow down. She toppled sideways, her front leg broken, the light blond of her underbelly exposed, but she kept bellowing, her head raised, her back legs working to push her up again. The bleating calf ran back toward her, and Nick aimed carefully. Two quick shots—one for the cow and the other for her calf.

Silva tried not to look, her heart thudding sick and heavy in her chest, bile rising in her throat. This wasn't anything anyone should ever have to do, anything anyone should ever see.

They chased the others, Ted and Nick trading shot after shot, the open land preventing the elk from taking cover or resting. Exhausted from the pursuit, the elk ran bunched together, the bulls' antlered heads extended at awkward angles, the calves falling behind. Nick and Ted didn't stop shooting until the last one collapsed—brown, twisted mounds of carcasses strung for a mile.

As the pilot called in the dead elks' location, Silva's stomach twisted, nausea coming on so suddenly she barely had time to lean out the open door, vomit spattering over the helicopter's side. The pilot slowed and leveled out as she heaved over and over, Ted passing a bag back to her, even though it was too late, nothing but bitter bile burning the back of her throat.

Ted leaned back, patted her on the knee. "At least you waited until it was over," he said as she wiped her face with the back of her hand.

"Who's going to take care of the carcasses?" Nick asked, his voice tight and his face drawn, everything about him tormented, trembling on the edge of anger and sorrow.

"The CWD crew was just waiting for the coordinates. They'll be on their way," Ted said. He turned to look at Silva. "Sorry you had to see that. Never should have come to this."

The pilot circled around, heading downcanyon as Nick and Ted looked for more elk. Hot wind blew dead grass, lifting dirt loose from the hillsides next to them, the Snake winding below. In the distance, acres of yellow star thistle shifted color as it blew, the sky such a deep indigo it seemed as if they were suspended in a fathomless sea instead of the air. But as they wrapped around the canyon toward the Larkins Ranch, they saw a dark smudge of smoke rising near Almost Paradise, its edges rimmed with orange spilling out like ribbons of dust.

Delores's warning: *There's a storm brewing. . . .*

The pilot altered direction, aiming toward the rising cloud, all of them trying to ascertain what it was and where it was coming from. With sinking dread, Silva knew—this was Len's storm. It had been coming for years. It had been coming all along.

Within moments, the acrid smell of char made its way into the helicopter, the smoke boiling up—a black billow rising like a mushroom cloud, the sky the color of a contusion. Flames licked the grass and brush, smoke engulfing the hills below the cemetery's palaver tree. Right where Silva had been hours earlier, her hand buried in bees.

The swarm. The certainty of it settled in the core of her stomach like cold lead. They had burned the bees, their retaliation for Fish and Game invading their land and killing their elk. Their retaliation for Nick's trespass. They had set their promised apocalypse in motion.

The helicopter pilot climbed, circling around the fire, his voice in their earpieces calling it in to the wildland-fire repeater, reporting on conditions and location. Heat radiated up through the helicopter's open doors and

flames leaped from grass to tree, rushing over the trail and down the hillsides with a kind of insatiability that left Silva paralyzed. Nick had talked
about how fast dry grass burned, desiccated thistle—how fire came like a
rush of wind. There was no stopping Len Dietz, just as there was no stopping flames from rushing through dead grass.

Smoke billowed thick all around them as an advance of hungry flames
rushed down the draw like a curse, eating everything in their wake. No
matter how quickly they responded to the fire, there would be no getting it
under control in these conditions without retardant planes and helicopters
dumping as fast as they could refill, and it would be too late by the time the
pilots gathered their gear, got in the air. It was too close, burning too fast,
Nick leaning so far out his door Silva was afraid his harness would break,
his expression a mask of anguish and fear as he gauged the fire's trajectory
just as he had the raft wreck.

Suddenly through the smoke, they had a view of the Almost Paradise
complex below them. Near the cemetery, there was a flurry of movement,
men with rifles slung over their shoulders lining up as the helicopter flew
over, one holding what looked like a rocket launcher in his hands, Len
Dietz standing behind them. Beside him was a boy Silva recognized—Isaac,
armed the same as the men, seemingly as ready for war as they were, looking
skyward, a lit blowtorch in his hand.

"They *started* that fire," Ted said, shock in his voice.

"The bees," Silva said, looking out with a sinking heart at Isaac standing
below the burning palaver tree, her chest tight with pain. "They've burned
the bees. . . ."

Standing among the graves of all the fallen women and girls, Len Dietz
stepped forward in a fighting stance and lifted a loudspeaker to his mouth.
"Your slaughter will not go unanswered. Your time of judgment is here," he
said, his voice cutting through the canyon, coming disembodied through the
air. "'Behold, the day is coming, burning like a furnace; and all the arrogant
and every evildoer will be chaff; and the coming day will set them ablaze so

that it will leave them neither root nor branch . . . burn for burn, wound for wound, bruise for bruise.'"

His men lifted their guns and yelled, "Burn for burn, wound for wound, bruise for bruise."

Len ushered Isaac to stand next to him as he spoke again. "'As a tongue of fire consumes stubble and dry grass collapses into the flame, so their root will become like rot and their blossom blow away as dust; for they have rejected the law of the Lord of Hosts and despised the word of the Holy One of Israel. . . . For the lips of an adulteress drip honey, but in the end she is bitter as wormwood. Her feet go down to death.'"

Len stopped then and lifted the boy's hand in the air. "Nick Larkins, behold your brother, Isaac."

Len's booming voice rang through the air as his men dropped to their knees and took aim, firing as one unit, muzzles flashing with light.

Veering off quickly, the pilot called in emergency codes, using the words *arson* and *under fire*, Isaac looking up at them with Nick's same blue-eyed, sinking gaze, standing next to Len Dietz as a son.

The rest of it came so closely together it seemed instantaneous: the quick *tata-tat-tat* of automatic rifle fire—like someone impatiently knocking on a hollow door, demanding entry—then a gray streak of screaming smoke and a rocking percussion so close it blotted Silva's ears and knocked the helicopter sideways. Darkness engulfed them, a whirlpool that sucked them down, spinning and banking, swallowed in smoke.

At first Silva thought the explosion was something that had happened inside her own brain, a distant ringing pain in her skull, everything as silent and dark as if she were being held deep underwater, insistent hands pulling at her, trying to lift her to the surface. A voice in her ears said, "Shots fired, repeat, shots fired. We're going down—" Someone pressed a wet cloth in her hands, telling her to breathe through its dampness, the haze of choking smoke everywhere, Nick slumped over next to her, unconscious. The pilot angled the helicopter downriver, sweeping so low over the water it looked as if it were about to take them captive.

The pilot radioed in that he was making an emergency landing and then called out a sharp warning through the headset as they went down, the helicopter tilting sideways before crash-landing with jarring impact on flat land a mile below the ranch, rotor blades whirring unevenly.

Silva sat dazed, her brain thick, the harness tight against her chest, her limbs immobilized, feeling as though she'd suddenly sunk into quicksand. Ted unbuckled his harness and came around the side to pull Nick out of his own harness, hoisting him away from the helicopter and laying him on the ground carefully, stabilizing his neck and head, calling for emergency responders, relaying Nick's vital signs—his heart and breathing rate elevated.

When Silva finally managed to get herself unbuckled, she found the ground with unstable legs and stumbled to Nick's side. She touched his face, his neck, crying for him to be okay.

He opened his eyes and looked at her with dilated pupils and tried to push himself up. Ted held him back, told him he couldn't go anywhere. Told him it was all okay, that he just needed to stay still and wait for the paramedics to arrive. But Silva knew where he was trying to go. *Juniper. The horses. The bees. The bonsai.*

Her feet found the trail's packed dirt, Ted calling her name over and over from somewhere behind as she started running, her legs moving under her faster and faster until finally it was quiet—just the uneven rhythm of her footsteps and the smoke pulling her forward, moving through a land she no longer knew except by the feel of it under her feet. A jagged line of fire rushed down the hills toward the ranch, black smoke mushrooming above, blotting the sky.

Somewhere along the way, she stumbled and fell hard, pebbles embedded in her palms and knees. A grasshopper landed on the back of her hand and perched there a moment before springing out of sight. Nick's story of the

neighbor's barn burning returned to her, the plague of locusts feeding themselves into the flames.

She kept running until she made it to the ranch lawn, fire already overtaking the back of the property where the hives were—the air so thick with
smoke that the bees wouldn't be able to see to escape, a rush of hot wind
crackling the air, driving the fire forward toward the apiary.

She ran through the smoke to them, picturing flames licking up the
hives, igniting the wax inside, consuming the bees she'd brought back along
with the brood they'd left behind, heat scorching their wings as the flames
overtook them. She couldn't see anything, couldn't breathe. She bent over
coughing until it felt like her lungs would collapse, her eyes and airways
burning as though they'd had embers pressed into them.

She ran for the hose, dragging it from the garden, where it tangled in
the wire fence, looping around itself like a snake coiling under threat. She
yanked until it came loose, but it was too short, would only reach the corner
of the yard, the smoke a wall, thick and choking, the air a gray haze, flames
eating up acre after acre, insatiable and unstoppable. She coughed until she
gagged, light-headed and dizzy, her lungs rejecting the air.

The flames had reached the old sheep shed in the back corner, and the
grayed boards cracked and popped as they ignited into a rushing flare,
sending burning embers to the trees at the yard's edge and onto the roof of
the house. Flames creeped up the tree trunks into the tree crowns that blew
up like torches, raining down burning needles, setting the house roof on fire,
the yellow tips of flames licking up from the shingles.

Juniper barked frantically from the house, and Silva dropped the hose and
ran. When she rushed up the steps and opened the door, the dog streaked
past her and disappeared into the smoky haze. Her voice was croaking and
weak as she called for him over and over again.

She ran with the larch and juniper bonsai to the river and settled them in
shallow water before going back for the spruce, cedar, bristlecone, and hackberry. Afterward, holding a wet rag over her nose and mouth, she heaped

all she could carry from the house in her arms, grabbing the picture of Nick and his mother from the wall along with one of his bee books, the house sides crackling into flames that cloaked the house in smoke—as though the fire were ashamed of its own dirty work, its final consummation, everything turned to ash, a scab of char, a blackened bit of nothing. First it would take the walls, then the ceiling and the floor, then the bedroom she and Nick had shared, watching as the mornings came in, imagining a life made whole.

Dizzy and coughing so hard she could hardly walk, she ran to the barn. Inside, Tiko's eyes were rolled back, the whites of his eyes like reflectors, his coat shiny with sweat. Thrashing, he kicked and reared against the wood stall, high-pitched screams rising from his throat. When Silva opened the stall and tried to reach him, he screamed and whirled, catching her with his back end, slamming her into the wall so hard she crumpled over. She pushed herself to her hands and knees and tried to get the stall door open as he reared up, pawing the air, crazed, his hooves coming down a foot from her head. He ran forward, ramming into the stall door so hard Silva thought he had broken his chest, but he bolted out, escaping from the barn corridor to the yard.

She crawled through the smoke to Sage's stall, where the mare lay stretched out on her side, heaving as if she'd been galloping, a green slag plastered on the smooth hair of her rump, sweat streaking her coat, her legs spayed out as if she were slipping on ice. Her neck pulsed with tremors as she tried over and over to get up, exposing the purple-gray of her gums as she squealed and lurched, her hooves grazing Silva's thigh, her neck arched in pain as Silva tried to pull her head off the floor, trying to help her get up.

"Oh god, no," Silva cried, holding Sage's head as she convulsed. "No, no, no," she sobbed, leaning over, retching on smoke that had grown thick and rancid, closing her diaphragm. Sobs came from somewhere so deep inside her they were soundless, racking her body. She was a curse, the black rot of loss pulsing raw and evident on her, infecting everything she touched, turning everything and everyone around her to ash. She should have let herself slide into the water a long time ago.

She crawled toward the river through the smoke, the house and barn engulfed in flames, the apiary already gone, smoke and embers and ash everywhere.

A plane roared overhead, and then a shower of liquid hit her, washing her skin crimson, the river running red as blood, fire retardant drenching the charred landscape, smoke rising in reedy tendrils from the ruins left behind her. But it was too late. It would always be too late. Closing her eyes, she curled tight against the anguish, this new, blooming pain so raw she couldn't breathe. What a fool she'd been to trust it could ever be different than what it'd always been.

CHAPTER FORTY-FOUR

Date: May 1, 2000
Title: In Eden
Subject: Honeysuckle Bonsai
Medium: Watercolor and graphite on cold-press
Size: 8×10

Dearest Eamon,

I sit outside in the dry heat of this desert spring, the landscape a ruddy expanse of flesh-colored stone and dirt and bluff, green studded with stunted brush and trees—wild bits of bonsai in the making. I have escaped back to Santa Fe—the place I called home after you, after Trawler. From the island to the desert. I'm nothing if not a picture of extremes.

I remember your story of the honeysuckle, your mentor gathering it in the wild from the base of Mount Fuji, drawn in by the lush fragrance of its blooms, and I think of your hands shaping, shaping, shaping it—all these years. All future growth directed by the vision of your sight. I wonder if it still looks the same now—twenty years later. If the lovers are still visible in its trunk, if we would still be able to see ourselves there. I remember it like I remember you—with a kind of clarity that hasn't waned. If I close my eyes, it's right there at arm's length, next to you, next to me—a reflection of our past, a presentation of our present, a casting forward to our future.

I painted it my first day free. It's like a rebirthing, coming into the light after being submerged for so long in the blackness. I have been able to do nothing but paint—filling one canvas after another after another, as if those months captive in the compound are spilling out in a long, wavering scream. The girls haunt my dreams. I left them there, half of them pregnant already—although that was the carefully curated plan, of course. High enough numbers that the rate of return pays off. It doesn't matter that one suffered an early miscarriage, or that a few others are medically at a high risk for complications, or that others will die in childbirth just like Shoshanna did before them, or that many of their babies won't make it past their first years for one tragic reason or another.

Faith got me out in the dark, taking me down to the river. I only hope she didn't suffer the consequences. Len was sure of his power over me, sure that, given enough time, enough wearing down, I, too, would become his, bowed to his authority.

Instead, I am here, trying to find healing, find my voice, enact my own version of recompense.

I have decided to send you my original twelve paintings—the Maidens of Almost Paradise. And also this art magazine showing you what has become of "In Eden" as it heads your way, one gallery at a time. A message in a bottle. Though I will keep these letters, this journal—not that I'm unwilling to share the depths of my tangled heart with you. I'm only afraid that once I do, there will be no coming back from it. From all I've done. A lifetime of running from myself. A lifetime of lostness.

I have put your packet in the mail—paintings of the girls and the art-show magazine with "In Eden." But I am afraid you won't answer, afraid that it's too late for me, for us—too late to ask for forgiveness, to ask for understanding, to ask, again, for your love, for a family of our definition, our own making.

I can only bare my heart here in these unsent letters, and on this cold-press paper run wet with watercolors—the color of my soul, of my longing, of my sorrow and my reclamation. The color of my love. My heart forever and always will be held here, for you, Eamon.

All my love,
Isabelle

CHAPTER FORTY-FIVE

She didn't remember anyone coming for her, or the journey to the hospital. Didn't remember anything but a series of colors shaping an amorphous world, like fresh paint bleeding over its own edges. Nurses talking to her, asking her questions she wouldn't answer, prodding her with cool, dry hands, quietly checking her vital signs, the room's blinds drawn, the lights dim. She refused to speak, refused to open her eyes until they left, day and night indistinguishable, everything an undeviating routine of beeping darkness.

They told her she had a concussion, that she was being treated for smoke inhalation, exposure, that she needed to rest without light. How could she when all that came was a flashing set of nightmares—scenes from hell, a torment real enough to send her cartwheeling into the fiery dark? She had no emotion left, only a sense of deafened blindness—a woman drowning in poisonous waters. Opening her mouth to accept her fate.

They told her Nick was in the ICU with a head injury, the pilot and Ted hospitalized as well. Said it was a miracle they'd all made it through—the fire, the rest of it, too.

A boy with his arm raised, standing hand in hand with Len Dietz. Feeling like she'd been thrown from a great height and was plummeting through a black void, tumbling down through a vortex with no end in sight.

She curled herself into the cloistered dark, her vocal cords tangled into a mass she didn't have the strength to unravel, her voice a thing so long in the past it seemed she'd never spoken—born mute and numb, without feeling or thought, and set adrift in the world, a foreign body forever without a home.

Her room was rife with the same sounds and smells of the room where Eamon had died, memory bearing down—the nurses' garbled voices, their lips moving out of sync, their eyes blinking ponderously, like puppets. Under the covers, she pressed her hands hard against the ridges of her hipbones, holding on to what was left of herself.

When they finally released her, she felt light, tippy, as if the floor were a tilt-a-whirl set into motion. When she looked at herself in the mirror, there was no recognizing the woman who stared back at her with blank, haunted eyes, the woman whose hands shook as she opened the door to leave, the woman she'd become, overtaken by grief until that was all there was. A scent in the air attached to her like a trailing.

She made her way to the ICU, hesitating a moment before walking in past the drawn curtain, Nick's face pale against white sheets, his head bandaged, the scar on his face red and angry. Old wounds newly made. Tubes, wires, blinking machines—the shock of the past and present colliding in breathless waves that crashed over her again. White carnations perched on his bedside table, machines beeping green lines on monitors, spiking and falling, making record of this moment, each heartbeat and breath. Three chickadees on a card singing, "Get Well, Get Well," from their open beaks.

He lay with his eyes closed, didn't move when Silva went to his side, his face battered and bruised, as though he'd grown tired of himself and tried to finish what had been started long ago—his father's leaving, his mother's death, Len's claiming of a brother lost and then found again. A life never truly his own to make.

She sat in the chair next to his bed and reached out to gently stroke the top of his hand, covered in a deep purple bruise from knuckles to wrist, as if his hand had been pressed between pieces of iron—a torture device cranked tight. What words could she say that would make any kind of difference? How she'd been too late, everything gone—what they'd worked so hard to shape. What Nick's life might have been if he'd known, if he'd been able to claim his brother as his own, raise him in the way he should have been raised. The missing blood link, genetic code like intimacy, matching alleles like love drawing you forth. *This is where I belong, this is who I belong to. . . .*

"I'm so sorry," she finally said, her voice as weak and broken as she was, but he didn't move, didn't open his eyes, his body flaccid under her hands. Then, ever so slowly, he drew himself away from her touch. Turned his head and body until his back was to her like a wall.

"It's all over. You should go," he said, facing away from her, his voice distant, as if it didn't belong to him anymore. A rejection of everything she'd thought might be possible.

She knew it then with a cold, hard sinking finality of her heart. Len had won. The fire had taken Nick from her as well.

———

She tried to imprint the way the sky met the hills, brand this picture forever in her mind, driving away. She had never stood a chance. None of them had. Wood stamped with the date of completion, ink bleeding into the grain, following the lines of growth. Wood turning to stone, turning into a solid mass of atoms—one element shifting into another, into a thing that once was. Bodies grown together as one torn up by the roots and burned into ash.

Corner inertia pulled her toward the river, and how easy it was to let the wheel follow—a brief instant of shoulder gravel, then weightless freedom, black water. A soundless river journey, her body stroking the silted depths of green shadows, just as her mother had, just as the woman had, the waters taking her before she could destroy anything or anyone else.

An eighteen-wheeler bellowed by, horn blasting, shaking her back to her own side of the line, that safety net of yellow, her fingers laced tight against the steering wheel's play. The road was lined with dry husks, ready to ignite; the blacktop like soft goo, entrapping the imprint of her tires, tracking her home.

She was the only one with windows down, the air a backward furnace sucking stands of her hair out the window. The cars she passed were air-conditioned tombs, their occupants waxen copies of people, immune to the heat as a steady rivulet of wet snaked down the gully of her backbone, a small river in its canyon of vertebrae and ribs.

The wavering road miraged into a lake ahead, masking ruinous scab land that radiated heat. Burned-out signs advertising cheap cigarettes, beer, and fuel. Shrunken towns replete with run-down trailers and dirt lawns, dented cars parked as if the drivers were in a hurry to nowhere—a fling with the neighbor, a snort of crank before the night shift. Small towns Silva hated, with their self-important speed limits, their empty cop cars parked at city limits as a warning. A double-wide on the bottom of a rise with a distinct line of black surrounding it—the hills blackened, the fence posts ringed charcoal, burned narrow at the ground. She gripped the wheel tight, feeling the panic and the heat, the dark-rolling smoke—people frantically digging fire line, snaking garden hose to wet their claim, save what was theirs, even if there was nothing left to save.

Each semi that passed sent the Dodge rocking, the roadsides littered with empty cans and broken beer bottles. She put her foot down, the needle lodged and quivering, the Dodge speed-rattling, threatening to fly into pieces and join the desert, nothing left but chunks of rusted metal. As though eating through the miles could redeem her, could save her from the ruin of her life.

The sage was interspersed with trees and creek-size rivers toting oversize names—*Raging*, *Dead Man*. The sharp points of distant mountain ranges showed in bas-relief against the sky, the land like a green memory. In an hour, she would be across the pass, back to what had always been.

By the time she got to the terminal, the last ferry was scheduled and the night mist had settled in deep layers of seeping wetness. She breathed in deeply as she paid for her ticket at the booth, the ticket man as tired and gray as the fog. Driving into the ferry lane, she clutched the receipt tight in her hand—*Trawler Island: passage for one adult, 1 vehicle under 20 feet*—the blanket of fog pulling her hair limp around her shoulders, the unaccustomed wetness chilling her to the bone. What this moisture could have done in the canyon—what it could have saved.

At the end of the dock, an old woman stood creased over her rod, crabs overlapping one another's slow movements in the bottom of a bucket next to her, the Sound still but for the quick slip of a seal, little swells rippling out behind it, shells and beer cans washed green under eight feet of water, battered pilings lining the shore—wet, brown pillars spatter-painted in gull guano, each one topped with a seagull or cormorant, perched there as if carved into the salt-raised grain.

No place had been able to save her; no place had been able to save anything after all.

Through the fog, the last ferry came, looming larger each minute. She wrapped her arms tight and stood on the dock a minute longer before getting in the Dodge, waiting for the ferry attendant to wave her on board the lower deck. She parked behind a Mercedes with gold Bellevue plate frames whose vanity plates proclaimed *JensLuv*. Silva set the Dodge's brake, left it in first gear, imagining it kicked loose, battering into the back of the car as the ferry started its slow plow through the Sound.

She walked slowly up the stairs to the upper passenger deck, winded, her seared airways aching. A wall of windows bordered empty rows of caramel-colored booths, the mainland already a blurred green haze outside, hidden in the mounting drizzle, the ferry's heat blasting in stifling gusts as passengers settled in with their coffee, glancing Silva's way as she passed.

On the deck, she lifted her face to the mist, the jolt of wet air dizzying, a balm for her scorched lungs. *Nick.* She resisted sinking to her knees, gripping the ferry's railing, clenching her jaw against crying. She wouldn't give herself the release of sorrowing. Not now. Not again.

She watched the horizon, cheeks tingling and damp. The wind blew her hair out in wet strings, plastering her mouth and neck. A gull sailed in front of the captain's upper window, wings outstretched. Others joined in, coasting above her, hitching a glide from the mainland. A group of boys ran around the deck opposite her in the mist, holding their arms out as if they were air-bound, too, their faces turned toward her like bright camera flashes.

The ferry docked at two other islands, letting passengers off, until only Silva and a handful of others were left on board. She didn't look up for fear she might recognize someone. Anything more, and she would lose the tenuous hold she had; the choking feeling would rise again, and her lungs and airways would sear closed despite the moisture imbuing the air, the water all around her.

When the ferry was close, Trawler right around the bend, she went back down to the bottom deck, the Dodge rocking back and forth as they docked, an attendant in work boots and reflective gear waving cars forward impatiently.

It was misting as she drove off the ramp. She rolled down the window and let in the wet, salted air. Manzanita lined the road, cedar and fir tall behind it. Shreds of rotting kelp purulent in the warm brine of tidal pools, the wavering arms of anemones, sea rocks covered in barnacles. Things she'd once known as well as herself. A blip in time, swallowed in an impression of memory she grasped at like a drowning person trying to hold on to a piece of waterlogged jetsam.

Everything looked the same—the red-and-white hotel above the cove, the café and gift shop, the Bait Shop's blackboard specials. The trees, the road, the smells. Everything that had once been all she thought she would ever want or need.

She drove with her window down, the air peppering her face. Streetlights hummed in the gray-fogged air and hatches of gnats clouded the lights. She drove down the rolling streets, past the docks, the cannery, and farther, until she found the cabin's overgrown turn by habit.

She wound through the massive cedars' trunks, damp forest duff mounded deep, moss and maidenhair ferns thick alongside the twin indents of the road, the familiar wet smell of humus and green things, the surrounding cedars like giants—roots pulled up from the earth, heartwood hollowed out. It was only a matter of time before they, too, toppled.

At the end of the drive the forest opened up, and there was the cabin, the trees, the shore.

She pulled up and turned off the truck. The magnolia off the porch gone wild, moss growing on the step planks and the roof, rusty needles covering the front lawn. Leaving ruin lying in her wake had become a repeated chorus to her life.

The front door lock had rusted, and it took her several tries to get the key to catch, the pin to turn. The thermometer hanging from the porch timbers read fifty-seven degrees. It was starting to rain—a quick deluge that soaked everything, dark stains seeping into the wood.

She stood in the middle of the empty living room. Above the kitchen sink, a steel wool had crumbled into a heap of rusted ash. A few blue enamel coffee cups and chipped plates still held place on the counter where she'd left them, dried heaps of dead bugs in the corners, the overhead light illuminating dust particles that drifted thick. Outside the window, chickadees twitted in the branches of the crabapple. She thought of Nick's get-well card, those birds singing their directive—*Get Well, Get Well*, as if you could just choose such a thing, deciding the path of your recovery.

She turned on the faucet, and it spewed bits of rusted iron, water that tasted like a wound. Water and blood, blood and water. Her own body. Her mother's body. The woman in the river. The girls in the compound.

She walked back to Eamon's room—the familiar corduroy of the log walls, his bed with its striped mattress, his old bonsai desk as filled with nature as the rest of the cabin—collections of nests and feathers, mosses and lichens, cones and dried fronds.

Finally, she went out to the woodpile and selected a smooth-grained cedar round. The dampened wood stack seemed insubstantial, the axe still chunked in the chopping block with its map of three-inch incisions, years of use spelled out in the chop marks. She split a rack of kindling and took it inside. The hearth was smooth and cold against her thighs as she crumpled damp newspaper, tilting kindling pieces into a teepee over top. She struck a match and cupped flame to paper, watching as it flared blue and then peaked into smoke. Tried not to not think of Nick sorting through the ashes, the black char left behind, sifting for whatever was left. Tried not to think of Juniper, swallowed by the canyon, like everyone and everything else.

Feeding a log in, her arm touched hot cast iron—the quick hiss of heat against flesh blooming red, blistering her skin. Eamon's old T-shirts made up the rag drawer. She tore one into strips and wrapped her wound. This wet world where she'd once belonged. This world that left her aching for Nick, for everything she'd thought could be hers.

She thought of Juniper and Tiko disappearing into the smoke, Sage lying still in her stall, and clutched her chest, choking back sobs. All she'd thought could be, all she'd held belief in.

She walked the wet trail to the beach, tangles of blackberry vines snagging her skin, the beach strewn with tracks—raccoon and gulls, the wide-splayed V-print of an island deer. Delicate clumps of blooming tufted saxifrage and Siberian miner's lettuce graced the hollow between forest and beach, shells studding the sand, Eamon's ashes joined with them.

A Swainson's thrush sang its night song, a sound like rain. She'd thought that whenever she finally went back to visit the island, Nick would be with her. Had pictured showing him all the island's secret places, teaching him everything she knew. Now that she was back and alone, she couldn't imagine Nick anywhere other than the canyon, her anywhere but with him.

The moon rose, nearly full, the air cold and damp. She took off her clothes, left them on the beach as she stepped into the water, this place that had defined her. She was surprised at the water's cold bite against her calves and thighs, the way it needled her stomach as she waded in deeper, her feet sinking in the silt of the rocky bottom, kelp waving its long leaves around her.

She stood hip-deep, looking out at the water's undulating expanse, the pull of the tide washing up against her body, rocking against her. Something small floated along the surface, and she waited until it reached her—a perfectly formed wreath bobbing gently on the swells, kelp and seagrass tangled together, adorned with tiny pale flowers like an aquatic bridal crown, except in the wreath's open, watery center, a tiny silver fish floated on its side, motionless. A funeral wreath delivered like an offering from the sea. But when she cupped her hand underneath it, the fish suddenly came to life, diving away so quickly she thought she must have imagined it.

The water pulled her in deeper, rising up her belly to her chest, until finally she let it fully take her, laying back and sucking in her breath as it swallowed her, prickling her scalp, washing over her closed eyes, her body sinking into its dark embrace. No matter how hard she tried to push it away, she felt the same familiar sureness she had before: everything she touched would crumble to nothingness. She'd never been meant to stay in this world.

The tide pulled her out as she sank lower and lower into the depths, her skin a muted white in the darkness, her hair floating around her face like a shroud—long tendrils waving outward with the seaweed, catching on the swell of her chest, her body turned sluggish and heavy, her lungs convulsing as they had in the smoke, the moon receding like a distant, wavering light showing through fathoms of years, finally claiming her as its own.

There was no going back. She was tired of fighting.

The moon disappeared as she descended into the darkness, sinking down until she could hold her breath no longer, her lungs feeling as if they would burst. Then, against her will, she flailed, convulsing in the black depths, sucking water in her mouth and nose to her lungs, her arms and legs churning as she choked, liquid coursing through her airways as she surged toward the surface.

Heaving and coughing, she splashed to shore, where she collapsed onto the beach, salt water running from her gasping mouth, from her nose and ears and eyes, streaming from her as it had from the woman onto the Snake's sunbaked rocks. She curled into a fetal position on the sand and rocks, digging her fingers in as she coughed and sobbed, trying to hold on to something, her hands like malformed appendages, as damaged and misshapen as the rest of her.

She remembered a small silver fish nosing bone in silt, the white ash spread of it like shock drawn long, a calcium-rich cloud shadow, a sea offering, what was left of Eamon settling below her submerged feet, shiny-edged bits glinting like teeth. Bones baked so hot they shimmered underwater like mica under glass: there were his hips and spine, the blades of his shoulders, his hands and skull. The bones of his face. A sea otter swimming and snuffing close by, trying to understand this new shape, this offering of grief, this marking of her passage: blood and bone, rivers and sea, hackberry and honeybees. The shores she'd stood on, casting her white stones.

Her body cold and quaking, the smell of raw woodsmoke drifting down from the fire she'd built, she wondered how she could survive the quiet burden of trees and tide, all the losses that had formed her life. A memory of land. A memory of water. The surviving silence of stone.

EPILOGUE

Isabelle set up her easel on the island's crescent beach cut out of the Salish Sea, the shoreline the same shape as the moon still pinned on the fog-hazed morning sky. On the beach's far end, the red-roofed lighthouse stood ready with its beacon of fenestrated light. The comfort of that scene: gulls and terns chattering and bobbing offshore, the morning foghorns sounding across the water's silvered surface with its reflection of sky. Endless, tranquil. The movement of her heart.

Nick and Silva walked hand in hand along the minus-tide's ridged sand and teeming tidal pools, the dog, Juniper, effulgent—wind sprinting ahead of them, then circling back in a run-by juke-out as they laughed and reached out, grazing his tail, his legs stretched in a speeding Superman pose, his feet flinging wet sand, his mouth wide in a toothy husky smile, his tattered ears folded back with the immense joy of it all.

Behind them, wild bluffs rose perpendicular to the beach, banks studded with manzanita and wild rose grown into alder and birch brush, and finally topped out in cedar, fir, and stately Sitka spruces in all their sparse, wind-blown beauty—bonsais grown into maturity. Intertwined in the evergreens was the bright auburn uprights of the madrones' trunks. The color of Silva's hair. The color Isabelle's hair used to be, too. Something febrile and alive, something that forced you to face the world on your own terms.

Isabelle set the angle of her easel, filled her jar of water, arranged her tubes of paint, selected her favorite brush, readied her palette and blotter, and stood there behind the cold-press paper making the first strokes of color against its blank, stippled whiteness.

Within a few quick flicks of her wrist, pigments began filling the unelaborated expanse of crevices, two figures emerging. She felt a trembling rising from her feet to her hands. *Eamon.*

This day—their anniversary. What he would have thought had he been there, witnessing this with her. Nick and Silva. The dog, too. Like something from a dream. Her own *granddaughter.* A grown woman. A woman who'd already become more than Isabelle could ever be.

The three of them—Nick, Silva, and Juniper—walked down to the lighthouse and nearly disappeared in the reflection of shore and water, the dog running through the tidal froth, his distant barking carrying on the air back to Isabelle, lighting her painting, lighting her face.

The trees on the bluffs blew sideways in the wind, their branches waving. Razor clams, hiding their phallic indecency, shot water spigots into the air while orange crabs scuttled along a water's edge piled with kelp grown pearlescent in its glaze of salt, sun, and cloud. The beginnings of an ephemeral but eternal archetypal scene—as if Isabelle were recording with her paints the first moments of humankind rising out of the muck, turning from fish into man and woman. Edenic.

She couldn't help but feel Eamon there with her. They had found their way back to each other after all. His spirit rose from the water, from the shore, from the trees, each one of them holding something of him. A reflection of love. A coming home. The scene Isabelle had been waiting to paint her whole life.

When Silva had told Isabelle that Eamon was gone, Isabelle had sunk to her knees on the shore in front of the cabin—the place Silva had put him to rest, his ashes spread there beneath the water, where he'd always be. Isabelle had held the pebbled sand in her hands and wept until she couldn't weep anymore. After her own early abandonment, after these twenty-some years apart, after her own eventual homecoming, Eamon was really, truly gone.

She'd had to force herself up. But then she'd carried on the way Eamon would have wanted her to, blotting her face, steadying her hands, going back to the cabin's warmth, the golden light of an early fall night illuminated through each windowpane. Back to Silva. Their granddaughter. Back to where she'd always been meant to be. Blood of her blood, flesh of her flesh. Chains of double-helixed DNA tracing them together through all these years, through all this time and space.

She painted fast, but with a sense of calm. This was her world. The world she'd always been coming to. The world she'd always been searching for. Delivered back unto her.

Nick and Silva and Juniper disappeared as distant specks hidden in beach grass, and then reemerged, walking back toward her. Out in the water, a spotted harbor seal lifted its dark, wet dog-face and regarded Isabelle for a long moment before slipping again below the surface. The wind kicked up, and with it the smell of woodsmoke and damp earth. Sand fleas burrowed and hopped around her bare feet, the cold seeping up from tide-wet sand. A new season coming in. An anniversary of change. A beginning. An ending. A starting over. A circling back.

On the ferry to Trawler, after the surprise of discovering their mutual destination, Nick had offered to give Isabelle a ride along with him and the dog. They had driven through town to Eamon's cabin in Nick's old jalopy of a truck, Juniper balanced on the front seat between them, panting the wet salt air, the bonsai and honeybees boxed behind in the pickup's bed. Driving down the winding, tree-lined driveway to the cabin, Isabelle had known: this was something new, something with meaning beyond what she'd always been trying to find, to define, to understand.

Silvania August Moonbeam Merigal. A child she hadn't known existed. A child, though, who she'd always felt in her heart, in her body, in her spirit. A child who was hers, who had been hers all along, waiting there on the island for her just as Eamon had before, arms wide open.

Silva had been standing there, outside the cabin, when Nick, Isabelle, and Juniper had driven up. As if she'd been expecting them, as if she'd known they were on their way, breaking a new path to her. And as soon as Isabelle had seen Silva, she had understood what she'd never been able to understand before: This was what she'd always wanted. This was what she'd always felt. This was what she'd always known to be true. This was the family she'd seen in her dreams.

She had stood back waiting, watching as Nick and Juniper and Silva reunited, Nick and Silva weeping as they embraced, Juniper yipping and whining as he jumped on Silva, licking her hands and face. Isabelle had stood there with her beating heart held in her hands. A wild, pulsing, wet thing. A thing with branching arteries, with muscles palpitating and contracting.

When she had finally walked to Silva, Isabelle knew that she was walking into a reflection: of herself, of what her life might have been, of her future. Their future. One story after another after another, intertwined, interwoven, interspersed—Silva. Nick. Eamon. Isabelle. A story made complete. A story made whole. A story with no start. A story with no end.

She painted as they walked back to her and kept painting as they drew near, Juniper running up to her in joyful greeting, his muzzle wet and sandy as he gave her hand a quick nuzzle before running back to Silva and leaping for a stick she threw out into the water, launching himself into the rolling swells and swimming with shoulder-lifting power.

Nick and Silva walked down to the waterline as Juniper swam back to the beach. Nick picked up a stone and brushed off the sand, gave Silva a challenging look before setting up his skipping throw, which ended in three quick hops. Silva's laugh was musical on the water as she selected her own stone and winged it, leaving widening dimples across a swath of the Sound long enough that its skips disappeared in the distance before it was overcome. Nick shrugged in defeat as Juniper bounced wetly around their feet, waving his sandy stick. Silva wrapped her arm in Nick's, reached up and touched his face. A caress that said everything anyone would ever need to know.

Isabelle rinsed her brushes, cleaned the paint from her hands, and walked down to join them. A fractured family of castoffs formed from the severed pieces that made up the sum of their existence. A fractured family fit back together. A fractured family made whole.